Corie Durrenberger
3 Candlewood Dr.
South Windsor, CT 06074

DON'T
LOOK
DOWN

"How about you do things your way, and I'll do them mine?" She stabbed a green bean. "And I'll solve this before the cops do. In fact, I'll bet you a hundred bucks that I put this all together before Castillo does."

"I'm not going to wager over something that could get you hurt."

"Ha," she retorted, shoveling in another mouthful and clearly perking up at the argument. "You won't wager because you know I'm right. My method against the cops'." Swallowing, she smiled darkly at him. "Come on, Rick. Bet me. Back up that hot accent with your big old wallet."

Obviously she was going to look into Kunz's death whether he wanted her to or not. Therefore, if he could use this opportunity to prove that her nefarious life couldn't get her results any better or faster than the police, it would be worthwhile.

"You're on," he said crisply, offering his hand. "One hundred dollars that Castillo and legitimate police work will solve this case and find the killer before you can manage it."

By Suzanne Enoch

Contemporary Titles

DON'T LOOK DOWN
FLIRTING WITH DANGER

Historical Titles

AN INVITATION TO SIN
SIN AND SENSIBILITY
ENGLAND'S PERFECT HERO
LONDON'S PERFECT SCOUNDREL
THE RAKE
A MATTER OF SCANDAL
MEET ME AT MIDNIGHT
REFORMING A RAKE
TAMING RAFE
BY LOVE UNDONE
STOLEN KISSES
LADY ROGUE

Suzanne Enoch

Don't Look Down

AVON BOOKS
An Imprint of HarperCollins*Publishers*

AVON BOOKS
An Imprint of HarperCollins*Publishers*
10 East 53rd Street
New York, New York 10022-5299

Copyright © 2006 by Suzanne Enoch
Excerpts from *Don't Look Down* copyright © 2006 by Suzanne Enoch; *Sex, Lies, and Online Dating* copyright © 2006 by Rachel Gibson; *Her Master and Commander* copyright © 2006 by Karen Hawkins; *Sword of Darkness* copyright © 2006 by Sherrilyn Kenyon
ISBN-13: 978-0-06-059364-3
ISBN-10: 0-06-059364-4
www.avonromance.com

First Avon Books paperback printing: January 2006

Avon Trademark Reg. U.S. Pat. Off. and in Other Countries, Marca Registrada, Hecho en U.S.A.
HarperCollins® is a registered trademark of HarperCollins Publishers Inc.

Printed in the U.S.A.

10 9 8 7 6 5 4 3 2 1

For my mom, Joan,
who always knows
both when I need to water my plants
and when I can use a good home-cooked meal—
and who takes care of both for me
when I'm on deadline.
I love you, Mom.

One

Devonshire, England
Wednesday, 1:51 a.m.

*H*eadlights blazing, a car slowed at the turn-off to the main house, hesitated, then accelerated down the road and into the dark again.

"Tourists," Samantha Jellicoe muttered, straightening from her crouch and watching the headlights disappear around the bend. The passersby, both native British and general fame-hunters on vacation, concentrated so much attention on the tall, ornate gates behind her and the barely visible estate house beyond that she could probably stand on her head and juggle and they still wouldn't notice her there in the shrubbery.

Tempting as scaring the shit out of some amateur paparazzi might be, *not* being seen was kind of the point at the moment. With another glance along the dark roadway, Samantha backed up into the middle of it and took a run at the wall, shoving her toes into a chink in the mortar halfway up and using that for leverage to clamber to the narrow and nicely finished top of the stone.

When she did a burglary, she actually preferred disconnecting the gate alarms and simply going in from the ground, but she happened to know that these gates had embedded wires running through buried pipelines out to the guard house on the north side of the Devonshire property. To deactivate the gates she would have to cut the power to the entire house, which would set off the battery-backed perimeter alarms.

With a slight grin she dropped to the lawn inside. "Not bad," she murmured to herself. Next she had to navigate past motion detectors and digital video recorders, plus the half-dozen security guards who patrolled the area around the house. Fortunately tonight was breezy, so the motion detectors would be overloaded and the guards tired of monitoring and resetting them. It was always better to go into a property on a windy night, though January in central England meant the windchill took the temperature down to somewhere around freezing.

Pulling a pair of pruners—which doubled as wire cutters—from her pocket, she lopped off a large leafy elm branch. Hefting it, she made her way along the wall to the nearest of the cameras mounted at regular intervals along the perimeter. Maybe her solution to the problem of the digital cameras was simplistic, but hell, she knew from experience that sometimes low-tech was the best way to beat the most complex of systems. Besides, she could see the headline: CHICK WITH STICK BEATS COUNTRY'S MOST SOPHISTICATED ALARM SYSTEM. Neaner, neaner.

Swinging the branch, she thudded it across the side and front of the camera, waited a few seconds, then did it again. Matching her pummeling to the rhythm of the wind, she smacked the side and the lens a few more times, then hauled back and slammed the casing hard with the thicker part of the branch. The camera jolted sideways, giving whoever was monitoring it a great view of a west wing chimney. After a few more swings, she flung the branch over the outside wall and made her way toward the house.

Somebody would probably be out in a few minutes to re-set the camera, but by then she'd be inside. Hauling ass out was a lot easier than sneaking into a place. Samantha drew a breath and headed east along the base of the house until she reached the slightly offset wall that designated the kitchen. Kudos to whichever aristocrat five hundred years ago had decided that the kitchen was too dangerous to be set fully into the main house.

The window frames on the ground floor were wired to the alarm system, and the glass was pressure sensitive. No punching through to get in, unless she wanted to wake up everybody in residence. Of course, no one was *in* residence, except for staff and security, but they could phone the police as easily as anybody else.

Making sure the pruners were secure in her pocket, she set a foot onto the narrow window ledge and boosted herself up. A few more careful footholds and she stood on top of the kitchen roof. Fifteen feet up and over, the library balcony beckoned to her.

Unslinging the rope she carried from over her shoulder, she pulled the pruners free and tied one side of the handle tight. On her first toss, it landed on the balcony, and she tugged on the rope to make certain the pruners were wedged tightly between the stone balustrades.

Her heart hammering with a welcome rush of adrenaline, Samantha wrapped her hands into the rope, then stepped off the kitchen roof. For a moment she hung there, swinging slowly back and forth in midair. Once she was certain the rope wouldn't give, she twined her legs into it and shimmied up to the balcony. God, that had been simple. Frequently, though, nerves were the only thing that divided the shirtless and smoking thieves who appeared on *Cops* from the ones nobody ever caught. Nerves and a well-made piece of gardening equipment. Totally worth the eighteen pounds she'd paid for it at the local nursery.

Hauling herself over the railing, she detached the pruners from the rope, tucking both back where they belonged. The full-length glass doors leading into the library were closed and locked, but they didn't worry her. They were wired, of course, but not pressure sensitive. Up this high, they would catch the evening easterly breezes and set off the alarms every five minutes. Nobody wanted to deal with that, even at the expense of inferior security.

She unwound the length of copper wire that braceleted her left wrist, tore off two pieces of duct tape from the miniroll in her pocket, and carefully inserted one end under each door to intercept and bypass the electrical circuit. That done, it was simple to pick the lock and shove open the doors in near total silence. "Piece of cake," she murmured, hopping down the shallow step and into the room.

The overhead lights flipped on, glaringly bright. Instinctively, Samantha dove sideways, crouching into the remains of the shadows. *Shit*. The servants all should have been in bed, and the owner was in London.

"This is interesting," a cool male voice drawled in a cultured, slightly faded British accent.

She lowered her shoulders. "What the fuck are you doing here?" she asked, stepping back into the middle of the room and trying to pretend that she hadn't nearly peed her pants. Despite her nearly foolproof, personally acquired information, obviously the owner *wasn't* in London.

He stepped away from the light switch. "I live here. Lose your key?"

For a moment Samantha just looked at him. Tall, dark-haired and dreamy, even in jeans and a sweatshirt Richard Addison resembled every young lady's wet dream. And that didn't take into account the fact that he was a multibillionaire, or that he did athletic stuff like ski and play polo for recreation. "I was practicing," she retorted, blowing out her breath. "How did you know I was coming in this way?"

"I've been watching you out the windows for half an hour. You're very stealthy."

"Now you're just being a smart ass."

He nodded, grinning. "Probably."

"And you have not been here for half an hour, because I hid out by the front gate for forty minutes while some skank pretended to have a flat tire."

"How do you know she was pretending?"

"Because she had a camera with a big-ass telephoto lens in her toolbox." She cocked her head at him, assessing his expression. He was damned hard to read; he concealed his emotions for a living. "I bet you got here about five minutes ago, while I was climbing the kitchen wall."

Rick cleared his throat. "Regardless of when I arrived, this is still the second time I've caught you breaking into one of my properties, Samantha."

So she'd been right about his arrival time. Annoyed as she was at being caught, she had to admit to a certain satisfaction that at the moment this billionaire wet dream belonged to her. "I wasn't trying to steal anything this time. Don't get bent out of shape."

"I'm not bent at all. An explanation, however, would be nice."

With a shrug she brushed past him, heading through the middle of the enormous library for the hall door. "I spent three hours today listening to John Harding complain about all the lowlifes and good-for-nothings who want to steal his art collection." She snorted. "As if any self-respecting thief would want his half-assed Russian miniatures. At least he used to collect silver crucifixes."

Bare feet padded behind her. "Correct me if I'm wrong, Samantha, but I thought you were going into the business of helping people *protect* their valuables. After all, as I recall, your last robbery ended in a large explosion and the near death of the homeowner as well as yourself."

"I know, I know. That's why I retired from the cat burglar business, remember. And that *was* how we met, Mr. Home-owner."

"I remember, my love. And I thought you were interested in taking on Harding as a client."

So had she. Apparently she was pickier than either of them had anticipated. "The preventing break-in stuff is okay. It's the talking to the marks that makes me—"

"Clients," he interrupted.

"What?"

"You said 'marks.' They're your clients now."

"Well, Harding *was* a mark. Once. And he's a boring ass-hole, not a client. I would never have talked with him if you hadn't asked me to."

She heard his slow exhalation of breath. "Splendid. You might have told me you'd robbed him before I went to the trouble of introducing you."

"I wanted to meet him."

"Does that give you a rush, to talk to your marks?"

Sam shrugged. "Not much of one. But any rush is a good rush."

"So you've said." He ran a palm down her spine. "Why is it that you never tried to rob me until that night in Palm Beach?"

She grinned. "Why, do you feel left out?"

"In a way, I suppose so. You already told me you only went after the best."

There were about a dozen flip responses she could make to that, but in all honesty, it was a question she'd asked herself. "I think it's because you and your collection were—are—so high-profile. Everybody knows what you own, so if somebody else showed up with it—"

"So my stupendous fame was all that saved me from you?"

"That's right. But before you start getting holier than thou on me, what are you doing here? You're supposed to be in London until tomorrow."

"My meeting ended early, so I decided to drive home—in time, I might add, to prove that you still can't get anything past me. Maybe *that's* the real reason you've never stolen from me, sweetheart."

Her spine stiffening, Sam stopped, facing him as they reached the hallway door. "What?"

He nodded. "I caught you red-handed in Florida three months ago, and now here in Devon. It's probably a good thing you did retire from the cat burglary business."

Oh, that was enough of that, the superior British ass. Samantha leaned up to kiss him, feeling the surprise of his mouth and then his arms slipping across her shoulders as his body relaxed. She slid the rope off her arm and twisted it around his hands, ducking from beneath his grip.

"Sam—"

She whipped the free end of the rope around him, pulling it tight and knotting his hands across the front of his ribs. "Who's slipping now?" she asked.

"Take this off," he snapped, the gloating humor leaving his voice and his expression.

"Nope. You've disparaged my abilities." She pushed

against his chest, and he sat down heavily in one of his Georgian reading chairs. "Apologize."

"Untie me."

Ooh, he was mad. Even if she'd been inclined to do so, letting him loose now seemed a supremely bad idea. Besides, she'd been working on a healthy adrenaline high that he'd managed to wreck. Before he could push to his feet, she tied him to the chair with the rest of the rope. "Maybe this'll convince you not to confront people breaking into your house unless you have something more substantial than charm to defend yourself with."

"You're the only one who breaks into my house, and I'm beginning to find it less amusing."

"Of course you are," she mused, stepping back to admire her handiwork. "I'm in charge."

Dark blue eyes met hers. "And apparently into bondage. Naughty, naughty."

"Apologize, Rick, and I'll let you go."

His jaw twitched, his gaze lowering to her mouth. "Let's say I'm calling your bluff. Do your worst."

"Ah." This was getting interesting. "My worst is pretty bad," she commented, her adrenaline beginning to recover. Tying up Rick Addison. Why hadn't she thought of this before? "Are you sure you're up for it?"

"Definitely," he returned, pushing toward her against the rope.

Slowly, Samantha leaned in and licked the curve of his left ear. "Good."

He turned his head, catching her mouth in a hard kiss. "So is this what I should expect every time you meet with a client?"

Samantha pulled her pruners from her back pocket, amused at the sudden wariness in his eyes. "Apparently," she returned, snipping the neck of his sweatshirt and then open-

ing up the front of the material to expose his chest and washboard abs. The first time she'd set eyes on him she'd thought
he looked more like a professional soccer player than a businessman, and she still couldn't quite control the way his
body affected her.

"Then I definitely encourage you to expand this business
of yours."

"I don't want to talk about business right now." Running
her hands up the warm skin of his chest, she followed the caress with her mouth. He moaned as her mouth closed over a
nipple, and she went wet.

"How about expansion?" he suggested, his cultured voice
a little unsteady at the edges.

With a chuckle she made her way back up to his mouth.
At least she seemed to have distracted him from the breaking and entering incident, though if he followed his usual
pattern, he'd call her on it later. It was weird, but after three
months she was almost getting to the point where she didn't
mind his questions or the way they made her do far too much
self-analysis, something she'd previously avoided with a
vengeance.

"At least untie my hands," he suggested.

"Nope. You lost. Suffer the consequences."

With a shaky breath, still a little unnerved at the way he
could break through every defense she had without even trying, she straddled his legs. Deepening their kiss to an open-
mouthed Frencher, tongues pushing and shoving as he tried
to win back a little dominance, she tangled her fingers into
his coal black hair. She could feel him between her thighs,
straining at his jeans, and with a satisfied sigh she wriggled
her hips.

"Christ," he grunted. "Take off your shirt and get up
here."

Well, that might be pushing who was in charge, but it sounded like a damned fine idea all the same. Pulling her black sweatshirt over her head, she dumped it to the floor, her bra following. She wasn't generally into power plays and domination, but there was something intoxicating about having him completely at her mercy. It didn't happen often. Lifting up, she offered her breasts to his mouth and tongue, groaning as his pinned hands went to work on the zipper of her black jeans. For a hostage he was quite enterprising, but she'd never had cause to doubt that.

Samantha gripped the spires on the back of the chair and arched against him. "You're nearly as nice as a good B and E," she murmured.

" 'Nearly as nice'?" he repeated, his voice muffled against her left tit. "And speaking of breaking and entering, take your damned pants off."

With a breathless chuckle she slid back off his thighs, shrugging out of her jeans and then flinging her underwear over the corner of the nearest bookshelf. "Your turn." Bending down, she unbuttoned the fastening of his jeans.

She knelt between his thighs and inch by inch began lowering his zipper. With each click of freeing metal teeth her breath came harder, while he lay his head back against the carved mahogany and took it. Finally he gave a clenched moan. "You're bloody killing me, you know."

"That's the idea of torture, isn't it?" As he came free but for the thin, tented material of his boxers, though, she couldn't stand it any longer, either.

Yanking his jeans and shorts down past his thighs, she climbed onto the chair again. She could have tortured him further, she supposed, but she wanted him at least as much as he wanted her. She always seemed to want him, far more badly and far more often than could possibly be normal.

Then again, she had very few long-term relationships to measure this one against. Her hands locked around the chair's arms to steady herself, she slowly sank onto his hard, ready cock.

Rick rocked his hips up against her, the most action he could make while tied to the chair. Firming her grip on the arms, she slid up and down the length of him as slowly as she could stand it, gasping for breath at the hard, filling sensation of him inside her. Rick leaned his head back again, pumping into her and obviously fighting for control. "Dammit, Samantha," he rasped.

She increased her pace, leaning against his chest as she plunged onto him hard and fast. "Let go, Rick," she breathed, biting his ear. "Come for me."

"Jesus," he grunted raggedly, pushing up into her again and again.

She came first, wildly, clenching onto the arms of the chair and flinging her head back as her body quaked. She felt his muscles contract beneath her, inside her, his animal growl of satisfaction—and then the chair collapsed beneath them.

They dropped to the floor in a tangle of limbs and rope and two-hundred-year-old armchair. After a stunned moment sprawled across him, Samantha lifted her head to look down at Rick. "Are you okay?"

He chuckled, twisting a hand free from the loosened ropes. "Not since I met you." Tangling his fist into her hair, he pulled her face down for another deep, long kiss. "And keep the rope handy. I may feel the need for payback, Yank."

"Mm. Promises, promises, Brit."

Two

Richard Addison awoke before Samantha. He usually did. When most people claimed to be night owls, they had no idea what they were talking about. Sam lived for nights, and with few exceptions she detested rising early.

Their sleeping habits were a pointed reminder of the differences between them. The necessities of running a worldwide conglomerate forced him to rise early and keep long hours. Until three months ago Samantha, on the other hand, had done most of her work at night. Cat burglaries, robberies, art and jewel heists, things he knew about in general terms but would probably never learn the specifics of—except for her last job. That one had been memorable. And if she hadn't been in his Palm Beach house trying to steal his priceless stone tablet, he would have been killed in the explosion that had literally thrown them together. She'd saved his life that night, and since then he'd made it his goal to save hers.

Richard leaned over to kiss Samantha softly on the cheek, then slipped out of the King George II bed and into the large adjoining private room. Once he'd called New York for an update on the Chinese tariff research he'd ordered, he buzzed the kitchen downstairs to request a pot of tea and headed into the shower. He had a bruise on one hip from the chair collapse last evening, but as far as he was concerned, the sex had been worth the damage.

Samantha had startled the hell out of him when she'd jumped through the library window. If he hadn't driven three hours to get home, and if he hadn't happened to begin his search for her in the library, he would have missed her arrival.

And thank God he hadn't; the only way to convince her she shouldn't return to her former—and extremely successful—life of crime seemed to be for him to stay one step ahead of her.

Mindful of the typical Devonshire weather in January, he shrugged on a heavy pullover sweater and his jeans before he left the residence on the upper floor of the north wing of Rawley House and headed downstairs to his office. The tea was waiting for him when he sat down behind his desk, and he held the warm cup in his hands for a blissful moment before he took a drink and logged onto his computer.

After eight o'clock he called his London offices to request the latest paperwork and updates on the pipe-fitting company he was in the midst of acquiring. He bumped the day's appointments so he wouldn't have to drive back into town until tomorrow, and had his assistant, Sarah, schedule a meeting for him with the Commerce secretary for after the weekend. That finished, he sat back to check the closing numbers for the American stock market, sipping his tea as he surfed.

Twenty minutes later he stood, stretching, and strolled into the chilly hallway. He'd provided an office for Samantha next to his, in what had historically been the estate manager's quarters. He hesitated before he put a hand on the door handle. Despite her colorful past, she'd been honest with him from the beginning, and if she said she'd decided to set up a small security business, then that was what she was doing. The problem, though, was twofold: One, a small business seemed more like a hobby than a permanent career change; and two, if her reaction to her interview with John Harding was any indication, apparently recommending alarm systems didn't provide enough of a rush to satisfy an adrenaline junkie. Richard frowned.

"I heard somewhere that you shouldn't frown, because your face could freeze like that," Samantha's voice came from a few steps away.

He just barely avoided jumping. "That's just a rumor," he returned, facing her, "perpetrated by people who sell cosmetics."

The sight of her stilled his breath, as it did nearly every time he set eyes on her. His best friend, his thief, his lover, his obsession—what she was coming to mean to him changed and evolved with every beat of his heart. Her parts—green eyes, auburn hair hanging to her shoulders, slim, athletic figure—drove him as mad as the whole of her.

"I thought so, damned antiwrinkle cream people," she commented, stepping by him to swing open her office door. "It's not locked. What were you looking for?"

"I thought I might lend a hand with your proposal for John Harding," he improvised, following her inside.

"I'm not sure I want to give Harding a proposal," she said, flipping on the lights. "I told you I'd rather focus on getting something manageable started in Florida before I open a worldwide megaconglomerate. I've never run a business before." Samantha offered him a fleeting grin. "Not a legitimate one, anyway."

Of course she would prefer to work in Florida. That was

where they'd met, and where she'd begun to put down a few tenuous roots. Taking her fingers, he pulled her closer for a kiss. "There's no such word as 'megaconglomerate,' Harding's a neighbor, and I need to stay in England for at least another fortnight."

"Not 'fortnight.' Two weeks. And I get it. You're telling me to keep busy while you're working," she commented, breaking his hold. "That's lame. I have my own business, and it has nothing to do with you, bub. I mean, shit. Next you'll tell me that you decided to turn the entire south wing of your house here into a public art gallery just because I said I liked art and you didn't want me to get bored."

That had only been part of the reason. "I enjoy art, as well. If I recall, you tried to steal some of it."

"Only one piece." She looked at him, green eyes speculative.

Time to go on the offensive before she figured out everything. "I'm setting up a public gallery because I want to. I asked you to help me because you've worked in museums, you have a damned fine eye for aesthetics, and I don't have to pay you. *And* you happen to know something about keeping my property secure. Besides, you have a nice ass."

"Mm-hm. Obviously you have a fine eye for beauty, yourself, Brit." She grabbed his hand again. "Now stop bugging me about starting my business and follow my nice ass into the gallery wing. I want to know what you think of the lighting we're setting up for the sculpture hall."

"Ah." That was Samantha and her mental sleight of hand; confront and redirect. But if she wanted to change the subject from business to art display, at least it stopped the argument for the time being. "And how much is this lighting going to cost me?" he asked, playing along.

Her quicksilver smile reappeared. "You don't want your

Rodin to look all glary with a cheap lighting system, now, do you?"

"It's far too early in the day for you to keep making up words, love," he returned, pleased to hear the genuine enthusiasm in her voice. "And I meant to ask you, if someone can break into Rawley Park as easily as you did last night, why are we moving my Rodin here, anyway?"

"*I* can break in. That doesn't mean anybody else could. Besides, it was a test. The idea is to keep improving security until I *can't* break in anymore."

"Is that how you're going to test all of your security work?"

"I don't know yet. It might be fun, though. There are companies who hire people like me just to test their security."

Wonderful. "Did you make those phone calls I suggested to get an idea of what you might charge for your services?"

Samantha sighed. "Rick, butt out. You go make your billions, and I'll work my stuff out for myself."

He wanted to keep pressing, mostly because once she did have a business established, it would be more difficult for her to throw her things into a knapsack and vanish into her former life. But he also recognized the expression on her face. She was someone who hated being handled as much as he did, and he'd been pushing hard.

"Fair enough. Might we at least have breakfast before I face the gallery?" He did genuinely like the idea of creating a public gallery, a place to display his priceless artworks and antiquities and to encourage their study and preservation. What he found annoying was the construction crew inside his house, tromping on his privacy and calling him "my lord." Democratic or not, his fellow Brits were unable to ignore a dusty old inherited title like the Marquisdom of Rawley. Thank God for Americans, and in particular for the one currently walking beside him.

"Fine. Breakfast first. Just remember that even though the gallery's a favor, you are paying me to do the security."

"I remember. You keep in mind, though, that this favor you're doing is costing me a small fortune."

She chuckled, her shoulders lowering. "Yes, but it'll look so nice when we're finished. You might even win an award."

"Lucky me. Why didn't you break in through the construction mess?"

"Because that's where I've got most of the live-action security stationed. And besides, it would be cheating."

His resident chef, Jean-Pierre Montagne, had prepared American pancakes for breakfast. As far as Richard knew, the culinary master had never lowered himself to such a thing before Sam's arrival, but she seemed to be as persuasive and charming with his Devonshire household staff as she was with his employees in Palm Beach. And pancakes happened to be her favorite breakfast meal.

After they ate, Samantha led him down to what they'd begun terming the gallery wing. Some time ago he'd given up trying to figure out why she had no trouble stealing anything from anyone but refused to rob museums or public collections—and in fact practically worshiped them. A sort of thieves' snobbery, he assumed. And where Sam was concerned, it made an odd and endearing kind of sense.

"I widened the alcove here," she said, indicating the blueprint she'd borrowed from the crew chief, "because I thought it'd be a great place for your blue Van Gogh. You need to view it from farther away to see the theme of loneliness and not get tangled up in the details of busy nightlife."

"I'm still amazed at how well you drew up the blueprints," he said, gazing at her profile.

She shrugged. "I practically learned how to read by looking at blueprints. Besides, nearly photographic memory, remember?" Sam tapped her skull.

It had more to do with innate talent and skill than memory, but he didn't want to swell her head any bigger than necessary. "Your memory doesn't explain how you know I own a blue Van Gogh," he said instead. "It's on loan to the Louvre."

"I'm subscribing to your monthly fan newsletter," she returned, her voice cool and only the upturn at the end indicating she thought she was being hilarious. "It's only $12.95 a year."

"And you're having it delivered here, I suppose?" he asked dryly. "Because that would be bloody splendid. Yes, Richard Addison subscribes to his own fan club newsletter."

"I'd do that, if *I* had a newsletter. But no, it goes to Stoney's house in Palm Beach and he forwards it to me."

"Wonderful. Your fence gets my newsletter."

"Former fence. He retired too, remember?"

Moving in behind her, Richard slid his arms around her waist, leaning in to kiss the nape of her neck. "How could I forget? And how is Walter?"

"Like you care."

"Hey, you care, so I care."

She shrugged against his chest. "Fine. I'm waiting for his call. He's . . . looking into something for me."

"Something legal?" he asked, keeping his voice amused. Walter "Stoney" Barstone was like the party-loving father to Sam's reformed alcoholic. The addiction in this case was thievery rather than liquor. And no, he didn't like Walter. Stoney was the closest thing Sam had to family, and he was a bloody bad influence on her. Rick wouldn't wager five pence that he was committed to his retirement, whatever he might say. An acquisitions relocation professional, as the fence called himself, didn't quit a very lucrative career just on a whim. And certainly not on someone else's whim.

"Like I'd tell you if it wasn't legal."

"Sam, you—"

The cell phone on her belt chimed the tune to "Raindrops Keep Falling on My Head" from *Butch Cassidy and the Sundance Kid*. Just the fact that she had a cell phone with a traceable number—whether he'd pushed her into it or not—spoke volumes about her intentions to join the legitimate world. "Speak of the devil," she muttered, sliding it off its clip and flipping it open. *"Hola."*

So she'd chosen a thief theme for Walter's ring. Richard wondered what tune she'd chosen for his calls. She listened for a moment in silence, then with a glance at him moved away down the gallery. He could hear her animatedly chatting about something, but obviously he wasn't supposed to know what was going on. He didn't like that much—and she would know it, too, damn it.

Taking a deep breath, he returned his attention to the blueprints. For someone who generally looked at building layouts with an eye toward breaking and entering, her plans for the gallery wing were amazing: simple, elegant, and designed for the artworks to be seen as the artist would have envisioned. It warmed his heart, and for the oddest reason; she enjoyed doing this, and he'd been able to provide her with the opportunity.

At the sound of her phone snapping closed, he faced her again. "And to repeat, how is Walter?"

"He's good," she returned, smiling. "He got the latest newsletter. You've apparently turned your fling with that mysterious Jellicoe into something more long-term, and have in fact invited her to move in to your massive and very private estate in Devonshire, England."

"Hm. Rumors, you know. Can't trust them."

"Right. I can't wait to check in on your fan board. I bet all the girls start flaming me again."

"What the devil are you talking about?"

"I told you, you have a website, hosted by Rick's Chicks. They don't like when you're dating anyone."

"I'd think they would be happy for me," he said dismissively, knowing she only kept track of such things because it annoyed him and amused her. "So that's the only reason Walter called?"

He saw the bare second of hesitation before she rejoined him at the drafting table. "No. He found a place with some good potential."

"For your office?"

"Maybe. He wants me to go back to Palm Beach to take a look at it."

He nodded, covering his frustration. As much as he wanted her to want to remain in England with him, he'd known the Palm Beach issue would surface eventually. "Give me a week, then, and I'll take a look at it with you."

Samantha cleared her throat. "It's apparently a pretty hot property."

"Have Walter tell them I'm interested. They'll wait."

A furrow dipped between her fine eyebrows. "You're not interested. I am."

"Same thing. Come on, let's—"

"It is not the same thing, Rick. For the last damned time this is my deal, okay?"

"I know that," he returned, wondering whether he was facing her independent streak, which was what had first attracted him to her, or her equally wide stubborn streak, which on occasion annoyed the hell out of him. "Someone as enterprising as you, though, might consider that I set up companies and make them profitable for a living—and that I'm rather successful at it. Furthermore, I have no objection to your making use of my experience, or my resources."

Samantha narrowed her eyes. "You have no objection?" she repeated.

Uh-oh. "I'm happy to offer my assistance," he revised, inwardly swearing at himself. She wasn't a leveraged buyout, and she wasn't a bloody employee. "I'd like to help," he tried again.

"I don't think you're offering help," she said stiffly. "You want to do it. Set up an international security firm, line up the clients you think would get the business going profitably and with minimum hassle. But I am not opening a satellite office of Addisco. This is my idea, my project, my shot. And *I* have to do it. By myself."

"Except for Walter, you mean. He gets to be included. It's an office—not a Picasso you can steal and fence."

"Oh, gee, thanks for clarifying that."

"My point is, you and Walter have experience at something that doesn't lend itself to establishing a legitimate business. I specialize in business, and it would be stupid not to take advantage of that fact."

"So now I'm being stupid? Why, because I want to do something without you, right? You know, Rick, I've made a fucking ton of money without your help—and without *my* help, you would have died three months ago."

He scowled. "What the hell does that have to do with setting up a business?"

The biting retort Samantha conjured came out of her chest as a frustrated growl. She'd tried to explain, numerous times, and he refused to listen. "I get it, you know. You want me to be obligated to you, and you want to be able to remind me endlessly that *you* were the reason I was able to succeed. That's not how I do business, legal or otherwise. So you can go to hell."

"If you try this on your own, I would imagine you'll get there first."

"Oh, that's enough of that, asshole," she snapped, turning on her heel and striding toward their private rooms. Or rather, *his* private rooms, which she shared. Buckingham damned Palace was smaller than this place.

"What does that mean?" he demanded, stomping after her.

"I'm going to Florida."

"In a week you're going to Florida."

"Ha!" *He still didn't get it.* "Think you can keep me here, rich guy?"

"It's for your own good. If you'd stop and use your brain instead of your bloody ego for a damned minute, you'd realize that you'd be better off if you waited for me."

"You think *my* ego's the problem?"

"You—"

"Hey, here's my advice to you," she retorted, flipping him the finger as she vaulted over the stair railing to the landing below, then did it again to reach the second floor well before him.

She knew what he was doing, trying to control her and the situation. That was how he'd made his billions. But this was her gig, her test, and if they continued with this escalated pushing and pulling as they had over the past few weeks, one or both of them were going to end up hospitalized or dead.

"Sam!" Rick bellowed, charging down the stairs after her.

She'd been a thief all her life except for the past three months, and some habits died harder than others. Dashing into the bedroom, she dove into the wardrobe and snatched out her knapsack. As many things as she'd been acquiring lately, everything she absolutely needed to survive stayed packed in that knapsack.

In the bedroom entryway he practically crashed into her, and she dodged beneath his grab. He was getting better at tracking her. After all, even for a rich guy he was in damned good shape, and she wasn't entirely certain she'd be able to take him in a brawl—especially since he'd been known to fight dirty.

Rick had given her a black Mini Cooper, mostly because she thought it was just too cool for words, and last night she'd left it parked half a mile from the estate. Rick had at least half a dozen cars of his own here in Devonshire, all but one of them currently in the large former stable he'd converted into a garage.

On her way out she snatched up her pruners, detouring through the garage and snapping the door cables as she dove out the front rolling doors. Behind her Rick skidded to a halt just in time to avoid getting brained, yelling at her to stop and quit fucking around. *Ha.* She'd barely begun. He'd have to go out through the front now, so she had at least three minutes on him. And she knew where her car was stashed, and he didn't.

His sleek blue James Bond BMW was parked on the drive, no doubt waiting for him to whisk her away on some picnic or fancy lunch or something, as he seemed to do on an alarmingly regular basis. From her first view of him three months ago, she wouldn't have thought him a romantic, but he seemed to have an uncanny sense of what she enjoyed and what she'd always longed to do. But fuck that. She refused to give him any points for being nice today.

Clutching the pruners like a knife, she plunged them into the right front tire of the BMW. At the hiss of air escaping, she yanked it out and went to work on the other three tires. It was a damned shame to disable such a hot car, but she was not going to let this turn into a chase. She'd told him she was leaving, and she meant it, damn it.

She left the pruners in the last tire, then sprinted down the long, sloping drive. His property extended for an obscene number of acres, but he'd been forced by the paparazzi and the public to put up a wall around the house itself. That was where his heaviest security could be found, and it was where she'd been concentrating on protecting both him and the collection of artworks he'd been relocating in anticipation of the gallery wing opening.

This morning, though, she didn't much care about setting off alarms, or any kind of stealth at all. The locks would be engaged on the main gate, so she simply scaled it, dropping down on the other side to the cobblestoned ground of the drive entry. That done, she hoofed it up the narrow road to the lake turnoff.

Sam couldn't help looking over her shoulder as she unlocked her car and tossed the knapsack onto the passenger seat. No sign of Rick, but he wouldn't be far behind. And he wouldn't be happy.

Even as she started the car and shot down the road toward the main highway, part of her enjoyed this. A little rush of adrenaline, no matter the reason, still helped to satisfy that deep craving inside her—the craving that hadn't been satisfied nearly enough lately. The craving that he wanted to lock behind a desk—probably in an office without even a window.

Flipping open her cell phone, she dialed British Airways. Using one of Rick's credit card numbers that she'd memorized, she booked a seat on the next open flight to Miami, and then arranged for a connecting flight to Palm Beach. Credit cards were good. She really should get one soon. As for paying him back, she'd wire him the damned cash as soon as she got to Florida. She wasn't going to owe him anything.

Sam watched out the tiny window as the plane took off. No sign of Rick at the terminal. For the first time she wondered if he might have decided not to come after her.

Sitting back, she shrugged. So what if she never saw him again? He wasn't any better than she was, but he was a hell of a lot more arrogant. She definitely didn't need that right now.

As she flipped open the *People* magazine she'd snagged in the airport, she found herself looking at him—at them, when they'd attended a movie premiere last month. He looked great in a black tuxedo, while she looked like she was trying not to cringe at the mass of camera flashes and yelling celebrity-holics. She definitely wouldn't miss that. And she wouldn't miss him.

Okay. Maybe she would miss him, but it didn't matter. After three straight months in England, she was going somewhere that for the previous three years she'd almost begun to think of as home. Except that right now in her mind "home" had the alarming tendency to be wherever Rick Addison was.

Mentally she shook herself. She didn't need him; she simply liked being around him. And she liked the sex. A lot. Even so, the promise she'd made to go straight hadn't been so much for him as it had been for herself. He didn't get to take the credit, and he wasn't going to do any of the work. It was up to her. Her life and the direction it took had always been up to her.

Three

Palm Beach, Florida
Thursday, 4:47 p.m.

*S*amantha picked the lock of the small, nondescript
house on the fringes of Palm Beach and slipped inside.
In the kitchen, a large shiny-headed, dark-skinned man sat
at the Formica-topped table and picked at a salad. A burger
still wrapped in its yellow paper covering sat on a plate one
seat over.

"About time you got here, honey," Stoney said, a grin
curving across his rounded face. "Your cheeseburger with
extra-tomato-hold-the-onion's getting cold."

"I was trying to surprise you," she returned, swooping in
to kiss him on the cheek before she dumped her knapsack in
the corner and dropped into the vacant chair. "How'd you
know I'd be here in time for dinner?"

"Check the answering machine," he said, pointing his elbow toward the counter.

She sighed, pretending that she wasn't actually relieved
that Rick was still in the chase. "How many messages did he
leave?"

"Three. I answered it the first time and then wised up. He's kinda pissed at you, sweetie."

"Well, it's mutual." *Kind of, anyway.* Actually, she mostly wanted to kick him until he apologized for being a jerk and agreed on a stack of Bibles that he would back the hell off and let her try this new experiment without his interference.

"You over with, then?"

Stoney would like that; he hadn't exactly approved of her relationship with one of the highest profile, wealthiest guys in the world any more than Rick liked her friendship with and reliance on the acquisitions relocation professional. Sam blew out her breath, trying to ignore the tightening of her chest when she thought of never seeing Addison again. "Hell if I know." She unwrapped the burger and dove in. "He was getting in my way. And I missed you."

"I missed you, too." For a long moment Stoney looked at her over a forkful of lettuce and shredded cheese, topped with fat-free Italian dressing. "You sure you want to go legit? Because I got a hell of an offer from Creese, a million for a night's work in Ven—"

"Shut up," she interrupted. "Don't tempt me."

"But—"

"The last job I pulled, Stoney, three people ended up getting killed. I think that's a sign."

"None of that was your fault. Without you there, it would have been worse. And Addison would have been a corpse, too."

That still upset her. "Maybe. But I'm starting to feel less like Cary Grant in *To Catch a Thief* and more like Bruce Willis in *Die Hard*." She shrugged. "It's not so fun when you have to watch out for falling body parts."

"And?" he prompted. "You've done a lot of jobs where nobody even chipped a nail. Besides, you could put up with a lot of crap for a million. It's for a lost Michelangelo, Sam. It's called *The Trinity*."

"Dammit, Stoney, I said not to tell me." *Michelangelo*. Shit. She loved Michelangelo. "I'm not doing it. I'm retired."

"Yeah, because he says so."

"Are all men deaf? Weren't you listening to me?"

"Yep. And I hear good, too."

"Good. Then hear this. *I* said no!"

"Okay, okay, but I'm not throwing away my Rolodex." Stoney chewed another mouthful of salad. "Just in case."

"That's probably a good idea," she conceded. "Is that why you're still living in this crappy house, too? Just in case?"

He chuckled. "Saying retired and thinking retired are two different things. And I've been keeping a low profile for so long I'm not sure I can do anything different. You have no idea how many bullets I sweated this morning when it dawned on me that you'd given Addison my damn phone number."

Samantha grimaced. "Your address, too."

"What?"

"Well, he's a pain in the ass sometimes, but if something happened to me, I wanted him to be able to get hold of you. Remember, I spent my first two weeks in England in the hospital with a concussion."

Stoney gave her a disgusted look. "I think you still have a concussion."

She cleared her throat. Time for a change of subject. "When can I see the office?"

"Since I had a good idea you were coming," he returned, glancing again at the phone, "I arranged for a tour in about half an hour. It's right on Worth Avenue, across the street from that Donner guy's office."

Sam smiled. "Really? I can get an office across from Tom Donner's? He'll hate that." Rick's closest friend or not,

Samantha didn't think she'd ever be able to see eye-to-eye with an attorney—especially one who was such a Boy Scout. Antagonizing Donner, though—that could be fun.

"I think the point is that you wanted me to find something swanky."

"Only swanky people are going to be able to afford my services. Our services."

"Right." His brow furrowed. "This is your gig, honey. I'll help with the paperwork."

"You don't sound very committed."

"I'm not. You're kind of stiff-arming me into it, don't you think?"

"Yep. I can't hang with you if you're still redistributing. And I like hanging with you."

Setting down his fork, Stoney took her fingers in his large hand. "You're my baby, baby. I've been looking after you since you were five, whenever your daddy went out on a job. But I hope you're really thinking hard about what this'll mean."

"It means I'll be legit, and I won't have to keep looking over my shoulder to see if Interpol found a fingerprint."

"Not just that. The whole high-profile thing. You're getting ready to advertise an office address. That means every cop in the world is going to know where to find you. And so will anybody you ever worked with, or for. And they're all gonna be worried that you're better than they are, or that if they cross Sam Jellicoe, she might just hand over evidence about them to the authorities."

She *had* been thinking about that, and it troubled her immensely. Still, it was her decision, and she wasn't going to let a bunch of high-line burglars and buyers and arrest-hungry cops—or idiot paparazzi—dictate her life. "I like pressure. Remember?"

"I remember. I also remember that you're crazy."

"Yep. Thanks for sticking with me, Stoney."

"I'd stick with you if you decided to spend the weekend in Venice stealing a Michelangelo, too."

She was tempted, dammit. "If I were an alcoholic, would you offer me a beer?"

"Is this beer worth a million bucks?"

"Knock it off, bucko."

As soon as they finished eating he drove them to Worth Avenue. She couldn't help noting that his red '93 Chevy pickup could use a detail and a tune-up, but she kept her observations to herself. After all, she had a hot blue Bentley Continental GT parked in Rick's stadium-sized garage at his massive estate just a couple of miles away. Stoney didn't precisely know that Rick had given her the car, because she knew exactly what her erstwhile fence would have to say about that particular gift. And he thought she'd been flirting with danger before. Ha.

Tom Donner's building—or more accurately, the location for the headquarters of the law firm of Donner, Rhodes and Chritchenson—was all reflective, glinting glass. Corporate, real estate, personal, and criminal legal defense all in one ultra-efficient, ultra-expensive location. The less noticeable building across the street lacked two stories on its opposite but had the same gleaming lines of glass and chrome.

"Which floor?" she asked as they parked in the two-story structure beside the building.

"Third. The whole northwest corner."

"Cool." Looking up at the building for a moment, she tried to imagine herself with not only an address, but a place of business.

"It's not cheap, baby. Are you ready to put your Milan retirement fund into renting an office?"

"Christ, how much is it?" she returned dubiously. Her Milan retirement fund, as both she and Stoney termed it, was nothing to sneeze at, but then she had always planned on retiring one day and using it to sustain her in extreme comfort for the remainder of her life. Her retirement had come early, and while affording Milan would still have been pretty easy, if she screwed up in the business world she'd be changing her plans to a retirement home in Fort Lauderdale.

"I'll let the realtor give you the figures. Her name's Kim."

The lobby had a concierge, a pair of elevators, and a marble floor the color and pattern of beach sand. God, it was so tasteful—which was precisely what she'd asked Stoney to look for. They stepped out on the third floor, covered in ivory-colored carpet with brown and green speckles. A series of pond and garden paintings guided the way down the north hallway.

"Monet," she noted automatically. "Prints, but nice frames."

"If they were real, *I'd* pay you to lift 'em."

A door at the far end of the hall opened. "Shut up," she muttered, assuming a smile and tucking her Gucci purse under her left arm as a petite salt and pepper brunette in one of those ubiquitous blue suit skirts from Neiman Marcus approached. "You must be Kim. I'm Sam. Thanks for meeting me this late."

The realtor gave her a confident smile and a firm handshake. "Walter and I have looked at seventeen different offices in the area. I'm excited that he liked this one enough to bring you in for approval."

"Let's take a look then, shall we?" Sam returned, gesturing her back toward the door. "*Seventeen* outings, Walter?"

Her former fence swatted her on the fanny as he passed her. "That's enough to qualify as at least two dates," he murmured. "I can't help it if she likes me."

"Hey, go for it, Sto . . ." She trailed off as she entered the office. A large reception area greeted them first, with a counter for the receptionist and a door on either side of that leading into the depths of the office. Five comfortably sized offices branched out from a squared-off, U-shaped hallway that ran from one reception door to the other. The corner office had a view of the beach and Lake Worth beyond—only the very rich could call a bay "a lake" and have it stick—from one wall-sized window, while the other looked at the law offices of Donner, Rhodes and Chritchenson across Worth Avenue.

While Kim listed off the amenities like central air-conditioning and marble restrooms shared by only two other office suites, Samantha gazed out the window. Weird. Three months after meeting Richard Addison she was preparing to set up an office fifty yards from that of his corporate attorney. Donner was going to crap his pants when he found out.

"Do you have any questions for me?" Kim asked.

"How much?" Sam returned, turning away from the window.

"Eleven thousand one hundred and twelve per month. That doesn't include phone or electricity, but it does cover your share of the concierge's wages, building security, elevator maintenance, water, liability insurance, and general common area upkeep."

"When can we occupy?"

"As soon as you sign the papers," Kim said, patting her briefcase. "Building management has informed me that there are four other interested parties, but taking into consideration your connections, they agreed to put a hold on the offices through midnight tonight."

Sam quickly erased her frown. "What connections would those be?"

Kim's smile twitched. "Walter mentioned that you're residing at Solano Dorado. That's Rick Addison's estate. And I always keep up on the local social news. It's important to my business. So of course I know that a Samantha Jellicoe's been dating Mr. Addison. That would be you, I presume."

Sending a glare at Stoney, Sam drew in a breath. Alfred the butler never told people Bruce Wayne's secret identity. "Yes, that's me. I hope you and the building management are aware that these offices will not be part of Rick Addison's business."

"Of course," the realtor returned, though from her expression, she hadn't been aware of any such thing.

"Then let's sign those papers."

"You're seriously ready to spend 10K on office furniture," Stoney said for the fourth time, his gaze on the road.

Samantha slouched beside him, her feet up on the dashboard as she composed an ad for an office receptionist. "We're swanky, remember?" she returned, glancing over at him. "I've spent most of my life rubbing elbows with rich marks, Stoney. Trust me, I know what they expect, and I know how to make them comfortable. Okay if I use your fax number until we get one set up at the office?"

"Sure. But don't you think it's kind of funny that if you quit spending your Milan retirement fund to make everybody else think you *look* rich, you would be rich? You can rub elbows with them without faking anything, baby."

"I'm not faking. I'm setting up an . . . ambience. It's good business."

"Yeah. If it doesn't give me a heart attack first."

She laughed. "And we thought thievery was dangerous."

He snickered. "Your dad would be so pissed off at you, spending your cash to go legit."

"I know." Samantha shrugged, crossing out a line. "I'm not Martin."

"I'll tell you what. Give me a couple of days to look into office furniture styles and shit."

"With Kim along to give you advice?"

Stoney grinned. "That is a fine idea, honey."

"Okay. I can work on getting clients, and you give me a couple of ideas about furniture."

"Works for me. Still not as fun as being in Venice, but . . . Uh-oh."

"What?" She looked up, to find him gazing down the street toward his house. Sam straightened.

A sleek green Jaguar, looking completely out of place in the old, shabby neighborhood, crouched at the curb. The driver was nowhere in sight, but of course she knew to whom it belonged. He'd made good time. Really good time.

"You want me to turn around?" Stoney asked dubiously.

"No. He probably heard your truck coming from a mile away, anyway."

They turned into the driveway. Stoney hung back, but she couldn't really blame him. She and Rick had argued before, but this wasn't about a thing or an incident; it was about *them*.

The front door was unlocked, and with a breath she pushed it open. She had a snappy entrance line ready, but when she saw him sitting at the nondescript Formica table in the kitchen and drinking lemonade from one of Stoney's palm tree glasses, she changed her mind. Neither did she care to put into words how . . . satisfying it felt to see him, or how her heart beat fast when he met her gaze. "How long have you been here?" she asked.

Cobalt blue glanced toward the wall and Stoney's sliding

eyes cat clock. "In Florida? Nearly two hours. At Walter's, about ten minutes."

"You busted my lock," Stoney said from the entryway.

"I'll buy you a new one," Rick returned, rising. "I took the liberty of throwing your knapsack into the car."

She frowned. "You can't—"

He lifted a hand. "You owe me a garage door and four tires. I would consider us even, though, if you'd come back to Solano Dorado with me."

"Bribery?"

"A business transaction. And besides, I'd like to yell at you, and I'd hate to have to do it here in front of Walter."

"I'd hate that, too," Stoney put in, strolling into the kitchen with the stack of paint samples they'd collected.

"Fine," she grumbled, not wanting Rick to think she needed Stoney for backup. "But don't expect me to apologize for the door or the tires. Or anything."

"We'll negotiate," he returned, pulling a piece of paper from his inside jacket pocket. "This came for you."

"You read my mail?"

"It was on my office fax at Solano Dorado."

"But you read it."

"It came to *my* fax number, darling."

She still didn't like it one damned bit. He'd been in town for half an hour, and despite knowing that she wanted him to back off, he couldn't resist snooping. Silently she added that to her list of grievances. Taking the fax, she offered Stoney a peck on the cheek as she headed back out the front door. "I'll see you in the morning."

"At the office?"

"Sure."

That sounded cool, to actually have an office where she

could meet people. Previously it had been mostly his kitchen table or dark restaurants or untraceable phone calls.

"So did you like the office Walter found?" Rick asked, catching up to her on the sidewalk.

"Yes." Silence. "We leased it half an hour ago."

He pulled open the passenger door of the Jag and offered a hand to help her in. Sam avoided his fingers, though, as she slid onto the warm leather seat. Touching him was important, and he liked the physical contact between them.

"Might I see it?"

"Probably not."

"Hm." He dropped in behind the wheel, and in a moment they'd peeled off down the street. "When I needed help solving a theft, I recruited you."

"No, I recruited *you*."

"Yes, maybe, but I agreed to it. Thievery is your area of expertise. Business is mine. Why won't you let me help you?"

"Rick, drop it, or the next time I take a trip you're not going to be able to find me."

He glanced at her before returning his attention to the road. "No. Look at it like I do, Samantha. This is obviously important to you. If you exclude me, then I've lost too much of you."

"You're jealous of me getting a job?" she asked incredulously.

"I'm jealous that you're trying to push me out of this part of your life, the part that's excited about trying something new and looking to the future."

Well, it was an explanation she hadn't expected. And it made her arguments seem selfish—though that had probably been the idea. He knew how to put together a persuasive proposal, after all. Hell, he did it for a living. But *she* hadn't been butting into *his* latest deal. "Sounds good, slick, but I said no."

"I got that. You disabled my car so I couldn't follow you, if you'll recall."

"I'm not trying to exclude you from knowing what's going on with me, Rick, but I don't want you to do this for me. I don't know why you don't get that."

"Try explaining it to me instead of just telling me to back off."

She sighed. "Okay. I've . . . I'm good at everything I try, you know?"

To her surprise, he gave a brief chuckle. "I've noticed that."

"But I've never tried this. And if you do the work, then it's not mine, and it doesn't mean anything. It doesn't mean I've done it." She thudded her fist into her thigh. "Does that make sense?"

They drove in silence for a moment. "Yes. More than I care to admit."

"It's about fucking time."

"Might I at least recommend clients?"

"As long as you don't assume I'm going to jump at every bone. I know swanky people, too, but mostly because I've robbed them."

"Good, and good God. Take a look at your fax."

She'd nearly forgotten it. Digging into her bag, she pulled out the sheet of paper and unfolded it. "Charles Kunz. He's a manufacturer, isn't he?"

"Plastics. His son Daniel and I play polo together. The father's a bit . . . abrasive, but—" He stopped, shooting a look at her. "You haven't stolen from them, have you?"

"Nope." Sam forced a smile. "I'm going to get that question a lot, aren't I?"

"Probably. Would you tell me if you *had* broken and entered?"

Probably not. "Maybe."

"Anyway, he wants to set up a meeting with you."

She perked up. "See? I haven't even been in town for twenty-four hours, and I'm getting clients already."

"You can use my office at Solano Dorado, if you'd like."

Whether he was just being generous or not, she didn't like it. "Don't piss me off again. I'll grab some folding chairs and meet him at *my* office tomorrow. It should be passable, if Stoney'll pretend to be the receptionist."

"I doubt folding chairs and Stoney will impress Charles Kunz."

She stuck her tongue out at him. "From the fax, he knows I'm just setting up," she returned, glancing at the sheet again. "And I'll have an ad for office help showing up in the paper tomorrow or the day after."

And she still hadn't given an inch. Richard wasn't accustomed to apologizing, and he knew he probably could have done a better job of it, but dammit, she could give him a little credit. Taking a breath, he concentrated on the road for a few moments, on the way the concrete and steel made way for palm trees and beach as they crossed the southern bridge, and on the way the sun reflected warm through the tinted glass of the Jaguar.

"Is Florida going to be home for you?" he finally asked, taking the main road cutoff leading to estate row.

Although he kept his eyes on the road, he could feel her glance. "I like it here," she said slowly. "Do you?"

"I wouldn't have bought Solano Dorado if I didn't."

"But you have that tax thing where you can only spend ten weeks a year in the States."

"I can be here longer. I just have to pay more."

"How much more?"

He pressed a button on his key chain and the heavy metal gates of Solano Dorado swung open. They headed up the long, winding drive past stands of palm trees and low hedges of tropical plants. "Not enough to keep me away if you want my company."

She cleared her throat. "I want your company."

He wanted to shout and sing and screw her until she begged for mercy, but instead he pulled up in front of the house and shut off the car. _Be patient_ was his mantra where she was concerned, though he often quashed it in favor of _enjoy it while you can._ "That's a good thing, considering that I find your company rather refreshing, myself."

Reinaldo emerged from the house, but Rick beat the housekeeper to Samantha's car door and pulled it open for her. This time when he offered his hand she accepted it. She had apparently decided he'd at least made his point, then. And thank God for that, because if he didn't get his hands on her in the next hour he was going to do himself some serious bodily injury.

"Hey, Reinaldo," she greeted the housekeeper, smiling.

"Miss Sam," the housekeeper returned in a light Cuban accent, "I'm to tell you that Hans has stocked peppermint ice cream and Diet Cokes."

"Is Hans married?" she asked, slinging her knapsack over her shoulder and strolling up the shallow steps to the front doors.

"Only to his antipasto," Richard put in, not giving her time to reconsider her phrasing. "Married" was one of those words she avoided, along with "love" and the combination of "future" and "together." He understood that, and he made allowances for it. With the way she'd grown up, the fact that she was able to admit to wanting him around at all was rather amazing.

She laughed, leading the way into the foyer. Catching up, he wrapped his fingers around hers and joined her on the way down the long hallway and up the stairs to what had previously been his private rooms, and were now theirs.

As soon as they were inside he closed the door and turned to pull her up against his front. "Hello," he murmured, leaning down to kiss her sweet mouth.

Her free hand slid around his shoulder. "It's only been like one day."

"And a whole other continent. I missed you, Samantha. I can't help it."

"I'm just irresistible."

She settled into him, arms around his waist and her face upturned. Richard kissed her slowly, deeply, relishing the sensation of her in his arms. When they were apart he always thought of her as being taller and sturdier; in reality she was slender and petite, and seemed totally unsuited for the life of crime she'd been living—and excelling at.

He wanted her badly. This was one of those times he intended to enjoy the moment. Slipping his hands beneath her pink, lacy-sleeved T-shirt, Richard ran his palms along the warm, smooth skin of her back, then twisted his fingers into the material and tugged it off over her head.

As he lowered his mouth to her throat she went boneless, and he swept her up into his arms and made his way to the bedroom with its huge blue bed. One-handed, she managed to undo his belt before he set her down, and she tugged it free as he sank over her on the soft coverlet.

"Rick?" she whispered, her voice not quite steady.

"Hm?" he returned, unfastening her cute pink bra and spreading his fingers across her pert tits.

"I'm glad you came to Florida."

He unzipped her jeans and yanked them down past her knees. "So am I."

She kicked her pants off completely. "I mean, I missed you, too. A little. Even though you're a jerk."

Unfastening his own jeans, Richard shoved them down and slid over her again, slowly sinking the length of his cock into her hot, tight depths. "You only missed me a little?" he managed, beginning his plunge.

"Christ. Maybe more . . . than a little."

"Good." Grunting, he continued his rhythmic assault while she clutched his shoulders, her legs sweeping around his hips as she met him thrust for thrust. With a gasp she arched her back and came. Faster than he wanted, he felt himself building too far to stop, so he gave into instinct and pumped into her hard and fast until he found his release.

"I'm going to have to stop using the word 'little' when I discuss you," she panted, guiding his face down to her shoulder as he relaxed against her.

"I'm going to have you start writing my fan club newsletter," he returned.

"Oh, you wouldn't want that."

Four

Samantha, with Rick seated beside her, drove the Bentley Continental GT to Worth Avenue. The car fit the street and the building to perfection, and if Rick hadn't gifted her with it, she would have purchased something like it. She'd long ago learned that blending with marks—clients—was the best way to earn their trust, and she couldn't very well set up a high-class security business and keep driving a Honda Civic. She hid a smile. Besides, that Civic had been stolen and then, with Stoney's help, ditched months ago.

"Are we going to Tom's office?" Rick asked, leaning an arm along the window frame.

"No. Mine." She slid into an open spot along the street and put the car in park. "You said you wanted to see it."

His gaze was on the tall building owned by Donner, Rhodes and Chritchenson on the far side of the street. "I do, but—"

"Come on. This way," she interrupted, enjoying his confusion. It didn't happen very often. "And no business advice."

"I'll do my damnedest." He followed her into the opposing building, through the tasteful lobby, and into the chrome elevator. "Five floors," he noted, taking in the short row of buttons and then the lighted one in the middle. "Third floor for you."

"Not the entire floor."

He smiled at her. "Not yet, anyway."

There he went again with his little pushes, trying to convince her to open offices worldwide and become some megasecurity advisor queen. The idea did appeal to her—for sometime in the future, if the legit career thing worked out. On the other hand, if she pretended to go along with his world-domination theme, it would give her an excuse to spend the weekend every so often in . . . Venice, say. Sam shook herself. Even with a chance to touch a Michelangelo and earn another million bucks, she was not going to Venice. Not, not, not.

She led Rick through the suite door and into the empty reception area. "Stoney's picking up some furniture catalogs."

Rick nodded but didn't say anything as they meandered through the unfurnished offices and the backside of reception. She tried to pretend that his opinion didn't matter to her, tried to pretend that his approval wasn't important whatever she might say to him—and not just as a multibillionaire businessman, but as her . . . lover, and her friend.

"It's champion," he said after a moment, smiling as he took another turn around the side office she'd already decided to claim for herself. "Well done, Samantha."

"Thanks."

Rick paused at the window. "And Tom's going to fill his knickers when he finds out your office is across the street from his."

Chuckling, Sam joined him. "That's what I thought. Isn't it great? But don't you tell Donner. I want to."

"There you are, honey," Stoney's voice came as he strolled into the office. He had an absurdly delicate purple orchid cradled in his large arms. "The building owners sent this as an office-warming present."

"Wow," she said, taking the orchid and doing a little more pretending that she hadn't noticed the way Rick and Stoney were pretty much ignoring each other. "Epidendrum." She felt Rick looking at her. "What?" she asked.

"I'd forgotten how much you like gardens and flowers," he returned in a quiet, intimate voice. "I'm going to tear up the area around the pool. It's time for an update, and it's yours."

Samantha swallowed. *A garden.* You couldn't roam the world and have a garden. He did know she'd always wanted one, but he couldn't possibly realize how much it meant to her. A garden meant a home. "From time to time," she whispered, taking his hand again in her free one, "you can be very nice."

"From time to time," he returned, tugging her closer, "you let me." Slowly he leaned down and kissed her softly on the mouth.

"Ahem," Stoney grumbled. "I plugged in a phone and a fax."

That had been fast. "Where did you get . . ." She trailed off at the quick head shake from Stoney. ". . . the phone numbers?" she finished.

"Kim set them up last night."

She checked her watch. Ten o'clock, probably a decent hour to return Charles Kunz's fax with a phone call—one she could now make from her own office. Samantha handed the orchid to Rick. "Thanks, Stoney. You two talk for a minute. I have to make a call."

"Sam—"

"I'll be right back."

Richard watched her vanish into the reception area, then

turned back to face Walter Barstone. He'd dealt with executives, disgruntled underlings, and slick lawyers, but Stoney was a new one. "Are you enjoying your retirement?"

"Not really. Is Sam enjoying hers?"

"She seems to be, yes."

The fence glanced toward the front of the office and back again. "You planning on staying long in Palm Beach?"

"Evidently."

"So she goes where she wants, and you follow? That's—"

"That's really none of your affair," Richard broke in. It was far more complicated than that, and he had no intention of discussing with Barstone that his business was essentially wherever he was. Location meant influence and prestige, but he could operate from anywhere.

"I mean, no offense, but you have a pretty busy life. And Sam's kind of a full-time deal all on her own. It just doesn't make much—"

"No offense," Richard cut in again, "but I don't think I need your advice."

"Then you don't—"

"Hey, Brit," Samantha crooned, prancing back into the room to take Rick's hand, "you wanna go on a date with me tonight?"

Richard couldn't resist sending Walter a smug look over her head. "I was going to ask you the same question, actually. There's a charity thing tonight, kind of a grand opening to the Palm Beach Season proper. It's bloody exclusive, but if you want, I'll inquire whether any tickets are still available. I thought you might find some potential clients there."

"Is this charity thing the one at the Everglades Club?"

He lowered one eyebrow. "Yes."

She snorted. "I already got us tickets."

Richard absorbed that. When he'd said the event was exclusive, he hadn't been kidding. "You did?"

"Yep." She kissed his cheek. "I have connections, too, you know."

"Who the devil did you call?"

"Charles Kunz's secretary. He wants to meet me at the club tonight. They're his extra tickets."

"So it's actually *my* connection you're using."

"You gave him to me."

"So I did."

The event at the Everglades Club was a dinner, dancing, and drinking fest for charity, an annual thing that marked the beginning of the Palm Beach winter season. Since Richard was rarely in town this early, he'd never attended before. In fact, he didn't particularly like their old-fashioned membership restrictions and had never applied to join the exclusive Everglades Club. When he was in Florida, for the most part he worked. Until now, apparently. As he'd been attempting to point out to Samantha, hers wasn't the only life that had been upended over the past three months.

The Kingdom Fittings project, for instance, was taking up too much of his time, particularly now that he needed to move the board of directors' meeting from London to Palm Beach. There was no going around them, especially since some farsighted individual had empowered them to accept or veto any purchase offers. Still, that made it a challenge, and he seemed unable to resist those.

At just after six he left his Solano Dorado office and made his way upstairs to change. Samantha wasn't in the room, but she had left her usual neatly folded shirt, jeans, and shoes under the nightstand on her side of the bed; he still hadn't been able to cure her of the idea that she might have to flee somewhere in the middle of the night.

He shrugged into his tuxedo and went into the bathroom to knot his black bow tie beneath the better light there. Samantha had left a yellow Post-It note on the mirror: "I'm on the pool deck."

Electric heat glided down his spine, sending his business frustration into something hotter and less tangible, and much more personal. It was just a bloody note, but it meant she'd considered he would look for her, and that she wanted to be found. With a glance over his shoulder, he removed the Post-It and tucked it into his breast pocket. The world knew him as a hard-assed businessman—he could guess what it would make of him if anyone learned that he saved the little notes from his lover.

Giving the bow tie a last tug, he went to the full-length glass doors that opened onto the small balcony and the pool deck below. He pushed them open and then stopped for a long moment on the balcony, looking down.

Samantha had chosen to wear red. He knew she liked to blend into situations, and the low-cut, sleeveless sheath of silk certainly would fit into the upper class elbow-rubbing bash, but he truly didn't see how anyone who got a glimpse of her would possibly be able to look away without noticing. She'd pinned up her wavy auburn hair, though wisps hung in front of her ears and across her forehead. She'd even gone with earrings, clip-on, of course—when she was working, she'd told him, she didn't wear any jewelry, in case something should fall off or could be seen on her and identified later.

As he stood on the balcony and watched, she wandered along the edging of grass, her gaze on the low mix of ferns and azaleas lining the half wall. "What are you doing?" he asked, heading down the stairs.

She faced him. "Were you serious about letting me replant here?" Her gaze sharpened as he joined her by the lighted pool. "And wow. James Bond. You look great."

"Thanks. I'll pass the compliment on to Armani."

"I so don't want to jump Armani's bones right now," she returned, grinning. "It ain't the tux, Brit." Reaching up, she readjusted his tie, though she seemed more interested in running her hands along his lapels.

If he could pick moments to last forever, this would be one of them. He covered her hands with his. "You look rather stunning, yourself," he murmured.

"Thanks. I found it at Ungaro's. I even cut off the tag so I can't return it."

Richard smiled down at her, hoping the expression didn't look as idiotically sappy as it felt. "Amazing. And yes, do whatever you like with the garden here. Unless you prefer somewhere else."

She raised up on her tiptoes and kissed him softly. "You don't have to keep giving me things. I'm here because of you. Not the Picassos."

"You don't like Picasso."

"You know what I mean. All I want from you is your trust."

Richard shifted to take her hand and guide her toward the front drive. "I do trust you."

"Mm-hm. I hear you talking, but—"

"It would be easier if you would accept at least some of what I have."

"Easier on you, you mean," she pointed out.

"All I'm saying is that I didn't acquire the Picassos or the

Bentley from being bad at what I do. My advice is as available to you as my . . ."

He'd almost said "heart." Jesus, she was making him insane—or he was doing it to himself.

"Your what?" she prompted, lifting an eyebrow, and her expression making it very clear that she had a good idea what he'd been about to say.

He'd take it as a positive sign that she hadn't turned and run. "My chef," he amended.

"I love your chef," she said, chuckling. "Hans makes the best cucumber sandwiches ever. And I appreciate your offering me the advice."

Deeply surprised until he considered that she hadn't said she would *accept* the advice, he opened the door of the stretched Mercedes-Benz S600 for her. "Right, then."

Limousines thronged the entrance to the Everglades Club, two deep and backed up for half a mile down Worth Avenue. Samantha watched through the tinted windows as they neared the red carpet and roped-off walkway. Press and onlookers lined both the street and the entire length of the entry.

"I didn't realize it would be this high profile," she muttered, starting to run her fingers through her carefully arranged hair and then stopping herself.

"It's the first event of the Season proper, remember?" Rick replied, taking her nervous fingers and squeezing them. "All the weres, ares, and wannabes are going to be here. You knew that."

"Yes, I did. It's just that cameras are here, too."

"You're eventually going to have to get used to it. Everybody knows who you are now, anyway. Another photo won't make anything worse."

"So speaks Mighty Fortress Man," she returned, concentrating on taking deep breaths.

"That's in private. In public, it's going to happen."

It would, for as long as they were together. And giving him up because of a few annoying photographers and reporters seemed the height of absurdity. Besides, as he'd said, the damage had been done. Her picture had been in *People* and even his fan club newsletter, for God's sake. And the Rick's Chicks flame girls regularly posted her photo, with moustache and horns added, on the website. Now all she could do was use her so-called fame to her advantage and get herself some damned clients, starting tonight. "So why is it I could get us tickets and you couldn't?"

"I could have," he protested. "You just beat me to it."

"Uh-huh. Sure. You keep telling yourself that."

He leaned forward. "Ben, just let us out here."

The driver nodded the back of his head at them. "No problem, Mr. Addison."

Sam looked at him, horrified. "Here? It's a long walk to the club."

He had the bad manners to chuckle at her. "I'm not going to get into the publicity game by fighting for a curbside entrance. I want to go inside and dance with you."

"Great."

Eventually they made it past the mobs of onlookers to the austere front doors. Despite her annoyance at him for parading her down the sidewalk, Samantha had to give Rick a few points for pretending not to notice that her grip on his hand was hard enough to break rocks, or that her smile to the crowd was more fake than the boobs of the top-heavy model preceding them.

If she could hear the numerous calls from the sidelines of "Ooh, it's Rick Addison" and "Look this way, Rick!", then her escort could hear them as well. Rick's attention, though, seemed divided only between the front doors and her.

"How are you faring?" he murmured.

"I think those girls on the left side with the signs are members of Rick's Chicks," she returned, mostly to see if she could rattle him.

"So are you, if you get the newsletter."

Sam smiled. She couldn't help it, even when the volume of camera flashes increased in response. "That's right. Ooh, Mr. Addison, you're so hot, sign my tit, will you?"

He leaned over, kissing her ear. "I am going to fuck you all night," he whispered.

Shivers went all the way down her spine. "I must have the deluxe fan club membership."

"Oh, that you do, Samantha. That you do."

They passed through the doors into the cool depths of the club. After three years in Palm Beach, she'd grown used to seeing the faces in the newspaper, but it was a little weird to have former Presidents, cosmetics executives, oil magnates, actors, and models all rubbing elbows together. And it was even weirder how many of them knew Rick and sought him out for a greeting or a word of investment advice.

"I wonder how many of these guys belong to your fan club," she murmured, reaching over to collect a glass of champagne and handing him another.

"Yes, well, I hope you've noticed how many of the men are looking at you," he returned, directing his famous smile at yet another acquaintance.

She had noticed the stares at her breasts and the assessing looks at her face and her ass. Those who didn't know she was Sam Jellicoe, security expert and Addison's current companion, were probably wondering who the hell she was.

Rick had been known to date actresses and models before, and while she wouldn't precisely put herself in that group, she did work out, after all. Something abruptly occurred to her. "Are any of your former girlfriends here?"

"I wouldn't doubt it. Why?"

"I don't know. I thought we could compare notes or something."

His brow lowered. "Don't you dare."

So she had found a sensitive subject. Admittedly, she'd managed to spend three months in England without running across his ex-wife, Patricia, but then she hadn't exactly been eager to make the lady's acquaintance. And unless she was greatly mistaken, she didn't think Rick had been eager for that, either.

"There's Charles Kunz," he muttered a moment later, nodding toward one of the three bars. "Do you want me to introduce you?"

A surprising rush of nervousness went through her. She'd done two or three security consultations for Rick and his cronies in England, but if she didn't blow it, Kunz would be the first official client of Jellicoe Security. Samantha stifled a frown. She needed a catchier name than that. "No, I'll take care of it," she said. "Besides, that girl by the door wearing that see-through white Band-Aid's been staring at you since we walked in. You should go say hi before her dress falls completely off."

She pulled her hand free, but Rick shifted to grip her arm. "I'll wander by to see you in a few minutes." Blue eyes met hers. "Good luck, Samantha."

"Luck's for schmucks, Brit, but thanks."

Swallowing, she made her way through the glitter and perfume toward the straight-shouldered man holding a half-full glass of liquor. "Mr. Kunz?" she offered, stopping in front of her latest mark—potential client—and noting from the faint odor on his breath that his drink of choice was vodka. Her late dad's poison of choice, as well.

He wasn't much taller than she was, and sported about a quarter of the hair. In a fight, unless he knew jujitsu or something, she could probably take him. When he faced her, though, the steely brown gaze said some of the things that Rick's did—this was a man used to being in charge of his world, and one accustomed to being obeyed. And she saw something else as well: worry. "Samantha Jellicoe," he returned, accepting her outstretched hand. "I've seen your picture."

"There've been a few of them floating around," she admitted. "Thank you for sending over the tickets for tonight."

"Free entry or not, I still expect Addison to make a donation. He brought his checkbook, I hope."

"You'd have to ask him, sir," she returned, making a mental adjustment to meet his direct manner. Blending in was always the key. "Would you like to discuss anything now, or should we set up an appointment?"

"Now's good. I hate wasting my time at these damned blue-blood things."

"All right. Why don't you start with telling me what your concerns are?"

For a moment he looked at her, his expression unchanged. "You went toe-to-toe with Peter Wallis."

"Once we figured out he was behind the theft of Rick's artworks, yes."

"I mean you physically fought him."

Sam pursed her lips, hoping her potential client wasn't into female mud wrestling or something. "He started it." Wallis had also been the one to give her the concussion that landed her in a London hospital for two weeks.

Kunz smiled, which she didn't think he did very often. "I know the rumors about you," he said, "and about your father's criminal record and how he died in prison."

"I haven't made a secret of any of that."

"No, you haven't. I don't quite believe that you never followed in your father's footsteps, though."

Now she was wondering whether this was some sort of Interpol sting. "If you don't trust me, Mr. Kunz, you should probably hire someone else."

"I didn't say I didn't trust you." He glanced around the noisy room. "I actually like what you've done with your life. It takes guts to push open that box and step outside of it, young lady."

"Thanks. What does all this mean for you, though?"

"Enough of the compliments, eh? Very well. I have a great deal of money and influence, and some people in my acquaintance who've been acting pretty interested in it, lately. And the people who work for me couldn't think outside their boxes if their lives—or mine—depended on it."

Samantha nodded. "Does it? Your life, I mean."

With another look around, he took a swallow of vodka. "Yes, I think it might."

"Then maybe what you need is a bodyguard. I can scrap with the best of them, but I'm more into preventive measures."

"I have been considering hiring a bodyguard," he returned, "but like you, I prefer a more passive and long-term solution."

"Then I'm your gal."

"Excellent."

Kunz drew a breath, his thin shoulders lowering. He'd been worried, she realized, that she might turn him down. Shit. She'd expected her services to be *wanted*, but being *needed*—that got the old heart pumping. "Look," she said, lowering her voice as much as she could in the loud room, "I'm not a big fan of carrying tales to the cops, but whatever security measures we decide on aren't going to be instantaneous. If you think this is an immediate threat, maybe you should think about talking to the PD."

"No. Success is based on the appearance of—"

"Success," she finished. "I've heard the lecture. And I'm not trying to dictate here, but in my book the number one rule is staying alive. If—"

Kunz chuckled. "I'll bet that's quite a book, Miss Jellicoe."

She found herself smiling back at him. "Sam. And I think you know that I'm not joking."

"I do know." He shifted, running a finger around the rim of his glass. "Perhaps I should—speak to someone, I mean. Do you have anyone in mind? Someone you trust?"

A cop she trusted. Talk about an oxymoron. Still . . . "I'll see wh—"

A loud bell chimed. "Dinner is served," a liveried employee of the club called.

A muscle in Kunz's cheek twitched. "Damn. I want to—" His gaze moved again. "Addison."

"Hello, Charles," Rick returned, coming up from behind her to offer his hand.

Kunz shook it. "Your Miss Jellicoe here is quite charming."

Rick smiled. "I think so."

"Okay, gentlemen," she said. "Enough with the compliments. We have a little more business, Rick. Give us a minute."

"No." Charles looked straight at her for a long moment, as though he had something else he wanted to say. She waited, but after a moment he cleared his throat. "Come by my house at two o'clock tomorrow. I want to set something up along the . . . lines we discussed."

"Will do. I'll see you tomorrow, Mr. Kunz."

"Charles. Yes. We'll talk then." He inclined his head. "Good evening, Addison, Sam."

She watched while he headed for the dining room and was intercepted by a taller, brown-haired version of himself. The son, Daniel, she guessed. What was it, who was it, that had him so concerned? He and Daniel looked chummy enough, though with the crowd in between it was impossible to overhear their conversation.

A moment later Rick nudged her shoulder. "Hungry?"

She shook herself. "You ever get that weird feeling that somebody's walked over your grave?"

He closed his hand over her shoulder and stepped around to face her. "You felt that? Then don't take the job, S—"

"Not me," she interrupted, ignoring for the moment that he was trying to give orders again. "Him. Charles."

Rick followed her gaze. "Really? My thought was that he's had a little too much to drink."

She watched as Daniel put a companionable arm around his father's shoulders and they joined the crowd streaming into the dining room. "Maybe. I still want to talk to him again later if I get a chance. Something big's bugging him."

"If something wasn't bothering him, he probably wouldn't have felt the need to call you."

"So you're saying I attract trouble."

"You attracted me," he said by way of answering. Rick held out his hand. "Come on, let's eat. Apparently dinner tonight is going to cost me ten thousand dollars, so I intend to enjoy it _and_ ask for seconds."

"I suppose," she muttered, taking his hand, "at least when you start the evening freaked out, it has to get better."

"Precisely," he returned, kissing her on the forehead. "So

get ready to consume thirty pounds of prime beef and at least a gallon of w—"

"Richard? Oh, good heavens, it *is* you! Richard!"

His hand gripped Samantha's convulsively, then relaxed again, and his face went absolutely still. *Shit*. This was bad, whatever it was. She'd only been joking about the ex-girlfriends thing, for God's sake. Even as she opened her mouth to ask whether he was all right, he turned around to face the cultured feminine voice.

"Good evening, Patricia," he said pleasantly, smiling. "Samantha, this is Patricia Wallis. Patricia, Samantha Jellicoe."

Patricia? The Patricia? And he'd been worried about exposing her to former girlfriends. Sam swung around to get a good look at the ex-Mrs. Addison. "Hi," she said, taking in the gorgeous black Vera Wang dress, three-inch black fuck-me heels, and coiffed mane of golden blond hair. She'd seen her picture, of course, but Patricia looked even better in person, the bitch.

"Hello. How very nice to meet you after all this time," the smooth voice returned in cultured, London-native Brit. Patricia held out her hand.

Sam shook it. The grip was a little weak and tentative, and Patricia slipped free before she released. Nervous then, Samantha decided, and trying not to show it. Walking up to her ex when he was in the presence of his new lover, though, had to take some guts.

"What are you doing here?" Rick asked, his face and voice still at ease but the expression in his eyes deathly cold. He didn't forgive betrayals easily.

"I came for the Season," Patricia returned. "A little excitement, you know. It's so dreary in London right now." She glanced around, avoiding his steady gaze. "I have something of a . . . dilemma. Might I come see you in the morning?"

Samantha expected him to refuse, but after a moment he nodded. "Nine o'clock," he said, for the first time his voice clipped at the end. "For breakfast."

"Splendid." With another hesitation Patricia put her hand on his arm, then took a half step closer and kissed him on the cheek. "Thank you, Richard."

"Hm," Sam mused when Patricia had strolled away. "I wouldn't have—"

"I don't want to discuss it," Rick muttered back, heading them toward the dining room again at something close to warp speed. "Not now."

"Okay. I think we busted our theory about the evening getting better, though."

Before he could answer, some supermodel appeared, clutching onto his arm, and they began an overenthusiastic discussion about winter holidays in Switzerland. Sam knew about those winter holidays, too, and the jewelry that rich vacationers stupidly insisted on toting with them, but she kept quiet. If he wanted to be distracted, she had no problem with that.

As they stepped through the double doors, she glimpsed one of the Society dames edging toward a side table. In a second, and with practiced aplomb, a small crystal inkwell vanished into the woman's handbag.

"Did you see that?" she murmured, gazing after the diamond-encrusted woman as she vanished into the depths of the dining room.

"What?" he asked, his tone impatient and his thoughts obviously still on the Ex.

"Nothing."

It figured. He wanted her to go straight, in the middle of a society where respectable charity women ripped off trinkets from the facilities. She saw things like that all the time; women, mostly, probably desperate for attention or a thrill. Usually it amused her, but tonight it bothered her—since she was skilled enough to palm wallets in her sleep, she was on restriction, but the clumsy, married-well herd could lift anything that wasn't nailed down, and without repercussions. Fucking hypocrites.

It wasn't that she wanted clearance to lift ashtrays—she didn't want to end up with a neat little collection of gaudy trinkets or something and call that her new life. When Rick handed her into a chair and then seated himself beside her, she spent a moment studying his remote expression. There were other ways to betray somebody than by sleeping around, and she wondered if he realized how close she sometimes felt to the edge. And whether he would forgive her if she slipped up.

Five

Saturday, 8:18 a.m.

Richard propped his head in his hand, watching Samantha as she slept. He felt as though he'd been kicked in the jaw last evening, but at least he'd done his manly duty and kept his promise to have sex with her all night.

He reached out and curled a strand of her hair behind her ear. When Samantha first set eyes on Patricia, he'd expected an interrogation at best, while his worst case scenario had involved slinging insults and a fistfight. But she'd come face-to-face with Patricia and hadn't said a word. In fact she'd been quiet and a little distant all evening. What did that mean?

Her enthusiasm when they returned home certainly hadn't waned. But she still hadn't asked him a single question about Patricia's presence or made a single comment about him inviting his ex-wife to breakfast this morning. And that made him uneasy.

Green eyes fluttered open, immediately awake and aware. "Good morning," she mumbled, rubbing her face into the pillow.

"Good morning. Why do you look so innocent when you're asleep?"

She smiled lazily, flipping onto her back and reaching up to touch his cheek. "I'm saving up so I can be devious later in the day without it showing."

"You do it very well, if I may say so."

"Thanks."

She studied his face for a moment, while he held still and let her look. *Honesty and trust.* Two things he would never have thought to find in a thief, and the two things he found most precious about her. And he needed to find a way to prove to her that he did trust her. "What?"

"Are you going to be okay this morning with Patricia coming to visit?"

She *had* been thinking about it. "It feels a little odd."

Samantha brushed aside the blankets and stood, naked and smooth and lovely as daylight. "I bet. All I'm going to say is do whatever you need to, Rick. Emphasis on *you.* She's the one who screwed around. You don't need to feel guilty about anything."

"Wow," he returned, rising from his side of the bed and reaching for a robe. "You sensed all that trouble on the horizon just from saying hello and shaking her hand?"

"She *is* trouble." Sam flashed her grin as she headed for the bathroom. "But then so am I."

"Yes, you are. I have to say, breakfast with the two of you is going to be bloody interesting."

She paused in the doorway. "I won't be here. I have to check in with Stoney and see if anybody's faxed over a résumé. And I have a meeting to get ready for."

"Kunz really got to you, didn't he?"

"Yes, but that's not why I'm leaving. If Patricia has something to say to you, she won't want me around."

The bathroom door closed, but he approached to lean against the door frame. "You're being very understanding."

"That's just me." For a moment he listened to the sound of water running and things clicking in the medicine cabinet. "And I really have enough to worry about today without getting into a catfight with Patricia Addison-Wallis."

So she *was* thinking about pummeling Patricia. "You would win," he commented. "I won't offer to help you put together a contract for Charles, but I'll be here composing an article for *CEO Magazine* if you want to run anything past me."

"I'll be fine." Silence. "Thanks."

"You're welcome."

Richard walked Samantha out to the Bentley, and then stood on the drive to watch her head out toward her new office. When he checked his watch, five minutes remained before nine o'clock. If Patricia kept to her old, familiar pattern, she would be at least twenty minutes late, but obviously Samantha couldn't know that, and obviously she hadn't wanted to chance running into her.

He blew out his breath, feeling ridiculous at the tension running through his shoulders. For Christ's sake, he sat opposite high-powered businessmen, attorneys, and heads of state on a regular basis without so much as flinching. In fact, he frequently caused *them* to flinch. And this morning, with his ex-wife coming by for breakfast, the tips of his fingers felt cold. Not nerves precisely, though he'd be much happier to have her back across the Atlantic. Three years ago he'd caught her in bed with his friend Peter Wallis. The . . . anger that he'd felt had frightened him, both because of its intensity and because of what, for a few blind, blistering seconds, he had considered doing.

To his surprise, a black rental Lexus rolled up to the house at precisely nine o'clock. *Hm.* She was anxious over something, then. "Patricia," he said, standing back as Reinaldo held open the car door for her.

"Richard. And Roberto, it's good to see you again." She'd dressed conservatively, for her, in what looked like a Prada blouse and skirt, a simple sky blue on top with a wild brown African print on the bottom, flowing and yet still managing to hug her well-honed curves.

The housekeeper didn't even blink at the misnomer. He'd lived through over a year of it, after all. "Mrs. Willis," Reinaldo returned instead, handing her off to Rick.

"That's Addison-Wallis," she said brightly, rolling her eyes for Richard's benefit as soon as the housekeeper's back was turned.

"Oh, yes, I forget, you have so many names," Reinaldo returned in an amazingly thick accent.

Richard threw Reinaldo a grin as he ushered Patricia toward the front door.

"Thank you for seeing me," she said. "I wasn't certain you would."

He'd arranged for breakfast in the dining room, mostly because he didn't want to have to listen to her chatting about the lovely poolside setting or the weather. "What brings you to Florida?"

"That's a new wall covering," she commented, slowing to run her hand along the textured adobe-style finish in the downstairs hall. "It's lovely. Have you restored the upstairs gallery?"

"Considering that your husband is the one who had it blown up," he returned, keeping his tone mild, "I really don't think that's any of your business."

"My ex-husband," she corrected, talking over the last part of his sentence. "I'm divorcing Peter."

Giving himself a moment to absorb that news, he gestured her into the dining room and the seat nearest the door. In his reluctance to have her there, he'd asked Hans to have breakfast ready rather than waiting to see what she might want to eat. Sitting opposite her, he nodded at one of the two servers, and the food began appearing from the direction of the kitchens.

"Aren't you going to say anything, Richard? I'm divorcing Peter."

"Why?"

"'Why?' He's in prison, on trial for killing two people, contracting another murder, and for smuggling and theft. Isn't that enough reason?"

"I don't know, Patricia. I'm unfamiliar with the workings of your moral compass."

"Richard, don't."

He took a breath. "I just find it a little surprising that you would come to Florida solely to confirm to me that you've made yet another mistake in judgment."

"I didn't know you were here," she shot back. Her jaw twitching, she reached for the bowl of strawberry jam and began spreading it on her toast. "But I'm glad to see you."

"I'll reserve judgment for my part."

"You were my first love, Richard. Nothing changes that. And the first eight months of our marriage were . . ." She fanned her hand in front of her face. ". . . exceptional." Patricia's gaze followed his hands as he cut up a slice of cantaloupe and ate it. "Is your friend going to be joining us?"

Richard narrowed his eyes. Past mistakes, past injuries, and poor judgment were one thing, but now she'd brought up the most important part of his present and—unless it killed him—his future. "Samantha had an appointment."

"I heard that she was setting up a security business. How do you feel about her working, when—"

"Patricia, why are you here?" he interrupted, finally allowing some of his annoyance to surface. "And don't give me that rubbish about the weather."

"Fine." She looked down, stabbing her over easy eggs into oblivion with her fork. "You didn't make things easy for me, you know, either before or after our marriage ended."

"I know that. Before was my fault. After is yours. I prefer to leave magnanimous gestures to the Pope."

"You—" She stopped herself, no doubt realizing that if she started flinging insults, she would end up out on the drive sitting on her arse. "I'm staying at a hotel here in Palm Beach. I had to leave London, and all the memories of Peter and those people—my former friends—he must have lied to. And I want your help to start over again. This time, I want to do things right. I'm living on a budget, trying to keep my priorities straight, making a go of being independent for once."

"If you're being independent, why do you want my help?" he returned, barely noting the rest of what she was saying.

"Well, I'm patterning myself after you," she said, with an unmistakable sniff. "I mean, look at you. You came out well, you've settled into your life, you have a new . . . friend, and you certainly aren't wanting for money. I need your advice, Richard. And your help and your understanding. Then I can be strong and independent."

She placed a hand over his, and he couldn't help notice her fingers shaking. He knew her well enough to be fairly certain that as proficient as she was at manipulating people, her show of helplessness wasn't an act.

"What sort of help do you want, then?" he asked reluctantly.

"I . . . I thought you might let me speak with one of Tom Donner's people, to get a perspective on what I can do in the divorce when half of Peter's—our—income was apparently derived from the sale of stolen objects. And I'd like to rent or purchase a small house here in Palm Beach, but I need someone to cosign the paperwork. This—"

"You expect me to help you move here?" he broke in.

She snapped her mouth closed, eyes wide and hurt. "It . . . it took everything I have to come here and see you." A well-timed tear ran down her cheek. "Tell me what I'm supposed to do. I can't stay in London. I need your help, Richard. Please."

"I'll consider it," he said, setting aside his fork with a clank and standing. "Now if you'll excuse me, I have to meet Samantha. Reinaldo will see you out."

"But—"

"You've asked enough for one day."

"You never used to go out of your way to meet me during the day," she muttered, just loud enough for him to hear.

He didn't reply; he wasn't certain how to do so, mainly because it was true. He'd never gone much out of his way, veered from his routine, to accommodate Patricia. It had never seemed necessary. She had been his wife, and her schedule had been designed to accommodate his. Samantha, on the other hand, was an all-consuming passion.

"Leave your hotel information with Reinaldo," he said over his shoulder, pulling open the dining room door. "I'll have Tom or somebody from his office give you a call."

"Oh, thank you, Richard. You have no idea what this means to me. Thank you so—"

He closed the door on her faux gratitude and went to collect his car. One thing he could count on about Patricia was that she never changed. Her surface charm and competence had been precisely what he'd wanted in a spouse—or so he'd thought. As it began to sink in that the depths were a mirror of the surface, and that neither were particularly interesting, he'd drifted away from her—until she'd taken the last giant leap into Peter's bed.

Three months ago he'd made a leap of his own, and he wasn't certain his feet had hit the ground yet. Richard climbed into his silver Mercedes SLR. When he did land, he knew where he wanted to be. And he was going to see her right now.

"How's that?" Stoney called, his voice muffled.

"Stoney, it's fine. Quit messing with it." Samantha blew out her breath, ruffling her bangs. "I don't care which radio station is on. I want to know where this fax machine came from and why the back is labeled 'Property of Dunbar Associates.'"

Her former fence appeared from the utility closet. "A radio station is all about ambience, baby. How you gonna catch rich, conservative clients when you have Puff Diddy bangin' it over the sound system?"

Lips twisting, Sam concentrated on looking through the blueprints of Charles Kunz's home. Some of her old contacts were still definitely worth keeping. If she'd gone through the city to get the plans, it would have taken six weeks. "You're a dork, Stoney. Where did you get—"

"Come on, admit it. You need a nice classical station. Soothing, elegant, and—"

"—and old. I'm not going to leave the office at the end of the day with gray hair and popping Geritol. Besides, it's commercial radio," she returned, deciding she almost preferred it when he was trying to talk her into the Venice caper. "What if some other security firm starts advertising over our sound system?"

"Just watch. You're—"

"The fax machine, Walter," she interrupted again, rubbing at her temple.

He plunked himself down on the folding chair opposite hers. "Don't yell at me because being legit isn't all balloons and daffodils, honey."

"Do I have to find Dunbar Associates and give them a call?"

"Not if we were in Venice."

"Stoney—"

"Fine. There is no Dunbar Associates. They went bankrupt. Big Bill Talmidge has been holding a few pieces of their office equipment, and he offered to make me a deal."

Big Bill Talmidge was a fence of much less refined taste than Stoney, but he did have a semilegitimate pawn business on the side. "Swear to me that it's not hot."

"It's not hot. Jeez. When did you get so squeamish?"

"Don't even ask me that, bub."

He sat there for a moment, and she could feel his gaze boring into the top of her head. Shifting, she flipped the blueprint to the next sheet, the electronic schematics of Kunz's estate, Coronado House. She knew precisely how she would break in, which gave her a good idea where to start beefing up the security. Like most residences, once somebody got inside, it was pretty much a free-for-all except for the safe and the paintings wired to the walls.

Yep, anybody could just wander in and mess with your things. Sam thunked her forehead against the surface of her desk. Damned Patricia was messing with her best thing right now. She was eating one of Hans's creations and probably regaling Rick with some tale of woe designed to win his heart back. And here she sat, figuring out how to protect a man's possessions without the use of sirens and gun turrets.

And when Rick decided to tell her about this morning, she

would of course be the understanding friend and confidante who only wanted him to be happy. *Shit*.

"Maybe you should take a break," Stoney finally suggested into the silence. "Go get a sandwich or something."

She slammed to her feet. "What, my first day at my own friggin' office, and you think I can't take it?"

Stoney held his hands up in surrender. "You're the one who looks like you're going to explode. Not me."

"I'm not going to expl . . ." She trailed off, the dim voice on the speaker above her head finally sinking in. "Did you hear that?"

"Hear what?"

"Change the station to news or something. I heard Kunz's name."

"You're being paranoid," he said, though he rose and headed back for the utility closet.

"There, stop there," she called after a moment.

"—astics millionaire Charles Kunz, longtime resident of Palm Beach. Kunz was sixty-two, and is survived by son Daniel and daughter Laurie. The death has been ruled a homicide in conjunction with a possible home invasion robbery, and police are investigating. And now for local traffic, we go to—"

"Jesus," Sam muttered, sinking back into her chair. The air shoved out of her lungs, as though she'd been kicked in the chest. Christ. Four days back in Florida, and people around her were dropping dead again. People she liked.

"Anybody here?" Rick's voice came from the direction of the reception desk.

She looked up to see Stoney in the doorway, his face somber. "Back here," he called, still gazing at her.

"If I'm not overstepping, you should have a little bell for clients to ring, in case there's no one at the front desk," Rick commented, his voice growing nearer until he appeared at Stoney's shoulder. He paused, looking from her to Stoney. "What's wrong?"

"There was just a thing on the news," she said slowly, reluctantly. "Charles Kunz is dead."

A thousand things ran through the back of his eyes. "What?" He came forward, stepping over the pile of electronics and security system books she'd been collecting to stop beside her at the desk. "Tell me what you know."

Samantha took a breath, trying to gather her thoughts. "Not much. A probable home invasion, probable homicide. It was just on the n—"

"Come on," he said, pulling her to her feet. "Tom'll be in his office. He can call the police department and we'll find out exactly what's happened."

Nodding, she stood. "I don't—"

"It's not your fault, whatever happened," he said sternly, towing her toward the front of the office.

"I know that. But he wanted my help. Badly. Christ, Rick, do you think he knew something was up?"

"A premonition? I don't believe in that, and neither do you."

"You believed that walking over my grave thing."

"I believe in your instincts," he countered. "And this is an unfortunate coincidence."

"How do—"

"He didn't ask for your help, Samantha," Rick interrupted as they entered the elevator. "He wanted you to present a business proposal to him, after which he would have decided whether to hire you or not."

No, that hadn't been what it felt like. Charles Kunz *had* asked for her help. "Maybe I could think it was just business, if he wasn't dead now."

"You're overreacting," he stated flatly. "If Charles had been truly worried about his safety, he should have called the police, and he should have hired another security firm months ago."

Rick always had a good handle on logic. "If you have this all wrapped up, then why are we going to see Donner?"

"To prove my point."

They entered the cool chrome and glass foyer of Donner's building and ascended in one of the half-dozen elevators to the top floor. Rick was handling her, as he handled any business situation. She didn't like it, usually, but for this one moment it was almost a relief to have someone else do the thinking. Her mind was engaged elsewhere, mainly on the last bit of her conversation with Kunz, where he'd wanted to ask more of her. He'd been seriously considering hiring a bodyguard, and she'd fairly easily convinced him to talk to the PD.

She should have found him after dinner and made certain he wasn't in any immediate danger. Instead she'd scheduled a meeting and had spent the rest of the evening trying to distract Rick from dour thoughts about Patricia. That might be what girlfriends did, but being with Rick didn't mean she should start ignoring her gut. Dammit.

"Mr. Addison!" the receptionist, seated behind a large golden plaque engraved with the name of the law firm, exclaimed. "We didn't expect you this morning. Just a moment, and I'll inform Mr. Donner that you're here."

Grateful for the momentary distraction, Sam took a breath. Hypotheses made her crazy. She needed reality for a minute. And in reality she was trying to start a business. She studied "Judy," as her name tag proclaimed her. Conservative dress and makeup, bland, pleasant expression, efficient at pushing phone buttons and knowing the names of clients, and with that smooth, professional voice required of high-class receptionists. So that's what she was supposed to be hiring. *Hm*. She could bet that the law firm's prospective clients never turned up dead. That was *her* thing, apparently.

"Rick!" Tall and lanky blond Texas, Tom Donner strode into the reception foyer. Grinning, the attorney grabbed Rick's hand and pumped it. "Thank God you're here. I almost had to attend the monthly finance meeting."

"Glad I could help." Rick stepped sideways and gestured at Sam. "You remember Samantha?"

The look Donner gave her was equal parts humor and annoyance. "You still haven't been arrested, Jellicoe?"

"Not yet. No real job for you yet either, eh, Yale?"

"Tom, do you have a few minutes?" Rick interjected.

"Sure. What'd she do this time?"

As he ushered them into the depths of the office, Sam stuck her tongue out at him. She hated attorneys as a rule, and it bugged her that deep down she actually respected this one.

As they passed by cubicles and elegant offices, Sam realized that the employees all seemed to know who Rick was, and that Rick knew all of their names as well. It didn't really surprise her—Rick probably considered them his employees, and he always knew who he had working for him. Details, he always said. It was all in the details. Kind of her philosophy, too—though her details were more of the corridor length and safe combination variety.

Donner's office sat in the corner of the building. So his office overlooked hers. That was a riot—or it would have been if she could have gotten the image of Charles Kunz and his half-empty vodka glass and his quiet look of worry out of her head.

"I heard you got an office," Donner said, eyeing her as he

took the seat behind his desk. "Rick said I would have to ask you where it is."

She jerked her thumb toward the nearest window. "Over there."

"North of Worth? That's a pretty good location."

"Nope. Over there. In that building." She stepped closer to the window. "See the office where the blinds are open? That's mine."

His jaw didn't precisely drop, but the gaping expression on his face was easy enough to read. "You're shitting me."

"Come over and have some coffee," she invited. "But you'll have to bring the coffee. We don't have a maker yet. Or cups. Don't bring Styrofoam, though. It's tacky."

" 'We?' " he repeated, glancing at Rick. "You two?"

Rick cleared his throat. "Samantha and Walter Barstone."

Both eyebrows shot up into Donner's blond hairline. "The *fence*?"

Samantha managed a smile. This was too good to ignore, whatever the circumstances. "Former fence. We're business partners now." She wondered if he knew who Dunbar Associates were, but hell, it was only a fax machine.

"Great." The attorney glanced at her office window again. "This is freaky."

"Thanks."

"It's not why we're here," Rick put in.

She was glad he'd brought it up; coming from her, it would sound too much like asking a favor, and if there was one thing she didn't want, it was to owe the damned lawyer one. Samantha took a breath and seated herself in one of the soft leather office chairs. Nice. She'd tell Stoney she liked leather.

"What's up, if giving me an aneurism wasn't the plan?"

Rick sat beside her, reaching over to hold her hand. Ownership, entanglement, whatever it meant, at the moment she didn't mind. "Have you heard the news about Charles Kunz?"

Donner nodded. "One of my criminal law guys was at the police station when the call came over the radio."

"Did he hear anything interesting?"

The attorney's gaze shifted from Rick to Samantha, his amused expression deepening to suspicion. "Why?"

"Curiosity," Rick returned.

"No, no, no. It's more than that. I can tell. Jellicoe had something to do with it. What? As your attorney, you need to let me know when—"

"I didn't have anything to do with it!" Samantha protested. "Jesus, you're paranoid."

"I'm experienced," Donner pointed out. "There's a difference. So what's your interest in Kunz?"

Sam would have answered, but subsided when Rick tightened his grip on her fingers. "He asked Samantha for a consult on his security yesterday," he supplied. "Before we tell that to anyone else, I'd prefer a few more details about his death."

"Great." Donner pushed to his feet again. "Wait here for a minute. I'll go make a few phone calls and see what I can find out."

After the door closed, Samantha pulled free of Rick's hand and rose to stride back and forth in front of the window. "Why do I have the feeling that he could have made those phone calls from right here?"

"He's trying to distance me—us—from any questions."

"What, does he have a video spy phone in here so his snitches could see us? He doesn't want me to hear what's going on."

Rick didn't look the least bit perturbed by Donner's flight.

"More likely he doesn't want you criticizing his methods of getting information, my love."

She took a minute to absorb that. "You mean I make him nervous?"

"I think if you wanted to, you could make a great many people nervous. You're rather brilliant, you know."

"Yeah, for a kid who had about two years total of regular school and did a lot of traveling."

He smiled, that warm, charming one that made her want to smother him with kisses and babble all kinds of mushy stuff. "No, for anyone. Just don't tell Tom I said so."

Flattered to her bones, Sam grinned at him. "Yes, he did spend all that money to go to Yale and everything."

Richard chuckled at her. "Actually Tom went on scholar-ship."

"Crap. Okay, he gets one point of credit."

At least he'd managed to distract her for a moment, he thought. Her first official bloody client, and Kunz had to turn up dead. Of course what had happened to Charles wasn't her fault, but Richard couldn't help noting her straight spine and the tense line across her shoulders. Kunz had made an impression on her, and she would have done a sterling job for him. Once Tom's report cleared up the details, he would be able to rid himself of the nagging sensation that she was taking this far too personally.

When Tom came back through the door, Richard stood a little abruptly. He had no intention of letting a bad start ruin her best chance to go straight—and to stay straight. "What have you got?"

"Kunz's daughter found him lying on the floor in his office with a bullet hole in his chest. She called the cops, and they're still going through the place. For sure a ton of cash is gone, and a set of ruby jewelry—all the stuff he had in his office safe. And they think some artwork."

Richard couldn't help glancing at Samantha. Other than the bullet hole, it sounded like something she might have done in her previous life. "Did he have any bloody alarm system at all?" he asked, finding that he was at least as angry at Kunz as he was at the man's killer. He might have taken some damned steps to protect himself and his property.

"Yes," Samantha answered.

Tom nodded as well. "Samaritans is falling all over themselves claiming that the alarm must not have been set. It never went off, so I wouldn't expect them to say anything different. 'Oops, it didn't work' probably wouldn't help their business." He turned his gaze back to Samantha. "You might want to keep that in mind, yourself."

She narrowed her green eyes. "Wow, with advice like that, it's no wonder you're so successful. Thanks, Yale."

"At least *my* first client didn't get killed," he retorted, gesturing at Richard.

"Which would be thanks to Samantha," Richard pointed out, "considering that she saved my life. And Kunz didn't sign any agreement with her, so he isn't—wasn't—her first client."

"Yes, he was," Samantha interrupted. "So goody for all of us, I'm glad Rick's still breathing, but—"

"Thanks," he said dryly, not taking her sarcasm personally.

"But can we be a little more constructive here? Do the police have any suspects?"

Tom cleared his throat. "My guy said they were still taking statements from family and staff. But what exactly is there to be worried about? The guy's dead, but you said there's no paperwork tying him to Jellicoe. She's clear." He paused. "Isn't she?"

"Yes, she's clear." Richard would never admit that for a

heartbeat he'd been worried. "It's curiosity," he continued. "I mean, the day after he inquired about getting increased security, he ended up dead. A bit odd, don't you think?"

"You want me to forward that info to the cops on your behalf?" Tom asked, settling back behind his desk.

Samantha shook her head. "His secretary knows he contacted me. She arranged for us to meet, and she sent me the tickets to the Everglades Club bash."

"Then the cops'll get in touch with you if they need to," the attorney returned, shrugging. "Is there anything else you want me to do?"

"No." Samantha grimaced. "Thanks, I guess."

"Yeah, don't get all mushy." Tom reached over to shake Richard's hand, but settled for a nod at Samantha. Evidently the attorney still remembered the first day they'd met, when she'd dumped him into the Solano Dorado pool after he'd grabbed her arm a little too vigorously.

She scooted out the door and to the elevator with a relief not even her considerable skills could disguise. The only place she seemed more reluctant to appear than an attorney's office was a police station.

"Does that help?" Richard asked as the elevator doors closed them in.

"I suppose so." She held his gaze for a long moment. "Do you ever have the feeling that even though everything looks okay, it's about to go all to hell?"

"Frequently," he returned, remembering that he hadn't told her yet about his agreement to help Patricia. If she found out before he could confess, the thin bond of trust between them might very well be smashed. Slowly, he reached out to touch her cheek, following the caress with a gentle kiss. He could stand a great many things, but not that. "Ready for the first wave?"

Samantha closed her eyes for a moment while she took a deep breath. "Okay. Hit me."

For a bare moment he debated what he wanted to tell her first—that Patricia wanted to move to Palm Beach, or that she'd requested his help to do it. "Patricia's divorcing Peter," he began, deciding to start with the least explosive news and work his way up.

She absorbed that for a heartbeat or two. "That's good. She really didn't know Peter was stealing from you, then."

"You thought that before."

"I know, but this kind of proves it. She does have some morals, anyway."

Richard snorted. "Not enough to keep her from shagging Peter while she was married to me, but enough for her to distance herself from him once he got arrested."

"I didn't say she had her priorities straight," Samantha returned, leading the way out of the elevator as the doors opened. "When you think about it, though, Peter's probably become really unpopular. She doesn't want to get thrown out of her circle of Society friends—what did you call them, Patty's Pack?"

"That term's not for public consumption. And speaking of Patricia's potential ostracization," he said, gazing at her profile and wondering how she would take this, "she wants to set up a household elsewhere than London."

Samantha stopped, suspicious emerald eyes glinting as she faced him. "Where?" she asked flatly.

"She's looking at—"

"Here," Samantha interrupted, crossing her arms over her pert tits. "Palm Beach."

There was no sense cushioning it now. "Yes, here. Palm Beach."

"She wants you back." Her gaze held his for a half-dozen

heartbeats before she broke away, increasing her pace through the lobby and into the warm air of eastern Florida in January.

Richard followed her, a dozen denials and rebuttals fighting for position. "She does not."

"Ooh, good retort. Prove it."

"She needs someone to cosign her paperwork, and I'm the only one she could think of to do it. I spend time here. Hence, Palm Beach."

"She needs—"

"And," he cut in, warming to the argument, "and, the Society here is the type she feels comfortable with, anyway. A good dozen of her Patty's Pack friends have winter homes here. I can't see her moving to Dirt, Nebraska. Can you?"

Samantha dove into the Bentley that waited at the curb and actually hesitated a moment before she unlocked the passenger door for him. "No, but I can see her in Paris or Venice or Milan or New York," she retorted. "But like you said, you're *here*. And hey, Mr. Denial, if she has her Patty's Pack friends in town, why is it again you're being recruited to cosign?"

Richard barely had time to close his door before she peeled away from the curb. "You're jealous," he announced.

"You're an asshole."

"Brilliant retort, Samantha. I stand cowed. Where are we going?"

"Back to Solano Dorado. I need to think." She shifted gears as they left Worth Avenue, hurtling them along the beach at just sublight speed. "Jesus, Addison, you are so blind," she finally exploded. "She comes in playing the damsel in distress, and you buy all of it."

"She did n—"

" 'Oh, Richard, I need your help,' " she mimicked, doing a

startlingly good impression of Patricia's soft, cultured Brit—especially since the two women had barely spoken a total of five words to one another. " 'I've left Peter, and I so badly want to make a new start, but I just don't know how to do it on my own. You're so big and strong and successful, can't you see it in your heart to help me?' " Samantha canted her eyes at him. "Did it go a little like that?"

Christ. "Maybe," he hedged. "But—"

"See? She wants you back."

"Well, she can't have me. I'm taken. But she asked for my help, and I'm partially the reason she's in this position."

"No, she put herself on her back and *then* you put her in the next position."

"Even so—"

"You can't resist putting on your shining armor, can you?" she said more calmly, blowing out her breath. "And if I know it, then she knows it, too."

"Honestly, Samantha, I think it's more a matter of Patricia actually being helpless than her acting that way to gain my assistance. I doubt she could find a grocery store on her own, much less the toothpaste aisle."

"But she's not after toothpaste."

As they stopped at a light, Richard leaned over and grabbed Samantha's face, kissing her hard on her surprised mouth. "Don't worry about this. You won't have to deal with her."

"Maybe not, but *you* will. And keep in mind that she's got a subscriber website where she gives advice about how not to get screwed in a divorce."

"She does?"

"Yes. Interesting stuff. You really need to spend more time surfing the 'net."

"Shit." Before Samantha could follow up her smug look

with more commentary, he took a breath. "I'll make dumping the website a condition of my helping her."

"Great. She won't need the site, anyway, because she'll be busy screwing you over in person, instead."

"No one screws me over, Samantha. Ever."

"Yet, smart guy. Yet."

Six

Saturday, 10:15 a.m.

*P*atricia Addison-Wallis lifted her sunglasses and sank down in the driver's seat of her rented black Lexus as a new model Bentley Continental GT sped past her down Ocean Boulevard. Jellicoe obviously had no regard for the law. But Patricia already knew that about the thieving bitch.

She considered following, but she had better things to do. They would be heading for Solano Dorado, and she had a spa appointment in forty minutes. If she cancelled with less than an hour's notice, she would be charged for the session regardless—and she needed to be frugal these days. With an aggravated sigh, Patricia pulled away from the curb and headed back north along the boulevard toward The Breakers Hotel.

Seeing Samantha Jellicoe with Richard was dismaying. A week or two should have been more than enough for him to purge the tramp from his system, and yet after three months they were still together. For heaven's sake, he was practically drooling on her. She'd always thought of him as dreadfully unyielding, and yet there he sat in the passenger seat while *that woman* drove his precious Bentley.

They thought she'd had no idea what Peter had been up to, stealing artworks from Richard's property here and selling them throughout Europe. Well, perhaps she hadn't known then, but she had picked up on a few things, especially after the arrest. Peter had had someone hire Jellicoe for a robbery. For weeks she'd looked into a way to prove it with other than Peter's word and have the bitch arrested, but nothing had come to her attention.

As she stopped at a traffic signal, Patricia looked at herself in the rearview mirror. The bad thing about Florida, even in winter, was that the bright sunlight made the corners of her eyes wrinkle. Thank goodness for the hotel spa. Especially with the dinner party tonight. Especially with Daniel still determined to attend, even with his father's death. It was for charity, after all, and one of Charles's favorites.

What a stroke of luck that Daniel had been across the room from her when she'd run into Richard and Jellicoe at the Everglades Club. Richard would have been much less inclined to aid her if he knew she was seeing someone. Patricia smiled. Not that she wouldn't drop Daniel in a hot minute if Richard should look her way again.

After all, she was simply human. She'd succumbed to a moment of weakness and fallen into another man's arms. It happened all the time—and with her and Richard's lifestyle, there had been so many temptations. She'd apologized repeatedly, offered to see a marriage counselor, but he hadn't wanted any of it. So she'd done what she had to in order to prove that she didn't sleep around on a regular basis. She'd married Peter Wallis. As for that marriage, well, Peter had been more obsessed with Richard than she was.

So now she was stuck with no husband, little money, and only the tentative beginnings of a boyfriend and a plan—and a former husband who was still one of the wealthiest, most handsome, and most charming men alive. And there sat Sam Jellicoe, driving a brand-new Bentley, sleeping in a thirty-room mansion, sharing a bed with *her* ex-husband, and apparently able to live life as illegally as she pleased.

Sam. What a stupid, masculine, unflattering name. But whatever anyone called her, the little bint had Richard. From what Patricia had been able to determine, they'd met the night of the explosion at Solano Dorado, when she'd gone to rob him. Did that turn him on now? Heavens. It must have been an early mid-life crisis, since he was only thirty-four. Well, if it was Sam's disregard for legal conventions that excited Richard, two could play at that game. She licked her ruby long-stay lipstick, her heartbeat accelerating. Even the thought of it—and of Richard—excited her, as well.

As she drove the Bentley around the last curve of the street fronting Solano Dorado, Samantha slammed on the brakes. A 1997 Ford Taurus blocked the front gates. Leaning against the back bumper, a wiry Hispanic man with a thick, graying moustache ate sunflower seeds.

"What the devil?" Rick grabbed onto the dash as they came to an abrupt stop.

"Tell me you invited Frank Castillo over for lunch," she said, watching as the police detective straightened to wave at them.

"No."

Her chest tightened. "So the homicide cop just showed up to say hello. That could happen, right?"

"Shall we find out, my love?" Rick said in a voice much more relaxed than hers.

She didn't want to find out any such thing. Hell, six months ago if she'd seen a cop at her front door she would have turned and run without looking back, whether she'd pulled a job or not. Only one thing kept her from making a U-turn now: The fact that she knew Frank, knew him to be an honest, intelligent cop. If she'd had her meeting with Charles Kunz, Castillo would have been the cop she recommended he should speak to.

"Let's go," she muttered, her teeth clenched, motioning Frank to get back into his car.

With a chuckle, Rick reached over to punch the gate button, and she fell in behind the Taurus as they cruised up the drive to the front door. She knew that Rick liked Frank Castillo; hell, he credited the cop with helping to save her life. That was a total exaggeration, since all Frank had done was make a long-distance call to the London cops to break down a door and arrest a suspect—it was just coincidence that she and Rick had nearly had the life beaten out of them behind that same door.

"Good morning, Frank," Rick said, climbing out of the Bentley as soon as she had it in park.

Samantha sat where she was for a moment. Stoney had told her several times that she had a radar for trouble and the bad sense to head straight into it. Frank's appearance alone meant something was wrong, and considering that she'd met a man yesterday who had died last night, she had a good idea why he was visiting. *Dammit.*

"Samantha, are you going to get out of the car?" Rick called.

No. With an irritated sigh, she shoved open the door and climbed out. "Hi, Frank," she said, going forward to shake the homicide cop's hand.

"Sam. You look great."

"Yeah, well, no offense, but I felt better before I saw you."

Castillo chuckled. "I don't doubt it. You know why I'm here, I assume?"

"Why don't you enlighten us, Frank?" Rick said, his fingers curling around Sam's.

Whether the gesture was out of support or to keep her from fleeing, she wasn't certain, but the contact did give her a certain amount of comfort—unless she did need to run and he tried to stop her. She wasn't going to prison. Not for anything.

"Charles Kunz. I'm working the case."

"Yes, we heard on the news that he'd been killed. I hope you don't think Samantha had anything to do with it." Rick took a small step closer to her. "She was with me all night."

"I think you'd probably say just about anything to protect her, Rick, but actually I'm just here to ask Sam a couple of questions about her meeting with Kunz yesterday. His secretary told me he'd had an appointment with you."

"I—"

"Do we need an attorney, Frank?" Rick interrupted her.

"No. Not yet, anyway."

"But I'm one of those 'persons of interest,' right?" Samantha insisted on clarity where cops and handcuffs were concerned.

"Not if your alibi checks out. There's a reason I said I'd interview you myself." The detective made a wry face. "Actually, I was kind of relieved when I found out Kunz had met with you, Sam. You have good instincts, and I thought you might have noticed if something was bothering him."

Okay, she didn't feel relieved, but at least Castillo seemed inclined to believe her. Maybe being acquainted with a cop did have an upside. "I was just going to get some lunch," she said. "Hungry?"

"Sure. Does your chef still make those cucumber sandwiches?"

"You bet."

Rick motioned Frank toward the front door and fell in beside him, Samantha just behind them. When she'd heard the news about Kunz, she'd thought of nothing more than the event itself and how it made her feel, and whether she might have been able to do something to prevent it. She was getting too complacent. Otherwise the sight of a cop at her front door would never have startled her so much. Hell, she wouldn't have been at her front door for a cop to find her. She'd made a mistake, and the present circumstance was pure luck. And she didn't operate on luck.

"Are you all right?" Rick whispered as she came through the front door.

Sam nodded. "I should have thought events through a little better."

"Most normal citizens wouldn't expect to see police at their door."

"I'm not a normal citizen, Rick."

He kissed her cheek. "And I thank God every day for that fact."

Wow. That was an absurdly nice thing for him to say. She only wished that she had time to dwell on it a little. She needed to be on her guard when cops were present, though. Even ones who might be inclined to think her innocent.

Rick called into the kitchen to request lunch, and then the three of them headed out poolside. Sam took the seat at the bistro table facing the front drive, even though it seemed a little late to start paying attention now. "What do you need?" she asked when she couldn't stand listening to the small talk between the two men any longer.

"Why did Kunz want to see you?" Castillo asked, pulling out his ubiquitous notepad and a pen.

"I'm starting a security business," she answered.

He glanced up at her. "I know. In fact, the whole PBPD knows that. Probably the FBI and Interpol too. Jellicoe Security."

"And what's the consensus?" Rick put in.

"Well, everybody's interested. Waiting to see what comes of it."

Sam crossed her ankles. "Meaning?"

"I'm not sure. I mean, if there's a rash of burglaries where you've been working, you're probably going—"

"There won't be," she interrupted. "The idea's to prevent them."

"Okay." He consulted his notepad again. "So did Kunz ask to see you, or did you solicit him?"

" 'Solicit'?" she repeated, lifting an eyebrow.

"Come on, Sam, I'm just looking for your take on this. If it was anybody else taking a five-minute meeting with a guy at a party, I probably would've sent Barney Fife to follow up. But you notice things."

Noticing things had saved her life on more than one occasion. And she did suppose that she owed Castillo. "He asked to see me."

"Anything specific?"

"Not really. He sent me tickets for the Everglades Club party. As far as I could tell, he was there dateless. His son, Daniel, was there, but they weren't standing together when I showed up. Kunz was drinking vodka. A little too much, I think. He wanted to talk business, but he had something to get off his chest. He said some people of his acquaintance had been acting pretty interested in his money and influence lately. From our conversation, he was seriously thinking about hiring a bodyguard. I suggested he talk to the police. It must have been serious, because he finally agreed. We were supposed to meet today at two to go over specifics."

Castillo jotted notes, his gaze lifting only when she paused. "Did he give you any more details?"

Samantha shook her head. "Nope." His parting expression nagged at her, and she sent a glance at Rick. "He was worried. Not just the usual nonspecific paranoia that wealthy people have. Really worried."

"Did he think his life was in danger?"

"You know, he didn't say word one about protecting his belongings. It was more about taking preventive measures in general. So yes, I think he suspected that somebody wanted him dead."

"Okay. Anything else?"

She drew a breath, hoping he wasn't going to start asking about her sources. "I looked over his blueprints this morning, to get ready for our meeting."

"And?"

"He has an existing security system, but it's got more holes in it than Chex cereal."

"Not a complicated job for a burglar, then?"

She hesitated. This was what had worried her, that her former compatriots would figure she'd turn snitch. Her life wouldn't be worth much if that ever happened. "Not if whoever went in there knew how the house was wired. Of course it could have just been dumb luck. Did the alarm go off?" she asked, even though she already knew. Hearing a version other than Donner's filtered one might be useful, though.

"No. Nobody knew anything was wrong until his daughter went looking to see why he'd missed breakfast."

"How many people live there?"

He consulted his notes again. "Eight, including the son and daughter."

"With that many people wandering around the place, probably just about anybody with a flashlight and a pair of plyers could have done it."

"So you think it was random?" Rick asked quietly.

There he was, trying to convince her that she hadn't ignored her instincts and dropped the ball. If Castillo hadn't been there, she'd probably have been unzipping Rick's trousers right now. God, she liked having him around sometimes. Even when he led her into thoughts and discussions she'd prefer not to traverse. "No, I don't, actually."

The detective's head lifted. "Why not?"

"Kunz is like Rick," she returned. "Used to being in charge, having people listen to him. Confident, a little arrogant. Oh, don't give me that look," she said when Rick's brow furrowed. "For you, that's a compliment." She drew a breath, returning to the subject at hand. "We got interrupted by dinner, or I think he might have told me more. After we ate, it got too . . . chaotic." And she'd let her attention drift from work to Rick.

The sandwiches and sodas arrived, and Castillo dug in. Rick followed suit, which made sense considering he probably hadn't eaten much breakfast with the Ex in attendance. Sam wasn't very hungry, even for cucumber and mayonnaise sandwiches.

"I agree that bodyguards means fear for yourself, not your cash. So you're positive about this, right?" Frank continued after half a sandwich had vanished.

"I'm positive that that was my impression."

Castillo chewed and swallowed. "That really isn't much to direct an investigation, Sam."

"That's not my problem."

"I know. It's mine." The detective sighed heavily.

"If it means anything, Rick wouldn't have agreed to talk to the cops without major consideration. Kunz wouldn't have done it lightly, either."

Dammit, she'd sensed that he needed her help. She wasn't typically anything close to a good Samaritan, but he'd sought her out for a reason. And intentionally or not, she'd let him down.

"Okay." Castillo took another bite of sandwich, washing it down with half a can of Diet Coke. "Anything else? General impressions?"

"I liked him." She studied the detective's competent, honest face for a moment. Thank God he'd been the detective assigned to investigate the explosion at Solano Dorado three months ago. If it had been any other cop, he might not have given her the chance to clear herself, and she might not have been able to stay around long enough to connect with Rick Addison. "Can you—will you—let me know if you find out anything?"

"I think I can arrange that." He consulted his watch. "Crap. I've gotta stop by the coroner's." Standing, he grabbed up the last quarter of sandwich. "Thanks for lunch."

"Any time, Frank. I'll see you out." Rick stood as well, pausing to smack a kiss on Samantha's hair. "Wait here, my love."

"Don't expect your sandwich to be waiting for you," she said automatically, settling back to look out over the pool.

If this was what the legit world felt like, she didn't like it. Samantha took a swallow of soda. She'd avoided ratting anybody out, but as long as Castillo felt like they were buddies, he would keep pushing her for information. And as long as she met these potential marks—clients—in person, she was apparently going to feel . . . responsible for them and their safety. That sucked.

Maybe, though, she didn't have to let this be the end of it. It was too late to save Kunz, but it wasn't too late for her to help figure out what had happened to him. Maybe that was what Charles Kunz had really wanted from her—to make sure somebody knew something was going on. And maybe to figure out what that something was.

Seven

*R*ichard stuck a finger in his mouth to lick off a drip of raspberry syrup. "And stop changing the subject."

"I'm not changing anything. You're the one who needs to fly back to London."

Fuck that. "I've already arranged to fly Leedmont and his board here to Palm Beach. I can purchase Kingdom Fittings here just as easily as I can do it in London."

"Ri—"

"So back to my point. You can't tell me that having Castillo here asking questions didn't bother you," he interrupted. "It bothered me."

Samantha looked as though she wanted to fling her Diet Coke in his face, but instead she curled her fingers around her fork and shoved another mouthful of French toast into her mouth. "And twenty-two hours later, he still won't let it go," she muttered thickly.

"Only because you still won't answer me."

"How many times do I have to tell you that I'm a big girl, Addison? Help your ex. Do your good deed. Go to London for your meeting, or do your negotiating here. I'll let you know if I need your help with friendly questions from the cop." She fluttered her eyelashes at him. "Unless you and Patricia are planning to move back in together or something first. Have you chosen your china?"

"Don't be an idiot."

"Hey, you married her. I didn't."

Yes, he had. And he had loved Patricia once, though that fact tended to horrify him now. Today he could ridicule Patricia's penchant for pretty clothes and perfect nails and befriending perfect people, but those same qualities had made her the perfect choice for a wife—especially to a man who traveled in circles where an arrogant belief in perfection was as common as diamonds and overloaded bank accounts.

"Rick?"

He shook himself. "Hm? Apologies. You had me reminiscing."

"I was joking about Patricia, you know."

Of course he knew that Samantha cared for him; she wouldn't have stayed about if she didn't. She would never say she needed him, because somewhere along the way she'd decided that needing meant needy—and only the self-sufficient survived in her world. But finally she'd been able to admit that she did *want* him about, and for someone of her diamond-hard exterior, that was something valuable.

"I know you were joking. I wasn't, though. I said I would help her, and I'll look into it. Nothing more."

"You might want to tell her that. She did once find her way into your pants, after all."

"Lovely." He reached across the table and took her fingers, fork and all. "I'm not leaving Palm Beach until I know that everything is all right with you and Castillo and the whole Kunz thing."

"I figured that." She made a face, freeing her fingers again. "I'm not going to just sit on my ass and let things blow over. Kunz asked for my help, whether he knew something specific or not. I let him down."

"Sam—"

"I did. And I let myself down. I mean, Christ, Kunz would have been my first real client. In a way, he still is."

He looked at her for a moment, trying to decide the best way to argue with her without making matters worse. "Since half the staff vouched for you being here night before last, you're not a suspect at the moment. But if you begin hanging about and asking questions, that could change. You have a reputation, whether anything's ever been proven or not."

She shot him her fleeting grin. "Don't worry about that. I doubt I'll be talking to anybody who would go to the cops."

That stopped him. Whatever he said now, it would probably push her further into this little game that he didn't want her to play. "Castillo said he'd keep you apprised of events," he said coolly. "If you frig about with suspects or witnesses or evidence, you could compromise the investigation, and Frank, and the way the police are looking at you."

"Yes, well, you do things your way, and I'll do them mine." She took another bite of French toast. "After all, you're the successful businessman, and I'm the successful thief. I think this is more up my alley than yours. I don't get caught."

"Except by me."

"Maybe, but I'm pretty sure I let you catch me."

He could dispute that, but it wouldn't help anything. Instead he finished off his cup of tea. "What do you have planned for today?"

"I'll head over to the office and check on Stoney. I think we have some receptionist applications."

"And then?"

"Oh, I thought I'd break into a couple of houses and maybe fence your new Rembrandt."

So that was how she intended to play it. Fine. "This isn't a usual day. I reserve the right to worry about you from time to time. If you think it shows a lack of trust on my part, you're wrong."

She stood, setting her napkin beside her plate and strolling around to stand behind him. "That's good. You didn't even flinch when I mentioned B and E. I'll be careful."

Richard tilted his head back to look up at her. "Promise?"

With a small smile she ran her hands down the sides of his upturned face before she placed a warm, soft, upside-down kiss on his mouth. "Promise," she murmured, and was gone.

He listened for movement in the hallway, but she was notoriously difficult to track once she'd gone into what she called "stealth mode." Even relaxed, she had a tendency to move as quietly and gracefully as . . . as anyone he'd ever seen.

And now she'd decided to go hunting for a killer. She thought of it as doing something for someone she'd let down, but his view was a little more cynical. Kunz had died, and she meant to plant herself right in the middle of something dangerous and more than likely illegal. Rick blew out his breath, rising. Her idea of careful and his degree of worry over her weren't quite at the same level, yet. Hell, they weren't even in the same hemisphere. He needed to make a few more phone calls than he'd planned.

Samantha asked for the Bentley to be brought around to the front drive, then braceleted an elastic band around her wrist and pulled her hair back to fix it in a ponytail as she descended the main staircase. That wasn't the image she wanted to take to Worth Avenue and her office, but she needed to stop by Stoney's house first, anyway. She kept an extra pair of binoculars there, along with other small equipment necessary for studying a mark and getting ready for a theft. Or now for investigating one, she supposed.

She'd told Rick she would stop by her office, and she would. Stoney had said he would put out some feelers to see if anybody in their circle had bagged some treasure over the past day or two. It would help if she knew exactly what had been stolen from Kunz's residence, but she'd do what she could.

She had some supplies at Solano Dorado, of course, but they were for extreme emergencies only, and she wouldn't put Rick at risk by leaving the house with them under the present circumstances. Castillo might say she wasn't a suspect, but he'd warned her that he wasn't the only one who knew she was in town—and he certainly wasn't the only one who knew the rumors about her previous life. The last thing she wanted was for the FBI or Interpol to knock on Rick Addison's front door and find her shiny set of lock picks.

Pulling open the front door, she nearly slammed into the person standing there, arm raised to knock. Instinctively she moved back and sideways, avoiding the collision. Only then did she note who'd come to visit.

"Patricia," she said, fingers clenching on the door handle. "Rick didn't say you were coming by this morning."

"He didn't know," the Ex returned, a tight smile on her face. "I took a chance on catching him at home."

"How did you get in?"

"I still know the gate code." Patricia gave a short laugh. "If I were you, I would have jumped over the wall, I suppose."

Great. Everybody knew she used to bend the law. Okay, shatter it into itty bitty little pieces. And they were changing the damned gate code today. "You probably would have set off the alarm if you did that," she returned, leaning back into the house. *"Reinaldo!"*

"Might I come in?" the Ex said, her cultured British accent tight as her gym club ass.

"I'll leave that for the housekeeper to decide," Sam returned, handing over control of the door to Reinaldo as he skidded into the foyer.

Edging past Patricia, she trotted down the steps and dropped into the Bentley. A black Lexus half blocked her exit, but she backed around it, close enough to hopefully annoy the crap out of the Ex. It shouldn't bother her that Patricia wanted help from Rick; he'd made it clear that he wanted as little as possible to do with her. When she thought about it, it was probably just the *idea* that Patricia had gone to Rick for help that bugged her. Patricia had screwed—literally— her chance with Rick, all on her own. Under those circumstances nothing in the world could have induced Samantha to face him again, and even less, to beg for his help.

Sam took a deep breath. Oh, yeah, it was easy to say she would stay an independent as she tooled over the unmarked Palm Beach bridge in a Bentley on her way to Worth Avenue and after spending the night having some really fine sex in a forty-acre estate. "Great, Sam. You stick to your principles, and you'll be fine. Or dead."

"No," Richard said into his desk phone, reflecting that, as Samantha had informed him on several occasions, he was perhaps too accustomed to getting what he wanted. "That's not necessary. If you'd just let Detective Castillo know I called, that will be sufficient. Yes, he knows how to reach me. Thank you."

He could call the chief of police to press for more information about Kunz's death, but once he became actively involved in the matter, attention would turn to Samantha as well. And if there was one thing he didn't want, it was for his actions to threaten her. Easy as it would be, he couldn't bulldoze through this. Apparently he needed a more delicate tool.

His intercom buzzed. "Mr. Addison?"

He pressed the button on the phone. "What is it, Reinaldo?"

"You have a visitor. Mrs. Wallis."

Bloody hell. "Where is she?"

"I showed her to the east sunroom."

"I'll be down in a moment." Swearing again, he released the intercom. When he'd first filed for divorce, dealing with Patricia and her things and her Patty's Pack friends had been infuriating. Now it was an annoyance—but more than that, as well. She was his greatest failure, and to be perfectly honest, he would have been much happier if she would just go away. Evidently she had a different idea.

Downstairs in the east sunroom he found her gazing at the Manet painting above the fireplace. "Patricia."

"I remember when you bought this. That auction at Christie's," she said, facing him. "We spent the night in Buckingham Palace, at the invitation of the Queen."

Clenching his jaw, Richard nodded. "I remember. What do you want? I told you I'd talk to Tom."

"I apologized, Richard. A million times." She came closer, pert and perfect in her blue Ralph Lauren blouse and pleated tan trousers. "And I've changed."

"Only your location. I have work to do, so tell me what you want, or please leave."

"What if I stole things from people?" she said abruptly, taking a slow step closer.

He froze for a heartbeat, then continued his stroll to the windows. "What?"

"What if I slipped into people's houses and into their

rooms and stole their valuables? We could be at a party, and while you distracted the host I could sneak into another room and take a diamond ring—or something—and no one would know who'd done it. No one but you and me."

Richard looked at her. So Samantha had been correct; Patricia wanted him back. For Christ's sake, what a mess this had all become. "You think your becoming some sort of cat burglar would be the thing to bring us back together?" he asked quietly, very aware of how carefully he had to tread right now. Apparently Patricia knew or had surmised a great deal more about Samantha than he'd realized.

"Stealing and killing do seem to be the new fashionable way to make a living in our world. And who fits into our world better than we do? Would that excite you, Richard, to know that we were in someone's house to steal from them, all the while they were serving us champagne and caviar?"

"You couldn't be anything like Samantha if you tried, Patricia," he said flatly. "If that's what you think you're attempting here, I suggest you give it up. If you had any idea what excites me about her, you wouldn't bother with this . . . pitiful attempt at one-upmanship—or whatever it is you think you're doing."

"But she's a thief. What else could possibly interest you about her?"

"Everything."

He could see the sudden hurt in her surprised, ice-cold expression. Obviously she'd thought her plan of attack through, and had decided that pretending she could be a better Samantha than Samantha was the best way to pique his interest. One bloody thief to be reformed was more than enough. Aside from that, he couldn't imagine Patricia doing what Samantha did. His ex-wife wasn't independent enough, or courageous enough, to put her life and her freedom in jeopardy on a regular basis for the sake of a thrill and a paycheck.

A muscle beneath her left eye twitched, and then she laughed. "Of course you find her interesting. She's different. And quite charming, in an odd sort of way. I was only joking about stealing things. I told you Peter was a poor influence on me. Please have Tom call me as soon as possible. I need to cut all my ties with Peter, and the sooner, the better. But it's not just legal assistance I need, Richard."

"Money? I thought you were being frugal."

"I am."

"Perhaps you should try shopping at Wal-Mart instead of buying Ralph Lauren, then."

"I have to fit in," she snapped, obviously annoyed. "You notice whether I'm wearing Ralph Lauren or Prada or Diane von Furstenberg, or whether I'm staying at Motel 6 or The Breakers. So does everyone else. I *am* trying to economize, but I don't think I should have to give up everyone and everything I'm accustomed to."

He looked at her skeptically. "I thought the idea was for you to find a new group of friends who weren't familiar with your life and your expensive tastes."

Her shoulders sagged. "My life is ruined. I have only a few friends left who understand what's happened to me, and even fewer who still want anything to do with me."

"It sounds as though you need to hire an image consultant. That's not my area of expertise." He took a step sideways and picked up the end table phone, punching the intercom. "Reinaldo? Please show Mrs. Wallis out."

"But—"

"Excuse me, I have a conference call."

Without waiting for her to reply, Richard strode out the door and back up the stairs. Just like yesterday, his first thought was that he wanted to see Samantha. Sternly, angrily, he pushed the idea aside and returned to his office. Damn Patricia. The last thing he needed was to smother Sam in order to reassure himself that she belonged to him, that she wasn't like Patricia, and that he wasn't the same man who'd loved that woman five years ago.

Patricia had been right about one thing; part of what excited him about Samantha, though he'd never admit to it, was that she was a thief. She had the ability to slip in and out of people's lives, to liberate their possessions, without them even being aware of it until after she was gone. The fact that he was aware of it, that even with all her skills she hadn't been able to slip out of his life—hadn't *wanted* to slip out of his life—made her presence all the more arousing. The shit of it was, she couldn't be allowed to do it any longer. How that would eventually alter their relationship, he didn't know, but it wasn't anything they could avoid. Not if they wanted to remain together. He wanted that, and he thought she probably did, as well.

As soon as he reached his desk, he dialed Tom Donner's direct office number. Helping Patricia had become a priority, if only so she would leave him alone. He had someone else to concentrate on—and making a mistake where Samantha was concerned could mean more than losing her. Where she was concerned, mistakes could be fatal.

Glancing around as she took her seat behind the wheel of the Lexus, Patricia favored Reginald with a forced smile. This was bad. Once she was back on the streets of Palm Beach, she was vulnerable. Daniel had certainly enjoyed their night together after her little experiment at the Harkley's dinner party. She'd enjoyed it, too. For heaven's sake, no wonder

Sam Jellicoe stole things. She'd never been so excited and aroused in her life.

Patricia fingered the diamond ring in her pocket as she turned down North Ocean Boulevard. It didn't make any sense. That American mutt stole things, and from the way she and Richard hung on each other at every event, they were shagging like bunnies. But when *she* did it—implied it, even—he told her to leave.

Now she was stuck with a stolen diamond ring—and with no one to help her. She couldn't make up some excuse to visit Lydia Harkley and put it back, because the police would instantly connect its disappearance and reappearance with her. She couldn't tell Rick, because he'd already all but called her an idiot for thinking of doing something like that. Even worse, he would only accuse her of trying to imitate that bitch, or something.

Wait a moment. *That bitch.* The idea stunned her. But Jellicoe would know what to do with the ring.

Patricia took a breath. If she were careful enough, she could even put the ring in Jellicoe's pocket or something. Then she could call the police and be a heroine. It would be the mutt the police would be after, and it would be the mutt going to jail, and it would be Richard left with no one.

Jellicoe had an office, Daniel had said, on Worth Avenue. Smiling, Patricia headed for the shopping district. Thievery *could* pay, after all.

Samantha stopped just inside the reception area of her office. Nine professionally dressed, fresh-faced people, all busily filling out printed sheets of paper, sat on plush leather couches along the back and side wall. Stoney stood behind the reception desk, a phone to his ear.

It wasn't so much the seven young women and two buff-looking guys that stopped Sam as it was the sight of the furniture—and of Stoney actually wearing a jacket and tie. "What the hell is going on?" she asked, shutting the main door behind her.

"Ah, Miss Jellicoe. Do you have a moment to see me in your office?" the big man returned, a white smile stretched way too thin on his dark face.

"Sure."

She headed through the nearest door leading to the back of reception and the hallway and offices behind. As she rounded the corner, Stoney's backside vanished into her office ahead of her, and she slowed a little to give herself a moment to think. Two things were weird: One, half the back office was piled with furniture from at least two different centuries; and two, he was wearing a damned suit.

"Where have you been?" he asked as soon as she entered the room.

"I had to run a couple of errands," she said. "Your next door neighbor was picking your roses again."

His gaze sharpened. "You were at my house? Which equipment did you pick up?"

"Binoculars and the spare set of lock picks." Samantha ran her finger along the edge of the desk that now occupied her office. "Um, this is real mahogany."

Stoney smiled. "It sure is. I knew you'd appreciate it. Don't get too attached to it, though. We only have this stuff for six weeks."

"Did you rent it? Why not just—"

"We're not renting."

Samantha returned to the office doorway and leaned out to look at the mismatched pile of tables and lamps and chairs in the common room. It was her taste. Stoney knew her better than anyone, so that was no surprise, but this was just . . . weird. "Okay, explain."

"We're storing it."

"Sto—"

"I know you're trying to stay on the straight and narrow, so you don't have anything to worry about, baby."

"But—"

"Hey, if you don't like it, find your own furniture."

Great. So now she could either piss Stoney off or risk getting busted for harboring stolen furniture. "Okay. I trust you. Who are the stiffs in the front room?"

"One of 'em is going to be your receptionist, I presume. They just started showing up. We shouldn't have published the address in the employment ad."

"Probably not."

"An hour ago there were twenty-three of them in there. I had to go across the street to see your Donner guy and get some application forms to give 'em something to do."

"We're popular already. That's good."

"It's good if you're here to help me out, Sam. Otherwise it sucks. The rest of the interviews are yours."

Samantha blinked. "Me? I'm not interviewing anybody. That's your job."

"No, it isn't. You said I'm a partner. That doesn't mean I get stuck doing interviews instead of depositing a quarter of a million bucks in my Swiss account. And I got the furniture, remember?"

"Don't be prissy, Stoney. Another few weeks like my last as a cat and you'd be wearing that suit to my funeral."

He grimaced. "Yeah. Okay. But right now I'm your business partner who's going to lunch."

"You—" She closed her mouth, eyeing his attire again. "You're going to lunch with the real estate chick, aren't you? Kim."

"That's none of your business, kiddo." He handed her a clipboard. "Here. I wrote down some questions to start you out. Good luck."

He left the office. Her heart jumping, Samantha hurried after him. "Wait a minute. When are you coming back?"

"If I'm lucky, tomorrow. The door key's in the right-hand door of the reception desk. Don't forget to set the alarm. The directions are in the same drawer."

"I don't need directions for an alarm," she shot back, still trotting behind him. This was ridiculous. She had a murder to investigate. And there were nine, *nine*, people in there, all waiting for her. "Stoney, I can't—"

"Sure you can. You're the boss."

He vanished through the reception door. She stopped short in front of it. *Crap.* Annoyed and even a little nervous, it didn't help to realize that she'd been abusing Stoney's support in this little venture, especially considering that he seemed more reluctant to retire than she'd realized. She was supposed to be able to take advantage of him, though. That's what family was for.

A mirror had been mounted on the back of the door to the reception area, probably so the suite's previous occupants could check their appearance before they emerged to greet a client. She looked at her reflection, hair still in a ponytail, a simple green T-shirt with a white shirt open over it, and blue jeans. Great. She had a change of clothes in the car, just in case, but everybody out front had already had a look at her.

Samantha blew out her breath. Okay, she could do this. Hell, compared with other situations she'd been in, this would be simple. Like Stoney had said, she was the boss. They all wanted something from her. Just another day in the life of Samantha Elizabeth Jellicoe.

She stepped out. "Okay, who's next?"

Nine faces looked at her, while she looked back at them. After a moment a fresh-faced girl who looked about her own age stood. "I think I am," she said in a soft Southern accent.

"Good. Come on back, and we'll have a chat."

After the third interview she had the hang of it—people liked to talk, so all she really needed to do was ask a leading question or two about which hours they could work and what kind of salary they were hoping for. Immediately she received a flood of information about the travails of single parenthood or unpaid college loans or bad backs or lousy ex-husbands. Sheesh. If people would learn to listen to themselves and think about impressions, they'd have a much better chance of getting a job, and she and Stoney would only have had three people to interview instead of twenty-three.

She showed victim number five back to the reception door. "Thanks for coming in. We'll be making our decision in the next few days."

"Thank you, Miss Jellicoe. I'm really looking forward to working with you," Amber said, taking a step closer. "And can I ask if your boyfriend ever comes by the office?"

Great. Another Rick's Chicks newsletter subscriber. "Yes, Stoney's here all the time," she returned, flashing a bright smile.

"But—"

Sam opened the door and nudged the girl out. "Thanks again. Next?"

One of the two guys, the one who looked like a hotel pool lifeguard complete with green-blond hair, stood. Before he could approach, though, another figure pushed by him.

"That would be me," Patricia Addison-Wallis said, her dazzling smile setting Sam back on her heels.

"I'm not hiring you," she said, before she could stop herself.

Patricia chuckled. "Of course not, my dear. I would never work for you. I did wonder if you had time for a cup of coffee."

"Wow. Rick tossed you out again, did he?"

With an annoyed glance at their now-rapt audience, Patricia grabbed her arm and practically towed her through the private door into the back. Obviously Patricia didn't know how little she liked being grabbed. Rather than setting the Ex on her ass, though, Sam pointed and allowed herself to be led toward the new coffee machine that had appeared in the small conference room.

"I have interviews," she said unnecessarily, reflecting that Patricia probably knew and didn't care about that.

"Yes, I saw. This is a lovely office. Who's your decorator? Trezise?"

"I'm the decorator." Well, Stoney was.

"Of course you are, dear." Patricia seated herself at the conference table. "It's very eclectic."

"So am I." Beginning to be a little amused, Samantha poured the Ex a cup of coffee. "Lots of sugar, I suppose?" she asked.

"Three cubes, please. Aren't you having any?"

Sam sat in the opposing chair. "I don't drink that shit. What's up, Patty? You don't mind me calling you Patty, do you?"

The smile tightened. "I prefer Patricia. I just thought we should chat. Being with Richard is a complicated prospect, after all, and since he's helping me so much, I thought perhaps I could help you."

"Help me," Samantha repeated. "You."

"Well, yes. Who has a better insight into Richard than I

do? We were married for nearly three years, however unfortunately it might have ended."

"It was unfortunate that he caught you screwing Peter Wallis, you mean," Samantha supplied. If they were going to chat, she wasn't going to pull any punches. Not with this woman. Not after knowing how much she'd hurt Rick. "You remember, the guy who tried to kill me and Rick."

"I had nothing to do with that." Patricia looked down into her coffee cup, idly stirring the sugar into the mix. "I made a terrible mistake with Richard, and then I made another one with Peter. It's not as though I'll forget. Ever."

Hm. Samantha had seen Rick when he decided he didn't like someone. He didn't change his mind, and his anger could be . . . devastating. On the other hand . . . "So you just want to chat," she mused, reaching into the pocket of her open shirt. "And to give me presents, I assume?" Her gaze on Patricia's face, she produced a diamond ring and set it on the table between them. "Nice ones, at that."

"How—" The Ex stared at her for a heartbeat, then burst into tears. "I hate this town! Nothing ever goes right for me."

"Considering that for a minute I thought you were feeling me up and I almost broke your nose, I'd say things went okay." Samantha stood up, going to the small refrigerator in the corner and getting a Diet Coke for herself. Yep, Stoney knew her real well. "So whose is this? It's not yours, or you wouldn't be giving it to me."

"I'm not giving it to you, stupid bitch."

So they were both being forthright. "Okay, you were planting it on me. Which doesn't answer my question. To whom does it belong?"

"Why should I tell you?" Patricia sat up straighter. "Because now it has your fingerprints on it. You took it. There. And I'm going to call the police."

Despite Samantha's immediate knee-jerk reaction to flee, she sat down again and popped the top on her soda. "Go ahead. What are you going to tell them?"

"That you stole that ring."

"And how do you know it's stolen?" Sam took a swallow of soda. "You should think this through, you know. The cops are pretty sharp around here." Well, some of them were, anyway.

"You told me you stole it."

"So I'm an idiot. And you're who, Lara Croft, Tomb Raider? Give me a break, Patty. Where'd it come from?"

"Patricia," the Ex snapped. "Don't patronize me."

"Don't try to frame me. Your hubby did that, and look what it got him."

"My *ex*-husband. Ex, ex, ex!"

"Like I give a shit. You just planted a ring on me. A stolen one, obviously." She took a breath, making a quick assessment of the situation. "And much as I hate to use the big guy for leverage, I've got Rick on my side. Spill."

"I hate you."

"That's fine with me." She pulled her cell phone off her belt and flipped it open. "He's speed dial number one, Patty."

"Patricia!" Patricia slammed her open hand on the table. "This is all your fault anyway! The way he looks at you . . . I thought, well, it worked for that bitch. Maybe it's his new touch, his early mid-life crisis that he likes to shag thieves. And then I mention to him how naughty it would be for the two of us, and he practically throws me out of the house."

"You can't really blame him for that."

"That used to be my house," Patricia continued. "And now I'm—I'm stuck with this stupid thing," and she waved a fist at the ring, "and you're going to ruin everything. Go ahead! I'll just go to jail! Maybe they'll put me in a cell next to Peter."

"No, you'd go to women's prison," Samantha corrected.

Sobbing, Patricia sank her head onto her folded arms. Samantha thought it was probably just for show, but the Ex did have some acting skills. Some pretty good ones. From what Rick had said and what she'd observed, though, this helpless routine might not be an act. She was a cold, arrogant snob, sure, but she also had the worst judgment in history.

Samantha picked up the ring. It was good quality platinum, and the diamond seemed genuine enough. Even without the benefit of a magnifier it still looked like maybe five carats. Wherever it had come from, once the owner noticed it was gone, the cops would be looking for it. She looked along the inside of the band. " 'For my love LH,' " she read. "Did you break in to get this, or just slip into somebody's bedroom when they weren't looking?"

"What does it matter?"

"It'll matter when the cops are called and the vic starts going over who was there when it went missing."

Patricia lifted her head. Her mascara was waterproof, but that didn't keep her eyes from being red and puffy. "The 'vic'?" she repeated. "What the bloody hell are you talking about?"

"The victim, Patty. Answer the question. Break-in, or convenience?"

"I was at the Harkleys' for a dinner party. I went upstairs to use the bathroom, and it was there in the bed stand of the master bedroom. I thought . . . I thought—"

"I know what you thought." Samantha closed her fingers around the ring. "The Harkleys." She remembered seeing them at the Everglades Club, an older couple with a ton of money inherited from mining and oil. And she remembered five years ago when they'd been in possession of a Mayan crystal skull. That thing had creeped her out. She'd never been happier to unload an item on a buyer. "When did you take it?"

"Last night."

From the expression on Patricia's face, Patricia had realized that she should cooperate with the questions. Nobody could fake hope, and Mrs. Addison-Wallis wore a large measure of it. Sam frowned. She was being a sap, and she was going to regret it. At the same time, she knew how much it must have hurt Patty to have Rick turn his back, whoever's fault it had been. The thought of him being there close enough to touch and not wanting anything to do with her . . . The pain of the idea slammed like a bullet into her chest.

And there was something else, too. The lure of danger, the thrill of going somewhere she wasn't supposed to be—it pulled at her. She'd turned down Venice; didn't she deserve something in return? Especially if she could write it off as a good deed.

"Samantha? Sam? Do you think . . . Would you . . ."

With a breath Sam put the ring back into her shirt pocket. A good deed. That's all it was. Something to give her some positive karma marks. "I'll take care of it. But if you breathe a word of this to anyone—*anyone*—I will see to it that you die a horrible, painful, slow death."

Whether she believed the threat or not, Patricia nodded vigorously. "I won't. I won't say a word. I swear it. I won't forget this, Samantha. If you ever need anything, you let me know."

"Right." Any more of this happy puppy dog crap, and she was going to puke. Especially when she was already humming with the thought of a quick B and E. Samantha stood. "I have some interviews to finish."

"Of course. I'll just let you get on with it, then."

Patricia led the way back to the reception door. Before she could pull it open, though, Sam blocked it with her hand. "One thing, Patty."

The Ex swallowed her obvious irritation. "Yes?"

"Stay away from Rick."

With a peal of laughter, Patricia headed through the reception area for the outside door. "Of course I will."

Yeah. Sam believed that.

Eight

Sunday, 11:48 p.m.

Richard stood in the library window, gazing down at the lighted front drive as the Bentley pulled up. He stayed where he was, sipping his brandy, as Samantha clambered from the car and trotted up the shallow marble steps, passing out of sight as she neared the front door.

She'd said she had a client to deal with, and that she would be home by midnight. She'd made it by twelve minutes. Whoever the new client was, he apparently kept late office hours. Rick gave a slow smile. The last time she'd met with a client, she'd come home and tied him up for chair-breaking sex. Not that he liked her being bored and frustrated, but it did seem to be his duty to help her work through those issues. And his day of coordinating meetings and re-vamping offers hadn't exactly been thrilling.

Refilling the snifter, he headed for the hallway and down the main staircase to meet her at the second landing. "How was it?" he asked, offering her a drink.

She took the snifter and sipped at it. "Boring. I'm sorry I missed dinner. Did you guys save me something?"

" 'You guys?' " he repeated. "Hans and myself, I presume?"

"You're my guys," she agreed, setting the snifter on the railing and stepping into the circle of his arms for a long, deep kiss. "You taste like brandy and chocolate," she murmured, snuggling into his chest.

"Brownies. Hans was quite upset you weren't here to sample them fresh from the oven. And yes, 'we' saved you some pot roast." Slowly he slid his arms around her waist, lowering his face into her wavy auburn hair. Paradise. But at the same time it didn't feel like wild sex night. "Come upstairs," he murmured. "I stole the can of whipped cream."

"Mm, fattening."

That wasn't quite the response he'd expected. The hard-on he'd been working on since she drove up faded a little. "Are you all right?"

"Fine. I brought a few receptionist applications to look at. I can do that over pot roast."

She slipped free from his arms, recaptured the brandy, and turned back downstairs. Rick studied her relaxed, graceful descent for a moment as he leaned his elbows on the railing. She did not look like a former thief who'd been dealing with frustrating and mundane duties all evening and needed to work off some adrenaline. "With whom did you meet?" he asked.

Samantha glanced at him over her shoulder. "Nobody you know. I don't think it's a job. More for practice, really. I'll be upstairs in a little bit." With that she vanished in the direction of the kitchen.

Richard knew her pattern by now. When she was bored or frustrated, she wanted to work it off—usually with him, naked. The woman who'd just headed in to eat pot roast was relaxed and sleepy. She'd already had her adrenaline fix tonight.

Worry teasing at him, Rick followed her. Hans had gone

to bed, but he'd left a covered plate in the oven with a note of directions. Detailed ones. Evidently the chef knew Samantha pretty well, too. "Mind if I keep you company?" Rick asked, sliding into the kitchen chair opposite her.

She nudged the brandy back in his direction, then stood to claim a Diet Sprite from the beverage refrigerator. "Sure. What's on your mind?"

"I think the more interesting question is what's on yours?"

Knocking her knuckles against a paper-filled folder as she passed by the table, Samantha picked up a hot pad and gingerly removed her plate from the oven. "Hiring a receptionist. You should have seen some of the applicants. There were a couple of guys, and I swear one of them is a body builder. He's at the top of my list."

"Very amusing. How do you know I'm not acquainted with your almost-client? Jellicoe Security only works with the best, and those are the people in my sphere, too."

"Snob."

"Who is it, Samantha?"

She glanced up at him as she peeled off the wrapping of tin foil. "You're cute when you're suspicious."

So much for beating around the bush, though another thought had occurred to him, anyway. "You were digging into Charles Kunz's life, weren't you? Frank told you he would keep you apprised. Leave the investigation to him."

"I figure I can find out more than he can, and much faster. Besides, it'll keep me out of other trouble. You want me to stay out of trouble, don't you?"

"I don't see how sneaking around in the dark and talking to your old cronies is staying out of trouble."

"How about you do things your way, and I'll do them mine?" She stabbed a green bean. "And I'll solve this before the cops do. In fact, I'll bet you a hundred bucks that I put this all together before Castillo does."

"I'm not going to wager over something that could get you hurt."

"Ha," she retorted, shoveling in another mouthful and clearly perking up at the argument. "You won't wager because you know I'm right. My method against the cops'." Swallowing, she smiled darkly at him. "Come on, Rick. Bet me. Back up that hot accent with your big old wallet."

Obviously she was going to look into Kunz's death whether he wanted her to or not. Therefore, if he could use this opportunity to prove that her nefarious life couldn't get her results any better or faster than the police, it would be worthwhile. He wanted her to stay straight, if for no other reason that if she didn't, eventually the trail of thefts she'd left would catch up to her. That could ruin him, but he wasn't precisely worried about himself. In addition, the mercenary part of him couldn't help thinking that if he could prove her wrong, he could use that to pull her further from her old life and into his.

"You're on," he said crisply, offering his hand. "One hundred dollars that Castillo and legitimate police work will solve this case and find the killer before you can manage it."

She dropped her fork and gripped his fingers. "Deal, Brit."

Castillo needed to work fast, because if Richard knew one thing, it was that Samantha hated to lose—and that she didn't do so often. He had his own connections, though, and as long as it was legal, he didn't see why he couldn't help out the Palm Beach Police Department. Civic duty and all that. Samantha would lose, and he would win—which as far as he was concerned, would be the bloody best thing for both of them.

                        * * *

Breaking into the Harkleys' and replacing the damned ring last night had been a piece of cake. They hadn't even updated security in the five years since she'd last gone in—which made the whole episode almost too easy. It had been okay, thrillwise, but definitely hadn't topped out the meter. On a hunch she'd lifted the videotape from the previous night while she disabled the equipment for her own moonlit stroll. Having a little extra ammunition to use against Patricia might come in handy.

The wager over pot roast, though—there were no maybes about that. It definitely had some potential. The first thing she needed to do was find out more about the jewelry and the paintings that had gone missing at the time of the murder. That might help answer the question of whether the plan had been murder *and* robbery, or whether one had just been a matter of convenience and bad luck.

She wasn't a big believer in luck, though, and so she decided to begin the morning with a phone call to Frank Castillo to give her a starting point. That, however, would entail getting out from under Rick Addison, and at the moment she was enjoying where she was far too much.

Gasping at the quickening slide of his hard body inside hers, Samantha lifted her ankles and locked them around his hips. "Rick," she moaned breathlessly, running her fingers around his flat male nipples.

Heat and arousal and safety. All three words were heady, and finding them all in the person of Rick Addison was enough to give her multiple orgasms. She was working on her third right now.

"Faster," she panted, lifting her hips to meet his humping.

"No," he grunted, catching her mouth in a hard, deep kiss. "I'm keeping you pinned here all morning."

What a way to go. "That's one way to win the bet," she

managed in between spasms of pure pleasure, then pulled him down hard and twisted. She ended on top, straddling him and fully impaled. "Oh, God," she murmured, lifting up and down on him. "But maybe I won't let you."

His elegant hands kneaded at her breasts, his hips rising to grind up into her over and over again. "That's cheating," he groaned.

After that both of them seemed to lose the ability to communicate verbally. Her entire body clenched and released. With a cry she collapsed on Rick's chest, while he held her hips down and finished himself off inside her.

She lay across him, panting, and waited for her second favorite part of their lovemaking. Slowly his arms lifted to wrap around her, not confining, but comfortable. Safe.

She'd been in several relationships before, all of them short-lived, and most of them ending because she got bored or lost interest, or needed to leave the country for a job and he decided she must have a lover somewhere else. She'd never been with anyone for three months, and she'd never craved anyone the way she did Richard Addison. And it wasn't just in bed; she liked talking with him, and eating with him, and the way he always made an excuse to hold her hand.

"Samantha?" he murmured, stroking her hair.

She kissed his throat, feeling his strong, fast pulse beneath her lips. Intoxicating—and she didn't use that term lightly, or often. Not until she'd met him, actually. "Hm?"

"I'm not going to try to change your mind about Kunz, but—"

"Good," she interrupted, straightening onto her hands to look down at him. "Because I'm not going to change my mind."

"Let me finish, Yank. Just be careful, will you? I want you to stay out of prison as much as you do."

She relaxed. "I'm always careful," she cooed, stretching her legs out beside his.

"No, you're not."

"I've been picking up some magazines for the office," she said, wrapping her free arm around his shoulder, resting her cheek on his chest. She liked to hear his heartbeat. "*Cosmo*, *Harper's Bazaar*, *Woman's Day*, stuff like that."

"And?"

"And did you know that after three months couples start to move out of their honeymoon period, noticing the flaws of their significant others and becoming less focused on sex?"

Rick snorted. "Then we're safe. I already know about your flaws, and I don't have any."

"Jackass."

"And as for becoming less focused on sex," he continued, pulling her farther across him and lifting her face to look up at her from inches away, "fuck that. I want you every minute of every day. You know how I feel about you."

Her chest tightening, Samantha slipped from his grasp and sat up. She hated when he talked like that—not because she didn't like hearing it, but because more and more, she did. If she let him, Rick would consume her, trap her into his life and make her think that was precisely what she wanted. It might be, eventually, but she couldn't let herself fall into it without analyzing who wanted what, and what was best for her.

Shit, she'd spent the entire twenty-four years of her life learning that she couldn't rely on anyone but herself, and that inevitably people would work toward their own safety and comfort and happiness rather than someone else's. And she wasn't an idiot, either. If she got caught while she was with Rick, his empire would pay for her blundering. So of course by pushing her to go straight he was looking out for himself as much as he was for her. It was the way of the world, even for big shots like Rick.

"Samantha?" he said quietly, sitting up beside her. "Don't go up the pole about it."

"I'm not freaking out. Even with the weird lingo you're cool—I've told you that." She shook herself. She'd done a B and E last night, and *he* didn't even know about it, much less the cops. But the fact that she couldn't—wouldn't—tell him about her foray . . . Fuck, she needed to focus. "But I think you're just trying to distract me and win the bet," she improvised.

He kissed her shoulder blade. "Have it your way, my love. I'm not in a hurry for anything but breakfast."

She drew a breath. "Yeah, yeah, yeah. Maybe I'll eventually come to my senses. I'm taking a shower. Stay out. And ask Hans if he'll make me up some pancakes, will you?"

Before she could scoot off the bed, Rick caught her hand. "You never told me that you'd be careful."

"I did yesterday."

"That was yesterday."

"All right, your lordship. I'll be careful."

As soon as she'd showered and they'd eaten breakfast down by the pool, Samantha jumped in the Bentley and headed into town. On the way she dialed Frank Castillo's cell phone. Whatever Rick might have assumed about her nefarious methods of investigation, she needed to know what had gone missing from Charles Kunz's house.

"Castillo."

"Frank. It's Sam Jellicoe. Do you have a sec?"

She could hear the surprise in his voice. "Sure. I'm in the office."

"Can I meet you somewhere?"

Silence. "Yeah. The office."

"Frank, don't be a—"

"Is this a favor for me or a favor for you, Sam?"

She scowled. "Fine. I'll come see you at the office," she said, her throat tightening.

"Okay. I'll grab a doughnut for you."

"Chocolate with sprinkles. See you in about fifteen."

Her hand was shaking when she flipped the phone closed with her chin. Her father must be whirling in his grave at the idea of his daughter volunteering to walk into a police station. New life, new insanity, she supposed. And she'd made a damned bet with Rick—one she wasn't going to lose. Especially not when that would mean failing Charles Kunz.

It dawned on her that she hadn't asked Rick about his visit with Patricia yesterday morning; considering what had transpired—the break-in she'd done last night to return the diamond ring—avoiding the subject altogether seemed the wisest thing to do. At the same time, he hadn't brought Patty up, either. With that knight-in-shining-armor crap he liked to do, his silence wasn't all that reassuring. At least Solano Dorado didn't have a guest house the Ex could move into—though thankfully that didn't feel like Rick's syle.

Secrets. They both kept them—and the better she came to know Rick, the less she liked that he had them. For perhaps the first time, she understood his frustration with her.

Her phone rang. She glanced at the caller ID. "Unknown," she mused, hitting the talk button. *"Hola."*

"Hello?" a deep English accent came back. "Samantha Jellicoe, please."

"Speaking."

"I called your office, and your assistant gave me this number. You deal in security, do you not?"

Great. Stoney wasn't happy, if he was giving strangers her

cell number. Sam changed lanes, shifting the phone to her other ear. She needed to get one of those hands-free things. "Yes, I do."

"I wonder if we could meet?"

"That depends," she said, turning right at the light. "Who are you?"

"Oh, yes. Well, that . . . that's a bit sticky. I need to ask for your discretion, first."

She frowned. "I'm very discreet."

"Very well." He cleared his throat, managing to make even that sound British. "My name is Leedmont. John Leedmont."

Samantha pulled over so fast that she nearly wrecked into a red Mercedes. Ignoring the honking, she put the Bentley in park. "John Leedmont of Kingdom Fittings?"

"You've heard of me."

"Rick Addison's buying your company. Of course I've heard of you."

"He's *attempting* to buy my comp—"

"What was it you wanted?" she interrupted. "Because if you're going to try bribery or something, I like chocolate— but Addison really doesn't take business advice from me."

"I'm afraid this is a personal matter, Miss Jellicoe, but I don't wish to discuss it over the phone."

"Right, you wanted to meet. How about my office, in an hour?"

"Absolutely not. How about Howley's on South Dixie in thirty minutes?"

He knew Palm Beach. And it was public enough to ease her paranoia a little. Sam checked her watch. "Forty minutes. I'll see you there."

She hung up, tossed her phone onto the passenger seat, and pulled into traffic again. That was bizarre, but considering how her week was going, that wasn't saying all that much.

John Leedmont, the British pipe fittings king, wanted to meet with her privately. She should call Rick, but it made more sense to figure out what the game was, first.

Samantha was almost thankful when she pulled into the police station parking lot. At least the sight of a dozen cop cars parked behind the building gave her something more immediate to worry about. She was insane.

At the front desk she asked for Castillo, and couldn't help looking around to see if they had wanted posters taped to the walls or something. True, her face wouldn't be on one, but that was only because the law didn't know who'd pulled all the robberies she'd done. She was public now, though, and they had all the time in the world to look into her past. Or to try to, anyway.

"Sam," Castillo's voice came, and she spun around.

"Frank." She stuck out her hand, absurdly relieved to see a relatively friendly face.

"Do you want to come on back to my cubicle?" he asked, his expression amused behind his thick, graying moustache. "Or we could stand out in the parking lot if that'd make you feel better."

"Funny," she grumbled, motioning him back the way he'd come. "Where's my damned doughnut?"

She could swear half the police department stopped what they were doing to eye her as she passed by. The robbery department had probably just gone on high alert or something. Shit.

"Here you go," Castillo said after a moment, taking a seat behind an ugly gray steel desk and shoving a napkin with a chocolate doughnut toward the guest chair.

"Where're my sprinkles?" she asked, reluctantly seating herself.

"SWAT came in early for drills. They took all the sprinkles."

"Okay." She took a breath. "I need a favor."

"I figured." The detective studied her for a moment. "You helped me solve an international triple murder. Aside from that, I like you. So I'll do what I can, but I'm not jeopardizing any investigation, and I'm not—"

"Jeez, Frank. I just wanted to know if you could tell me exactly what was stolen from the Kunz estate."

"Sam . . ."

She could hear the reluctance in his voice. "He came to me looking for help," she said, "and so did you. I just want to know what's missing."

He blew out his breath. "Okay, but if this gets out, I'll know where it came from."

"Like I have anybody to tell." Not anybody who'd tell a cop about it, anyway.

"It was ruby jewelry that turned up missing. An entire collection. Kunz had bought them about ten years ago from a private collector. Something about Flemish royalty."

That rang a bell. "The Gugenthal collection," she said after a moment.

Castillo looked at her. "Right. And you knew that because . . ."

"Rubies and Flemish royalty. I keep up on things."

"I guess so."

"How much was taken?"

"From preliminary insurance reports, something around twelve million bucks in cash and jewelry."

Sam tapped her fingers on her thigh. "And the artwork?"

"One Van Gogh and an O'Keeffe."

"That's a weird pairing."

"They were both in his office," Castillo supplied, checking his notes. "Apparently he'd just come back from a collection trip."

Hm. If that were the case, things the family had never known existed could be missing, as well. Another complication. "But nothing turned up missing from anywhere else in the house?"

"Nope."

"So it was a murder first, with the robbery maybe just to cover it up."

Sitting back in his chair, Castillo took a bite of his own doughnut, buttermilk glazed. "You think like a cop. Did you know that?"

Great. "Thanks, I guess. Any clue which it is?"

"What do *you* think?"

"Me?" There were a few other things she knew—or suspected—but that was her own business. Helping the cops wouldn't do anything but lose her the bet. "Kunz knew something was going to go to hell, and from somewhere close by," she offered. "People like him don't have many weak points, and they don't let an outsider see one unless they can't help it. And if it was just the jewelry or the cash he was worried about, he could have had the stuff moved to a safe deposit box or something."

The detective had set aside his doughnut to jot down more notes. "That makes sense. And it all fits with your bodyguard theory."

"When's the funeral?" Samantha asked abruptly. She didn't attend many of those; when her friends or colleagues died, she usually wasn't in a position to come into the open. She wanted to attend Charles Kunz's, though, if she could, both to let him know that she intended to keep the promise she'd made, and to see what—or who—crawled into the sunlight to attend, as well.

"Day after tomorrow. It's gonna be private, but I'm going

from the PD." He took a breath. "Do you want to be my date?"

Their relationship had definitely changed since their first meeting, when he'd pulled a gun on her. "Rick might get an invite. If he doesn't, then yes, I'd appreciate it."

"You got it. But Sam, if you're asking me this stuff because you're trying to solve the case, don't. It's my job, and I'll take care of it. I don't want you screwing it up. And between you and me, there're enough people around who'd like to see you take a wrong step that you shouldn't even be crossing the street on your own."

With a smile, she stood. "Frank, I have no idea what you're talking about. My father was the thief, and he was convicted for it. Remember? I'm the art and security expert."

"Yeah, and I'm Fidel Castro. Stay off my radar—and everybody else's."

"Don't worry about that, Fidel. I'll call you tomorrow."

As quickly as she could do so without looking like a fleeing felon, Samantha left the police department. *Man.* That had rattled her more than a B and E gone bad. Taking deep breaths, she jumped back into the Bentley and headed for Howley's.

She'd only seen John Leedmont once, when she'd met Rick at his London office for lunch right as the CEO of Kingdom Fittings had been leaving. He was tall and distinguished, and she'd had the urge to start singing, "The Very Model of a Modern Major General" from *The Pirates of Penzance*.

When she walked into Howley's to see him seated at one of the Formica tables, her first thought was that he didn't look as music-inspiring today. No, he looked worried. It was getting to the point where everybody who wanted to talk to her was worried about something. Happy people, though, probably wouldn't need her services.

"Leedmont," she said, pulling out the chair opposite.

He half rose, doing the British bowing thing as she sat. "Miss Jellicoe. Thank you for seeing me."

"Sure. What's up?"

"You do security work."

"You already asked me that. The answer's still yes." A waitress came by, and she ordered a Diet Coke.

"And you've promised your discretion. If this were to become public, I would be ruined. And I would make certain that Addison never got his hands on Kingdom Fittings."

Sam sat back. "Gosh, you make this sound so attractive. Are you offering anything besides threats?"

"A flat fee of ten thousand dollars, American."

It wasn't much as fees traditionally went for her, but it was just about enough to cover her first month's office rent. "That sounds okay," she said slowly, "but I still want to know what the gig is, first."

"The gig. Right." He cleared his throat again. "This was slipped under my hotel room door this morning." With a deep breath he pulled an envelope from his inside coat pocket and set it between them on the table.

Immediately wary, Sam dropped her hands into her lap. She wasn't going to be tricked into touching someone else's stolen property or dirty money in public. "Why don't you open it and show me?" she suggested.

"I'd prefer not to do so here."

"You set up this meeting. I consult on security installation, and this isn't looking like that."

"No, it isn't. But I still need your help." Grimacing, he opened the envelope and set the contents on the table in front of her.

Samantha looked down. "Crap."

The waitress appeared with her soda, and Sam slammed

the photo upside down. Once they were alone again, she flipped it upright once more. Grainy, probably taken with a telephoto lens and at night, she couldn't tell who the woman was. That white moustache, though, was hard to miss.

"So you got a blow job," she said, keeping her voice pitched so no one at the closest tables could overhear. "Good for you."

"Did you read the photo's border?"

She held the photo closer. In small black letters along the white border of the picture she could just make out the words *$50,000, P.O. Box 13452, Palm Beach 33411-3452.*

Samantha looked at the picture again. It had been taken from above, looking down into the front seat of the convertible. The steering wheel was on the left, and the woman, with black straight hair and no facial features visible, wore a red tube top and white shorts. "This was taken here," she said. "And you got into town what, yesterday?"

"She practically leapt into the car."

"And right onto your cock. Amazing."

"But she didn't. I didn't receive anything, and I didn't pay her for any services. She asked for a ride, and I gave her one."

"If you ever watch *Cops*, you'll see that about ninety-five percent of the johns they bust say that same thing." She glanced up again at the bony hands gripping a cup of tea. "You're married," she stated, taking in the thick gold band on his left ring finger. "And this isn't your wife."

"No, it's not."

"Then pay the money."

"Not without an assurance that this picture will never surface again, and that I'll never receive another copy with a request for an additional sum of money at a later date."

"How did she end up with her face in your lap, if you're telling the truth?"

"I am telling the truth. She chose the place we should pull over," he said after a moment, reluctance edging his voice, "and when I stopped the car to let her out, she dropped her lighter, then leaned over to get it. That lasted for maybe a second, and then she got out of the car and thanked me, and I continued back to the hotel. Until this morning, I thought that was the end of it. My good deed, as it were."

"There's no such thing as a good deed," Sam returned, despite herself beginning to believe him. "So you think somebody paid her to set you up?"

"I don't know how else to explain it." Reaching over, he flipped the photo on its face again. "Will you help me, Miss Jellicoe?"

"I don't have much experience with blackmail," she hedged, keenly aware that Stoney was probably going ballistic back at the office waiting for her.

"If this had happened in London, I would have had people to contact who I could trust to assist me. Here, though I have many acquaintances, I wouldn't precisely say that I trust any of them."

"Especially after somebody took that picture."

"Precisely. And calling my people in now would bring too much negative attention. I know that you handled a delicate situation for Addison, and my gut tells me that I can trust you. Any information about why this happened would be helpful, though of course you will only receive the fee if I receive the original photo, the negative if there is one, and a reasonable assurance that any and all copies have been destroyed."

"If it was digital, you could be pretty much screwed, pardon the pun."

"I still want to know who took the picture."

She liked a man who tried to maintain a reasonable handle on reality even when his life was going to shit. "I'll see what I can do," she said, sweeping the photo back into the envelope. "Where are you staying?"

"The Chesterfield. Room 223."

"I'll be in touch." Finishing off her soda, she stood.

"I won't have this hanging over my head while I'm negotiating with Addison," he said distinctly.

Hey, she hadn't even seen any money yet, and he was already making threats and ultimatums—not that she could blame him. "I'll call you tomorrow morning," she amended, tucking the envelope under her arm and heading back to the car.

To her surprise, her office reception area was empty of applicants when she reached the suite. The leather couches were more noticeable, and they were very nice. She wondered again to whom they belonged. "Stoney?" she called, heading into the back.

"In here," he called. "Your office."

"Hey, you have your own office, man," she returned. "The big corner one. Stop stealing my peppermin—"

She stopped as she rounded the doorway. Stoney sat in her chair, facing the doorway. In one of the two opposing chairs, her blond hair in a ponytail that looked a great deal like Samantha's, sat Patricia.

"What the hell are you doing here?"

Patricia flowed to her feet. "I just wanted to chat. To see how your evening was."

"Right. Why don't we go down the street for a cup of coffee?" If there was one thing she didn't want, it was for Stoney to find out what she'd been up to last night, and for whom she'd done it—especially after she'd turned down the Venice gig. The only thing worse than that would be if Rick figured it out. "Starbucks or something?"

"Oh, yes." With a polite nod at Stoney, Patricia joined her

in the hallway. "That black man is very large," she whispered as Sam gestured her toward the lobby.

"Yes, he grew up that way. To repeat, what the hell are you doing here?"

"I wanted to know what happened with the ring. You don't just expect me to sit about and wait for the police to come knock on my door."

"One could only hope."

"I beg your pardon? You said you would help me. If you think you can use this to try to poison Richard against me, I will make certain you get the blame for it."

Samantha bit back her first response. She'd been careful in her conversation with Castillo not to admit to ever doing anything illegal. With Patricia she needed to be at least as cautious—especially now that she'd broken into a house for the Ex. Yep, her instincts had been right on the money when she'd lifted that surveillance tape. "I made sure the police won't be knocking anywhere around you, Patty. Play nice, and I'll keep it that way."

"What is that supposed to mean?" Patricia asked stiffly.

"I hope you don't have to find out." There. That seemed vague enough, considering that she didn't know precisely what was on the tape yet.

"Fine."

"Good. I have work to do now, if you don't mind." Sam hit the elevator call button and then turned back toward the office.

"But I thought we were going to have coffee."

Samantha closed her eyes for a moment. *Crap.* She already needed to pee. "One cup," she said, turning around again.

The Starbucks down the street had a half-dozen tables clustered on the sidewalk outside. As they reached it, Patricia took a seat at one of the empty tables. "I'd like a mocha latte," she said, setting her Vera Wang purse on her lap.

"So go order it," Sam returned, leaning against the wall. "I don't even like coffee."

Patricia cleared her throat. "I don't like to order things," she said in a lower voice. "It's so confusing in there."

More like it was beneath her dignity. With a deep breath Samantha pushed away and entered the shop. Okay, so her motives for tolerating Patty were selfish; she was genuinely curious about the woman who'd netted Rick Addison, little as he seemed to like Patty now. Luckily Starbuck's had non-coffee strawberry freezes, so she ordered one of those along with the Ex's mocha latte. She paid, hefted the cups, and headed for the door. Now Patricia owed her four bucks in addition to her freedom. In the doorway, though, she paused.

A tall, golden-haired man about her age sat in the chair beside Patricia. He was good-looking, with a Florida tan, Ray-Bans, and a Body by Jake set of abs. Something about him seemed very familiar, and she spent a moment studying him. *Damn,* if it wasn't Daniel Kunz. Charles's son.

He leaned over and kissed Patricia on the mouth, then pushed his chair back and stood. Not wanting him to escape until she'd gotten a little more information on this very interesting turn of events, Sam shoved open the glass door. "Here you go, Patty," she said, setting the mocha on the table. "Who's your friend?"

Patricia's cheeks actually reddened. "He—I—"

While Patricia stumbled around, he stuck out his hand. "Hi. I'm Daniel Kunz. You're Sam Jellicoe."

"I am. And I was sorry to hear about your dad," she said, shaking his hand. Strong grip, no hesitation.

"Thanks." Both his grip and his gaze lingered for a moment before he freed her hand and looked back at Patricia. "I'll see you for lunch, right?"

"Of course, Daniel."

"It was nice to meet you, Sam," he said, nodding. He gave Patricia another swift kiss on the lips, then headed down the street toward the cluster of high-rent office buildings.

Now this was interesting—and possibly extremely useful. Samantha took a sip of frozen strawberry while she waited for Patricia to put together whatever version she wanted of what had just occurred.

"Daniel's an old family friend," the Ex said after a moment, as she fiddled with the cardboard wrapper around her coffee cup. "He's very friendly."

"Right. He didn't kiss *me* like that. He's the one who got you into the Everglades Club, isn't he?" That made sense; if even Rick had trouble getting tickets at the high-profile event, it would have been impossible for someone who hadn't been to Palm Beach for three years. Especially for someone with a relatively limited income.

"You can't tell Richard!" she burst out. "Just because I'm lonely doesn't mean I'm interested in Daniel. We're just friends."

"You said that already." Samantha pursed her lips. Obviously Patricia was consumed with the impression she might be making on Rick, but Sam tended to look at this a little differently. Daniel Kunz had been wearing a white polo shirt and shorts, looking like he was fresh off the tennis court. Fit, relaxed, and well-rested, and thinking of both food and females—that hadn't just been a casual look he'd given her. He was a guy who liked to get laid, and that had definitely been on his mind.

What he hadn't looked like was a son who'd just lost his father, or even a close acquaintance grieving for a friend.

Neither did he look worried that what had happened to Dad might happen to him. "Where are you having lunch with him?" she asked.

Patricia hesitated. "At his home. I'm helping him set things up for the wake."

"Take me with you."

"What? No!"

"Daniel's father was a . . . friend of mine," Samantha hedged. If she'd had a chance to know him better, she thought that might have been true. "I'd like to help."

"We don't need your help. I doubt you've ever thrown a party in your life."

"I've attended plenty of them." Of course she'd attended so she could case the joint and then rob it later, but that was beside the point. "Besides, I thought maybe I could assist my friend Detective Castillo. He was assigned to Charles's case."

"You're friends with a policeman?" Patricia lifted a delicately arched eyebrow. "How fascinating."

"Be fascinated all you want, but you're taking me to lunch."

"I am not."

Okay, time for the gloves to come off. "I have the video of you taking that ring."

She blanched. "You—"

"I took it for your protection, and I kept it for mine. Don't make me deliver it to my detective friend."

Patricia clutched the coffee cup so hard the plastic lid popped off. "You wouldn't dare."

"I'd dare just about anything. All I want is access to that house."

"I don't suppose I have a choice, if you're going to blackmail me."

Wow, that was definitely the theme of the day. "That's right. I'm blackmailing you. What time should I pick you up?"

"Noon. I'm staying at The Breakers. Don't come in. I'll meet you out under the portico."

"The Breakers. Nice. They have a great spa. No Motel 6 for you?"

"In your dreams," Patricia muttered.

She said something else into her mocha, but Samantha couldn't make it out. Sam didn't much care what it was, anyway; she'd found a way to get into the Kunz house. Who would have thought that Patricia Addison-Wallis stealing a ring might be useful?

Nine

"I hope you're not planning on signing this thing," Tom Donner said, flipping through the thirty-page contract. "This guy's got some balls. I'm surprised he got cornered into selling at all."

"One might almost think he's trying to make me overvalue Kingdom Fittings. Draw up our version of the deal, and we'll see if we can get Leedmont to see the light." Richard leaned against the back of his chair, facing away from the conference table and toward his koi pond in the front of the estate. "He did come out to Palm Beach, so maybe he's willing to listen to reason. Take out the nontermination clause, put in a tiered benefit program for long-term employees, and let's make the board of directors a reasonable counteroffer that doesn't have me supporting them for the rest of their lives."

"Gotcha."

For a long moment Richard heard nothing but papers rustling. Somewhere out there, beyond the pond and the stands of palm trees, hidden among the walls of glass and steel, Samantha Jellicoe was hunting. He should have kept his bloody mouth shut. Instead, in trying to prove to her that she could live without resorting to old habits, he'd pushed her into using them. Talking about cutting off his nose to spite his face. Now he needed to make sure she lost this wager—for both of their sakes.

"Did you bring the police report?" he finally asked.

"I brought it. The captain wasn't happy about handing it over. I'm starting to owe people favors, Rick. And that means *you* owe people favors."

"I'll deal with it." Richard turned around, picking up the folder Tom slid at him. "Anything interesting?"

"We never used to work this way."

"Things change."

"Gee, I wonder why." Tom exhaled noisily. "The report's not complete, since the investigation's ongoing."

"They haven't made much progress."

"The murder only happened a couple of days ago. I get why Jellicoe's interested in this; besides the whole thief thing, she feels—"

"What do you mean, 'the whole thief thing'?"

"Well, she was the top cat burglar around here, and now somebody's pulled a job right under her nose. Bet that pissed her off."

"It's not like that," Richard said stiffly.

"Fine. Then she just feels guilty about letting Kunz down. Totally selfless stuff."

"And your point is?"

"Why are *you* asking me to get police reports, instead of her?"

If it had been anyone else, Richard wouldn't have answered. Tom, though, had been his closest friend for better than ten years. And Tom provided a certain balance of opinion where Samantha was concerned—a balance that otherwise didn't exist.

"I made a wager with Samantha," he said gruffly, settling into his chair to look through the police report more closely. Tom was right; there wasn't much there.

"What kind of wager?"

"A hundred dollars that the police could solve the murder through legitimate means more quickly than she could do it through whatever methods she could conjure."

"A hundred bucks is chump change for you guys."

"The amount's not the point. It could have been a nickle and we'd be treating it the same way."

"So you pretty much dared her to break the law," Tom offered.

"No. She was going to break the law, anyway. I told her the investigation could be done better by the authorities."

"Hence the favor-owing to get confidential police reports that Kunz's family hasn't even seen."

Richard glanced up at the attorney. "I'm just keeping track of my team. And I'll continue to do so."

"Right. Anything else you want me to get for you? China patterns in the Kunz pantry? Or should I just go work on this twelve million dollar international pipe fittings deal?"

"Actually," Richard returned, keeping a tight hold of his heating temper, "can you have your secretary set up a lunch for me with the governor? Today, if possible. Tomorrow's acceptable."

"Rick—"

"Never try to out-sarcasm a Brit, Tom. And I'm going to win this wager. You get the new proposal ready."

Rick stood, taking the folder with him as he left the conference room. Donner might be right about his focus, but logic had no place in obsession. She was out there, and if he couldn't know where, he at least could know what she was doing. And to know that, he needed to think like she would. Hopefully the report would give him some clues.

True, he'd taken the side of the law. That didn't mean that he just had to sit on his ass and watch, however. Nobody had said he couldn't nudge things a little if he saw a direction.

"Rick."

He turned around as Tom caught up to him along the gallery hallway. "What?"

"Don't get pissed at me or anything, but if you want this Kingdom Fittings deal, it's gonna take more than having my team rewrite the proposal. You still have to convince Leedmont to sell. He's the key vote."

"I'm working on it."

"No, you're not. You're working on winning a hundred dollar bet, not a twelve million dollar company."

"I'm doing both. And I'm coordinating that humanitarian relief program in eastern Africa, chairing a committee on solar power applications, reviewing a preliminary profit statement, revamping a propo—"

"Okay. I get it."

"So if you're going to begin that crap about Samantha being too big a risk and bad for my health or whatever it was you tried the last time I was in Florida, save your breath. Do your job."

"I am."

Richard took a step back toward Donner. "Samantha's not going anywhere if I can help it. If you can't deal with that, feel free to fax or e-mail me your letter of resignation."

"Jesus, Rick. I'm not going after Jellicoe." Tom cleared his throat. "I'm just saying I've never seen you lose focus during a negotiation. Not even when you were dumping Patricia. This is dif—"

"It *is* different." Taking a deep breath, Richard forced himself to back down. "I'm not losing focus. I'm expanding it. She's been clean for three months, but I'm getting this feeling that she's . . . looking for an excuse to slip."

"It's gotta be tough, I'll admit. Like being a stuntman at the top of your game and being forced to work at kids' parties as a clown or something."

"Thanks for the analogy."

"Yeah, well, I didn't finish. What if she gets offered work in the new Vin Diesel movie or something? You think she'll keep making balloon animals?"

"She'd better."

"Uh-huh. That'll work. Threats."

"Well, hopefully I'm more important to her than her old life," Richard returned, tired of bloody theoretical scenarios. "If the two of us part company, it won't be because of something I have or haven't done. I'm not making a mistake with Samantha. If it comes down to it, everything else can go to hell. I love her."

"Okay. That's what I needed to know." Tom gripped his shoulder, then continued past him toward the front door. "I'll make sure nothing goes to hell. I'll be at the office if you need something."

Richard watched him head down the stairs. "Thank you, Tom."

"Yeah, if you want to thank me, quit firing me."

"No promises."

The cell phone on his belt rang in the familiar tri-tone that meant Samantha was calling. Shaking himself, he flipped it open. "Are you in jail yet?" he asked.

"Been there and gone, studmuffin. I'm—"

"What?" he interrupted, turning back into his office and closing the door as one of the security guards strolled down the hallway on patrol. "Are you all right? What happened?"

"Yeesh. And I thought you'd be pissed that I called you 'studmuffin,' " her voice came back, relaxed and amused.

She wasn't in any immediate danger, then. Good as she was at playing games, he could still read her voice. Rolling his shoulders, he sat behind his desk. "I was saving that for later."

"Okay, then. I just stopped by Castillo's office. Don't have a heart attack."

Richard took a moment to absorb that. It was significant, both that she'd voluntarily visited a police station, and that she'd told him about it. "All right. No heart attack."

"Good. I just wanted to let you know that I'm going to Charles's funeral with Frank if you're not going. Are you?"

"The card came by messenger this morning," he returned. "I thought you might want to go."

"Great. I'll call Frank and cancel on him. And I might have something else going that I'll tell you about, but I need to figure a couple points out, first."

She was getting very good at making him insane. "That's fine," he said coolly, refusing to take the bait. Trust. Whether he trusted her to stay out of trouble or not, she had to believe that he did.

"Okay." She was silent for a moment. "Rick?"

"Yes, my love?"

"I'm glad you didn't stay in England."

"So am I."

He smiled, lowering his shoulders as he clicked off the call. From her, an admission like that was as telling as a kiss or a caress. Answering Tom Donner's question was simple:

as long as Samantha continued to try his way of life, yes, he would risk losing a deal or two. With a slight smile he dialed his New York office and then logged onto his computer for a joint statement review. He didn't plan on losing anything.

Samantha entered the small Pompano Beach television repair shop. A harried-looking woman relayed information from the cell phone at her ear to the young, scraggly-haired guy sitting on a stool behind the counter. A large TV squatted between them, wires and guts hanging out.

"Hey, Tony," she said, and the tech looked up.

"Julie. He's in the back."

With a nod Samantha picked her way through the clutter to the door at the back of the shop. Tony thought she was a druggy and his boss her dealer, but that was fine with her. "Bobby. How's it going?"

The round man with thinning hair seated in a chair that looked far too flimsy for his girth, lowered his biker magazine. "Julie Samacco," he rumbled. "Long time no see."

Jeez. She cringed every time she heard that pseudonym. Thank God Rick didn't know about it, or he'd die laughing. Still, it served its purpose, and it was easy to remember. "I've been out of town," she returned. "I've got a question for you. An answer is worth a hundred." She placed five twenties on a nearby TV.

"Ask away."

Bobby LeBaron was one of those low-rent fences who'd buy bronze candlesticks and toasters. From the variety of high-value items that had gone missing from the Kunz estate, the burglar hadn't been a high-price cat on contract for a particular buyer. A street hood couldn't have gotten in and out without alerting the household, but any burglar with experience could have. And Bobby knew a lot of those guys.

"You know anything about a cat with a recent load of cash money on hand?"

"Nope."

"Okay, how about rubies or a Van Gogh?" They were both pretty much out of his class, but it couldn't hurt to ask.

"Nope."

"Would you mind asking around for me? It's worth another hundred."

With a grunt of effort Bobby stood. "You know what kind of shop this is?"

Samantha frowned. "Yes."

"Television repair. You know what that means?"

"Enlighten me, Bobby."

"It means we got a lot of TVs. And they're on all day. We get talk shows, soaps, repeats of entertainment shows from the night before. Shit like that."

The hairs at the back of her neck began to prick. "Good for you," she returned, making note of the screwdriver a few inches from her left hand. She'd always thought of Bobby LeBaron as crude and a little sleazy, but otherwise harmless. On rare occasion she'd been wrong, though, and she wasn't going to ignore the suspicion creeping up her spine.

"Yeah, good for us. I especially like *Hollywood at Seven.* They show movie premieres, like the one for the new Russell Crowe film in London two months ago."

Shit. She didn't mind that a few of her higher-class contacts knew who she was, but dumpers like Bobby would sell her out to the cops. Hell, she only knew him because he and Stoney used to go to the track together on occasion when she was a kid. Of course the cops knew where she lived now, and Bobby didn't have anything more on her than they did. It was just the damned principle of the thing. "So do you not know anything because I didn't tell you my real name, or because you actually don't know anything?"

Brown eyes fixed her with an annoyed gaze. "Shit. I had Martin Jellicoe's kid running my track bets, and Stoney never even told me. You really going legit?"

"Probably."

"Damn shame. No. I ain't heard of any cat with a new wad of cash or any million-buck paintings. And if you're straight, from now on you make an appointment like my other customers."

"That's fine." As Samantha turned back for the door, she retrieved eighty dollars from the pile she'd set down. "Then I pay the same rates as your other customers. Your sign out front says twenty bucks per consultation. Have a nice day."

"Bitch."

She let him have the last word. After all, she had an answer and eighty bucks back. The shady life could be costly, and she might need the cash elsewhere.

"How many jobs have you lined up for Jellicoe Security?"

"One." Samantha turned her back so Stoney could zip the back of her yellow Chanel dress. She'd pulled the blinds on her office window—no sense in giving Donner a thrill—but she needed to look the part when she picked up Patty for lunch.

Stoney zipped. "The Kunz one, or a real one where you get paid money?"

"A real one. And a 10K flat fee."

"Well, that'll keep us in Diet Cokes, anyway. Whose house? One of Addison's buddies?"

Samantha hesitated. "It's not a house, and it's definitely not one of Rick's friends. Just the opposite."

"Right." He stepped backward as she turned around. "It's me, Sam. The guy who told you the tooth fairy was fake."

Samantha's lips twitched in a quick grin. That had been an interesting conversation. "It's not my fault I thought she was a cat burglar."

"Who wouldn't?" he returned. "The point being, you can tell me what's going on. I know you're still working on Kunz."

"Oh, so like I'm making up this new client?" She wiggled her fingers in front of her. "Woooo, he's invisible."

"As long as his money's not invisible. Somebody needs to pay for your services."

"I know that. And he will. But this is kind of . . . strange, so I'm going to talk to Rick first."

He looked at her. "But not to me."

"The client's not a business rival of yours. I'm trying to be good, Stoney, but I'm new at it."

"And so far this seems like so much more fun than earning a million bucks for two days' work in Venice."

She closed her eyes for a second. Jesus. With Stoney and Rick pulling her in exact opposite directions, she was going to split in two. "Maybe it's not more fun, but I'm trying to acquire a taste for doing the right thing, okay?"

Stoney took a deep breath. "Okay. Anything new with the dead, nonpaying client, then?"

"I'm still trying to figure out just what happened. What if it meant something that he died right after he contacted me about security?"

"Maybe it did, but that doesn't make it your fault—or your problem. What *is* your problem is twelve thousand dollars in rent you have to pay every month, and it sounds like you have something going with that. Of course it also sounds like you're trying to do it all yourself and you're getting stretched a little thin."

"Business sucks."

"Sam—"

"Okay, okay. I don't mean that. Not yet, anyway. Just give me a couple of days. Then we'll put some business ads in newspapers and on the radio and start acting like a real company."

"It's a deal. For now. I'll go through the call-backs. And hey, how many paintings do you think we need for the decor in here?"

Sam hesitated. "That depends. Where are the paintings coming from?"

"Same place as the furniture. I'll take care of it."

"Six week rentals again?"

He grinned. "I don't know yet."

Samantha dug into her purse, making sure she had a couple of paper clips and some copper wire in addition to her keys. The tools of the trade—of her trade, anyway. Rick had once accused her of trying to be MacGyver, but hell, Mac could build a plane out of paper clips. She could just open doors with them.

"Are you going to tell me where you're going, all fancied up?"

Somebody should know, just in case. "I'm going to lunch with Patricia. She's taking me over to the Kunz place."

Stoney stopped in his tracks. "You're doing what?"

"She knows the son. Daniel. I said I'd go to help out with setting up tables and decorations and shit for the wake."

"Oh, my good glory," he said quietly, grabbing her arm. "Just remember two things, Samantha Elizabeth Jellicoe."

The middle name. Uh-oh.

"One, you can get as close to these people as you want, but don't you ever forget that you've stolen from half of them. They aren't your friends. They're your marks."

"Clients," she corrected. "They're my clients now. Potential ones, anyway. What's number two?"

"Number two, whatever I think of you pretending to settle down with Rick Addison, he's got it bad for you. You hanging out with his ex is a bad idea. A very bad idea."

She wasn't all that sure she was pretending anything. "I'm getting information about Kunz. That's all."

"Sure it is."

Sure it was.

Patricia was waiting at the edge of The Breakers' covered valet drop off. She'd donned a nice dress of pastel greens and yellows with metallic beads around the waist and hem. It had to be either a Donna Karan or a Marc Jacobs. Samantha stifled a grin as she unlocked the passenger door. Before, she'd made a point of knowing which designers were hot because she had to mingle with marks who spent a great deal of their income looking fashionable. Now with Rick as her companion she'd become one of the fashion elite.

Patricia had also put a white billowy scarf over her hair and donned a dark pair of sunglasses. Evidently she didn't want anyone to recognize her and realize with whom she was driving about town.

"Nice scarf," Samantha said as she roared out of the drive and headed toward North Ocean Boulevard.

"It was a gift," Patricia said stiffly.

"From Daniel?"

"That's none of your affair."

Samantha smiled again. "I'm just trying to make conversation."

The sunglasses lowered for a moment as blue eyes gazed over the rims at her. "I don't like you."

"I'm not your biggest fan either, Patty. What you did to Rick was—"

"No worse than what he did to me."

"What the hell are you talking about?"

"He ignored me. Oh, when it was convenient or he needed a companion he would take me out to dinners or lunches or parties, but that was it. The rest of the time he had his meetings in Tokyo, his contract-signings in Milan . . . Half the time I didn't even know where he was. And after a while I really didn't care."

"He said you didn't like to travel."

"There's a difference between travel and what he did. Who wants to fly to Tokyo to be left in a hotel for three days? After the first three months of being on a plane and not even knowing where we'd landed I'd had enough of that, believe me. You'll see."

Samantha glanced sideways at her passenger. Rick had been making an effort to be around as much as he could, but it was all too precious and still too new to use for bragging rights with Patty. And she had no guarantee that the Ex wasn't describing her own future, anyway. She'd be long gone, though, before she ever got as desperate as Patty.

"Hey, I just stick around because he's got two personal chefs," she said instead.

Patricia waved her hand dismissively. "Anyone can have a personal chef," she returned. "Peter and I had one. I had to let her go when Peter was arrested. Damned legal fees. Now I just have a woman who comes in to cook and clean for me."

"So you still have the house in London," Samantha said, pulling up to the wrought-iron gates of the Kunz estate. Coronado House lacked a few acres and several thousand square feet on Solano Dorado, but just about everything outside of Donald Trump's Mar-a-Lago did.

"My attorney will be putting it on the market any day now. Unfortunately, Peter's lawyers have already put some sort of lien on it."

"More legal fees?" Putting down her window, Sam pressed the call box.

"By the time this trial and the appeals are finished, I'll be a complete pauper. Peter's so selfish, doing this to me. He might have just admitted to everything and gone to jail. Then at least I would have been left with something."

"Who's calling?" the voice on the intercom said.

Better not to confuse anybody until she was inside, Sam decided. "Patricia Addison-Wallis, to see Daniel."

"And who are you?" the voice demanded.

"Oh, for heaven's sake," Patricia grumbled, leaning across Samantha. "She's a friend. I will not sit out here and be interrogated."

The gate swung open.

"Very nice," Samantha complimented.

"It has nothing to do with you," Patricia returned. "It's unseemly to be seen waiting out here."

The Coronado House estate boasted only two stories, and the sprawl of the building wasn't as pronounced as Solano Dorado. The architecture of both were in the same Mediterranean revival style, as most of the large properties in Palm Beach were—the architect Addison Mizner was practically worshiped as a god around here. Everything worth anything had to be built in the image favored by him.

She'd seen the blueprints, but they didn't describe the decor. Surprisingly, once a stern-faced butler wearing a black band around one arm showed them into the foyer, Coronado House's homage to old Spain ended. The foyer was more of an atrium, a steel-domed spiderweb filled in with glass and open to the light of the Florida sky above. Tropical plants hung from the web in wire baskets, while towering palms softened the lines of the staircase and the open, arched entryways into other rooms of the house.

Where everything in Rick's house reflected an ageless antiquity and sophistication, Coronado spoke of manipulated wilderness. "This is nice," Samantha said, turning a slow circle and not surprised that she preferred Rick's understated control and sense of elegance.

"Hm," Patricia murmured. "I always feel like I should have bug spray to hand."

" 'Always?' " Sam repeated. "How many times have you been here?"

"Patricia," a female voice said from above them.

Sam turned to look as a slender, brunette-haired woman in hip-hugging black Versace slacks and a white peasant shirt glided down the curving staircase. Now that she knew Daniel's face, recognizing another Kunz of similar age was simple. This had to be Laurie, the daughter. Kunz's late wife must have been a Miss America to overcome her husband's lack of stature and stick appendages in their offspring.

"Thank you so much for coming by to help me with this," Laurie continued as she descended. "Everything is just so . . . overwhelming. Whoever thought of holding a party when someone dies obviously never had to do it himself."

"I'm so pleased I could help," Patricia said warmly, going forward to greet Laurie and give her a fake two-cheek kiss at the bottom of the stairs.

"With all the events already scheduled for the Season, it's been almost impossible to find a caterer." Laurie returned the almost kisses and then faced Samantha. "You're Samantha Jellicoe," she said.

"Patricia said you might need some more help," Sam offered, not approaching or offering her hand or her cheeks. *Whoo*. She knew hostility when it was being beamed at her.

"Are you certain you're not here to steal something?"

Alarms began going off in Sam's skull. "Excuse me?" she

returned, deciding on a tone of disdainful disbelief and declining to point out that from her observations the Kunz wake was more likely to be targeted by bored society dames than by her. She refused to be surprised any longer by the number of people who knew her secret identity.

"I don't know why my father wanted to hire you," Laurie went on, navigating a slow circle around Samantha, "but I found the file he was making up on you."

"A file?" Patricia said, coming back to life. "What kind of file?"

"Newspaper clippings of her appearances with your ex-husband, a few archived Internet articles about her father—he died in prison, did you know?—and some notes on robberies my father thought she'd probably done."

Great. An ambush. "Thinking's easy," Samantha returned. "Proof's hard. My dad did some crappy things. He paid for them." And for some that were hers. "We're not all like our parents though, are we, Laurie?"

"I didn't know you were bringing friends, Patricia," Daniel's smooth voice came from the doorway to the left.

He'd changed into jeans and a loose polo shirt, the quintessential Florida trust-fund beach bum down to his black flip-flops. His gaze, as this morning, focused on Sam rather than Patricia.

"Oh, she's not a friend," Patricia said, brushing past her to reach Daniel. "She doesn't really know anyone in Palm Beach, and I felt sorry for her."

This was becoming more and more interesting. Much as Samantha had wanted to see the rest of the house, the information she was getting right there in the foyer was probably more useful than taking in the view. She knew the layout already from the blueprints. The hostility, though, was beginning to interfere with the task at hand. She needed to analyze all of this, but not while people were trying to accuse her of things.

"I know a few people in Palm Beach," she noted, keeping her attention on Daniel. It was instinct, she supposed, always looking for an opening, a weakness, a way to get whatever it was she wanted. And she sensed that she was more likely to get it from him than from Laurie. "I'm only here because I liked your dad. Good luck finding a caterer."

Not waiting for the butler to return and open the front door for her, she headed back out to the drive and the Bentley. She wasn't worried about Patricia; the lady, despite her obvious helplessness in some areas, had a genuine gift for getting what she wanted. With one exception.

Once she was back out on the street, Sam pulled out her phone and speed-dialed Rick. Her father had always taught her that the first person she needed to think of and be concerned about was herself. That had changed over the past few months, and that weakness was probably the main reason she'd decided to retire from a life of crime. Whether she was annoyed with him or not, frustrated at the way he kept trying to manipulate her life into what he wanted it to be or not, his was still the first image she thought of in the morning and the last one she conjured at night. And if she knew him at all, by now he'd probably hunted up a few leads of his own.

"I was just thinking of you," his voice came, without preamble.

She smiled. "Were you? What did I do this time?"

"Nothing. I decided to have a Diet Coke."

Samantha laughed. "Great. You associate me with a soft drink."

"It's rather your signature, don't you think?"

"I suppose it could be worse."

He was silent for a moment. "What's up?"

God, he always knew. But she could use that to her advantage. "Nothing much. My lunch date cancelled."

"How fortunate that I was just about to head out to Café l'Europe for lunch, then."

"Oh, you were, were you? The Diet Coke was just to whet your appetite?"

"I was thirsty. Are you anywhere close enough to join me?"

"Sure. Twenty minutes?"

"I'll see you there."

To paraphrase Sherlock Holmes, something was afoot. Her tingling Spider sense said that nothing about Charles Kunz's murder had been ordinary, or accidental. At least some of the answers were still at Coronado House. Unless she was mistaken, she'd seen some of the clues already. And maybe Rick had a few more for her, if she asked the right way.

Ten

As Richard handed his SLR key over to a parking valet, Samantha walked up to him from down the street. She would have parked the Bentley around the corner; she hated giving up her keys and the location of her car to someone else.

Something troubled her. He'd heard it in her voice over the phone, and he could see it now, in her face. Richard drew a breath, advancing the last few steps to meet her. "You look great," he said, taking her hands and spreading them to view her better in her short yellow dress and matching sandals.

She'd been meeting someone who would expect these clothes. He could probably make a few guesses, but it would mean more if she told him. He'd always been patient, but since becoming acquainted with Samantha, he'd learned to turn it into something of an art form.

"So do you," she said, leaning in to place a peck on his lips while she smoothed the lapels of his charcoal gray jacket.

"That won't do," he returned, tugging her in against him

and lowering his mouth over hers. Heat speared through him at the touch, as it always did. Obsession. It seemed the more refined his tastes, the more primitive his needs. And she'd moved to the top of his list practically from the moment they'd met. He'd stopped trying to figure it out logically, because logic obviously had nothing to do with it.

"Okay, you look really great," she amended, favoring him with a smile as she freed her mouth and one of her hands. "Buy me some chow."

"I don't believe they serve 'chow' at Café l'Europe, but I'll see what I can do. A chili dog, perhaps?"

"With bratwurst."

"If you eat that, you're not coming home."

The maitre'd nodded as they entered the restaurant. Despite the small crowd waiting for seats in the bistro, a table in the formal dining room would have been reserved for them—or it should have been, since he'd called to make reservations the moment he'd hung up with Samantha. After a bare moment of well-disguised scrambling the head waiter appeared to lead them through the cool, dim room to a place against the large front window.

"Thank you, Edward," Rick said, shaking the waiter's hand before he held the chair for Samantha.

"How much did you slip him?" Sam murmured, sitting.

He took the seat across from her. "That's gauche. My thanks will appear in the tip." Another waiter appeared, and he requested an iced tea for himself and a Diet Coke for Samantha.

She waited until they were alone again, then tapped his finger with her spoon. "You already ate, didn't you?"

"I had an apple," he conceded, leaving out the roast chicken and fresh bread and thankful he always carried breath mints.

"You're a good guy, Rick."

He smiled. "I keep telling you that."

Her smile joined his, her thoughtful green eyes studying his face. "Do you know what I want to do right now?"

Rick placed the cloth napkin across his lap. He should have asked for a less conspicuous table. "Tell me."

Samantha picked up a bread stick, examined it for a moment, then slowly licked the length of it. "Mm, salty goodness," she murmured.

"Christ. Cease and desist before I split my zipper."

"Oh, then I would have to sit on your lap in my short dress to protect your modesty." She leaned forward, gazing at him serenely. "Comfortable?"

He snorted, not certain whether she was actually feeling that randy or whether she was trying to distract him from asking any sticky questions. "No. My only consolation is that later I'm going to see to it that you do everything you just suggested."

Samantha straightened again, biting off the end of the bread stick. "Until then, can I run something by you?"

And there she went, changing personas again. "I'm supposed to be able to think now?" he returned, torn between amusement and umbrage. "You forced all the blood out of my brain."

"You're still smarter than the average bear." She took another bite. "What's your opinion of the Kunz kids?"

His brain began to refill, deflating his cock. All business now. "That depends."

"On what?"

"On whether this is about the wager or not. The wager that *you* made, by the way."

Samantha blew him a raspberry. "Okay, whatever. I can always con my way into their house and find out for myself." She sat back and finished off the bread stick. "Or maybe

Laurie needs a new best friend." She grinned without humor. "Or maybe Daniel does."

Bloody smashing. "What do you want to know?"

"How well do you know Daniel?"

"Daniel. Better than a passing acquaintance, not quite a friend," he returned.

"What's your opinion of him? What's he like?"

Richard looked around, making certain no other diners could overhear their conversation. One didn't criticize one's fellows in public—only in select company who wouldn't credit you with the gossip. "Officially he's a vice president in the Kunz Manufacturing Company. Unofficially, I doubt he's ever gone into the office except to shag his father's latest secretary."

"He doesn't seem stupid," she commented, angling her eyes beyond him and straightening. "Not from what I've seen, anyway."

He didn't need to look to know the waiter was approaching with their drinks. Samantha ordered the fettuccine while he requested a table salad with vinaigrette. As soon as the waiter left again, Samantha shoved the basket of bread sticks across the table in his direction.

"Table salad? I hope your first lunch was heartier, because you're going to need more energy than that for later, babe."

At least she hadn't gotten into any mortal danger this morning on whatever mission had required that sexy, sophisticated yellow dress, or she wouldn't have been so horny for him. He wondered whether she realized how well he could read her. "I'll manage," he returned, wishing they could forego lunch altogether, "and no, Daniel's not stupid. He's just lazy about business."

"All the money came from Daddy's efforts, right?"

"Yes. He and Charles always seemed to get along well,

though. Charles might have been disappointed with his lack of ambition, but Daniel did bring in some tennis and yachting trophies. I think that satisfied everyone concerned."

"For putting him somewhere between acquaintance and friend, you seem to know his character pretty well."

He nodded. "I'm observant."

"What about the daughter, Laurie?"

"Laurie owns a real estate agency," he commented, beginning to wonder whether this was Samantha being idly curious, or something more. As he'd said, he'd made most of his fortune by being observant. "She's the smart sibling. Again, as far as I could tell, Charles seemed to dote on her, even more than on Daniel."

"Probably because she was earning her own paycheck. So what happened to Mom?"

"Cancer. Nine years ago or so, I believe."

"Who did that affect the most?"

No sympathy from Samantha, but then her mother had dropped out of her life when she'd been five. "I don't really know. Daniel would still have been in high school. Laurie too, or just starting college. I didn't know them, then."

"Okay." Ice cubes tinkled as she swirled her glass. She frowned into her soda. "Have you ever been inside their house?"

"Coronado? Once, for a Fourth of July party. Sorry, but I really didn't notice security."

"That's all right. I don't know what I'm looking for, anyway. I have the specs on the blueprints."

"So this *is* about the wager."

Samantha grinned. "Maybe."

"Mm-hm. Change the subject."

"Fine. How was your morning?"

"I rejected a sales offer from Leedmont and sent it back

with Tom for revisions, and called Sarah in London to arrange for the rest of the Kingdom Fittings board to fly to Palm Beach on my dime."

"Rick, you don't—"

He lifted a hand. "If I don't get to give you business suggestions, love, you don't get to give them to me."

Her eyes narrowed. "Speaking of which, there's something I should probably tell you."

"So tell me."

"You won't like it."

Richard gazed at her. "That's never stopped you be—"

"Who's that?" she interrupted, her gaze somewhere beyond his shoulder.

Somewhat glad the chaos of his diverse business had prepared him a little for Samantha's quicksilver mind, he shifted to glance casually behind him. "Who?"

"The guy with Laurie Kunz."

"How do you know that's Laurie?" She'd never set eyes on the older Kunz sibling that he knew of.

She shot him an annoyed look as the waiter appeared with their lunch. As he set the plates on the table, Samantha touched his hand and smiled up at him. "Could you help me?" she cooed, all clueless green eyes and open innocence. "I wanted to give my condolences to Laurie Kunz, but I can't remember the name of the man with her."

The man actually blushed. "I—" He looked over his shoulder. "Oh. That's Aubrey Pendleton." The waiter leaned closer. "He's a walker."

"Oh, really?" Samantha lifted an eyebrow. "Thank you so much."

"No problem, Miss Jellicoe."

Richard dug into his salad. He didn't know why, but there were times—frequent times—that he felt like he was back in public school where Samantha was concerned. If only it were that simple, that he could get her name tattooed over his heart and he would know she wasn't playing a game. Changing the chameleon aspect of her character might change the essence of who she was—and he wasn't certain he wanted that. "Feel better now?" he asked finally.

"Definitely. Aubrey Pendleton's not a bad-looking guy."

In the guise of taking a sip of iced tea, Rick sent the bistro crowd another look. Tall, with blond hair just going silver and a George Hamilton tan, Pendleton had the handsome, ageless look of precisely what he was—a professional escort. No female in Palm Beach liked to attend a society event alone, so walkers like Pendleton made themselves available for escort duties to young and old women, alike. His presence with Laurie Kunz was a little surprising, since she'd never lacked for company as far as Richard knew, but perhaps he was just a friend of the family.

Samantha knew more than she was admitting, but this wasn't the setting to explore that. They both knew that things couldn't continue with them pursuing contrary agendas and with her apparently pushing the limits—or threatening to—where the wager was concerned, but he'd been doing his homework over the past three months. Watching and listening frequently netted him more than confrontation. The last time he'd pushed his agenda on her, she'd headed for the airport. With the Kingdom Fittings deal pending, he didn't have the time to go chasing after her again. *Honey, Rick, not vinegar.*

She paused as she lifted a bite to her mouth. "He's not as pretty as you are, of course."

"Thanks."

With a chuckle she sipped her soda. "I'm just clarifying. And thanks for meeting me for lunch."

"My pleasure." Yes, honey was definitely the way to go.

Her grin deepened. "Do you think we'll eventually end up killing one another?"

Richard grinned back at her. "Probably."

When they left the restaurant they both turned their cell phones back on. Samantha's rang immediately, in Stoney's telltale "Raindrops" theme. "*Hola*," she said out of habit. Blending was the key, and just because the call came from Stoney's cell phone didn't mean it was Stoney calling.

"Honey, I think I found something you might be interested in. Can you meet me at Gressin's Antiques?"

"I'm about fifteen minutes away." She looked toward Worth Avenue. "Who's at the office?"

"A sign that says 'Back in five minutes,'" her former fence returned. "Coming?"

"I'll be right there."

Before she could head down the street to where she'd stashed the Bentley, Rick snagged her arm. "What were you going to tell me that I won't like?"

She might have been the one with the near photographic memory, but he never forgot anything, either. Crap. She needed to tell him about Leedmont, but she was pretty sure how he would react—and she needed to meet up with Stoney. Still, the longer she kept quiet, the worse it would be when she spilled the story. "One thing first. I don't know all the details yet, but whatever happens, you have to pretend you don't know anything about it."

"That's a bit vague."

Sam folded her arms across her chest. "I'm serious, Rick. I'm pretty sure I shouldn't be telling you this at all. It's got to be an ethics thing. So you have to promise me."

He didn't like it; she could see that on his face. People like Rick didn't appreciate being dictated to. But they didn't like being left out of the loop, either. After a long few moments he nodded. "I'll remain ignorant, whatever you tell me. Unless it endangers your health or mine. I promise."

Blowing out her breath, Sam took a last look around. As long as they didn't start yelling, nobody was close enough to have a clue what they were talking about. "I got a paying gig this morning."

"I'm not surprised."

"Thanks," she returned, meaning it. "It's not actually in my area of expertise, but the client didn't have anywhere else to go, and I think he's being screwed over."

"Okay."

"The client is John Leedmont."

Rick blinked. "The same John Leedmont with whom I'm fighting over Kingdom Fittings."

"Yes."

"I see." His lips thinning, he took a few steps down the street and then returned to her again. "What did he hire you for?"

Samantha shook her head. Ethics might be a sticky area, but she did know a couple of things about it. "That's between him and me."

"Sam—"

"No, Rick. I told you because you two are doing business, and I didn't want you to get blind-sided. I'm not telling you the details."

"You know you can trust me not to betray your confidences."

"I know I can. But that's not my point. If you want to fight about it, okay, but I'd rather not."

"Fuck," he muttered. "I don't expect you to tattle to me. But I didn't expect that your first paying client would be someone whose company I'm trying to take over, either. What if—"

She put a hand over his lips. "If any 'what ifs' show up, I'll give talking to you some serious thought."

"All right." With a slight smile he tucked a strand of her hair behind her ear. "Thank you for telling me."

"Hey, I'm trying."

Whew. Considering that she'd been anticipating a knock-down drag-out, that had gone pretty well. All this time he'd been trying to butt into her business, and now she'd landed in the middle of his. He kept his balance pretty well. She liked that. Maybe he was learning, after all.

Rick's phone gave a four-tone ring. "Donner," he said.

"That's my cue to take off. I have to meet Stoney."

He caught her hand again before she could head down the street. "Hold on a minute. There's another charity dinner tomorrow. If we're going, I need to call for tickets," he said, lifting the phone. "Tom."

As Rick listened to the attorney, his grip tightened around her wrist. She looked up from her watch as he snapped the phone closed without even saying good-bye, his gaze practically boring a hole through her.

"What now?" she asked, freeing her arm and taking a subtle step backward.

"Katie Donner. You remember Kate?"

"Of course. Tom's wife. Is she all right?"

"She saw you."

Sam frowned. "Then she should have said hello."

"You were driving the Bentley. Actually you were stopped at the front gate of Coronado House."

Shit. She'd nearly forgotten that bit of nonsense. "I didn't want to have to explain it to you," she said slowly, easing back another step. *Don't get trapped. Don't ever get trapped.* That was in the top three lessons for thievery her father had taught her.

"Explain it anyway." He stopped, taking a deep breath that shook around the edges. "What the devil were you doing with Patricia—and at Coronado House? That wasn't just mild curiosity before, was it? You went inside."

And this was why she preferred blending and anonymity. Too damned many people knew her now. "Fine. Patricia knows Daniel, and I wanted a way into the house that didn't look totally bogus. It didn't work, though, because apparently Daddy Kunz did some background on me, and both kids know about the Jellicoe legacy. I took off and called you for lunch. The end."

"So you used my ex-wife to gain illegal entry into a house."

"There was nothing illegal about it."

"And you lied to me about your acquaintance with Daniel and Laurie."

She frowned. "Okay, I lied. I'm trying to win the bet."

"A wager I'm beginning to regret agreeing to." Blue eyes continued to glare at her. "How did you know that Patricia is acquainted with Daniel?"

"I saw them talking together," she lied. The ring thing and everything surrounding it were still between her and Patty. She'd given her word about that—and with his obvious suspicions, no way was she going to confess to a B and E, whether it had been to return an item rather than take one or not.

"So you just rang her up and asked to join her at Coronado House, and she agreed," he said, his rich voice thin with sarcasm.

"Pretty much. I think she's still trying to size up our relationship. Yours and mine. Looking for clues and shit. So I used her, and she used me. And everybody goes home happy."

"Everyone but me, apparently. Didn't it occur to you that I would prefer you not become chummy with my ex-wife, or did you just not care?"

"Maybe this just isn't about you," she retorted as the valet arrived with the silver SLR. "If you'll remember," she continued, as Rick slid into the driver's seat, "you didn't ask me whether I approved of you helping Patty with her little problems, but I didn't throw a tantrum about it."

She left him in the SLR and started down the street in the opposite direction, toward the Bentley. Damn it, nobody got under her skin like he did.

The SLR slammed into reverse, coming into the corner of her vision as he backed around the corner, matching her pace. "Samantha!"

"I'm busy," she snapped, increasing her pace and knowing the two of them probably looked like complete looney tunes. But dammit, she'd been making concessions, trying to at least keep him apprised of what she was investigating, if not how.

The car continued to back up beside her. "I'm not going to stop arguing just because you walk away," he said after a moment.

She stopped, leaning through the open passenger window. "Good," she muttered, meeting his gaze and then retreating again. "But you'd better have a good reason to fight. Patty isn't one. I'll see you later. I have a meeting with Stoney."

Samantha continued on, pretending not to be listening as the car window slid up, the gears changed, and the engine revved as it headed into drive again. That car was definitely worth the half million he'd paid for it last month. She was abruptly worried that the time would come when Rick wouldn't bother to argue, though, that he would realize that every time he conceded the point, he actually won. Or even worse, that he would decide her supposed lifestyle wasn't worth the risk to him or his company.

But hell, so far she liked playing with fire—as long as she never looked down. In a way, it made her whole life an adrenaline rush. If she got dizzy and fell, then it would be her own damned fault.

Before she went into Gressin's Antiques, Sam spent a moment looking through the front window. Furniture, chandeliers, vases, a nineteenth-century rocking horse—decorator items. She frowned, wiping the expression away before she pushed the door open and entered. Nothing from the Gugenthal collection of jewelry or any self-respecting Van Gogh or O'Keeffe would be in here, even if someone had tried to fence them at a legit antique establishment.

"Sam," Stoney's voice came from the far right corner deep inside the shop.

She spied his domed forehead through a forest of fringed lampshades and headed through the clutter in his direction. "We already have office furniture," she said in a low voice as she reached him. "Or is this the next installment?"

"Very funny." He fingered a small mahogany wooden jewelry box. "Isn't this nice?"

"It's very pretty. What—"

He flipped open the lid. A large ornate "G" in gold leaf decorated the inside of the red crushed velvet lid.

"Gugenthal?" she muttered. "A bit gauche, isn't it?"

"That's kinda my point, sugar," the big man returned. "It's not exactly up to the specs of the rest of the collection—like maybe it dates from right before the Gugenthals had to sell out."

"Ah, a poor attempt at a return to the glory days. If you can't make it expensive, make it loud." She closed the lid again, gently turning the box over to look for any markings. "It is handmade," she conceded after a moment, running a finger over the carved emblem of what looked like a tiny pine tree. "Probably in Belgium. It could be from the Gugenthal family, then. But what—"

"I asked when it came in. The owner said yesterday."

"Hold on." She flipped open her phone and dialed, at least as horrified as she was amused that she had this particular number memorized. "Frank? It's Sam. By any chance were any jewelry boxes listed among the stolen items for Kunz?"

"Nope," the detective answered after a minute. "Why, did you find something?"

"Maybe. Mostly I was wondering how organized the theft was. Stuff scattered around, or laser surgery?"

It wasn't entirely a lie, and it seemed to satisfy Castillo. "Mostly scattered around, I would guess. That's a good analogy. Mind if I use it in my next briefing?"

"Be my guest. Just don't give me any credit for it."

"Like I want anyone to know that I know you."

She hung up, turning back to look at the box again. "It wasn't reported stolen."

"That doesn't make it any prettier."

Sam rubbed her temple. "Okay, I'll go with this scenario: It's ugly, it's empty, so let's get rid of it. I mean, relatively crappy as it is, I'd still put it at what, five, six hundred bucks?"

Stoney nodded. "Seven twenty-five with store markup."

"That's not very sentimental of the family—if it came from Coronado House. The patriarch did maybe die in the room with it, after all."

Her former fence grimaced. "That's the part I'm not sure about. The timing's right, but you said Daniel was a brown-haired tan guy."

"Yes."

"The seller was blond."

"You didn't get a name?"

"I asked, but you know how snobby antique dealers are. 'A blond gentleman' was all I could get."

Samantha grinned. "Point me in the snob's direction."

Stoney gestured her toward the front of the store and then headed for the exit. At least somebody knew and appreciated how she worked enough to give her a little space.

She liked antique shops, and not just because on rare occasion she'd been able to acquire a contracted item from one of the more elite establishments—and breaking into a business was just simpler than breaking into a house. This particular store was mid-range, and she'd never explored it before. Fleetingly she wondered whether this was where the high-society ladies dumped the stuff they lifted at parties.

The owner had probably never been handsome, and now that he'd thinned down and lost his butt as older men tended to do, he'd become almost the stereotypical poster boy for nerdy old snob. He even wore Coke-bottle-thick round glasses, poor guy.

"Hi," she said, favoring him with a bright smile as she reached the cluttered counter.

"Good afternoon. You're the young lady interested in the seventeenth-century mahogany jewelry box?"

"Early twentieth century, you mean," she corrected. "The nails in the hinges are aluminum."

"So you know your jewelry boxes," the dealer conceded, setting aside the newspaper he'd been perusing. "Your companion said you did."

"They're a hobby of mine. I always ask Mr. Barstone to keep an eye out for them." She shifted, leaning an elbow on the counter and favoring him with a view of her pink bra. "It's Danish, isn't it? Or Flemish, rather."

"According to the craftsman's signature, yes."

"Was it an estate piece?"

"The gentleman who brought it in said it had been a gift. He's brought me pieces before, and I have no reason to doubt him."

"Do you think he has any more boxes in his possession? Flemish, but older?"

"He may have access to some," the dealer said grudgingly.

Sam recognized the hesitation, and the reason behind it. She sent him a coy smile. "I might have access to some things that would benefit you, if you help me out."

"B-Beg pardon?"

She leaned closer, making sure he could see the pink lacy B-cups. "You know. You scratch my back, I'll scratch yours."

"Oh, my." Fumbling for the Rolodex, he nodded so vigorously she worried that he would break a vertebrae. "I'll give you Mr. Pendleton's number. I'm sure he won't mind."

"That's great," Sam returned, using every bit of her experience to keep from batting an eye at the name. Pendleton. Aubrey Pendleton, Laurie's walker?

She thanked the antique dealer again and made her way outside to where Stoney leaned against his Chevy and sucked on a fast food soda. "Was I right?" he asked.

"Looks like it. The seller was Aubrey Pendleton. I saw him an hour ago with Laurie Kunz."

"Damn, I'm good," Stoney stated, polishing off his soda and pushing away from the truck. "I'd better get back to the office. We've got some file cabinets and a conference table coming in."

She refused to rise to the bait and ask where *this* furniture had originated. "I'll follow you. I have to make a few phone calls." She needed to find a walker, and she wanted to know from Leedmont at which street corner the girl had jumped into his car, and where they'd stopped when she'd fallen onto his lap. Hm. Sometimes it definitely felt like the good old days were more glamorous than her new gig.

Eleven

Monday, 2:40 p.m.

"How long are you going to stare out my window?" Tom Donner asked, looking up from the pile of paperwork on his desk.

Rick looked back down at the revised list of demands from Leedmont. "I'm not staring," he grunted. "I was glancing."

"You've been glancing a lot."

"I'm a little worried."

"Jellicoe seems able to take care of herself."

She could, but it wasn't precisely what she was doing as much as it was with whom she was doing it. Patricia, Leedmont—she couldn't get much more tangled in his life, and yet she continued to protest whenever he offered his advice on her affairs.

"I knew I shouldn't have called you when Kate phoned me."

"You should always call me." All he needed was for ex-wives and current lovers to mouch about together and no one to tell him about it.

"Yeah, well, I thought it was kinda interesting. I didn't know you'd go Pompeii."

"You bloody well did. Otherwise you would have had Kate call me with the news. You wanted Sam and me to argue."

"Okay, maybe I did."

Rick spared a moment to glare at the attorney. "And why is that?"

"Jellicoe's used to looking for weak spots in security. She figures Patricia'll know all of yours, so of course she wants to buddy up. Face it, Rick. You're just another mark."

"I'm nobody's mark, Tom," he retorted. "And if you repeat those sentiments to me or to anyone else, I'm going to stop pretending to fire you and do it for real."

"Can I just say that you're crazy, then?"

"You can say that." Today he would agree with the assessment. "Once." He blew out his breath. Keeping his . . . frustration bottled up like this was going to give him a heart attack. Damn it, he was used to action. See a problem, handle it. Make it go away, or turn it to his advantage. Having someone else able to dictate the direction he went—that was new. And it was extremely difficult, however important it was that he give her space.

"Well," Tom continued after a long moment of silence, "from what you said, Jellicoe was using Patricia to win your bet. I doubt the two of them would get together to go shopping. It was probably just a onetime thing."

God, he hoped so. At times he wished Samantha was the kind of girl who just went shopping. But if they'd met at Neiman Marcus, he would never have gotten to know the real Sam Jellicoe. She would never voluntarily reveal her secrets to anyone. Only the fact that he'd caught her breaking into Solano Dorado and then the two of them had nearly been blown up five minutes after that—that was the only reason he'd gotten to know the real Samantha Jellicoe. And he thanked his stars that they'd both survived that first meeting, and for every day with her since then.

Richard forced his attention back to the paperwork in front of him. "Do you have that employment clause for me?"

"It should be coming off the printer right now."

Rick nodded. "I'll take it with me and look it over tonight. If it passes muster, I'll send it over to Leedmont. It would be nice if he was on my side when the rest of the board votes on it."

"I get the impression that he's more stubborn than he is sensible."

And for that reason it would have been handy to know why Leedmont had hired Samantha. "I don't need him if I get a unanimous vote from the rest of the board. He would just make everything easier. I figure the best way to proceed is to get the new proposal to the board just before they get on the plane. That'll give them a few uninterrupted hours to mull over their futures without Leedmont to persuade them to reject my offer."

"You'd better stow some booze on the plane for 'em, too," Tom said, following him to his secretary's printer outside the office door. "They'll need it."

"One would hope so."

He waited while Shelly put the revised paperwork into a folder, then headed out to the parking garage and his SLR. Before he settled in to look over the contract revisions, he was going to make good on Tom's suggestion and have a drink. A large one.

"So you're saying it's wrong for me to use a potential source of information just because she happens to have a history with the guy I'm sleeping with."

"Sam, all I said is that I'm staying out of it." Stoney didn't bother to hide his grin as he went back to checking off office furniture from a list on a clipboard. A list he wouldn't show her. "I'm in Illinois, I'm so far out of it."

"I would have told him if something important came up. But she was barely worth the gas money I spent." Of course, Patricia was also pretty much still at her mercy as long as she had the surveillance tape of her lifting that ring. But the more people who knew about it, the less pull she would have. For that reason she was keeping her trap shut about the deal with Patty. "Actually, I don't know what Rick even saw in her."

"Whoop, I'm moving farther away. Now I'm in Idaho. And don't follow me."

Samantha spun another circle in the cushy green reception chair. Even with the good news and potential lead of the Gugenthal jewelry box, foremost in her mind was the stupid argument with Rick. Of course he'd been mad that she was hanging out with Patty—whether the woman half drove her nuts or not. Thank God she hadn't kept Leedmont a secret from him. "Stoney, you're my Yoda. Advise me and shit."

"Three months ago I told you hooking up with Richard Addison was a mistake. Everything after that's your own fault, honey. I'm the one who lined up the paying vacation for you in Venice." He examined a file cabinet serial number and checked it off his clipboard list.

"We're not going to find Jimmy Hoffa in one of these, are we?" she asked, rapping a knuckle against the metal cabinet.

"If we do, you have to do the TV interviews." Stoney drew a breath. "Okay. One piece of advice. If you like Addison, and if your hanging out with his ex-wife upsets him, don't do it."

"Wiser words were never spoken," a low Southern drawl came from the doorway.

Samantha whirled in her chair. Tall, athletic, and fiftyish, Aubrey Pendleton strolled into their reception area. "Mr. Pendleton," she said, standing.

She offered her hand and he took it, though instead of the standard "Pleased to meet you" handshake, he brought her knuckles to his lips. "You must be Samantha Jellicoe. Your call surprised me."

"Why is that?" she asked, withdrawing her fingers.

"Ladies with Rick Addison for a companion usually don't need another gentleman's services," he returned, nodding at Stoney. "Aubrey Pendleton."

"Walter Barstone," Stoney responded, stepping forward to offer his own hand.

Aubrey didn't kiss Stoney's knuckles, which was probably a good thing. Sam went around to the reception door and opened it, gesturing Mr. Pendleton to join her. Taking in the bare walls, muted paint color, and eclectic collection of furniture, he complied.

"This place used to belong to an insurance company," he commented, following her toward her office. "Gossip was they couldn't afford the rent."

"Great," Stoney grunted from behind them.

Pendleton offered a smile of perfect teeth. "Personally I thought they either attracted the wrong clientele, or chose the wrong area of town for their business. With your connections, I doubt you'll have any problems."

Jeez. Everybody knew who she was and with whom she was sleeping. Sam wondered what else he might know. "Speaking of connections," she said, imitating his easy, confidence-inspiring style of conversation, "I happened into Gressin's Antiques this afternoon. You wouldn't by chance have any other Flemish jewelry boxes available for purchase, would you?"

"Ah, very smooth, Miss Jellicoe. My compliments."

She smiled. "Sam's fine."

"I never call a lady by her nickname," he returned. "She deserves to be addressed with more respect than that. Might I call you Miss Samantha?"

"Sure." Rick rarely called her Sam, but she figured that was just his British showing. That whole respect thing, though—that was nice. "Jewelry boxes?"

They sat in her office guest chairs, while Stoney went back to checking off furniture. She swore her desk chair had changed style twice and color three times.

"Jewelry boxes," Pendleton repeated. "You know, a nice selection of grand master prints would give you a fine sense of elegance in here."

So he wanted to chat around the topic. Okay, she could do that. "There're already some Monets in the common hallway."

"Too European," he drawled, sounding dismissive. "Something closer to home. O'Keeffe, maybe."

"Desert life? Not really quintessential Palm Beach."

He chuckled. "Diego Rivera, then."

Sam cocked her head at him. "Is this an art quiz? Rivera's South American, but he's definitely not upper crust art guy. Why don't you hit me with a few naked natives like Gauguin?"

Nodding, he sat back in the chair and crossed his ankles. "Laurie Kunz gave me the jewelry box two days ago and asked if I'd get rid of it for her. She said she'd never liked it, and that with the trust tied up for the time being, she could use the ready cash for tipping the extra people they were bringing in for the wake."

She took a moment to study both his expression and the tone of his voice. "You didn't approve," she finally said.

"Charles and I and a few other gentlemen used to play poker on Thursday evenings when he was in town."

"You liked him."

"Yes, I did."

"So did I," she admitted.

Pendleton nodded. "And he liked his collections. I offered to loan Laurie some ready funds. She had no reason to dispose of that box except for the fact that she could do it. I didn't think it was seemly."

"But you went to lunch with her today."

His white-toothed smile appeared again. "One must make a living, Miss Samantha. And there are families one doesn't cross if one wishes to remain inside the Palm Beach social circle."

"Gossiping to me—or anybody—seems like a bad way to stay popular," she noted.

"No, having information is vital, and knowing with whom to share it is at least as important." He stretched out an elegant hand to touch her knee. "I'm choosing to share it with you."

"Why?"

"Our occupations aren't all that different, my dear. We both largely . . . live off the efforts of other people. Or you *did,* rather. You'll have to let me know how well having a legitimate occupation agrees with you."

Sam laughed. "If I knew what you were talking about, I'd definitely keep you apprised."

"Fair enough, though I assure you that I am the very soul of discretion. Is there anything else?"

She hesitated for a bare moment. Living off her instincts had never steered her wrong before, and she sensed that she could trust Aubrey Pendleton. "Do you know of anybody setting up rich guys or tourists with a prostitute and then taking photos for blackmail?"

"I've heard whispers about some low-brow scam with a woman and photos. And something about a post office box."

Bingo. "I had a feeling it wasn't a onetime thing. No clue about who's behind it?"

Aubrey chuckled. "Darlin', whoever it is, he's not part of the Palm Beach social circle. I've seen things like this before. The beau monde would rather pay a few dollars than ever acknowledge the mosquito by calling the police and reporting it."

"Okay. Thanks."

"My pleasure. This is exciting, actually, investigating murder and mayhem. I feel very *CSI Miami.*"

Samantha smiled. He did seem to be enjoying this, and he'd certainly been forthcoming. One more question couldn't hurt. "Do you think his kids had anything to do with Kunz's murder?"

He lifted both eyebrows. "Whatever my newfound penchant for excitement, I would not knowingly associate with murderers. Between you and me, they're spoiled little shits, but killers? I don't think so."

Crap. Back to square one—though she wasn't eliminating them on just one person's say-so. "Thanks again, Mr. Pendleton."

"Aubrey, please. And keep me informed on all fronts, if you would. I find it fascinating."

"It's a deal."

Aubrey stood, offering her an elegant, old-fashioned bow. "Call me anytime at all, for business or for pleasure." He smiled again, Southern gentleman to his bones. "And by the way, in my experience there are two ways to make a man forget an argument: food, and sex."

Now *this* was getting interesting. "How many of your female companions know that you have so much knowledge about men?"

With a wink he slipped through the doorway. "About as many as know I came here to talk to you."

"I'll keep that in mind," she said, just loud enough for him to hear. Aubrey Pendleton was right—they both had some secrets.

When Rick got home there were already two messages waiting for him from Shelly in Tom's office. He called her back, only to discover that the *Wall Street Journal* had been calling to confirm his buyout of Kingdom Fittings.

"Splendid," he muttered. There was nothing like media interest to start raising the price of things. They hadn't even agreed on terms yet, much less sale price. "Put them off until Friday, at least," he instructed. "Tell them I'm attending a funeral tomorrow."

As he hung up the phone it rang again, and he automatically picked it up. Not many people had his private office number. "Addison."

"Hello, Richard," Patricia's cultured voice came.

He frowned. "I'm a bit busy right now, Patricia. I'll call you back later."

"I was just wondering whether you'd spoken to Tom. I'm quite anxious to get settled here."

"And why is that again?" he asked. However lightly he might pretend to take Samantha's warnings, he wouldn't disregard them. Patricia rarely did anything that didn't benefit herself. "Why Palm Beach?"

"We already discussed that."

"Let's discuss it again, shall we?"

She laughed, a sound he used to find attractive. Now it

sounded more like warning bells. "Why not Palm Beach? As I said, the weather's nice, it's far from Peter's circle of influence and acquaintances, and it actually has a society and a season for the aristocracy—or what passes for them in America. Besides, most of my remaining friends have winter homes here."

Right. The damned Patty's Pack gossip brigade. They'd commiserate with her, obviously—or she wouldn't be so keen on living there—but they wouldn't fund her new life. Apparently that was his job. "What if I asked you to settle somewhere else?" he suggested. "What if I offered to pay for it?"

For a moment she didn't say anything. "Is that American mutt of yours afraid of the competition?" she finally snapped, the smooth veneer coming off her tone.

"Samantha's not afraid of anything," he returned. "I'm trying to do *you* a favor. Not her. And she's not a mutt, darling," pride goaded him into saying. Samantha might not have a pedigreed bloodline, but she was probably the purest person he'd ever met.

"Whatever helps your fantasy life, darling," she returned, then audibly drew a breath. "Please help me, Richard. I don't have anywhere else to turn. Peter betrayed every man I know, including you, and you're the only one I can still . . . count on."

Even when he was aware of it, he still couldn't help what Samantha termed his "knight in shining armor" tendencies. "Tom's looking into it. I'll have him call you tomorrow."

"Oh, thank you, Richard."

Rick tightened his grip on the phone. "If you want to thank me, Patricia, stay away from Samantha."

"Tell the mutt to stay away from me. It's certainly not my idea to be seen with her."

The phone clicked dead, and he hung up. Surprisingly, he wasn't as angry as he was bemused. His girlfriend seemed in pursuit of his ex-wife, who wouldn't leave *him* alone. He certainly led a strange life, these days.

At the knock against his open office door, he turned around. *Speak of the devil.* "Hi."

Samantha eyed him for a long moment before she stepped into the room. "Are we still fighting?"

"I don't know. Are we?"

"In a way, I hope so. Somebody just told me the two best ways to make a man forget an argument are food and sex."

Richard closed the proposal file. "That's interesting," he said, standing to approach her. "Because you do look very hot in that dress."

She grinned. "Thanks. I was actually thinking about Hans's chocolate pie, though." Slipping backward, she retreated down the hallway.

For a moment he stood in the doorway, watching the soft sway of her hips as she retreated and feeling the blood leave his brain to head downward. So they weren't arguing. Nothing was settled, but neither did he intend to spend the night sleeping alone. "I like pie," he said, catching up to take her hand.

"I thought you'd still be pissed off," she noted, sending him a sideways glance.

"I'm a big boy. Besides, I like to keep you on your toes."

"You're good at it." At the head of the stairs she stopped. "I grew up not being able to tell anyone what my father and I did for a living," she said unexpectedly. "I'm used to secrets. And in all honesty, I knew you'd get mad if you found out I was talking to Patricia. So I kept my mouth shut. I didn't mean to make you angry."

Slowly, Rick drew her toward him. "I married her. Denying that would be abysmally stupid. And I loved her for a time, as well."

She started to pull away. "Rick—"

"I know, I know." He smiled. "I just wanted to say that my scope of experience is wider now, and that I'd like to think I'm wiser and more cautious." He leaned forward, tipping her chin up with his fingers, and kissed her. "You may think it's a weakness to admit certain things, but I happen to think it's a strength. And so I've decided that you're just going to have to get used to hearing it. I love you, Samantha."

"You—"

He stopped her protest or whatever it was going to be with another kiss, deep and slow. "I love you," he whispered, nudging her backward until her hips came against the balcony railing, "I love you."

She didn't answer, and he didn't expect her to, but from the way her arms swept around his shoulders, fingers digging into muscles as she met his mouth hungrily, she felt something. More than something. Whatever it was that prevented her from saying the words, he understood the emotion.

"Mr. Addison?"

With a stifled curse Richard tore his mouth from Samantha's and looked around her down to the foyer where his housekeeper stood. "What is it, Reinaldo?"

"Sorry, sir, but dinner is ready."

Samantha licked his ear. "Mm, and I'm so hungry," she murmured.

Christ. "Have everything set out in the dining room, and then give everyone the rest of the night off."

The Cuban gave a quick grin. "Right away, sir."

"My, aren't you generous?" Samantha murmured.

He ran his hands down her back, stopping to cup her bum and pull her against him. "Not in the least. Do you know how much I want you?"

Her responding moan made him hard. "I have a good idea," she breathed, shifting her hips against him.

"Good. Now just walk in front of me to the dining room so I can keep a little dignity."

Samantha laughed. "If you weren't so generously endowed, you wouldn't have that problem."

He released her, motioning her to precede him down the stairs. "Yes, but then we'd have another problem entirely."

"True. I'd rather have the first one."

As they reached the first floor he moved up behind her, shifting her hair forward on her shoulders so he could kiss the back of her neck. "Maybe I am generous," he conceded, welcome heat running just under his skin, "because I intend to give you my entire endowment."

She gave a near silent, shaky breath. "You just made me wet," she whispered.

If they didn't stop this, he'd never make it to the dining room. And Reinaldo had best have gotten everyone out of there.

The dining room was thankfully deserted, with two places set opposite one another at one end of the long table. Tonight's dinner had apparently been entirely in honor of Samantha and her tastes, because a steaming pot of chili sat midway between the settings, with piles of nachos on both plates. Farther down the table a chocolate pie topped with whipped cream sat awaiting dessert.

"Oh, yes," she crowed, dropping into one of the chairs. "Hans is a genius." She crunched into a nacho, turning to look up at him with half-melted cheese strung down her chin.

With a smile he leaned around to nibble the straying

cheese. While she stood up to spoon chili onto her chips and cheese, he grabbed his own plate and moved it to the place beside her.

"Here," she said, cupping her hand under a generous load of chili and nachos.

It was spicier than he expected, but as she shifted to undo his shirt buttons while he chewed, he wasn't about to comment. He fed her the next chip, using the moment to squat down and pull off her yellow sandals. His shoes came off next, and then she stood so he could unzip the back of her Chanel dress, kissing the warm skin of her shoulders as he exposed it.

"It occurs to me that nachos aren't the most fragrant of foods," he said, lowering the dress to her feet. Oh, my. She'd worn her pink bra and panties with the lace around the edges.

"We're both eating them," she returned, arching her back as he ran his fingers down her spine.

He turned her to face him, kissing her deeply. She was right; she tasted like chili and peppers—which was actually quite fitting for her. Shifting his attention to her throat, Richard slid his hands around to the fastening of her bra. All the teasing at lunch and then the argument—in a sense, Samantha knew what she was talking about. It wasn't difficult to channel all that frustration into arousal.

He pulled the bra straps from her shoulders. Laughing a little unsteadily, Samantha fed him another chip. Denied a better use of his mouth for the moment, he ran his fingers across her nipples, relishing the sound of her gasp. Good God, she turned him on.

Moving back a step to unfasten his trousers and drop his shirt to the floor, he still couldn't take his eyes off her. She consumed him, and only at times like this, when he was about to be inside her, to hear her moan with pleasure and to make her come, did he feel like she belonged to him. When she ran her palms slowly along his abdomen and then leaned in to lick his left nipple, he nearly lost control. "Jesus," he managed, shuddering.

Samantha chuckled, the sound reverberating into his chest. "You're so easy."

Richard slid a hand into her cute underwear, moving his fingers upward to feel the damp warmth inside her. "I'm not the only one."

"Okay, that's enough teasing, buddy," she moaned, writhing against him. "I want the main course."

"I'm not through with the appetizer," he returned, lifting her onto the edge of the table and pulling her panties down in the same motion. He flung them somewhere over his shoulder.

"Hey! I've lost track of the number of pairs of underwear I've lost since I met you," she protested in a voice thick with passion and amusement.

"I'll buy you a store." Rick sat in her vacated chair and leaned in to kiss the insides of her thighs.

Samantha shoved the plates aside and lay back. Moving in, he licked along her soft folds. Abruptly she jumped, sitting up to grab his hair and yank his face away from her. "Jesus Christ!"

He blinked. "What? Did I—"

"Those peppers sting, man," she panted, laughing breathlessly. "Do it again."

So there was an unexpected benefit to spicy foods and sex. Richard went to work again with his fingers and his mouth, ruthless and relentless as she squirmed beneath him.

"All right, enough, enough," she finally begged. "Come up here and fuck me, Rick."

He wanted to; the wait was killing him. But he wasn't finished with torturing her yet. It was payback time. "I haven't had dessert, yet," he murmured, reaching over to hook the pie and slide it closer.

Two fingers of whipped cream plopped onto each of her breasts, and he leaned along her body to lick them clean, one finger still pressed inside her. She bucked and came, crying out his name. That nearly did him in. *Not yet*, he commanded his cock, taking deep breaths and striving for control.

Samantha hammered her fists on the tabletop and gasped for air. "You're killing me, you British bastard."

He grinned. "What a way to go, though."

Sitting up, she kissed him, licking cream from his chin. "I believe in fair play, you know," she murmured, dipping her hand into the pie.

Richard eyed her warily. "Samantha, might I remind you—"

She grasped his hard cock, smearing chocolate and whipped cream along its length. "Uh-oh. We'll have to clean that up, now."

Oh, boy. Pushing him back down into the chair, she slid off the table to kneel between his thighs. He lost the power of speech as her warm mouth closed around him. All he could do was tangle his hands into her hair and try to force himself to breathe and not ejaculate until he was bloody ready to do so. And that meant not until he was inside her.

Her darting, caressing tongue along his length was too much. "Stop, stop," he groaned when he couldn't stand the torture any longer, pulling her away. He snagged a napkin to swipe off the remains of the chocolate, then knelt to face her. Pushing her backward off balance onto the marble floor, he half fell on top of her, taking her mouth and adjusting himself to push inside her.

With no time for finesse, he simply pinned her to the floor

and thrust madly until he came with a rush. Growling her name, he collapsed on top of her.

Her arms tightened around his shoulders and then slowly relaxed again. "I told you we'd probably kill each other," she gasped.

He kissed her again, more slowly and gently this time. "And I told you I liked pie."

Twelve

*S*amantha hated funerals. She'd attended only three in her life—one for Stoney's mom, another for an old colleague of her dad's who'd retired to a country without extradition, and the third for her dad, himself—though that had been a tiny service just outside the prison where he'd been doing time, and she'd watched from a nearby hill through binoculars while a few Feds and the prison padre stood around and a quartet of fellow prisoners dug the hole and dumped the casket in.

This one was unlike any of those, but at the same time it was exactly the same. A good two hundred mourners stood under white tent canopies or sat in white wood chairs, accompanied by several thousand dollars' worth of mourning bouquets and wreaths, and attired in several million dollars' worth of suits and dresses and jewelry. But just like the others, it was too quiet, and for someone like her, who counted on knowing what to say and to whom to speak, there weren't any words to use.

"You okay?" Rick whispered, his arm close around her shoulders.

For once she didn't mind the confining contact. In fact, she welcomed it, and snuggled closer into the circle of his arm and chest. "Yes. I mean, I barely knew him."

"You knew him better than some of his friends, I'd wager," he returned in the same low tone, nodding toward the loose group of mostly older gentlemen who sat at one end of the grave site. From what Aubrey had told her, they were probably Kunz's poker buddies.

The police were keeping the press a respectful distance away, but in the murmuring quiet she could still hear the click of shutters. Again this time she didn't mind. Though she recognized a great many of the fellow mourners, a few were unknown. And odds were that at least a few of those would have their faces and names in the local papers tomorrow. At this moment they were all suspects, and she wanted to know everything about them.

"Laurie's looked better," Rick commented, as the central group of mourners disembarked from their limousines and made their way to the site through the scattering of tasteful gravestones and mausoleums.

"Black's not her color," Sam agreed, watching the brother and sister approach arm in arm.

"That's a tad catty, don't you think?"

"Her nose isn't even red. How do you mean she's looked better?"

He shrugged against her. "I don't really know. I guess it's just a thing you say at funerals."

Sam twisted her head to look up at him. "I'm serious. Does she look like someone who's lost a parent, when they were apparently close enough that they lived in the same house? Yesterday was the first time I've seen her."

"I don't know, Samantha," he whispered back. "And it's a big house. Sharing it with a family member doesn't necessarily mean they were close."

"Speaking from experience, are we?"

"Shh. We can delve into my private closet another time. But I told you, Charles doted on both his children."

"Right. I just don't see that from looking at the two of them." She scanned the growing crowd again, trying not to linger on the coffin being carefully set onto its lowering mechanism. "I'm missing something," she grumbled. "I know I am, and I have no idea what."

"Rick, Sam," Castillo's voice came from behind them.

"Hello, Frank," she answered over her shoulder. "Anything new?"

She felt the tug on the back of her chair as the detective pulled himself forward. "Nothing. I've got guys checking pawnshops and fences between here and Miami. We've run all the prints in the house, and they all belong to family and staff and friends."

"So you're figuring it was family, staff, or a friend who did it," she returned, for the moment setting aside the fact that she wouldn't have left prints if she'd done the robbery.

"Yeah, well, being in the cop business, I kind of need some proof, and that leaves a lot of people to look at," Castillo noted. "You notice anything screwy here?"

"Laurie's nose isn't red," Rick contributed, tightening his hand on her shoulder. "Can we do this elsewhere? It's not seemly."

Her chair bumped as Castillo released it. "Right."

She wasn't sure if the admonition was snobbery or Rick's British sense of decorum or something else entirely, but it surprised her into silence. "Are you okay?" she murmured.

"Bad memories," he said quietly. "Let's just pay our respects and go."

"I need to go to the wake," she put in after a moment. "But if you don't want to, I'll hook up with Fr—"

"I'm going with you, my love."

She leaned in to kiss his cheek, then settled back as the ceremony began. Casting her gaze around the crowd, she looked for . . . something. It seemed stupid that somebody might show up and do a tapdance over Kunz's grave, but she knew she could read people, and someone had done this. Someone had killed Charles.

As her eyes reached Daniel Kunz, she was surprised to see that he was already gazing at her. He looked tired, more so than his sister, but his eyes were dry as well. Maybe the family just weren't criers. He held her gaze steadily, and she looked away first.

She'd seen that look in men's eyes before, most notably Rick's. Daniel was interested. And that brought up something else she'd practically forgotten: Patricia. Where was she? Was she so obsessed with looking available and vulnerable in Rick's estimation that she'd forgone the opportunity to make good with Daniel?

Then she spotted Patty, seated toward the front but so swathed in black hat, black netting, black sunglasses, and black Vera Wang that she looked nearly unrecognizable. The charitable, honorable thing for Sam to do, she knew, would be to keep her mouth shut about the Ex's presence.

"Patricia's here," she murmured, indicating the direction with one finger.

"I wonder who invited her?" Rick said.

"It's kind of the place to be today. She is in the good seats, though."

The testimonials began, led by a series of Charles's poker

buddies and fellow Everglades Club members. She wondered why they hadn't done this in a church, but the fashionable clothes and surrounding pack of press answered that.
Somebody wanted publicity, or at least a photo op. Which
meant one of the family, since they would have been the
ones to make the arrangements. Then again, everybody in
Palm Beach society liked publicity. It didn't make anyone a
killer, but everything meant something.

Finally Laurie moved to the front and spoke for a few
minutes about her father's contributions to the community,
and then how he'd supported her in her decision to go into
real estate and how proud he'd been of both her achieve-
ments and Daniel's, including the yachting trophy Daniel
had brought home last year. Then the priest came forward
again with the final benediction, and the reminder that the
wake would be at Coronado House. Daniel never spoke.

As the mourners began dispersing, Rick stood. "It was a
nice service," he said, pulling her up beside him.

"It was sad."

With a small smile, Rick put his hands on both her shoulders and kissed her forehead. "Charles is lucky he spoke
with you that night."

She kissed him back, this time on the lips. "Why do you
say that?"

"Because now he can be certain that one way or another,
someone will find out what happened." Wrapping her hand
around his jacket sleeve, he headed them toward the waiting
stretched Mercedes-Benz S600.

"Does this mean you're on my side now?"

"I want whoever killed Charles to go to prison. I maintain
my position that the police can handle it without your assistance and that they'll solve this before you do. And I wish
you would limit your participation to chats with Frank."

"Frank and I exchange information." She knew why he'd made the wager and why he was sticking to his guns, but she couldn't sit around and do nothing. She wasn't wired that way. And he liked the way she *was* wired. "Honestly, what would you be saying if I did what you wanted? If I kept my hands completely out of the cookie jar? If I never had cookies again?"

"I'd say, 'Thank God, I can rest a little easier because I know she's safe,'" he answered promptly.

"Sure. And with my new free time I could knit you turtlenecks and learn to play the piano. What a hoot I'd be. You'd probably retire so you wouldn't have to miss a second of my exciting company."

For a long moment he gazed at her. "I think you should try living a normal life before you dismiss it as mundane."

Mundane. That was the thing she never wanted to be. And that was what Rick didn't get, that if she totally gave up her old life, it would change everything in her and everything between them. She'd be just another of the women in his life, nothing special, nothing out of the ordinary. Mundane.

"I'm not sure I know what normal is," she said, because he would expect her to answer with something flip. *He* was the one who needed to imagine her in a normal life before he tried to force it on her.

In silence they joined the train of vehicles, mostly chauffeured, entering and exiting the gates of Coronado House in an unending circle. "We don't have to stay long," she said, drawing a hard breath as she patted Rick's knee. Nothing unusual here. Just the same old nonmundane Sam. "I just want to look around and see who's talking to whom."

"From what you told me about the other day, you may not be all that welcome, Samantha."

"I will be if you're here, sweetie."

"Wonderful. Now I'm your passport to larceny."

Samantha wandered out of the foyer and front sitting area and made her way toward the courtyard at the center of Coronado House. As far as she could tell, there'd never been much difference between an upper class wake and a straight party, and this wasn't any different.

Rick was out of sight somewhere behind her, but he could take care of himself. Hell, he schmoozed people and shit for a living. She schmoozed their possessions—or rather, she used to. It would have been an easy gig today.

The open air courtyard was nearly as crowded as the inside, but it gave her a view through Charles's office window without actually having to barge into the room. She leaned against a palm tree to take a good look. None of the windows were broken or cracked, which didn't surprise her, but the thin lines of molding were all even and slightly sun-faded to the same degree. Whoever'd gotten into the office hadn't gone through those windows.

A hand brushed her bare arm. "Hi."

She jumped, leaning around the palm tree. *Shit*. "Daniel. Hi. That was a nice service."

"Thanks, I guess. I'm glad you're here."

"You are?"

Daniel nodded. He'd shed his jacket, but still looked like a model straight out of *Hunk* magazine in his dark blue shirt and gray tie and slacks. "Laurie was a little hard on you yesterday," he said with a disarming smile. "She's having a rough time with all this stuff going on."

"Well, you found a caterer, anyway," she returned, gesturing at a passing plate full of crackers and paté.

"Luckily she's got a lot of connections through her business." Daniel reached out and flicked a strand of her hair behind her ear. "So I wanted to apologize."

"That's not necessary." *As if apologizing was what he was doing.* "You both have a lot on your minds."

"Yes, we do." Moving closer, he wrapped a hand around her arm. "Hey, you like art and antiques, don't you?"

"Sure."

"Come and take a look at this."

For a brief moment she weighed her instinct to stay clear of Daniel against what she might find out if she went with him. The opportunity was too good to pass up.

He didn't take her hand, but his guiding grip on her arm made it clear that they were together. The presumed possession annoyed her, though the same gesture from Rick in most instances gave her warm, fuzzy feelings that led to all kinds of worries about the future and her independence.

To her surprise, they didn't go to a secluded poolside cabana or anything like that, but straight to Charles's office. Okay, it was either really good luck on her part, or kind of freaky on his. Not under any circumstances would she consider making out in the office of someone they'd buried an hour earlier.

"What do you think?" Daniel asked, gesturing at a small glass case that stood on a long mahogany credenza.

She relaxed a fraction. He wasn't going for a full frontal assault, anyway. Shaking herself, she went forward to take a closer look, noting the large Renoir over the right-hand wall. A fake Renoir, she decided after a second. Normally it would have taken her a little longer to make that determination, but the overlarge painting, together with the thick division between the office and the bathroom on the other side, yelled "safe." Nobody with any taste put a genuine painting somewhere it would have to be taken on and off the wall or set into a panel with hinges. Skin oils, fingerprints, and general banging around were all terrible for resale values.

She bent down to look into the four-sided case Daniel had indicated. "It's nice," she said after a moment, taking in the thin, elongated, featureless bronze woman encased within.

"Do you know what it is?" he asked, leaning in to look at her through the right angle of the glass.

"Do *you*?"

He straightened when she did. "Not a clue. I couldn't find it on any inventory or insurance list."

"Has it been here long?"

"I never noticed it before last week. Dad had just gotten back from Germany, so I thought maybe he bought it there. He's always—was always—doing that."

So Charles's love of art wasn't shared by his son. "Well," she said, bending briefly to look at it again and thinking that he'd probably grab her ass if she lingered in that position, "it's not an antique, and it's really not from a medium that I follow."

"Shit. So you don't know wh—"

"But I would guess it's probably a Giacometti, maybe a prototype for one of his full-size works."

He took a step closer, brushing the line of her wrist with his thumb. "How much is something like that worth?"

So he figured he needed to flirt to get information. Normally—prior to three months ago—she wouldn't have hesitated to follow the same game plan. Now, though, she had a very jealous Brit in the other room and his ex-wife lurking somewhere around. She shrugged. "A couple of years ago one of his full-size sculptures went for somewhere over three million."

"Wow."

"There're a lot of fakes and reproductions out there."

"Dad wouldn't buy either one." Daniel cupped her chin, tilting her face up toward his. "Are you sure the London lord's not too dull for you?"

She smiled. "I thought you had a London lady, yourself."

"Patricia? I hate limiting my options." He leaned in and touched his lips to hers.

She could have stopped him, dropped him to the floor if she wanted to, but unless she was greatly mistaken, Daniel had something to do with the real story of Coronado House. Neither, though, did she make any attempt to kiss him back. "That was a little presumptuous, don't you think?"

He tilted his head, golden-brown hair falling across one eye. "That depends on what you do next." He waited for a moment, then smiled. "I didn't think you'd run." Digging into his pocket, he produced a business card. "My cell number's on the back. It's private."

"You have these made up in advance?" she asked, flipping the card over to see the handwritten set of numbers.

"I was hoping you'd come by." He touched her cheek again. "I'm a generous guy, Sam. I share what I have. Keep that in mind."

She smiled carefully. "Are you trying to bribe me or something?"

Daniel shook his head. "I'm trying to seduce you."

"There you are, Samantha," Rick's voice came from the doorway before she could reply with something ballsy but noncommittal. "I have that conference phone call— Ah, Daniel." Still wearing the friendly, bland expression he generally conjured for big gatherings, he approached Daniel. And she didn't think for a moment that he hadn't seen the caress. "My condolences."

"Thanks, Rick. I was just asking Sam if she had any idea

what that was," Daniel returned, jabbing a thumb toward the case.

Rick's gaze didn't leave Daniel's face. "She knows her art." Slowly he held out his hand to her. When Sam gripped his fingers, they were shaking a little. "My apologies, but I need—"

"No problem. Thanks again, Sam."

"Any time."

As they made their way toward the front door, Rick pulled out his cell phone and dialed Ben, his driver, to meet them on the drive. Samantha tucked Daniel's business card into her purse and kept her mouth shut.

Once they were in the limo, Rick sat forward. "Ben, a little privacy, please."

"Yes, sir."

Silently the opaque divider slid up from the back of the front seat. Since she had no idea how he would react to her little meeting with Daniel, Samantha decided to counter-attack first. "Rick—"

"Be quiet. I need to think."

"Hey, I didn't kiss *him*."

He gazed at her for a moment. "I noticed. Why did he think kissing you would be a good idea? Other than your general attractiveness, of course."

Well, no shouting, anyway. "I think he figured he had to give me something for the information about the sculpture."

"And he didn't have a quarter in his pocket?"

"I don't know. I didn't check his pockets."

"Any further insights? If it won't jeopardize the wager, of course."

"As if. I'm so far ahead I can't even see Castillo," she lied.

"So unbelt."

She blinked. "Jeez. Horny much?"

"What? No. I mean spill it, Yank."

"You should have said that in the first place."

"I did. Quit stalling."

"Fine. I think he's the most important thing in his life," she returned, relaxing against his side. If he didn't trust her, he was doing a good job of hiding it. "Nobody's availability or interest matters except his own. And I didn't kick him in the nards because there's something going on at that house. I know there is, Rick. And I think he knows what it is."

With a sigh he looped his arms around her, pulling her closer against him. "Is there any reason I shouldn't turn his business into dust?"

Okay. Now *that* sounded like Rick. "Because until last week it was his dad's business, and because right now he's just smarmy and selfish. You can ruin him if he had something to do with Charles getting killed." She kissed his throat. "I thought you'd be way more pissed off."

"Sometimes I surprise myself. I was ready to be. If you'd been anyone else, I would have been. My loved ones don't precisely have a good track record in fidelity where I'm concerned."

Christ, she hadn't even thought of that. He'd come upon Patricia rolling around with his former college roommate, and that hadn't exactly gone well for anyone. "I don't even like him," she offered.

"I know that. And honestly, you're just so bloody cute that I can't resist you." He kissed her, deep and soft.

"Well, thank goodness for that," she said, pretending he hadn't just practically given her an orgasm.

"What now?"

"I have to talk to Castillo again." And she was probably going to have to make a phone call, after she figured out a way to keep Daniel Kunz interested but still at a safe distance.

"Isn't that cheating?"

"My way encompasses any and all means of getting information, buddy. I just have to put it together before the cops."

"Don't expect me to wish you luck."

"Luck's for chumps."

So Samantha had decided to use Daniel—and Patricia—to help her solve her puzzle. Richard scowled as he sat at his desk in front of the stack of paperwork that had just arrived from London. This damned wager had been designed to teach her a lesson, not to give her the means to drive him insane.

He blew out his breath. Under the best of conditions he wasn't accustomed to sitting about and waiting for a situation to resolve itself. Whatever else he had on his plate, assisting Castillo and the Palm Beach Police Department wouldn't be cheating; it would simply be putting his ample experience, resources, and contacts to good use.

If Samantha thought Daniel had information, then Laurie might know something useful, as well. And besides, she owned a real estate business, and he'd promised to help Patricia find a place in Palm Beach. With a grim smile he pulled out his Palm Pilot, found Laurie's business phone number, and left a message for her to give him a call. Samantha wasn't the only one who could play the charm game.

"Rick?" Samantha leaned her head into the room as she knocked on the door frame.

"Come in," he said, shutting off the Pilot and dumping it into his desk drawer. He took in her jeans shorts and green T-shirt. "You're not going into work?"

"No. Stoney's got a date, and I . . . just want the rest of the day off."

He stood, keenly aware of the quiet sadness in her voice. A thief with more compassion than most of Kunz's supposed friends and even his family. And paperwork or not, his job immediately became attempting to cheer her up. "A date? Walter?"

"Well, yes." She smiled. "I loaned him the Bentley."

"You . . . It's your car."

"And don't you forget it, babe." She shifted her gaze to his credenza. "You don't happen to have a big piece of graph paper, do you?"

"I imagine I do." He went to the supply cabinet and rifled through it until he found a half-used pad. "Doing a detail of Charles's office?"

"That's a good idea. I will now." She gave him a peck on the cheek as she took the pad. "Thanks."

"What was it for before I gave you that brilliant idea?"

"The pool area. I thought I'd do some sketches and go through some garden magazines."

"You can hire a landscape architect, you know."

She flashed her smile at him. "You sure you don't want to give me a spot where nobody can see the results?"

"I trust you. I'm just saying—"

"No, today's a good day to look at flowers, I think. That whole 'normal' thing you were talking about. I think I can do plants without puking. You can come carry my pencil for me, if you want."

Samantha was inviting him in. That didn't happen very often, and he counted every instance like it was a precious grain of gold. "I have to check in with Tom, and then you've got a deal."

"Okay. I'll be out by the pool."

Sam set her stack of gardening magazines down on one of the wrought-iron poolside tables and plunked a fresh, chilled can of Diet Coke beside them. She had a few ideas about what she wanted to do, but considering this was her first venture into gardening and that Rick used Solano Dorado as both a meeting and a showplace—and that every inside room on the west wing had a view of the pool—she wasn't about to dig up so much as a weed without getting at least his tacit approval first.

As she sat down and opened the tablet of graph paper, though, Rick's other suggestion pulled at her. Everything meant something, and there had been clues aplenty in Charles's office—whether the police would view them that way or not.

The police. That in itself was a little curious, that the scene of the murder would be open to the public less than a week after the act, and before any suspects had even been named. She knew from experience that the Palm Beach PD was accustomed to dealing with the rich and famous and that they were typically protective and deferential, but this was Castillo's case, and he was good at what he did. Hell, he'd nearly caught *her*, once.

Slowly she sketched what she remembered of the wall into which the safe was set. She'd never had any formal art training, but she'd spent most of her life around famous works of art, and she'd been told on several occasions that she had talent. It kind of amused her—the art thief who could draw.

More valuable was her near photographic memory, and she had more than a hunch that it was why she was so bothered today. She'd seen something, and until she realized what it was, it was going to keep eating at her.

The pencil sketch of the wall and the Renoir print didn't tell her anything, so she moved on to the desk and the credenza, re-creating on the page what she'd seen in person a few hours ago. She paused as she began work on the case holding the Giacometti figure. *Wait a minute.*

If it was actually a prototype for *Standing Woman*, Alberto Giacometti's most famous work, it was probably worth nearly a million. In all honesty, unless someone was familiar with Giacometti, it didn't look all that impressive, but she had recognized it—and so would a cat burglar good enough to leave no sign of entry or exit. From what Daniel had said, it wasn't listed on any insurance form. That would make it much less complicated to fence. In addition, it had been sitting out in plain sight, with no alarm wired to it, during the robbery and murder.

Instead, however, the killer had opted to take the time to break into the safe and then steal cash and well-documented jewelry, and the more recognizable Van Gogh and O'Keeffe. Interesting, and not very bright. Considering Daniel's ignorance of the woman's value, its being left behind definitely didn't speak well for his innocence. She wondered whether Laurie knew any more about art, modern or otherwise, than her brother did.

For the first time she realized that she specifically suspected Daniel. It seemed like it should be a huge deal, but it didn't *feel* that way—it was as though she'd been aware of it all along. Unless he'd hired someone to kill his father, his ignorance about art made the crime circumstances logical. Just about everybody knew Van Gogh and O'Keeffe, and the value of rubies and cash were no-brainers.

What she needed was someone with a little more insight into the Kunz family. Checking over her shoulder to see whether Rick was approaching, she pulled her cell phone off her belt and dialed.

"Hello," the smooth Southern drawl came after only one ring.

"Aubrey, it's Samantha Jellicoe. Can you talk?"

"No one's ever been able to stop me from doing that before, darlin'. I thought you'd be at the wake. I've been lookin' for you."

"Are you still there?"

"I never miss a party, whatever the circumstances."

"Sorry. I'll call you later, then."

"Hold on a second." She waited, hearing the echo of voices and some sort of reggae music playing in the background. Hm. She'd thought Charles more of a classical music type. But not much about the funeral or the wake had seemed to be about him. "All right, Miss Samantha," he continued after another moment, "I'm in the library."

"Alone?" she prompted. If anybody overheard their conversation, she would lose any leverage she had with Daniel and his libido.

"I doubt most of the guests know where the library is. What's troubling you?"

"What's the most famous thing the Kunzes own?"

He stayed silent for a moment. "The Gugenthal rubies, I would say. Charles has—had—a Manet in the upstairs sitting room, but he didn't show it much."

"But he showed it to you."

"He thought I'd appreciate it. And I did."

"And what one thing in the family was worth the most?"

"The rubies. Do you have a suspect in mind? This is getting very exciting."

She grinned at the enthusiasm in his voice. Apparently Aubrey Pendleton had been feeling rather starved for intellectual stimulation. Charles probably hadn't had time to show off his new acquisitions to his friend. Now they belonged to someone else—someone more interested in dollar signs than in truth and beauty. "Nothing for sure," she answered. "Would you do me a favor, though? If somebody in the family circle asks you if you know a good, reliable fence, would you give them Walter's name?" She recited Stoney's old business number, and heard Aubrey pull out a paper and scratch it down.

"I'm going to have to get my private dick license after this," he said.

"I don't think anybody actually refers to themselves as dicks anymore."

"I'm obviously still a novice."

"You're a quick study, Aubrey. Thanks again."

"Thank *you*, darlin'. I'll keep you posted."

"Aubrey?" Rick's voice came from right behind her as she flipped the phone closed.

"Jesus. You're getting better at sneaking."

"I wasn't sneaking. Aubrey Pendleton? The walker?"

She twisted to face him, noting that he'd changed into shorts, as well. Yummy. He had great soccer athlete legs, and didn't show them off nearly enough. "Yes. He's pretty interesting." Sam caught the expression in his cool gaze, and she tugged on his hand to pull him into the chair beside her. "Don't worry. He's a bigger fan of you, blue eyes, than of me."

Rick lifted an eyebrow. "Really?"

"Yes. That's a trade secret, though. And he's helping me out."

"His secret's safe with me." He picked up her soda and took a drink. "What have you got so far?"

It took a second before she remembered that he was talking about her ideas for the garden. "Nothing much," she confessed. "I was kind of distracted."

He tucked a strand of hair behind her ear. Funny, the gesture from Daniel left her vaguely disgusted, but Rick's fingers brushing her temple made her shiver. "Then let's just sit and drink your soda."

That sounded surprisingly nice. "Can we look at garden pictures?" she asked, tugging the magazine stack closer.

She needed to run a short errand to Lantana Road so she could scout out the probable perch for Leedmont's photographer, but she preferred not to do that in broad daylight, and she didn't quite feel . . . together enough to be stealthy and clever tonight. And since she was on hold with the Kunz thing until after the wake and until she could take a few minutes to talk to Frank Castillo again, she might as well relax for a day. And spending time with Rick doing nothing was still new and rare enough that it didn't feel either ordinary or mundane.

"I would like that," he returned, smiling.

Thirteen

Wednesday, 7:18 a.m.

The great white shark shot up through the murky water, straight at her. Samantha's eyes flew open and she sat up, a scream rising in her throat. At the sound of the *Jaws* theme ringing from the nightstand, she swallowed her shriek and grabbed the phone. "Fuck," she muttered, lifting it. "Do you know what damn time it is?"

"Did you want me to ask around for you or not, cupcake?" Bobby LeBaron's voice returned.

She pushed mangled bed hair out of her eyes, glancing around for Rick even though he was probably already in his office, working. "What did you find out?"

"First things first, Jellicoe. This is gonna cost you."

"I told you it would be worth a hundred bucks."

"Uh-uh. Richard Addison's squeeze can pay a thousand bucks for what I've got."

Samantha blew out her breath. Greedy son of a bitch. Still, she'd played this game before. "Two hundred, or go sell it to somebody else."

He hesitated. She could practically hear the wheels turning in his brain. "I want the cash up front."

Well, it wasn't going to get any better than that. "Are you at your shop?"

"Yep. Some of us work early hours."

"And some of us work late hours. I'll be there in half an hour."

"Use the back door. I don't open till ten."

Samantha closed her phone and dove into the closet for some clothes. Whatever the info was, it was about damned time something had turned up. Suspicions or not, she needed that pesky proof Castillo was always harping about.

She brushed her teeth and pulled her hair back into a tail, then headed down the hall for Rick's office. "'Morning," she said, leaning in.

He looked up from his computer. "Is it later than I think, or is something deathly wrong?" he asked, glancing at the clock.

"Nothing's wrong," she said, walking in to plant a kiss on his wavy black hair. "I have to go follow up on something."

"A clue?"

"Maybe. I'll probably go by the office too, so I'll see you later."

Rick caught her fingers as she brushed by him. "Do you need a sidekick?"

"No. It's just conversation-type stuff." Cool. He'd asked instead of demanded. Her heart did a funny little flop. Certain as she was about his feelings, the fact that he'd begun making concessions to her odd way of life felt . . . good. She kissed him again, this time on his sensuous mouth. "I'll call in and let you know I'm not dead."

With a quick grin he went back to the computer. "That would be nice. Take the SLR."

* * *

Samantha pulled into one of the loading area slots at the back of the strip mall. The SLR wasn't the most subtle car in the world, but she didn't plan on staying long.

She rapped on the white metal door. Taking into account that Bobby would have to actually stand to answer her knock, she wasn't surprised when she had to wait nearly three minutes before the knob rattled and opened.

"Okay, what've you got?" she asked, slipping into the back of the shop and putting a couple of feet between her and the fence.

Panting, he closed the door and leaned back against it. She didn't like that; his bulk alone made him a formidable barricade. The front windows and door were barred, but in an emergency she could probably put a TV through something and get out. He'd never catch her in the open.

"Where's the cash?" he asked.

Pulling the wad out of the pocket of her light jacket, she set it on a cabinet. "Right here. But you don't get to keep it if I don't like what you have to say."

"Oh, you'll like it. You're looking for a real Van Gogh, right? Blue lily pads?"

That was it. "Where did you see it?"

"I didn't. I got a call. Some guy with one of those Darth Vader voice changers looking for names of fences who might handle that kind of merchandise."

"And what did you tell him?"

He held out one meaty hand. "Cash first, cupcake."

Since he'd identified the Van Gogh, his information was probably legit. With a frown she handed it over, evading his fingers when he tried to close them over hers. "Talk, Bobby."

"You know, I was thinking. Addison's got a shitload of valuables. We could work out something to relocate 'em. It'd be sweet. And you could probably empty half the house before he ever caught on."

Samantha folded her arms across her chest. "You know, the money was for information, but the ass-kicking is gonna be for free."

"All right, all right. I told him I could probably help him out if he came by before nine o'clock this morning."

She glanced at her watch. Nearly eight o'clock. "Okay. You don't mind if I hang out, do you?"

"Damn right I do. You're bad for business, Jellicoe. The guys I hang out with know you're straight. You hide anywhere you want, as long as nobody sees you. *I* don't even want to see you."

"Fine. Is he coming to the front or the back door?"

He shrugged. "Don't know. Get lost."

"Get out of the fucking way."

With a rumble of amusement Bobby lugged himself sideways. Before he could change his mind, Sam grabbed the doorknob and yanked it open.

"It feels weird, don't it?" Bobby said to her backside.

"What?"

"Not being wanted by the scum you used to be too good to hang out with."

She turned around to face him. "You took my cash, Bobby. If you rat me out to this guy, you're really not gonna be happy with me."

The SLR couldn't stay, but she wasn't sure where she could park it and have it still be there when she went back to it. Next time she went out looking for bad guys, she was taking a less obvious and way less valuable damn car. Finally she decided to park it behind the gas station on the corner. It was less than ideal for tailing somebody, but she didn't have much time to plan this out.

At eight-fifteen she climbed the drain pipe beside Bobby's back door and settled herself onto the flat roof. Even this early and in January it was already warm up there, and she shed her jacket, using it to lean her elbows on. She could just smell the doughnuts from the coffee shop at one end of the strip mall, and her stomach rumbled in response. Since Bobby's instructions had been "before nine," though, she needed to stay where she was.

At twenty-eight past, an '84 Chevy pulled up to the back of the shop. She didn't recognize the guy who got out, but as he reached into the backseat and pulled out a stereo, she relaxed again. Apparently Bobby did most of his fencing work before regular business hours. Great. As long as the cops didn't drive up and find her staked out on the roof, she didn't much care what he did. Stereo guy left a few minutes later minus the stereo, and she settled down again.

It was past eight-forty when another car pulled into the loading area. Samantha leaned over the edge of the roof to get a look. A shiny black BMW. Okay, that was interesting. That car didn't fit in any better than hers did.

The car slowed down, then moved past the TV shop and circled around to the front. Somebody was nervous. Crawling on her elbows and knees, she edged toward the front of the roof. The BMW's windows were tinted, and she couldn't make out anything more than that there was one person in the front seat.

After two minutes the driver door swung open a few inches, then wider. Sam held her breath. This was the guy. Whoever stepped out of the car was the one who had killed Charles Kunz.

Her waist began playing "Raindrops Keep Fallin' on My Head." Loudly.

Shit, shit, shit. She grabbed the phone and turned it off. As she did, the door below slammed closed again. The BMW started up and squealed into reverse. She'd just been made.

Lurching to her feet, she swung over the narrow ledge and dropped to the ground. She sprinted for her car, but by the time she crossed the lot the BMW was gone westbound down the boulevard. She'd caught the damned license number, but had also seen the Enterprise rental sticker on the bumper. Whoever had the Van Gogh knew a little bit about protecting himself.

"Fuck," she growled, hurling the cell phone into the passenger seat. *That* was why she didn't carry phones with her when she was on the job.

Now she had to decide whether to let Frank have the license number—which would be a difficult decision considering that unless she gave up Bobby LeBaron, there was nothing illegal or suspicious about anyone driving to a TV repair shop. In the meantime, she had an Enterprise office to break into, now, unless she could figure out something more efficient. This just kept getting better and better.

"I am *not* going to pretend to work for Rick Addison," Stoney stated, folding his arms.

"It's to help me, not him," Samantha returned, putting the silver SLR into park. "Come on. You busted up my stakeout. You owe me."

"You should have told me what you were doing. I can't believe you went to see Bobby LeBaron instead of me."

"You're retired. I needed somebody who isn't."

"That's it. I'm unretiring."

"No, you are not." Thank God he didn't know about the Harkley break-in. This was bad enough. "Come on, Stoney, we can argue later. By the way, somebody might call you looking to unload an Alberto Giacometti prototype. Act like you're interested."

He nodded. "I might be, actually. Who's liberat—"

"For the last time," she broke in, "if I'm retired, you're retired. No working with some hack who gets you tossed into jail. You're my only family, remember?"

"I remember. Of course I also remember you telling me to hook up with somebody else for Venice."

"That's because I knew you couldn't find anybody else who could pull that job."

"Yeah. And it's a damned shame to see the world's best cat losing her nerve."

She scowled. "I didn't lose anything. Knock it off."

Patting her knee, he sent her a grin. "Whatever you say, honey. And the Giacometti?"

"The Kunz estate owns it. But with the homicide investigation ongoing, the insurance company isn't releasing anything. That statue, though, isn't on the insurance roster."

"Sweet deal."

"*You are retired.* Now are you going to help me with this other crap, or not?"

He sighed. "What is it?"

"Just go into the Enterprise office and give 'em this license number," she said, handing over the piece of paper. "Tell them Rick was in an accident and whoever drove this car is the only witness. We need a name and a phone number."

"And you can't do it because . . . ?"

"Because I don't work for Rick. People know my face."

Stoney slammed the passenger door open. "Too many damned people know your face. I'll be right back."

This was the best and most legal way she could come up with to get information on the driver of the BMW. Rick wouldn't like that she was throwing his name around, but as she'd said, her methods encompassed anything and everything that would win her the bet. Of course she'd already spend two hundred and twenty bucks to win a one hundred dollar bet, but the money had always been beside the point.

Stoney came back just as she was about to start chewing her fingernails. "Did you get it?" she asked as he dropped back into the car.

"Yeah, but you're not gonna like it." He handed over a neatly printed piece of paper.

" 'John Smith?' You're kidding me, right?"

"Apparently the guy had fake ID. I did get an address on top of the phone number, though."

She looked at it. "It's the marina. The Sailfish Club."

"What?"

"The address. The phone number probably is, too."

"Sorry, honey. Dead end."

Slowly, she pocketed the paper. "I don't think so. It's probably somebody who knows the Sailfish Club. I wouldn't pick it as a phony address. Would you?"

"No. That's pretty slim, though."

"I know. But it's something. Now I have to figure out what to do with it."

Stretching, Samantha checked her watch. Just before ten p.m. She'd delayed going to Lantana Road for two days, but she couldn't put it off any longer. Beside her on the deep couch Rick was scribbling in the margins of the revised Leedmont proposal.

She smiled. Most business tycoons of her acquaintance were hands-on to some extent, but Rick had raised it to an art form. He'd told her before that he enjoyed what he did, but she would have known that just from the way he worked a contract. Changing a word or two could alter the course of millions of dollars, and he knew every trick in the book. Heck, he'd probably written the book.

He looked up at her. "What?"

"I was just thinking you'd look cute with a pair of those granny reading glasses on."

"Mm. Are you going to eat the rest of the popcorn? I'm only asking because you've been hogging the bowl."

"You're not watching the movie, so you can't have any popcorn," she countered, indicating the mammoth screen that had dropped from its recess in the ceiling.

"I am watching the movie."

"Prove it: What's the name of the monster with the wings?"

Rick set aside his paperwork. "That's a trick question. The winged monster with one head is Rodan, and the one with three heads is Monster X."

With a grin she handed over the popcorn bowl. "Excellent. I have to run an errand. I'll be back by eleven-thirty."

He stood when she did. "I'll go with you."

"No, you won't. It's nothing dangerous. I just have to match a picture with a location, and before you ask, because of lighting and stuff I can't do it during the day."

"Okay." Blue eyes studied her face. "But at least tell me where you're going."

That was fair. He hadn't asked a single question about her trip to Bobby LeBaron's. "A little north of downtown."

"By eleven-thirty."

"Yep." She wrapped her hands into the front of his T-shirt and pulled him in for a kiss. "Tell me how the movie ends."

"You already know."

"Not for me. For you. It's a quiz."

"Great. Sam, be careful," he said, running his hands down her shoulders to take her fingers. "I like all your parts arranged just as they are."

"No sweat."

Sheesh. She was just going to look at something, for

Pete's sake. To be a successful thief, she needed to have total self-confidence and a good measure of caution—and the
ability to drop the latter in favor of complete recklessness at
a moment's notice. Maybe she wasn't stealing tonight, but
the same rules applied. And she was looking forward to it so
much, the ache physically hurt.

She headed down to the garage. Stoney had the Bentley,
but this time she wanted something less conspicuous, anyway. She stopped just inside the garage door. "Inconspicu-
ous. Right." Not in this garage.

After a moment she flipped open the key rack and lifted
the set of keys for the '65 Mustang. Penchant for smooth sophistication or not, Rick was still a guy. And guys loved
muscle cars.

It was cherry red with the personalized plate RA 65, but
neither would matter much at night. She punched open the
garage door and roared down the drive. Hot dog.

The gates swung open on command, and she headed
northwest. It would be too much to hope that the hooker and
the photographer would be working tonight, but she could
do a little research, regardless.

Leedmont had told her that he'd stopped somewhere
along Lantana Road. That was still a pretty nice section of
town, which made sense. A rich guy wouldn't want to pull
over either for fun or to do a good deed if he thought he
might get mugged or car-jacked. At ten o'clock on a Thursday night, though, the area was pretty deserted.

Samantha turned into a McDonald's parking lot and
pulled out the photo Leedmont had given her. He hadn't
been sure of the exact location along the street where the girl
had bent over him, but at the time he wouldn't have thought
it very significant.

From the angle of the picture, the photographer was on a

third floor. There were several two-story shops where he could have waited on the roof, and a handful of apartments and condo buildings, too.

At least she knew which direction Leedmont had been heading along the street, which halved the number of possible perches. Streetlight placement narrowed it down even further. It would be easier to do this from above looking down, but at this point she wasn't willing to break into that many places. Two or three, sure, but not ten or twelve.

She made one speed limit pass from east to west, then circled around to do it again more slowly. Her thief's eye allowed her to eliminate a couple of rooftops as too exposed, and a handful of apartments with flower pots and cats sitting on the windowsills. Not that flower and cat people couldn't take blackmail photos, but they definitely fell to the bottom of the list.

She stopped again, this time at a gas station, and sketched out the south side of the street over a four-block stretch, then crossed out the least likely positions and ones that obviously didn't match with the photo's street lighting.

"Six," she counted aloud. Two apartments, a condo, and three rooftops.

The next step was to get the apartment numbers and see what she could come up with on the Internet to find names that went with them. But before she could let her fingers do the walking, her feet needed to do some.

She parked and headed up to the apartment building. The glass doors were locked, with an intercom on the side. Entry by permission only.

"Right."

She pulled a paper clip and a magnet out of her shorts pocket. In twelve seconds she had the door open and slipped into the building.

She stopped on the third floor in front of the first of the two possibilities. Knocking, she donned a slightly off-center smile for the benefit of the peephole. "Rob?" she called. "Robby?"

The door clicked and opened. A dark-haired man who looked to be tired and in his early thirties gazed at her. "There's no Robby here," he said.

"No? I'm sure this is the apartment number he gave me." Deepening her smile, she leaned against the door frame.

Beyond him the television played some song sung by dancing Muppets. As she risked a glance into the depths of the main room, a short version of the guy at the door wobbled past.

"There's still no Robby here."

"Okay. Sorry to bother you. I'll give him a call."

She backed off, and he shut the door. One down, one more in this building to go. And then it was the condo and the rooftops. Counting down ten doorways, she stopped and knocked again. "Hello? Robby?"

Nothing.

Samantha waited a few beats, then knocked again. "Rob? Are you okay? I thought we were supposed to meet tonight, cutie pie." That sounded fairly harmless, she decided. If she came across as a kook or a stalker, nobody in their right mind would open the door.

The apartment beyond the door was absolutely silent. The window from the street had been dark, but that didn't necessarily mean anything. Still, she couldn't leave without taking a look inside.

"Okay, Robby," she called, "I hope you're not naked, because I'm using my key." Or paper clip.

She stepped into the dark family room and quickly closed the door behind her. If somebody was lurking, she didn't want to be silhouetted in the light from the hallway. For a long moment she stood still, listening, then slipped a pair of leather gloves out of her purse and pulled them on.

By now in her career she'd gotten good at sensing her surroundings, and her gut told her that no one was home. Leaving the lights off, she made her way around a couch and coffee table, stopping to check the stack of mail there and dimly note the name Al Sandretti as the addressee before she went on to the window.

If this had been her place, she would have put a half-dozen potted plants—probably a few ferns and some orchids—on the deep windowsill. Al Sandretti, though, had left it bare. Well, not entirely bare, she noted as she twisted the lever to open the wood blinds an inch or so. Street light flooded in to reveal a camera sitting on one end of the sill.

Instead of picking it up, she fingered the blinds and looked down at the street. A low thrill ran through her bones. The angle matched Leedmont's photo exactly.

"Bingo," she breathed.

Samantha picked up the camera. It was a .35 millimeter film rather than digital, and that surprised her. The ease with which the photographer could post digital pictures on the Internet probably didn't matter, though, if he was only concerned with getting a check. Of course the guy could be a technophobe, but whys and wherefores were beside the point.

All that mattered at the moment was that film meant a finite number of copies and a master negative. Setting down the camera, she went searching.

It was a fairly small space, and the search only took a few minutes. Whatever the guy did for a living during the day, he kept the stuff for his night job organized. The two-drawer file cabinet in the bedroom was locked, but it only took a second to open it. In neat alphabetical order about fifty files, each one with a varying number of photos and a negative, filled both drawers.

The photographer obviously went to a one-hour photo shop and got double or triple prints. Leedmont had been right—some of the files had notations of three and four and even five separate payments. Apparently Al Sandretti just sent out regular requests until a mark got tired of paying. She couldn't tell if the mark's wife got brought into the game after that, or not.

While she had no problem with a guy getting shaken down for cheating on his significant other, at least half the photos she looked at could easily have been setups like Leedmont's. And whether Sandretti ever followed through with his threats, it would be almost impossible for the mark to deny fooling around with a hooker and have anybody believe it.

Sam pursed her lips. "What the hell," she decided, and began emptying all the files into one. She was one of the good guys now. And besides, this was just sleazy.

Finished, she closed and locked the drawers again, hefted the bulky folder she'd removed, and headed for the door. Just inside, she pulled off her gloves, opened the door with one of them, and then stepped out and closed it with the loose glove again. Bye-bye fingerprints.

Stuffing the gloves back into her purse, she made her way to the elevator. The nearer of the two opened as she reached it. Sam took a small step back, flashing a smile as a large, tanned Schwarzenegger wannabe emerged.

"Hey, babe," he rumbled, taking in her chest as they passed.

"Hi," she returned shyly, edging into the elevator sideways to partially shield the folder from his view. Unless every instinct she possessed was wrong, that was Al San-dretti. Yipes. Who knew the Incredible Hulk was for real?

Normally she didn't run into her victims on the way out of their place. The encounter sent her adrenaline through the roof as she trotted back to the Mustang.

The whole gig had been way too easy. She'd anticipated having to stake out the post office box and doing more sleuth work from there to find the photo .bmp file or the negative.

She put the folder on the passenger seat beside her and started the car. Leedmont was going to be happy—and she'd just made ten grand.

Not a bad night's work, if she said so, herself.

At forty-two minutes past eleven Richard sat on the edge of the bed to pull on his athletic shoes. "North of downtown" was fairly vague, but it gave him a place to begin looking.

Ben said she'd taken the Mustang, which meant she hadn't been heading anywhere particularly posh or secretive. In addition, she'd worn her shorts and a T-shirt. That still left a great many places for someone of her skills to be.

Stopping in his office, he unlocked the back cabinet and pulled out a Glock .30, which he dumped into his jacket pocket. Wherever she was, he was going prepared to get her out. To the outside world, being twelve minutes late was barely worth mention. Samantha Jellicoe worked in increments of a second—and in her line of work, former or not, any of those seconds could kill her.

He'd already called her cell phone three times, but as he headed down the stairs to the main floor he dialed it again. A second later the faint strain of the James Bond theme echoed up from the direction of the kitchen and garage hallway.

The sound stopped. *"Hola,"* her voice came over the phone. "I'm only ten minutes late."

She appeared in the foyer below him, the phone still to her ear. Richard lowered his as he finished his descent, sharp relief digging into his chest. He wanted to grab her, but she'd be offended by his lack of faith in her abilities. "The James Bond theme?" he said instead.

"It seemed appropriate." Samantha looked him up and down, stopping directly in front of him. "Going somewhere?"

"Not now. You've got to change my ring."

"Nope. You're James Bond." Leaning closer, she placed a soft, slow kiss on his lips. "Thanks for being ready to charge to the rescue."

"Yes, well, it's what I do."

"Mm-hm. And it just so happens that I'm in the mood to be shaken and stirred. What do you think about that?"

He grinned, taking her free hand to head with her back to the bedroom. Whatever she'd been up to, she was back and she was safe. "I'm at your service."

Richard was downstairs finishing breakfast and reading the *Wall Street Journal* when Laurie Kunz called. After a few minutes of pleasantries and chitchat, she agreed to meet him at her office that morning.

She was of course a professional businesswoman. At the same time, though, Samantha's comments about how deeply the Kunz offspring had or hadn't been affected by their father's murder stayed with him. She'd tossed and turned for the past two nights—which he knew because she'd nearly brained him twice—and had even gotten out of bed to watch television for an hour or so before dawn. As far as he knew, she was still in bed. Laurie, though, who had buried her father two days ago, was up by seven and making business appointments.

"Business as usual," he muttered, sipping tea. Perhaps she had her own way of grieving, but to a casual observer it didn't look well. And appearance was everything in Palm Beach society. On the other hand, he was becoming accustomed to noticing things that the rest of society might not.

His phone rang again as Samantha staggered into the dining room and grabbed a chocolate doughnut off the sideboard. "Good morning, my love," he drawled, looking at the number ID as he picked up the phone. "It's Sarah."

She nodded, slumping into the chair beside him and only smiling when Reinaldo appeared with a chilled glass of Diet Coke. Richard stifled a grin as his London secretary briefed him on the day's schedule. Halfway through, though, he stopped her.

"They're coming in tomorrow," he said, frowning. "Saturday. For a Monday meeting."

"That was my understanding as well, sir," his secretary's efficient voice came. "But when I checked with Mr. Leedmont's office to confirm the flight details, they informed me that the rest of the Kingdom board will be landing in Miami at one o'clock today, your time. And the meeting has been moved up to ten a.m. on Saturday."

Shit. "Why didn't they let me know?"

He could hear her hesitation over the phone. "They claim to have done so, sir, but I'm positive we never received anything. I triple-checked e-mail and all of my voice-mail messages and I—"

"I'd believe you before I believe them, Sarah," he broke in. Richard knew as well as anyone that in a buyout, the contract was only a small part of the process. Nerves weighed at least as heavily. "We'll adjust. Did you inform Ben?"

"Yes, it's on his updated schedule. And I've arranged for a half-dozen rooms at The Chesterfield, since that's where Mr. Leedmont is staying."

"Excellent. Thank you for the heads-up, Sarah. Please e-mail me the latest list of attendees, and send it on to Donner's office, as well."

He shut the phone off and thunked it onto the table, swearing under his breath.

"What's wrong?" Samantha asked.

"Leedmont's up to something. He's flying the rest of his board in a day early, and he's moved up the meeting to tomorrow."

"But isn't this *your* meeting?"

"Apparently I was informed of the schedule change."

She snorted. "This is one of those alternate reality problems, I bet. Happens all the time in *Star Trek*."

Of course nothing like a schedule change would faze her. "Mm-hm."

"On the other hand, maybe Leedmont just wants them to be able to enjoy the nice Florida weather."

"Your other theory's better."

"Thanks. So move the meeting back where it was."

"I can't. That would mean that I'm petty and I can't handle him." He wondered briefly whether she knew anything helpful, but refrained from asking. She'd said she would let him know if her work affected his. Richard blew out his breath. "I should just write off the whole bloody thing. We could go fishing instead."

"Ooh. Fishing." She shook her head. "I pulled you too far into my mess and distracted you when you've got your own deal working. I'm sorry."

"Nobody pulls me anywhere I don't want to go. Not even you. Truth be told, I'm just not that interested in it. It's a good investment, but plastic pipe fittings don't really—how do you Yanks put it?—float my boat."

"So you power through it and look for something that interests you more for the next time," she stated, her face surprisingly serious. "Don't you? I mean, what would Rick Addison do if suddenly he just didn't like his line of work anymore?"

He took her fingers. "Is this about me, or about you?"

Samantha shrugged. "I don't know. You're bored about a meeting that could net you eight million bucks, and I have your business rival and a nonpaying dead guy for clients. Maybe we should move to Detroit and sell auto parts."

Laughing, Richard kissed her delicate thief's fingers. "Now that would be boring. Even with you for a partner."

She sighed deeply. "I suppose you're right. Okay. I'm going in to work. What's on your new and improved schedule?"

"I'd best finish the contract revisions so Tom's office can put together our proposal, and I've got a little work to do on Patricia's project."

"Great. Just remember, I suggested auto parts." With a nod she started to her feet, swiping her soda as she went.

Richard hooked an arm around her waist and pulled her back across his lap. "Let's go out to dinner tonight. You choose the place."

"You have a big meeting tomorrow now."

"I'll manage. I want to go to dinner with you."

"That's better than fishing, anyway." She cupped his cheek with her free hand and kissed him. "It's a date. And can I borrow the Mustang again? Stoney's still got the Bentley."

He was about to suggest that Ben drive her to work, but Ben needed to head for Miami to pick up the Leedmont board of directors. "Certainly. Just don't scratch it."

"You never said that about the Bentley."

"The Bentley's yours. I'm not giving over my man car to anyone."

She laughed. Hugging him, she licked the curve of his ear. "Too bad Reinaldo's here," she whispered. "You would get *so* lucky right now."

She bounced off his lap and vanished down the hall, still laughing. Grimacing, Rick went back pretending to read the *Journal* until he could stand without embarrassing himself.

There was no sign of the Bentley when Samantha pulled into the parking structure. She put the Mustang into park, but stopped her hand halfway to turning off the car. What was she going to do here at her office, anyway? Sift through receptionist applications? For all she knew, Stoney had already hired somebody. Orchestrate a marketing campaign? Ooh, that was good. Maybe she could find a tactful way to advertise that her first potential client had actually been murdered the day before he'd hired her, and that she handled hooker blackmail on the side.

"Fuck," she muttered, yanking Daniel Kunz's business card out of her pocket. She needed to get all of this resolved before she could move on to mundane things like ordering her own business cards. And there was that damned word again. *Mundane*.

It took five rings before the connection went through. "This had better be important," Daniel's gravelly, annoyed voice came.

Oops. She'd forgotten it was barely eight o'clock. "Hi, Daniel. It's me, S—"

"Hey," he interrupted, his voice sharpening. "Give me a number, and I'll call you back in five."

She gave him the number and hung up. Hm. No names

from his end. The name "Sam" wasn't all that suspicious—unless the other person he didn't want to include in the conversation knew who "Sam" was. So Daniel and Patricia were sleeping together. And Daniel was making a play for her, at the same time. "Slime."

She took the five minutes to call Castillo.

"Did you go to the wake?" Frank asked as soon as the call connected.

"Didn't you?"

"Yeah, right. Anything interesting?"

"How come I could just walk into Charles's office at Coronado House?" she returned. "Did you run out of yellow tape?"

"Hey, if it was up to me the whole house would be covered with crime scene tape. But it's not, and Forensics pulled all the prints and took all the photos they needed. So is that why you're calling me? To make fun of my tape distribution?"

"If anybody in the family sells something of Charles's now, is that okay?"

"Technically not. It's a murder investigation; and even if it wasn't, insurance has the assets impounded. Lots of hands want a piece of his pie. Why?"

She wasn't about to mention the BMW, especially if it warned Daniel that she was snooping in his direction. Samantha narrowed her eyes. "I have a hunch about something. If it happens, I'll let you know. But which hands are you talking about?"

"Sam, if you know some—"

"Frank, which hands?"

"Christ. I liked it better when you weren't calling me. Pretty much the usual—a sister and her family, two business partners, and his kids."

"Two business partners?"

"Yep. Nobody's been ruled out but . . . well, between you and me, they just want their business assets unfrozen."

Maybe so, but whether her money was on Daniel or not, she wasn't turning her back on anyone. "Okay. Thanks."

"Sam, I expect you to tell me if you know any—"

She hung up on him. That was the problem—in her line of work, there wasn't that much difference between knowing and suspecting. Frank, though, required pesky things like evidence.

The Bentley rolled in beside her. "Okay," Stoney said as he climbed out of the car, "I can kind of see why you like tooling around in one of these."

"Ha!" she chortled. "I told you so. How are you going to go back to the crapmobile after this?"

"Maybe I'll take a look around for something," he admitted, leaning into the open passenger window of the Mustang. "But it's gonna be a little less showy. Maybe a Lexus."

"That's a start," she conceded. "Hey, get in here for a sec."

He complied, climbing into the Mustang and closing the door, then manually rolling up the window. He knew the game. No sense letting any of their legitimate business neighbors overhear their private conversations.

"What's up now? I'm not pretending to be Addison's butler again."

"Nothing like that. Has anybody called you about the Giacometti?"

"Nope. No sculpture, and no paintings."

Damn. She hoped she hadn't scared the thief off. At least he hadn't seen her face—but she hadn't seen his, either. "Okay. If—"

Her phone rang. Five minutes on the dot. Samantha's heart thudded a little as she answered. The old adrenaline rush. "Hello?"

"Sam," Daniel's voice came. "I thought you might be calling."

"Oh," she returned, injecting coyness into her tone, "and why is that?"

He chuckled. "Did the Brit burst a blood vessel when he saw us together?"

"No, I think he believed the story about the Giacometti. So did you have anything special in mind, or did you just want to know if I would call?"

"That depends," he returned, all smooth charm. "How do you feel about boats?"

Boats. Boats meant water, which meant isolation and sharks and drowning and not the remotest chance of escape. It was bad enough that Rick kept trying to talk her into going deep sea fishing. "I like cars better."

"Well, you'll like this boat. Meet me at the Sailfish Club docks, slip thirty-eight, in half an hour."

"I'm not—"

"Come on, Sam. I'll be a perfect gentleman. Let me dazzle you with my charm and good looks."

"All right. Half an hour."

"What the hell was that?" Stoney demanded as she returned the phone to her belt.

"I'm following a hunch." At the Sailfish Club. Interesting.

"A hunch about whom?" he asked distinctly, disapproval written all across his broad face.

"Daniel Kunz," she returned. Keeping secrets from Stoney was both counterproductive and potentially dangerous—if she did vanish, someone needed to know where she'd gone.

"I saw his picture in the paper the other morning," Stoney said, gazing out the front window. "He's not bad-looking."

"Oh, come on. It's just business, and you know it."

"*I* may know it, but I notice that you took that phone call here and not at Rick's."

"Why make waves when I'm just trying to get a peek below the surface? Now get out of the car. I have to go to the pier."

He didn't budge. "I don't like this, Sam. You should tell Addison or somebody."

"Why? What possible difference would it make?"

"It would make a difference."

As far as her safety was concerned, she'd told the person she needed to, but she knew what Stoney meant. For a guy who'd never been married, he had a pretty good handle on relationships. "Fine. I'll drop in and tell Donner," she decided. Then if the attorney ratted her out to Rick, at least she'd already be on the boat.

"Okay." He pushed his door open again and climbed out of the Mustang. "And by the way, are we ever going to hire a receptionist?"

"I thought maybe—Yes. Just keep . . . doing what you're doing, and I'll be back on track in a couple of days. I made 10K last night. I just have to call Leedmont and pick up the check."

"As long as we're making some money, then. I won't even point out that 10K's chump change for you."

"Thanks," she said dryly.

"Just don't get killed working for the dead guy." Shaking his head, he left the parking garage. Sam drew a breath, then followed, though she headed across Worth Avenue to the glass and chrome building housing Donner, Rhodes and Chritchenson. She wasn't surprised that the Boy Scout would be at work already, but she was surprised that he agreed to see her without delay.

"What did you do now?" he asked, making a show of lounging behind his big mahogany desk.

"Nothing."

"Right. You're here socially."

It was tempting to argue with the lawyer just on principle, but she only had twenty-five minutes before she was supposed to be at slip 38. "I'm going on a boat with Daniel Kunz," she said, folding her arms across her chest. "I'm only telling you in case something happens to me, so Rick won't wonder where I disappeared to."

" 'On a boat with . . .' " he repeated, straightening a little. "What the hell for?"

"Because he invited me."

"That's a pile of sh—"

"I think he might have had something to do with his dad's death, or at least with the robbery. So tattle on me if you think it's necessary, but I just wanted somebody Rick trusts—somebody I . . . trust, to know."

"Wow. I bet that hurt."

"Shut up, Yale. Don't you have some contract work to do for Rick?" She pushed away from the window and headed for the door again. "The board's flying in early, and that meeting's Saturday, now."

"He already called me. I'm not the one who's distracted," he retorted.

"Rick's pretty focused. If he wasn't, it would probably be because somebody keeps tattling to him about his girlfriend's whereabouts when she's investigating a murder." *So there.*

"I've only got Rick's best interests in mind."

She stuck her tongue out at him. "So do I." With that she slipped back into the main office and out to the elevators.

Okay, so it was both Rick's and her own best interests she had in mind. And maybe they were occasionally at cross purposes. This morning, though, with the limited amount of time she had to figure it out, just doing what she did best seemed the logical course of action. Even if that something included Daniel Kunz and a boat.

Fourteen

Samantha parked the Mustang at the Sailfish Club at the edge of Lake Worth and found slip 38 without any problem. Daniel stood on the pier waiting for her, a picnic basket in one hand. She looked past his shoulder toward the water.

"That's not a boat," she stated, pushing away the memory of her shark dream the other morning. She'd already changed LeBaron's ring tone.

He laughed. "Technically, it's a yacht. A small one. Watch your step," he said, offering her a hand to help her over the railing.

She could have made it over the railing with her eyes closed, but Daniel obviously liked to show off, so she took his hand and made a dainty jump on board. "What's it called?"

"She," he amended, climbing aboard himself, "is called *The Destiny*."

"Nice. Yours, or the family's?"

"Mine now, or it will be as soon as the paperwork goes through. Dad bought it for me, mostly."

Had that been impatience in his voice? That pesky homicide investigation might be delaying his plans. She'd keep that in mind. "Because you race them?"

"Because I win. Like I said, she's small, but she's got a big engine."

"Ah. Just the way I like 'em."

"Good." With a charming smile, he set down the basket and headed up the ladder to the small bridge. "Can you untie that line at the bow?" he asked, gesturing.

"Sure. That's the front, right?"

"Yes, it's the front."

So far, so good. The more ignorant she could be, the more he could talk and be the big man on campus—or on yacht, rather. As she untied the heavy line she automatically noted where all the life preservers on deck were and surreptitiously kicked the box in the bow labeled RAFT. It felt solid enough. Locked, but that wasn't a problem.

Even knowing where all the emergency gear was didn't leave her feeling any better. On land she could always find a way out in case of trouble. On the water that proposition was much more complicated. Planes or boats—both left her feeling distinctly uneasy.

"Come on up," Daniel said as the yacht rumbled away from the pier.

With a deep breath, Sam climbed the narrow ladder to join him. "This is nice," she lied, resting a hand on the console to steady herself. "How often do you go out?"

"As often as I can." He glanced at her. "Rick's got a yacht here. Don't you go out with him?"

"He's never asked me. I don't even know where it's parked."

Daniel chuckled again. "Berthed, you mean. That's it, actually, right there."

He pointed at the gleaming white yacht tied to one of the neighboring piers. It was easily the largest boat at the club, and probably on all of Lake Worth, dwarfing the sailboats around it. Unlike *The Destiny*, it had obviously been built for luxury rather than for speed. "Do you know its—her—name?"

"It used to be *The Britannica*," he returned, "but he had it rechristened a couple of weeks ago."

"Really?"

Daniel nodded. "Mm-hm. To *The Jellicoe*."

She blinked. "The what?"

"You didn't know?"

"He didn't tell me."

"If I named a yacht after someone, I'd tell them."

"So would I." Well, that was interesting, but it certainly wasn't the topic she'd come aboard to discuss. And out on the water she wasn't going to lose her focus. "Why did you give me your number the other day," she asked slowly, "when you knew Rick had named his yacht after me?"

"Because I saw you looking at me when Patricia introduced us, and then you were looking at me again when you made her drag you to Coronado House with that lame excuse about the wake decorations." He turned away, angling the yacht under the bridge and into the open water of the Atlantic Ocean. "And then at the wake I was watching *you*. As soon as somebody started talking to Rick, you left him. I thought you might have been looking for me."

Maybe, but not for the reasons he thought. "You're pretty sure of yourself."

He pushed the throttle forward, and the boat accelerated. "I know what I like," he said flatly.

At least they seemed to be heading up the coast rather than straight out to sea. "And what is that?" she purred, wishing she'd added swimming laps to her exercise regimen.

"First tell me: Is it true that your father was Martin Jelli-coe, the cat burglar?"

"It's true."

"Did *you* ever steal from anyone?"

So that was it. He wanted a confession from her to put them on more even footing—not that he'd confessed to do-ing anything. Yet.

"I might have," she returned, covering her reluctance with a smile.

"What was it like?"

"I don't like to air my sins in public," she said, putting a hand on his arm.

He gave her that charming smile again. "Come on, you can trust me. I like sin."

"I'll bet you do. If I show you mine, you have to show me yours."

"We'll see. I told you I'd be a perfect gentleman today."

Pushing him harder would put him on the defensive. And luckily she had stories to spare even if she needed to get spe-cific; the statute of limitations had run out on some of her jobs, after all. "All right. It's a rush. Pure adrenaline."

"I get that," he said, grinning into the wind. "I extreme ski. It's wild."

For a while they talked about skiing and yacht races, mostly so he would get comfortable with bragging and shooting off his mouth while she listened and made admir-ing sounds. After about twenty minutes he began heading closer to the shore, easing them in toward a small inlet.

"Between you and me, you still do it, don't you?" he asked abruptly. "Steal things."

For a brief second Sam wondered whether he was doing some investigating of his own. Did he think *she'd* killed Kunz? That would make him totally innocent, though, and she didn't believe that in any of her deeply suspicious bones. More likely he was hunting for a potential scapegoat in case something should go wrong. In that case, he was looking at the wrong girl. "Not for a long time. It's not good for my health."

He nodded, throttling down. "I get that, too. Busted my leg in three places my last time in Vail. Good thing there're other ways to get the rush." Daniel sniffed, pinching his nose.

Great. It could be a motive for the robbery, though. Samantha forced a laugh. "That's what I hear, but I think stealing's easier on the wallet." She looked at the shoreline. "Pretty. Where are we?"

"My private lunch and recreation spot."

"Mm-hm. Do you and Patricia come here?"

Daniel ran a strand of her windblown hair through his fingers. "I'm here with you."

She allowed the caress, but figured that it gave her a little more room to push. "Maybe I'm getting too personal, but your dad was killed during a robbery. I expected you wouldn't be that thrilled with taking a thief, former or not, to lunch."

"This is about attraction, not my dad," he returned, using both hands to play with her hair now.

He leaned in and kissed her. She allowed that, too. "Hey, I thought you were being a gentleman today," she said, pushing him slowly away. It took more control than she expected to make the gesture seem reluctant. Pretty face or not, he made her skin crawl. Rick said she had her own sense of honor, unconventional or not, and Daniel was treading all over it.

"What about attraction? I know you feel it."

"Maybe I do." Sam gave him an assessing look. "But honestly, Daniel, I need more than a boat ride to convince me that you can do more for me than Rick Addison can."

"Man, you're mercenary," he said, laughing again.

She could say the same thing about him, though she kept her commentary to herself. Considering that he'd attended a funeral day before yesterday, he seemed in quite the good mood, in fact—as if he thought he'd gotten away with murder or something. Had easygoing Daniel done it, though, or had he hired somebody? She would love to know whether he'd rented a BMW. "I'm just practical."

"Fair enough."

He released the anchor into the water and shut off the engine. The absolute lack of concern with which he viewed her presence, considering she could easily have been involved in his father's demise, actually shook her a little. It wasn't exactly an admission of guilt on his part, but if he was already *that* sure she hadn't done it, it was because he knew who *had*. Sliding down the short ladder, he picked up the picnic basket and set it on the small, built-in table on deck.

"Hungry?"

"Sure. What've you got?"

"It's a little early for lunch, so I had the cook pack mostly fruit and bread and cheese. And a bottle of wine, in case it's not too early for that."

"My goodness," she drawled, joining him, "someone might almost think you're trying to impress me."

"You're already impressed, or you wouldn't be here. Patricia calls you the American mutt, but I figure you've got more sophistication than most women I know."

"Thanks, I think."

"No, really. Patricia wouldn't know a piece of art from a piece of toast. She knows fashion, but that's about as deep as it gets."

"And you like deep?"

"I like that you're deep." Daniel set out a plate with grapes and orange slices, motioning her to sit as he took the bench opposite her. "So what do you do for fun?"

"For fun. I'm starting a security business, but you already know that."

"You have one of those phones that has different rings for different people, don't you? Does it help you keep your clients straight?"

So he wanted to know about her phone. That wasn't good. "I keep my phone on vibrate." She grinned. "I like it that way."

"I bet. So if my dad had hired you, what would you have done to protect Coronado House?"

"I haven't really thought about it," she lied. "It does work out better for me that he was killed before we signed a contract, doesn't it?"

"Come on," he cajoled. "You can speculate, can't you? More video cameras? Motion sensors? Some of those infrared beams?"

"What does it matter? It's too late now."

"Yeah, but that guy knew right where he was going, how to get in, where my dad was, how to get out. Do you think any of that technical shit would have stopped him?"

Christ. Now he was fishing for compliments. She looked him in the eye. "No. He was too good. The best I've seen, from what I can tell. Do the police have any clues?"

"Not a one. If he's that good, maybe you know him." He popped a grape into his mouth. "Maybe he's famous."

Was she reading too much into the conversation because she wanted him to be guilty? Was he really pushing his luck as far as she suspected? "*I* wasn't that good," she lied, looking down and feigning disappointment or shame or something that would make him feel even more superior.

"I bet you could hang with the big boys, Sam. I'd let you hang with me."

She looked up again, smiling. "Are you one of the big boys?"

He leaned closer, to whisper into her ear. "The biggest."

Samantha chuckled. "And wealthy, too. You *are* starting to look better and better."

Daniel angled his head toward the belowdeck hatch. "So do you want to fool around?"

At least he'd asked, instead of just jumping on her. She wasn't sure she could drive the damned boat back on her own. "I'm still not entirely convinced."

He stood. "Okay, but I'm going down to freshen up. I'll be right back."

"I'll be here, enjoying the view."

As Daniel disappeared through the squat door, Samantha sat back. Given her suspicions, she'd expected him to be more defensive and considerably more evasive. Of course, she hadn't expected that he would be high; that made reading him both easier and more difficult. Quickly she opened her phone and set it to vibrate—not that she had any idea if anybody could reach her out here.

She glanced toward the hatch. He was probably getting higher right now—which could explain his pressing need for cash and his assumption that he would get away with murder. Had Charles doted on him, as Rick had claimed? It would be difficult to prove. Families, especially wealthy ones, tended not to advertise their internal problems. She needed to get a look at Charles's legal documents to see whether Daniel's funds had been restricted for any reason.

A quick, hard beat of excitement ran through her. All she needed was a little proof, and she could go to Castillo. And best of all, turning in Daniel would be hugely different from turning in one of her former compatriots. No torn loyalties, no risk of reprisals.

Of course she still had to get back to shore intact and then find a way to get a look at those documents. And finding the paintings and the rubies would definitely help. Samantha sighed. Apparently she was going to have to make nice with Tom Donner again.

When Daniel emerged into the sunlight again his smile was even broader—and he actually had a small streak of powder on his upper lip. Daniel Kunz was either really clever, or really arrogant and stupid.

"You missed a spot," she noted, pointing at his lip.

With a sheepish chuckle, he ducked his head to wipe his nose clean. "So, where were we?"

"You were about to say that you've done some naughty things in your life, and that you would invite me to join you on the next one."

"Yeah," he agreed, nodding as he reached for the bottle of wine. "We could be like the modern Bonnie and Clyde. We'd be so hot together."

"I imagine we would. You make an interesting proposition."

He handed her a glass of wine and took one, himself. "Here's to interesting propositions."

She took a swallow. *And to interesting conclusions.* "So tell me how you learned to race yachts."

Rick pulled into the small parking lot outside Paradise Real Estate at five minutes before ten. Laurie drove a BMW, and there was no sign of it yet, so he shut off the SLR's engine and called Tom.

"Donner," the attorney answered after one ring.

"Tom, did you get the e-mail I sent?"

"Rick." Silence. "Yeah, it's right here. Are you coming in today?"

"This afternoon. I have something to take care of, first."

"Okay. No problem. We'll have the updated pages ready for you."

Richard actually held the phone away from his ear and looked at it. "You remember that the board's coming in early," he said after a moment. The way Tom obsessed over details, he should have been close to hysterics right then.

"You only called me an hour ago. We'll be ready. I'll talk to you la—"

"What's going on, Tom?" he interrupted.

"Nothing's going on. We're just busy."

"Is something bothering you? I told you I'd be ready for this."

"I know." More silence. "'Bye."

The line went dead. Something was definitely up. In fact, he couldn't remember the last time Tom had hung up on *him*. He moved to hit the redial button, but a gleaming silver BMW pulled to a stop beside him. Shit. All right, he'd figure out what was bothering Tom later. It wasn't as if he had nothing else to accomplish today.

"Laurie," he said, stepping out of his car to hold her door open for her. "Thank you for returning my call. I know this is short notice."

"Don't worry; I'll make sure you pay for it down the line." She took his hand, holding it rather than shaking. "Let's take my car. I've got all the maps and printouts."

With a nod he went around to her passenger door and slid in. He would have preferred to drive, but if driving made her feel more in command of the situation, he had no problem with it. Especially since he had more on his mind than real estate.

"So, Rick—you don't mind me calling you Rick, do you?"

"Not at all."

"So, Rick, why didn't you approach me day before yesterday to arrange a showing?"

"You seemed to have enough on your plate. I wouldn't have disturbed you for business."

"Business is business," she said as they turned out onto the street and headed south. "There's always time for it."

That used to be his motto, until he'd met Samantha. His work ethic had slid into a definite secondary position, though he hadn't realized it until lately. And it didn't bother him nearly as much as he'd expected it to, or nearly as much as it would have a year ago.

Richard sent Laurie a sideways glance as she checked her mirror. He knew how to use people, to manipulate them into seeing his point of view, and he'd never lost any sleep over that fact. He did it the way some people were doctors and others were mechanics. And he happened to do it very well. Today he meant to use those skills to figure out whether Laurie Kunz had had anything to do with her father's death. He'd been raised in the elite circle of which she was a part. Those people used money as a weapon. He had a shitload of ammunition.

The question was how hard to push. His own parents had died when he was still a teenager, but even half a continent away at a boarding school in Switzerland and separated from them for nearly a year, he hadn't felt equal to any kind of task at all for several weeks. The fact that Laurie was out making real estate deals this morning didn't make her guilty, but it did make him suspicious.

"My condolences again on the loss of your father," he offered.

"Thank you. It's been difficult, but Daniel and I are coping."

"The two of you have always been quite close, haven't you?"

"We try. It seems like the older we get, the more our interests diverge." She signaled, turning left into a cozy tract of two-story houses. As she steered past a street game of soccer, she smiled. "Don't worry; I'm not showing you one of these. There're some custom homes on the hill."

"I trust you."

"Speaking of which, you're not thinking of selling Solano Dorado, are you? Because I'd be very hurt if you didn't let me handle the sale."

"No, no. I promised a friend I'd help her relocate to this area."

" 'A friend,' " Laurie repeated. "Would it bother you if I mentioned that I personally wouldn't be . . . sad if you were to end up single again? Not that I wish your relationship with Miss Jellicoe ill, of course."

He sent her another glance, making sure she saw it this time. "I'm flattered."

Laurie smiled again. "Good."

The houses along the crest of the hill were several degrees above those they overlooked. In addition they all seemed to have nice views of the ocean. Large yards, good for entertaining, and a half-dozen rooms, large foyers, and grand curving staircases. He made mental note of everything as they toured the homes she'd selected, but kept his focus on the realtor. The more he could get her to talk, the more he would find out.

"Are you going to keep Coronado House?"

"I'm sure we will. Dad was very fond of it."

Kunz had also been killed in that same house, but Richard didn't mention that. "You and Daniel both?" he continued instead.

She looked at him sideways as she showed him out of the house they'd just finished touring. "We'll stay together unless I get a better offer. What do you think?"

Her. Not Daniel. "What do I think?" he repeated. Of the house?"

"All right."

He grinned back at her. "I'm thinking something more intimate. A condo—in a high rise. A yard would be at the bottom of the list." Patricia would require a home where *she*
could be the centerpiece. A garden would just be wasted
space where she would complain about the cost of hiring
someone to maintain the landscaping. But this outing had
not been about his ex-wife as much as it was about Laurie
and his impression of her.

"I have two on my list that might suit," Laurie said, not con-
sulting her notes; she would have every listing memorized.

"Let's take a look," he returned, gesturing her back to the
car. "If you have time."

"I have time for you." They headed back down the hill.

"I should buy you lunch, then, for your trouble."

"It's no trouble, Rick, but lunch would be great."

He nodded. "How about the Blue Anchor Pub in Delray
Beach?"

"That's the pub that came from England, isn't it?"

"Transported stone by stone. There's even supposed to be
a two-hundred-year-old London ghost there. A murderess or
some such thing." Actually, Bertha was reportedly a murder
victim, but the other depiction fit his purposes better.

"Ooh, spooky. It's a date." Laurie didn't bat an eye. If she
was a murderess herself, she was a cool-headed one.

"Good." Perhaps a word like "murderess" hadn't bothered
her, but it was all part of the test.

"You haven't mentioned what you think of Daniel and Patricia," she said conversationally.

Richard kept his gaze on the road, but just barely. If he
hadn't had nearly twenty years of practice at hiding his
thoughts and feelings, he wouldn't have made it. *Daniel
and Patricia*? Abruptly a few things made sense. That was

why Samantha had chosen to use Patricia to get into the Coronado estate. Which meant that Samantha *knew*, damn her. "I didn't think it was any of my affair," he said smoothly.

"That's very . . . British of you, I guess. I was surprised to hear your voice on my answering machine, though. Your ex-wife and my brother are boffing, and aside from that, Patricia seems to think that you have some sort of vendetta against her."

"She flatters herself."

"Ah. *Now* you sound annoyed."

He laughed. "What's annoying is people dwelling on the past. There's no profit, personally or in business, in looking behind you."

"I'd like to think I'm a forward-looking gal, myself."

Nodding, Rick turned his gaze out the window, though every ounce of his attention was on the woman in the driver's seat beside him. "I've noticed that people who spend too much time in the past tend not to have a plan for the future."

"We seem to have a great deal in common." Laurie chuckled. "You know, I always wondered why you didn't ask me out after one of those charity polo matches you and Daniel love so much."

He nearly had once, a few months after his divorce. She was what had once been his type: attractive, self-assured, and used to being in the public eye. "You always had someone else attending with you," he returned.

"As if that would have stopped you."

That had been precisely what stopped him. He would never touch another man's woman. That was one stricture he'd had even before the stickiness with Patricia and Peter. It was that sense of fidelity that he, and Samantha— surprisingly, given her haphazard lifestyle—believed in.

Given Laurie's participation in his pseudo-flirtation, she didn't seem as particular.

"Will your business concerns change at all with your father gone?" he asked, curving back to his topic of choice.

She shrugged. "Almost everything was put into a trust last year. Daniel and I have some decisions to make, and depending on what comes of it, I may divest myself of Paradise Realty." Laurie sent him a smile. "Not before I've found the ideal property for you, of course. My clients never leave unsatisfied."

"I don't doubt it. But what would you do if you gave up your business?"

"Spoken like a true workaholic. I'd travel, I think, and my dad's business would be more than enough to keep me occupied."

"Charles would like that you're willing to take over for him, I'd wager."

"It would be stupid to let all of his work and connections fall into the hands of the sharks."

He wondered if she would consider him a shark. As for what she was, he had a few ideas. Most people clung to the familiar in the face of tragedy and upheaval. Laurie was already considering changing careers. To Richard, that said she wasn't all that fond of the real estate business. On the other hand, lack of satisfaction with a profession didn't make anyone a murderer. Still, he meant to find a way to go through some of her business records.

By the time they'd finished looking through the two condos, Richard thought he'd found an acceptable residence for Patricia, but he meant to keep the search going a bit longer, anyway. While he'd discovered a few more things about Laurie Kunz, nothing definitively pointed toward her as a suspect in her father's murder. What he did have was a split-ting headache, something that he assumed James Bond would never confess to.

But he didn't intend to end this meeting empty-handed. Samantha wouldn't be wasting time, and he—and the police—had a wager to win. "Is Daniel planning on joining you in the boardroom?"

"I doubt it," she returned easily. "Business doesn't interest him very much."

"It's a good thing he has you, then."

"Ha. Tell him th—"

His phone rang, in Tom's four-tone signal. "Yes?" he answered as he flipped it open.

"Okay, I can't stand it anymore," the attorney's voice came. "Jellicoe went boating with Daniel Kunz."

The breath froze in Richard's throat. "Beg pardon?" he returned, keeping his expression perfectly still.

"She came in this morning and told me, then dared me to rat her out. But I don't want to get blamed for not telling you if something happens, and I don't want to be caught in the middle of your little whirlwind, so I—"

Rick snapped the phone closed. "My apologies, Laurie," he said easily, "but I'll need to reschedule our lunch. Would you mind driving me back to your office?"

She smiled. "No problem. I'm available any time. And I want to know more about the ghost."

"Let's do this again on Tuesday. Ten o'clock?"

"It's a date."

Fifteen minutes later they pulled up beside his SLR and Richard left the BMW. With a wave, Laurie backed out of the lot again and vanished in the direction of Coronado House. Richard closed himself inside the SLR and sat very still for half a minute. Then he pushed in the key, pushed the start engine button, and headed toward the Sailfish Club.

Samantha helped tie the yacht back to the dock, then blew Daniel a kiss as she headed back up toward dry land and her car. He stayed on board, ostensibly to polish something, but she figured the boat was probably where he generally went to powder his nose. Tension ran through her shoulders as she reached the parking lot. He hadn't been threatening, hadn't done more than kiss her once and make a few naughty suggestions, and she still felt as though she'd made a narrow escape from a shitted-up burglary.

"Samantha," Rick's low voice came from in front of her, and she lifted her head. The gull-winged SLR was parked right next to the red Mustang, and Rick Addison leaned against the bumper.

"Fucking great," she muttered, mustering a smile. "Hi."

"You went out on the water with Daniel Kunz?" he asked, straightening.

"Are you chasing me around town, now? Because that's not going to work."

"Tom ratted you out."

She shook her head, not even surprised. "I knew Captain Tight-Ass wouldn't be able to resist telling you."

"Then why'd you tell him?"

"Because I'm not an idiot." She stopped in front of him, trying to gauge his mood. "Are you going to kiss me or shoot me?" she finally asked.

"I really don't know." He reached out and straightened her sleeve. "Did you know that Daniel is seeing Patricia?"

"Yes."

"And you didn't tell me because . . ."

Samantha squinted one eye at him. "And when did you name your yacht *The Jellicoe*?"

He blinked. "Don't change the sub—"

"Some guys tattoo their girlfriend's names on their arms and shit. You named a boat after me."

"I don't like tattoos."

Unable to help herself, she smiled. "You're so damned cool, Rick. I'm the biggest boat in the marina."

Rick blew out his breath. "What the hell am I supposed to do with you?" he murmured, taking her fingers and drawing her in close to kiss her.

She closed her eyes, relishing in the warm, intimate contact. "I'll tattoo your name on my fanny, if you'd like."

He made a choking sound that might have been laughter. "I don't want to see my name on your fanny. I don't need directions."

That was definitely true. With the memory of her morning fresh in her mind and the relief that Rick wasn't mad at her, she abruptly needed . . . She didn't know what, but Rick could provide it. She stepped forward and wrapped her arms around his shoulders, resting her head against his neck.

After a heartbeat his arms joined around her waist, and he pulled her tightly against him. "Are you all right?" he asked quietly.

She nodded, unwilling to let him—to let this moment—go. And Daniel thought he could offer her more than Rick could. Ha. Daniel didn't know the first thing she needed, or wanted. "Rick?"

"Mm-hm?"

"I think Daniel did it. I think he either hired someone, or did it himself."

"You— Fuck." He didn't ask her what proof she had, or

how she knew. Instead, he slid a hand up her back, rocking her slowly back and forth and letting her hold on for as long as she wanted to.

Finally Sam took a breath. *Pull it together, Jellicoe.* "Sorry," she muttered, lifting her head.

"For what?" He cupped her face in both hands. "I'm actually relieved. I was beginning to think the only thing we needed to worry about where you were concerned was Kryptonite."

"Oh, ha ha. I just wasn't ready for ocean travel with a probable murderer."

"Speaking of which, don't ever do that again, Samantha. Not even if you tell Donner first. Not unless you want me to have a heart attack before I hit thirty-five."

"No, I don't want that." She kissed him on the chin. "We should get out of here before Daniel sees us together."

He lifted an eyebrow even as he held open the Mustang driver's door for her. "And why don't we want him to see us together?"

"Because I'm sneaking out to see him behind your back, and he's working on seducing me away from you."

For a long heartbeat he didn't say anything. "Oh. He'd best be going to jail for something, then," he finally murmured. "Otherwise I will be, for beating the shit out of him."

She didn't bother telling him to keep his testosterone in check; she knew what his hot buttons were, and she knew that by his actions Daniel had pushed several of them. All the same, his response had felt almost . . . underheated. Sam took a quick breath. He'd taken her demand for a little trust seriously. Of course, even with a huge meeting tomorrow he'd still charged out to Lake Worth to check up on her, but she would have done the same for him. They both knew how dangerous their lives could get.

At the same time, it was a little frightening to realize how much she was coming to rely on him for his opinion, his advice, just his presence. She wasn't used to relying on anyone but herself. That was in the top five thieves' rules as taught by Martin Jellicoe. Never count on anyone but yourself. She'd begun to wonder, though, whether Martin had simply never met anyone he thought he *could* trust. She had.

"I'm going in to Tom's," he said, slowly letting his hands course down her shoulders.

"I need to get into the office, too, before somebody declares it abandoned and repossesses Stoney's furniture. And I need to figure out how I'm going to prove any of my hunches to Castillo. Proof sucks."

"Yes, my dear. But it's necessary if you want to win the wager." He kissed her again, then helped her into the car and closed the door for her.

That was Rick, always the British gentleman no matter what else might be going on. They were both headed for Worth Avenue, and she wasn't the least bit surprised when he fell in behind her and stayed within a car length or two for the entire drive. She thought she'd made it extremely clear that she knew how to take care of herself, but apparently his ancestors had been actual knights in shining armor—and Rick had obviously inherited their "rescue the damsel" mentality.

She crossed Olive Avenue, and Rick got stuck at the light. She half expected him to run the red, but he didn't. Today, at least, the knight was obeying the law.

The Mustang lurched forward as metal ground into metal. Samantha's forehead smacked hard into the steering wheel. "Shit!"

Dazed, she automatically put on the brake as she looked in the now-crooked rearview mirror. A big blue pickup filled the entire mirror. With a roar it shot toward the back end of the Mustang again.

Shoving down the accelerator, she made a hard right onto a small side street. The pickup clipped her right bumper and skidded around behind her.

Okay. This was on purpose. Her heart hammering more from adrenaline than fear, she punched it again. The Mustang had a V-12 engine, and the pickup had a hemi. A pretty even match, except that she wasn't going to let this turn into a chase.

She screeched a left turn, then another, heading back to the main street. As soon as the pickup driver figured out what she was doing he roared up onto her bumper again.

They connected, knocking her forward even when she braced against it. With only inches separating them, she slammed on the brakes.

The pickup thunked into her again. With all her strength she steered straight for a light pole. The pickup engine screamed as it tried to accelerate her into the metal post while she tried to stop.

Or not. Taking a breath, she waited until the last possible second, hit the accelerator, and spun the wheel left. The right side of the Mustang scraped into the pole and bounced off. The pickup slammed squarely into it.

Fishtailing wildly, Sam brought the Mustang to a limping stop. She jumped out and ran back to the truck. Whoever it was, they were getting their ass kicked.

"Hey!" she yelled, yanking at the dented driver door. "What the fuck are you—"

A baseball bat crashed through the tinted glass straight at her head. Instinctively she ducked the blow and the shower of safety glass, but just barely.

"You bitch!" a male voice roared. The door shoved open and Al Sandretti lunged toward her, bat swinging.

Samantha dodged sideways, aiming a kick at his groin. She hit a muscular thigh and he stumbled, grabbing at her foot. Jesus, he was big. If he got hold of her, he'd break her in half.

Neighbors were starting to emerge from their houses, though she noted their presence only enough to keep Schwarzenegger and the bat well away from them. Pissed as he was, she didn't think he would care who he swung at. "Come on, big boy," she taunted, backing along the street.

"Where are my fucking photos?" he roared. "You're fucking dead!"

She dodged again, looking for an opening and hoping someone was dialing 911. Her heel cracked into the curb and she went over backward. With a gasp she rolled sideways just as the bat dug into the parkway where her head had been.

Rolling onto her back again she pistoned both legs straight into his knees. He staggered back, spitting and grunting. Christ, the guy was built like a fucking tree stump.

Doing a backflip onto her feet, she jabbed at his face and nearly took a fist to the gut.

"Come on, bitch. Let's d—"

Sandretti stumbled forward onto his knees. Sam side-stepped as Rick backed up a few steps, then charged forward again with a flying kick and rammed both feet between big Al's shoulder blades. As the guy dropped, Rick followed up with two hard, quick jabs to his kidneys.

Sandretti groaned and started up on his hands and knees again. Sam kicked him in the side of the head. With a grunt he collapsed.

She bent over to take a breath. When she straightened,

Rick had the baseball bat clenched in both hands. His face was white and furious, and she didn't doubt for a second that he would bludgeon Sandretti into paste.

"Stop!" she gasped, grabbing his arms and forcing him backward with all her weight.

He moved about a step, but it got his attention. "He—What—Who the hell is that?"

"Al Sandretti."

"Is this because of Kunz?"

Sam shook her head, taking the bat out of his trembling hands. "It's part of the Leedmont thing."

As sirens approached, Rick touched her forehead. His fingers came away bloody. "I saw him hit your car," he said in a more even voice. "Christ. I thought—"

"Hey, I'm okay," she returned, taking his hand and clutching his fingers. "I have a hard head."

"And thank God for that." Abruptly his tense shoulders lowered, and he gathered her in for a tight hug.

"I broke your man car," she said, her voice muffled against his chest. She could feel the hard, fast beat of his heart against her cheek. He'd really been worried about her.

"*He* broke my man car," Rick amended, separating from her as the cops rolled up. "And he's going to fucking pay for it, the wanker. Do you want me to take care of this?"

He'd asked instead of jumping in. *Wow.* "No, I can deal."

By the time she finished explaining how she'd found a folder with some weird photos in it in the McDonald's parking lot and had been on her way to give them to Detective Castillo and how this guy must have seen her do it and panicked, she almost believed herself. It didn't hurt that she had the folder in her trunk to hand over, or that a bunch of the neighbors and Rick Addison could corroborate various parts of the story. She slipped the Leedmont photos under her shirt without anybody noticing, signed a statement, then climbed into the passenger seat of the SLR.

"Are you certain you're all right?" Rick asked, sliding behind the wheel. He feathered her hair behind her ear, and she shivered.

"I'm fine. A little headache, but I've had much worse." It was the last time she would take a car with personalized plates on a gig, though.

"I remember." He leaned over and kissed her, surprisingly gentle. "You actually went toe-to-toe with that brute."

"You told me not to scratch your car. He made me mad."

Rick smiled. "I love you."

She felt her cheeks warm. "And I'm glad you can do that karate flying kick thing. Take me to the office, will you?"

For a long moment he gazed at her before he nodded and put the SLR in gear. "Sure."

He let her off at the front steps, then headed for the parking structure. The Bentley was where Stoney had left it; at least he seemed to be serious about helping her, whatever his private reservations. Hell, he'd already logged more office time than she had.

"Hey," she called as she stepped into the reception room. "I'm back."

Stoney shoved open the hallway door to join her. "Good. What the hell happened to you?" He motioned at her head.

"Not much. I'll tell you later."

"Fine. I'm going to lunch."

"Sheesh. Was it something I said?"

"Nope. I have a lunch date. And I got a call on that Giacometti. I went ahead and scheduled a meeting for tonight."

She grabbed his arm to stop him. "Wait a minute. Who called?"

"I don't know. They used one of those Darth Vader voice

changers." He grinned. "Very James Bond—and very amateur."

The same guy who'd called Bobby, then. "Okay. We'll go over strategy when you get back."

"Like I don't know how to take in property of questionable origin."

"You're not—"

"See you later, honey."

Sighing, Sam headed back to her office to call Leedmont. Stoney had left her the dwindling pile of résumés and a small stack of phone messages, most of which said something along the lines of "I hadn't heard from you, so I accepted a job with fill-in-the-blank." Crap. Her desk had gone from mahogany to oak, and she was beginning to wonder whether it was safe to put her pencils away.

After she set up an early Saturday morning meeting with Leedmont, she started to go through the remaining applications again, weeding out the ones who had found work elsewhere, but after a minute or two she set it aside. Instead she picked up her desk phone and dialed Aubrey Pendleton.

"Hello, darlin'," he answered.

Samantha smiled at his tone. "Hi. Could I ask you a question?"

"Ask me for the moon and the stars, and I'll deliver them."

"You're in a good mood."

"A lovely lady just sent me a case of 1935 French wine."

"Wow, you must be a good date."

"Try me."

A little good-natured, nonserious flirting was good for her, especially after the surreal attempted seduction on the yacht and the pro wrestling match. "I might. But who asked you for the phone number?"

"The phone number? No one. I've been carrying it around

just in case, but it's been quiet. I must say, you've started a terrible craving for adventure in me. I'm not sure how I'll go back to being merely charming."

"I wouldn't call you 'merely' anything, Aubrey."

"Oh, you're making me blush. Oops, my date's on the other line. I have to go."

"Okay. Thanks."

So whoever had called Stoney hadn't gotten the number from Aubrey. It wasn't that surprising, she supposed; in the right circles, Walter Barstone had a reputation for being one of the best in the world. Through him she'd managed to make a nice-sized fortune, after all. And though he worked primarily with her, it wasn't an exclusive relationship. Not professionally, anyway.

She had some strands, now, but she needed to find a way to weave them into a web. And then she needed to catch a fly—a fly with a cocaine addiction, and who went by the name Daniel Kunz.

Fifteen

Friday, 7:17 p.m.

*B*y seven in the evening, Richard felt they'd nailed the contract. It was closer than he liked to cut things, but even if Leedmont intended some sort of preemptive strike, he'd still be ready. He left Tom wrapping up a few phone calls and headed across the street to pick up Samantha and see where she'd decided on for dinner.

The offices sharing the third floor seemed to have emptied out for the day, but when he tried Jellicoe Security's door, it turned and opened. "Samantha?" he called.

"In my office," her voice came from the back.

"You should lock this door when you're the only one here," he said, still shaken by that hug she'd given him at the pier, though the fight with Al Sandretti—whoever he was— had nearly driven her embrace from his mind.

"A locked door wouldn't even slow down most of the people I know," she returned, joining him in reception. "You hungry?"

She had a nice bruise on her forehead, which he brushed with his fingertips. "Starving."

Samantha grinned, wrapping her hand around his arm. "Well, do we go home and change, or pick a place suited to our current wardrobe?"

They were both in jeans and shirts, and in the middle of the winter season at Palm Beach, that meant their dining possibilities were severely limited. "That depends on what you're hungry for."

"If I told you what I was hungry for, we'd never make it out of the office," she returned, laughing. "But how about Mexican?"

"I'll rely on you."

He couldn't help mauling her in the elevator. If they'd descended more than three floors, he would have had her out of her pants. She could investigate all she pleased, but the more she put herself into danger, the more she flirted with other men to get information, the more he liked to remind her what waited for her at home.

"Randy much?" she joked, pushing him out of the elevator when they reached the lobby.

With a calm nod at the concierge he led the way through the side door to the parking garage. Patricia would have called such a display undignified. For her, everything had been about appearance. Samantha's concern was that admitting to liking him too much would somehow trap her, keep her from being the person she'd grown up to be. She'd loosened up her defenses over the past few months, and he wasn't going to give up until she realized he was an asset rather than a liability. Not when the alternative would mean losing her.

"What about the SLR?" Samantha asked, sliding behind the wheel of the Bentley. Thank goodness Walter was better at taking care of borrowed automobiles than she was.

He moved around to climb in beside her. "We'll pick it up later."

"You're so romantic. Can't spend a minute without me."

"Shut up and drive."

She kept her good mood all through dinner, even after recommending some sort of tomato and pepper salsa so spicy it nearly took off the roof of his mouth. Apparently that was some sort of American humor, but he didn't mind. He liked hearing her laugh. She hadn't done much of it since they'd returned to Florida.

"Are you okay for your meeting tomorrow?" she asked abruptly as they drove back to the parking garage. She had to be in a good mood, because she handed him the keys to the Bentley. "I can quiz you or something."

"It'd be nice to know what Leedmont was plotting, but I think I'll manage."

"Hm. Well, I'm meeting him first thing in the morning, so if he's got dynamite in his pockets, I'll let you know. Come on, let me quiz you. I probably know tons about pipe rings and fittings."

"I'm terrified."

Her phone rang, though he didn't recognize the tone. From her expression, she didn't recognize it or the number. *"Hola,"* she said.

He watched her face as her expression closed down and her skin went gray. Alarmed, he pulled to the side of the street and put the car into park. "Samantha."

When she held the flat of her hand out to stop him from talking, her fingers shook. Richard grasped her hand. Whatever was going on, he wanted her to know—if she didn't already—that she had his support.

"Okay. I'll handle it," she finally said. "Don't worry." Her voice broke as she slowly closed the phone.

"Sam?"

"That was Stoney. He's in jail."

"In—What happened?"

Samantha drew a breath, obviously working to pull herself together. "He couldn't say much, but about two minutes after he took possession of a Giacometti prototype, the cops rammed open his door."

Richard started to comment, then closed his mouth. He knew very well what both Walter and Samantha did for a living when they'd all met. And he would have to be very careful about what he said next. "I thought Walter retired when you did."

"He did. He was doing me a goddamned favor."

"You? Samantha, you promised me that y—"

"Shut up. I need to think for a minute."

Panic shoving into his chest, he grabbed her shoulder. "Are the police going to come after you for this?"

She looked at him so blankly for a heartbeat that he knew the answer before she spoke. "No. No. It's not like that. He wasn't even supposed to take it. I just needed to know who was trying to sell it to him. I told him . . ." She growled, slamming her fist against the dashboard. "It doesn't matter. I have to get him out of there."

For a brief moment he pictured her breaking into the city jail. "*We* will get him out," he countered, shaking her to make certain that sank in. "I'll call Tom right now."

What he didn't say was that he wasn't sure what the attorney would be able to do. Samantha had just said that Stoney had taken in some sort of stolen property. And he'd done that previously, too many times to count. If circumstances had simply caught up to him . . . From what Samantha had intimated on numerous occasions, Walter could be spending a very long time in prison.

Even as he dialed Tom, he was also considering that removing Walter Barstone from Samantha's life, painful as it would be for her, might also serve her for the better. He'd been trying to pull her away from her criminal past, and Walter obviously still had a pretty tight hold on her.

As Katie Donner answered the phone, Richard exited the car. It wouldn't do for Samantha to overhear his responses to whatever disparaging remarks Tom might make. The two of them had a tricky enough relationship as it was.

When he slipped back into the Bentley, she was sitting in the passenger seat, staring out the front window. This all had to hurt. She let so few people into her life, and Stoney was closer to her than anyone else. Maybe even than him.

"Okay. Tom said he'll—"

"I'm going to the police station. I have to bail him out."

"Wait a minute, Samantha. You need to listen to me."

She glared at him. "Why, so you can talk me out of something? Do you think I'm going to leave Stoney in jail for one second longer than I have to?"

"No, I don't. But I also think that before you charge into the police station, we should let Tom have a few minutes to find out what exactly Walter is being charged with. If the Giacometti has something to do with you, it's possible that whoever turned him in might have mentioned your name."

"I didn't steal it, Rick."

"I didn't suggest that you did," he retorted, though the thought had crossed his mind. "You know about it, though, which means someone else might know about you." He drew a breath, shuddering at the thought of what jail or prison would do to her. "In fact, maybe we should consider relocating back to London."

"No. I had to sit in the shadows and watch while Martin

got sent to prison for the rest of his life. He died there. I'm not abandoning Stoney." Her voice broke again. "I can't."

"You won't have to. Right now we need to go home, though, and wait for Tom's call."

She shook her head. "No. I need to look into some things." Before he could stop her, she'd opened the door and stepped onto the sidewalk.

"Samantha, for Christ's sake—"

"I'll call you. And give me the SLR keys, or I'll have to hot-wire it."

There were times as a businessman that he'd had to acknowledge defeat. He recognized this as one of them. Digging into his pocket, he found the Mercedes key and tossed it to her through the open door. "Be careful."

"I will."

For a minute she didn't think he would leave, but with a last concerned look he screeched back into the street.

Samantha walked three blocks to the parking garage and found the SLR. In less than an hour she could have Stoney out. It would mean pulling a gun, which she'd never done in her entire career, but she could do that. Getting into the station wouldn't be a problem, even for someone of much less skill than herself. Getting out would be more difficult, but she could do that too.

The part she wasn't sure about, the one thing that made her hesitate, was the knowledge that afterward she would have to run. She'd have Stoney, yes, but she wouldn't have Rick. She'd never have him again. Because even if he wanted her after the jailbreak, he was too public. People always knew where he was, and the second she tried to see him again she'd be arrested.

"Fuck," she muttered, bending to rest her forehead on the

steering wheel. She banged her head against the stretched leather, feeling the sharp stab of pain from her sore forehead. "Think, Sam. Think."

If Aubrey had supplied Stoney's phone number to anyone, this would have been simple. Whoever had contacted her fence, though, had found him on their own. Still, she'd only told one person about the probable value of the Giacometti. It had to be Daniel.

Why, though, had he set Stoney up? Was this to plant evidence for the robbery and murder? She lifted her head, ice drilling into her chest. Stoney's house wasn't exactly high security. Once someone found it, breaking in was kid's play.

Starting the Mercedes, she headed for the west part of town. Getting to Stoney's house took what was probably the longest twenty minutes of her life. When she turned the corner onto his street, though, she stopped. One, two, three police cars, lights spinning, cordoned off half the block.

"Shit." She flipped off her lights, backing up until she could turn down the cross street.

She'd been so obsessed with doing all of this investigating her own way that she'd left Stoney completely open and unprotected. Anybody who watched the office would know that they worked together, and anybody who'd researched her as well as Charles had would have deduced that she used Stoney as her fence. This was her fault. All of it.

"Okay, okay. Get it together." If this had been Daniel, then he knew he'd hurt her. He would be ready for it if she confronted him. Hell, he might even have set something up on his yacht that could incriminate her. She ran the morning through her mind. She'd had her hands on the wine bottle and a glass, plus railings and the windshield and the mooring line.

It felt selfish, worrying about her own skin while Stoney

was being booked and photographed and fingerprinted, but that was the nature of the game. Besides, if the cops were going to move on her, she needed to be ready for it.

And so did Rick. Dammit. He had a huge meeting tomorrow. All he needed was for Castillo or somebody else to interrupt with a search warrant. In his world, appearance was everything. Three months ago, she and he had more than ruined Peter Wallis's life with proof of murder and robbery; they'd ruined his business and his future—and his marriage.

The best, fastest, easiest place to get answers was still Stoney. And she'd meant what she'd told Rick—she wasn't leaving her friend in jail for a second longer than she had to.

With a deep breath, Sam put the car into gear. Rick probably still had a pistol in the glove box, but she would make him one concession—she'd try to do this legally, first. She exited the parking structure and turned left, heading for jail.

Halfway home Richard changed direction, and fifteen minutes later pulled into Tom Donner's driveway. He only pounded on the door twice before Tom yanked it open.

"Keep it down, will you, Rick?" he snapped, stepping aside. "Mike's got to be at school at seven in the morning for an away game."

"Apologies," he said, lowering his voice. Damn. And Samantha accused him of being too civilized. "What did you find out?" Richard headed toward the stairs and Tom's office.

"I'm working on it. I told you to go home, and I'll call you."

"I prefer to be more involved."

Tom entered the office behind him and closed the door. "That's not very comforting. I'm doing my best, okay? It's a Friday night, and honestly, my area of expertise is in reading and modifying contracts, looking for tax loopholes, and putting together corporation documents—not working for criminals or trying to find ways to get them released from jail."

Richard faced him, surprise cooling the heat in his veins. "So you pick now to stage your holier than thou rebellion?"

"I warned you before, Rick—I don't like digging into shit for Jellicoe. Now you're asking me to help get her fence out of jail, and twelve hours before the Kingdom meeting? What the hell's wrong with you?"

For a heartbeat Richard closed his eyes. He and Tom had been friends for better than ten years. And he understood what the attorney was questioning—whether he was willing to throw everything over for Samantha. "I understand your reservations," he said, keeping his tone even and quiet. "I understand that you're a straight shooter. Hell, that's why I hired you in the first place. But I'm not asking you to lie for Walter Barstone, or to do anything illegal on his behalf or anyone else's. I'm asking you to find out what's going on. That's all."

"I—"

"I could do it myself," he interrupted, stepping back toward Tom. "I will, if you won't. She loves him, all right? Consider Walter to be her father. I am not going to sit on my bum while she does God knows what to try to see him set free. I am going to know what's going on, and if it takes using some of my influence to aid him in either his bail or his defense, I will use it."

Tom folded his arms across his chest, not backing down. "Do you have any idea how much this could cost you? And I'm not talking about dollar figures, though eight million in one day comes to mind."

"I know. And as my attorney, I'm asking you to carry out my orders." He drew a breath. "As my friend, I'm asking you to do what you can to help me."

"Shit. Shit, shit, shit. I told you she was trouble. But did you listen to me? No, you went right ahead just like you always do and—"

"Before you say another word, you might want to consider it very carefully, Tom. You need to find a different song. That one's getting old."

Donner inflated like a puffer fish, then abruptly blew out his breath. "I've got five phone calls out, to the watch commander, the chief of detectives, the chief of police, the district attorney, and Judge William Bryson. This time, you will owe somebody a favor."

"I can live with that."

"Okay." Tom nodded. "Go home, Rick. I'm working on finding out exactly what Barstone was arrested for, and what the D.A. is going to charge him with. I will call you as soon as I know anything. I promise."

Every part of Richard rebelled against simply retreating somewhere and waiting for someone else to take action. On the other hand, he wasn't going to accomplish anything by invading the Donners' house and glowering. Uttering a quiet expletive, he brushed past the attorney and headed downstairs again. "As soon as you know anything," he repeated.

Sam sat in a metal chair behind a glass partition and waited. It was past visiting hours, but she'd stepped on every toe and charmed every ass she needed to in order to get a seat on that chair. Castillo would probably be pissed at the freedom with which she'd thrown his name around, but at heart she was a thief—and she would steal whatever she needed to, including the detective's name, to get what she wanted.

The door at the far end of the room opened and a sheriff emerged, Stoney beside him. Her throat tightened. He still wore his street clothes, but the belt with the loops was new, as were the two sets of handcuffs running through it. The sheriff guided him to the chair on the opposite side of the partition, then retreated to the doorway again.

"Did you set me up?" Stoney asked quietly, dark eyes on hers.

"What? No!" The words ripped from her throat. "How could you think that?"

"What am I supposed to think?" he hissed back. "You give me a job, cops bust down my door, evidence planted in my damned closet, how—"

"Stop!" she began, lowering her voice when the cop by the door stirred. "Stop. First, you weren't supposed to buy the sculpture; I just wanted to know who was selling. Second, th—"

"I didn't buy it. I went to the meet and nobody was there. So I went home to eat a sandwich."

"But the cops found the sculpture."

"Yeah, in my damned front closet."

She gazed at him, a half-dozen scenarios crowding through her skull. "You were set up."

"No shit. If it wasn't you—"

"Of course it wasn't."

He took a more even breath. "I really didn't think so, but I'm kinda pissed off right now. What about your boyfriend? I know he doesn't like me very much."

"Oh, for crying out loud. It wasn't Rick."

"But you know who did it, so spill."

"I think it was Daniel Kunz. Getting you accused would definitely take any heat off him. And it might be a warning to me, to back off."

"So I'm just the scapegoat. Great." He leaned forward an inch or so. "In that case, get me the fuck out of here, Sam."

She could see it in his eyes, behind the anger. He'd fenced

every job she and Martin had ever pulled. Even with just
one year for every caper, he was looking at forty plus years
in prison. And he knew it, and he was scared. "I'm trying,"
she muttered back, "but they've got a seventy-two hour hold
on you."

"I can't do this, Sam. Please, honey."

For a heartbeat she thought of the Glock in the car. She
could do it, but it wouldn't help. It might even be what
Daniel was hoping for, that she'd break Stoney out. Then
the cops would have their suspects. "Stoney, I'll come up
with a plan. I promise. But right now you're probably safer
here."

"Bullshit."

"There's something going on, and at least now I know
you're not going to end up with a bullet in your chest."

His eyes narrowed. "Don't you leave me here, dammit. I
told you we should have gone to Venice. But no, you had to
stay here with your pretty boy and play detective. So help
me, I—"

She stood, backing away. Another second of this and she
was either going to cry or jump the partition and hit him.
"You're just going to have to trust me, Stoney. I'm sorry."

He rose as well, and the sheriff immediately approached.
"Sam—"

"I'll get you out as soon as I can, Stoney, but you have to
trust me. I love you."

When she returned to the safety of the SLR, she did cry.
This was what her lame attempt to go straight had gotten
her—her only family in jail. And they wouldn't even confirm the charges, which to her said they were still trying to
pile them on. She didn't doubt that by Monday one of them
would be the murder of Charles Kunz.

This had to be Daniel's doing. Threats behind her back,

and offers of seduction to her face. Okay, she couldn't confront him without something to back up her suspicions, but she could talk to someone with whom he was well acquainted. "Patricia," she murmured, putting the car into gear again. Rick's ex, Peter's ex, Patricia Addison-Wallis seemed to have a knack for associating with the wrong men. And the two of them needed to have a little chat.

Rick sat in the Donners' driveway, the Bentley idling. This was the crux of the conflict between himself and Samantha. He'd gone through legal channels—every channel possible—while she was off somewhere using her own methods of detection. He couldn't guess how she felt at the moment, but he knew quite well what he was feeling: useless. And that simply wasn't acceptable.

Samantha hadn't told him much, but he was good at paying attention. Walter had been arrested with a Giacometti. And it happened that he'd seen one on Charles's desk when he'd gone to find Daniel trying to maul Samantha there. If he confronted Daniel, dearly as he would love to beat the shit out of him, he might jeopardize both what Samantha was trying to do, and whatever Castillo was investigating.

He paused, his inconclusive but very interesting conversation with Laurie Kunz running through his head. Picking up his cell, he rang Tom again.

"What? I know you're still in my damned driveway."

"Paradise Realty. I want all their paperwork."

"What the hell for?"

"And whatever you can get of Kunz family wills and trusts," Richard continued, ignoring the commentary. "I'll want them right after the Kingdom meeting tomorrow."

"You're going to have to pay for my therapy, after this."

"I'll pay for you and Kate and the kids to spend a week in Cancun."

"Deal."

He hung up the phone. It so happened that Laurie had given him another direction to consider, as well. Apparently Patricia and Daniel had some kind of relationship. And Patricia owed him at least one favor.

Against her better judgment, Samantha let a valet park the SLR at The Breakers. She didn't have time to be squeamish tonight. In the lobby she found a house phone and dialed reception.

"Good evening, how may I direct your call?"

"Guest Patricia Addison-Wallis, please."

"Just a moment."

The phone rattled and answered after the third ring. "Yes?" Patricia's scratchy voice came.

Apparently Patricia had nothing better to do on a Friday night than go to bed early. Which meant Daniel was elsewhere, and could have been up to anything. "Miss Addison-Wallis?" she drawled. "The hotel would like to gift you with a complementary bottle of champagne."

"Well, thank you," Patty said, her voice perkier.

"Certainly. I have your room number as 816. We'll send—"

"I'm in 401," she interrupted.

"Oh, yes. My apologies. Eight sixteen is the time the order request came in. Your champagne will be up momentarily."

"Thank you."

Sam hung up. "Schmuck," she muttered, heading for the bar to swipe a champagne bottle.

That done, she took an elevator to the fourth floor. Patricia had the floor's suite—an odd choice for someone trying to live on a budget, but she couldn't begin to figure out the workings of the Ex's mind. She knocked, holding the bottle up in front of the peephole.

"You might at least have put it on ice," Patricia said, pulling open the door. "I expected more from—Oh, it's you. Get out of here."

"Thanks," Samantha answered, pushing past Patricia and closing the door behind her, then tossing the bottle onto a chair. "We need to talk."

"I'm busy. Go away."

Samantha glanced through the open bedroom door. It belatedly occurred to her that Daniel might have been in bed with her and that was the reason Patricia had made it an early night, but only one side of the bed was turned down, and the television was on. "I can see you're busy," she returned. "You and Jay Leno."

Patricia pulled the monogrammed Breakers bathrobe closer around herself. "What do you want, then?"

"I want to have a little chat about Daniel."

"Why, Richard isn't enough? You have to steal every man away from me?"

"Excuse me?" Sam lifted an eyebrow. "One, you and Rick have been divorced for like three years. Two, as far as Daniel is concerned, yuck."

"You kissed him. And don't try to deny it, because I saw you."

Great. This was not the conversation Sam wanted to have, and it wasn't one she had time for, either. "If you want to get technical, *he* kissed *me*, but trust me, he's all yours. Now have a seat."

Patricia went to the coffee table for a cigarette. "You are

not going to order me about, and we are not going to have a chat. Get out before I call security."

"Then call security, and I'll ask them if they can verify where you were this evening, and on the night Charles Kunz was killed."

"What?" Patricia's ivory-colored skin went a shade lighter. "I did not—Oh, no, you don't. You are not going to do this to me again. My life was ruined—*ruined*—after Peter went to jail. I'm still paying for it. This is not going to—"

"Hey, Patty. Peter tried to blow me up, and then he fractured my skull. Quit screwing criminals who're trying to hurt me and mine, and I'll stay out of your life."

"Sod off, Jellicoe. If you think Daniel is trying to hurt Richard, you're mad."

"Not Rick. When's the last time you saw Daniel?"

"I'm not going to answer anything. You're trespassing, and I want you to leave."

"I don't care what you w—"

The door rattled with the force of a knock, and both women jumped. "Now what?" Patricia sniffed, going to the door.

Rick strode into the room. "Patricia, we need to talk," he snapped, then saw Samantha and stopped dead. "What are you doing here?"

For a moment Samantha just looked at him. They'd obviously come to the same conclusion, and he'd elected not to remain at home and wait for someone else's report. He'd come because he thought she might need help saving Stoney. And he had so much more to lose than she did if he let himself get entangled in this mess. But he would know that, too.

"Hi," she said.

"Hi."

"I called Patricia and pretended to be room service to find out her room number," Sam commented, tilting her head to watch him approach. "How did you find her?"

"I asked the front desk."

"Show-off."

"They like me here," he continued, his expression easing as he walked toward her.

"Obviously."

"I presume you're here to ask some questions about Daniel," he said, brushing her hand as he passed her and sank onto the couch. "Anything interesting?"

"We're still at the hostile greetings stage. Have you heard anything new?"

"No. Tom's working on it." He turned his attention to his ex-wife. "So, Patricia, where's Daniel?"

"Daniel?" Patricia stammered, lighting her cigarette. "I don't know what you're talking about." She jabbed the glowing tip in Samantha's direction. "And she's a bloody liar, anyway."

"This isn't about Sam. It's about Daniel. When is the last time you saw him?"

"Richard—"

"Sit down and answer the question, Patricia. I don't want to have to resort to threats. It's not dignified."

Satisfying as it was for her to see Rick finally letting loose on the Ex, she knew that ganging up on Patricia was likely to leave her feeling the persecuted martyr. Once Patricia decided it was her lot in life to suffer, they'd never get anything out of her. And if she'd been in Patricia's shoes, she'd rather go to jail than confess her new errors to the ex-husband on whom she hadn't quite given up.

She sat down beside him. "Rick, leave this to me," she

murmured, while Patricia continued to aim disparaging remarks at her.

"She's *my* ex-wife," he returned. "I'm involved, too."

"I know you are. And you coming here . . . We'll talk about that later. But she won't confess anything to you. She might to me."

Rick looked at her. "Don't shut me out of this."

Samantha kissed him on the cheek. She couldn't help herself. "I'm not. But she's not going to admit to you that she's sleeping with Daniel, and you know it. This is a girl thing."

For a long moment she thought he wouldn't move. Finally, though, he blew out his breath and stood. "I'm going to find Castillo," he muttered, gripping her fingers. "And I'm going to see if I can find out where Daniel is."

She frowned. "I don't want him to know why—"

"He won't know why I'm asking." Rick planted a kiss on her lips. "We have a polo match on Monday, and it can't hurt to go over strategy. See? I learn things about subterfuge from you every day." Placing his hands on both her shoulders, he held her there for a moment. "Just be careful, Samantha," he whispered. "I mean it."

"I will be." The honest concern in his face was almost too much to take. Jeez. Who would have thought that nearly getting blown up with a guy three months ago would have turned into this, where he'd become so . . . precious to her? "And I'm sorry I took off like that. I couldn't think."

He smiled. "Take off whenever you want. Just make sure you come back—and in one piece."

"Deal."

Patricia had holed up in a chair in the corner to glower at both of them. Sam rose to close the door behind Rick, then faced the Ex again. "Okay. It's like this: my friend was arrested tonight for being in possession of a genuine Giacometti prototype."

"A what? And why does this concern Daniel and me?"

"It's a piece of art. And the last time I saw it was at Coronado House, when Daniel showed it to me and asked me how much I thought it was worth."

"Then your friend shouldn't have stolen it."

Sam clenched her jaw. "He was framed, and now whoever *did* steal it is missing out on making about a million dollars for it."

"A mill—"

"I thought that might get your attention. So did you notice or hear Daniel mention anything about getting rid of it?"

"We don't talk about art or money."

"Not about money at all? Does he know you're trying to move to Palm Beach?"

"Richard is assisting me with that," Patricia said stiffly.

"Okay, let me ask you this: Why does a person who might need money intentionally lose a chance to make a lot of it?"

"Why don't you just go away?"

"I'll tell you why," Samantha said slowly, reasoning it out in her own head as she spoke. "Because he's creating a chance to make even more."

"What?"

It made sense. The cops hadn't said, but she would be willing to bet that one of the Gugenthal rubies had been found with the Giacometti sculpture. In one move Daniel would have managed to get himself out from under any suspicion for the theft and the murder, and pin it on someone else. And since he undoubtedly had the rest of the rubies, he'd be free to sell them elsewhere while the state prosecuted Stoney for having them and refusing to divulge their whereabouts. And from her best information they would be worth something around three million, even at pennies on the dollar. All untaxed and unreported, for any recreational purposes he could come up with. Plus he'd have the inheritance free and clear.

She explained it as best she could to Patricia, putting up with the insults and insinuations the entire time. After an hour she finally seemed to be getting through.

"You're saying Daniel killed his own father," Patty said around her third cigarette.

"That's what I'm saying. And even if he didn't, he did the robbery. Which means that when he gets arrested for it—and I will make sure that he does—you are once again going to be dragged through the papers for having a relationship with a thief and probable murderer."

For a moment she thought Patty had swallowed her tongue. "This is your fault," she finally spat. "I don't know how, but it's your fault."

"It's not my fault, but I'm going to give you a way to help yourself out of this. If you work with me, I'll make sure the cops know you've been in on the investigation all along, and that you came to me with your initial suspicions about an old family friend and his cocaine habit."

Patricia took another long drag, blowing smoke out through her lips. Then she ground out the butt. "What do I have to do?"

Sixteen

Saturday, 1:02 a.m.

Richard sat on the sofa in the bedroom suite, his cell phone and a notepad beside him, while he flipped channels on the plasma television. Every time he changed a channel the time came up across the bottom, and he'd been counting every minute.

Finally, a little after one o'clock in the morning, the door opened behind him and then closed again. "Hi," he said over his shoulder.

"You didn't have to wait up," Samantha said, flinging her purse onto the side table and sinking onto the couch beside him. "You have a big day tomorrow. Today, I mean."

"And face your stinging sarcasm when you came in and had to wake me up?" he returned, finally relaxing as she settled in against his side and drew his free arm around her shoulders.

"Is there anything new?"

"We can't get Walter out of jail until Monday at the earliest. He's going in front of a judge and they're going to formally charge him then. That's when his attorney will ask for bail and—"

"I went to see him," she interrupted.

"Walter?" It abruptly felt as though reality had slipped out of focus. Twice in a week now Samantha had voluntarily visited a police station. "Did you find out anything new?"

She shrugged, burrowing a little closer against him. "Just that he's scared shitless to be there and that he wants out now."

"I'm sorry," he returned quietly. "With the weekend, they can hold him an extra day without filing any—"

"I know the drill." The line of her shoulders remained straight and tight. It had been a long evening for her.

"Tom's got Bill Rhodes on the case. He'll get bail on Monday."

"Don't you think maybe it's too high profile, having one of the senior partners of a prestigious law firm representing a fence?"

Richard shrugged. "Maybe. It could work in our favor, though. Donner, Rhodes and Chritchenson wouldn't risk its reputation on a thug."

"'A thug,'" she repeated. "Don't let Stoney hear you say that. You'll hurt his feelings."

"I said he *wasn't* a thug, my love."

"I know. I think my sense of humor is broken."

"You're just tired. What say we hit this again in the morning?"

"Stoney said the guy who called him for a meet never showed up, and then the cops busted into his house and found the Giacometti in his front closet. Did Donner find out anything else?"

"Yes." He didn't want to answer, because it would start a whole new line of questions, and they both needed to get some sleep. At the same time, he knew her well enough to realize that they weren't going anywhere until he gave her the information. "The police received an anonymous tip that the guy who'd killed Charles Kunz had gone back in for another piece, and gave the location where Stoney would be. He was there, and they found the Giacometti the caller had mentioned, and—"

"And a Gugenthal ruby, right?"

He frowned. It had taken Tom three hours to find out what the cops had inventoried during the arrest. "You might have called me if you had that bit of information."

"I didn't have it."

"Then how—"

"A hunch. And I'll bet it was the least valuable one in the set."

"I don't know that, yet. Castillo might." He rested his cheek against the top of her head. "And did you get anything useful from Patricia?"

"It's too early to tell. I probably shouldn't have given her the whole night to think things over, but I doubt she'll tip off Daniel. After Peter, I don't think she trusts her taste in men all that much."

At least she hadn't included him in that little cluster of miscreants. "And what, precisely, is she thinking over?"

"I'll let you know tomorrow afternoon."

"Samantha—"

With a deep sigh she stood, tugging him to his feet beside her. "Bed, please."

"It'll be all right, you know."

She mustered a small, grim smile. "I know it will be. I'm going to make it that way."

"*We* will make it that way," he amended, hiding his alarm in a tight hug. If Samantha went over to the dark side, God help whoever crossed her.

* * *

Samantha's first stop of the morning was to Ungaro's, where she purchased an expensive emerald necklace in an antique gold setting that matched the pictures she'd seen of the Gugenthal collection pretty closely. Then she went to a teeny bopper accessories store and bought a big cheap ruby necklace. That done, it only took a few of her more delicate thieves' tools to replace the emerald with the glass ruby.

It was a big hunch she was going to play, but it was the best one she could think of. For most of her life she'd lived by relying on her instincts, and she wasn't going to alter that just because it was Stoney's life at risk as well as her own.

Rick hadn't looked all that pleased to see her putting on a sleeveless flower print Valentino dress that morning, but since he'd been busy donning a black Armani suit and a deep blue tie for his meeting, neither of them had spent much time on conversation. He hated when she wished him luck, probably for the same reasons she hated the term, so she'd settled for a simple "You look yummy" and left to run her errands.

For stop number three she drove to the Chesterfield Hotel. It surprised her that John Leedmont had agreed to meet there, especially with the rest of the Kingdom Fittings board of directors roaming the halls. On the other hand, Leedmont had a big meeting in a few hours, and he probably wasn't up for a clandestine rendezvous in a coffeehouse.

Leedmont answered his door just a couple of seconds after she knocked. He was nervous—though she wasn't sure yet whether it was because of her or because he was within two hours of meeting an Addison charge full on.

"Miss Jellicoe," he said, stepping back to motion her into the room. "Were you able to find my blackmailer?"

She nodded, handing over the envelope containing the photo and negative. "There you go."

Leedmont opened it, pulling out the contents and examining the two items. "Did you have any trouble?"

Sam shrugged, resisting the urge to touch her bruised forehead, buried under an inch of makeup. "He wrecked my car, but I kicked his ass, so all in all I'd say it worked out."

"He won't . . . cause me any further difficulties?"

"No. He had quite the business going with his little candid camera game. I imagine he'll be heading to jail for a couple of years."

"And my involvement?"

"No such animal. You're one hundred percent not involved."

"You didn't keep any copies of the photo for yourself?"

Sam offered him a smile, though she wasn't particularly amused. "So I could blackmail you into working with Rick, maybe? This is between you and me. I didn't keep anything, and he doesn't know anything. Hell, you could even not pay me and I wouldn't say anything to him." She let her smile deepen. "But I wouldn't recommend going that route."

"I don't imagine you would."

Leedmont reached into his jacket pocket and produced a check, which he handed to her. She pocketed it without checking the value.

"By the way," she added, heading for the door, "I believe you about the circumstances. Your photographer set more guys up than just you. And Miss Hooker's gonna have some long, nervous evenings while the cops look for her."

"Thank you."

Shrugging, she pulled open the door. "You seem like a good guy. I'm glad you came to me."

"Miss Jellicoe?"

She stopped halfway into the hall. "Yes?"

He motioned her back into the room. "Might I ask you a private question?"

"Okay. I can't guarantee an answer."

"Fair enough."

Sam closed the door again, leaning one hand on the handle. With a ton of other shit to take care of today, she really didn't have time for this. On the other hand, she was trying to start a business, and it couldn't hurt to make a good impression on her first paying client—even if this hadn't been remotely related to building security.

"Richard Addison," he said.

"Like I said, this is between y—"

"You and me. I know. I only wanted to ask your opinion of him."

Deeply surprised, Samantha considered her answer. "I'm living with the guy, so I must think he's okay."

"That's not precisely what I meant."

She grimaced. "All right. I don't trust many people, but I trust Rick Addison. How's that?"

He nodded. "Better. Thank you again."

"Sure."

She returned to the Bentley and headed out on her last errand of the morning. Thankfully, Patricia was already dressed and waiting for her in the lobby of The Breakers. Samantha eyed her for a moment. "You'll do," she said.

"Oh, praise from the mutt," Patricia returned, holding out her hand. "Where is it?"

Sam handed her the necklace. "Just remember, it was a gift. Don't be self-conscious about it."

The Ex fastened it behind her neck. "I know how to wear jewelry, thank you very much."

Gazing at Patricia's neck critically, Samantha nodded. "Looks good. And where did you get it?"

With a pained sigh, Patricia followed her to the Bentley and recited, "Daniel gave it to me at dinner the other night.

He said I should be showered in rubies and emeralds."

"Bathed. He said you should be bathed in rubies and emeralds."

"What?"

"Being showered in them would hurt."

"Bitch," the Ex muttered, allowing herself to be handed into the passenger seat by a valet.

"Slut," Sam returned, tipping the other valet and climbing in on her own. This valet thing wasn't all that bad, though she'd hate to rely on having her car delivered to her while she was trying to make a getaway.

"I still don't understand how this is going to help anything," Patricia said, fiddling with the short hem of her white and yellow Ralph Lauren.

"It's simple. A charity lunch with us sitting at the same table as Laurie Kunz. She'll see you wearing the ruby, ask where you got it, and we'll take it from there."

"But you said Daniel robbed his father."

"I'm betting Laurie will think so, too. I want to see her reaction."

"I think you don't know anything, and you're just trying to ruin my life again."

"If I'm wrong, then you get a nice necklace."

"It's not even real."

"The setting's real gold." Ruthlessly Samantha kept her growing annoyance in check. This was for Stoney. And it was for her, though she couldn't help thinking that if she'd just dropped her pursuit of Charles's killer, none of this subterfuge would have been necessary.

Fifteen minutes later they pulled up to the gated drive of Casa Nobles. Samantha showed the guard at the gate her invitation—which had actually been sent to "Miss Samantha

Jalico and guest" at Rick's address. Hell, it wasn't perfect, but it did signal that she'd been accepted into Palm Beach society to some degree.

"I still can't believe I'm attending as your guest," Patricia muttered as they pulled into the curving drive.

"I'm sure you would have been invited if they'd known you would be in town," Samantha said soothingly. "But this way, you're the secret weapon in a robbery and murder investigation."

"Yes, I am." Patricia led the way up the shallow Spanish-style steps to the double front doors of Casa Nobles. "And don't you forget it."

The luncheon at Casa Nobles was hosted by Mrs. Cynthia Landham-Glass, the daughter of the inventor of vending machines or some such thing, and the wife of the owner of the largest string of Lexus dealerships in the country. Cynthia herself stood in the doorway greeting the all-female guest list.

"Patricia!" she exclaimed, giving the Ex the traditional two-cheek miss-kiss. "I had no idea you were in town. I'm so glad you were able to attend."

"Yes, Samantha asked if I would join her. She's new to this sort of thing, so I agreed to be her guide."

Samantha smiled as the stretched-tight face and Botox lips turned in her direction. "Hello. Thank you for inviting me."

"My pleasure, Samantha. Rick Addison is well-respected for his philanthropy."

"He's been encouraging me to become more involved in local society," she returned, adopting the lofty airs of the two women. "He even sent his checkbook with me today."

Well, he hadn't objected when she'd lifted it from his pocket, anyway. She'd tell him later.

"Splendid. SPERM will be delighted to see how generous Rick Addison and Samantha Jellicoe are."

" 'SPERM?' " Samantha repeated in a low voice as she followed Patricia through the house.

"Sam!"

She looked up as a petite blonde emerged from the patio and the spread of tables beyond. "Kate," she returned with a genuine smile as Donner's wife embraced her. "I didn't know you'd be here."

"And no one told me you were attending. SPERM is a favorite cause of mine."

Samantha leaned closer. "And what the hell does SPERM stand for?"

Kate Donner chuckled. "The Society for the Protection of the Environment and Range of Manatees," she recited. "I like them because they have a sense of humor. And it is a good cause."

"I'll take your word for it."

"Hello, Kate," Patricia said. "What a nice surprise."

Kate glanced in the Ex's direction. "Patricia. I heard you were lurking around town."

"I don't 'lurk.' "

"Skulking, then." Wrapping her arm around Samantha's, Kate guided her toward the patio. "What are you doing with her?" she whispered, her fresh, tanned face folding into a frown.

"Rick knows," Sam returned. "It's business."

"Thank goodness. When I saw the two of you together the other day, I—"

"You told Yale, and he ratted me out to Rick. Thanks for that, by the way."

Annoyed as she still was at the complications that had

caused, Sam couldn't help but like Kate. She had from the moment they'd met. Even better, Kate obviously didn't like Patricia. At the same time, satisfying as ditching Patty would be, Sam needed her.

"Tom doesn't keep things from Rick. And at heart he's a huge gossip. I should have called you first, but I was so . . . surprised, I didn't think of it."

"No problem." Samantha took a breath. "Kate, would you mind . . . sitting elsewhere? I need some space around Patricia and me. I can't exp—"

"What you're doing won't get Rick into trouble, will it?" she asked. "Because I won't allow that. Especially because getting Rick into trouble will get Tom into trouble."

"It won't get Rick into trouble. I swear it." Samantha hoped she wasn't being overly optimistic. Crossing her fingers, though, would be a bit blatant.

Without a backward glance, Kate returned to the group of women with whom she'd been chatting. The invitations all had table numbers on them, though Samantha had erased hers and Patricia's. They were going to sit at Laurie Kunz's table. If Laurie didn't see the necklace, they might as well be at Taco Bell.

Finally she spied Charles Kunz's daughter, seated at table number eleven. Swiftly, she pulled a pen from her purse and etched the corresponding number onto her invitation. "Let's go," she said over her shoulder.

She'd taken a few steps before she realized that Patricia wasn't following.

"What is it?" she said, returning.

"I did not come here to be embarrassed and humiliated," Patricia snapped, her voice shaking a little.

"I didn't embarrass you. I will if you don't go through

with this, though. And not just because you're dating Daniel. I haven't forgotten that whole stolen ring thing, Patty. I still have the tape, so I pretty much own you."

"I'm not talking about you. I meant Kate Donner. She used to be *my* friend. All these women used to fall over themselves to be my friend. And now they invite *you* to their parties."

Samantha gazed at her for a minute. "Under other circumstances I might feel some compassion for you," she finally said, "but today I'm trying to get my friend out of jail. You made your bed, Patricia."

Patricia stomped her yellow sandal. "I made a mistake. A stupid mistake. And you stepped in to take advantage when you had no right. You've ruined everything."

"So make it right."

Patricia pinned her with a pale blue glare. "What a stupid thing to say."

Sam grinned. "It made sense to me. Help me, and I'll give you credit for discovering a murderer. That's the beginning and end of this partnership."

"It had better be."

Four other women were already seated at the table, and another three were headed in that direction. Grabbing Patricia's hand, Samantha towed her to their chairs and sat before anyone could dispute their ownership of the seats.

"Miss Kunz," Samantha said, "I wanted to give you my condolences again. It's nice that you're not giving up your charitable activities."

"My father was a great supporter of wildlife," Laurie returned. "I didn't realize that you and Patricia really are friends. How . . . interesting."

"Richard asked me to guide her about society," Patricia put in, embellishing the lie she'd begun earlier.

That was fine with Samantha. Just looking at the tables directly around them, she recognized occupants of three houses she'd robbed over the years. She'd hobnobbed with them before, but only when it gave her an opportunity to case their houses. Now they would happily invite her in, because gossip linked her with Rick Addison. Weird.

"It just so happens that I've been guiding Richard around at the same time," Laurie contributed, favoring Samantha with another smile. "He's quite the charmer."

"You and Richard?" Patricia broke in.

For once Patricia's obsession with her ex-husband was useful. It saved Samantha from having to ask that question herself. Whether she would have to beat the crap out of Laurie would depend on how she answered the question.

"Yes. We've been looking at real estate."

Samantha rotated her shoulders, forcing herself to relax. One thing was for sure—whether she was good at chitchatting or not, she preferred a straight B and E to all this fake politeness and artifice. And Rick owed her an explanation as to why he'd selected Laurie to be his realtor, especially after all the shit he'd fed her about honesty and questioning whom she chose to hang out with.

The rest of their table filled up, and two older women were left standing there, looking from one guest to another. "I thought this was our table," one of them said.

Samantha sipped iced tea, gave a commiserating look, and kept her mouth shut. Finally one of the hostesses appeared and led them to the two empty seats at table eight, where she and Patricia had originally been assigned. As trays of shrimp salads appeared, Mrs. Cynthia Landham-Glass took the podium by the pool and began her speech about the charity while Samantha kept her attention on Laurie Kunz.

Ideally Laurie would have seen Patricia's necklace already and blurted out some sort of accusation about her brother, but she seemed engrossed with lunch and with chatting to the ladies at all the surrounding tables. She was firmly entrenched in Palm Beach society, and if anything, her father's death had only helped with that. Now she had the sympathy card to play—and that, together with her family's longtime residence, would get her into practically anyplace she wanted.

After twenty minutes of being charming, Patricia leaned toward her. "She hasn't seen it," she murmured, dragging her fork through the chicken capellini.

"Be patient. She will."

"What am I supposed to do, stick my tits in her face?"

"If it comes to that," Samantha returned. "Ask her to pass the sugar."

Patricia blew out her breath. "Laurie, love, would you mind passing me the butter?" she asked. Apparently substituting butter was her way of improvising.

Samantha kept her eyes on Laurie and saw the exact moment she noticed Patricia's necklace. Green eyes widened, then narrowed again. Her next glance was at Sam, who lowered her gaze to her lunch in time to avoid contact.

"Where did you get that lovely necklace, Patricia?" Laurie asked.

Patricia buttered a piece of bread. "This? Daniel gave it to me over dinner the other evening." She smiled. "He said I should be showered in rubies and emeralds, and that this was only the beginning. Your brother is quite the romantic."

Not bad. Sam waited a beat, then leaned over to finger the ruby. She gave a low whistle. "That's quite a beginning."

For a moment Patricia simply basked while all the ladies leaned in to look at her neck and offer various compliments.

Laurie didn't, but then she already knew where the ruby had come from—or she thought she did. What was it like, Sam wondered, to realize that your kid brother had killed your dad? She supposed she could have been more tactful about making her suspicions known, but as far as she was concerned, nobody in that house had been cleared.

For the rest of lunch she watched. Laurie chatted and applauded readily enough, but she picked at both her capellini and dessert, and several times fingered the cell phone on the table beside her elbow. She wanted to call Daniel, no doubt, though Sam wasn't entirely certain whether it was to accuse her brother of murder or of giving away stolen rubies.

Lunch began to break up, and Samantha wrote out a donation check. As she replaced the checkbook in her purse, she pulled out the note she'd written that morning and slipped it under Laurie's cell phone.

The next step was the hardest. Now she had to wait.

Seventeen

Saturday, 3:45 p.m.

"Is she home?" Richard asked without preamble as Reinaldo met him at the front door.

"Miss Sam came in just a few minutes ago. I believe she was going to change and go for a swim."

Nodding, Rick tugged his tie loose and headed for the stairs. "Have Hans put out a half-dozen steaks. I'm going to barbecue for the Donners tonight. They'll be here at six."

"Very good. Hans is working on a Boston cream pie for dessert. Is that—"

"That's splendid," Rick interrupted, for a second debating cancelling dinner in favor of another night of pie sex. He almost immediately changed his mind, though; he wasn't going to wait that long.

Outside the bedroom door he moved into stealth mode, slipping off his shoes and inching the door handle down until it opened. They had other things to deal with, and Walter was still in jail, but damn it all, that didn't change one unavoidable fact: he was a man who wanted to get laid. Hell, he'd even brought home the Kunz and Paradise Realty paperwork instead of staying at Donner's office to look at it there, despite the risk of Samantha finding them.

He spotted her immediately, one hand on the back of the deep blue couch as she slipped on her flip-flops. She had on a red bikini, and his mouth actually went dry. Samantha was a slender woman, but round in all the right places, and well-toned muscles played beneath her smooth skin.

Moving fast, he took the two carpeted steps in one bound and tackled her around the waist, throwing both of them onto the soft cushions of the couch. She yelped, giving him a hard elbow in the ribs before she realized who it was.

"Damn it, Rick, you scared the hell out of me," she protested, twisting underneath him until she was on her back.

"Score one for me," he returned, lowering his head to kiss her.

She kissed him back, giving his lower lip a gentle nip. Mm, life was good. His tie slipped onto the floor, followed by his jacket.

"I take it your meeting went well," she mused, reaching between them to unbutton his shirt. "You're the pipe fitting king of the world now, right?"

"Right."

"Neat. Maybe I'll branch out into security and plumbing installation."

"Ah. And tell me why Leedmont said I should thank you?"

Samantha looked up at him, grinning. "Because he asked my opinion of you, and I told him how sad and nerdy you are and how you've always wanted to own a pipe-fittings company."

"I see." He didn't know whether to take her seriously or not. Whatever she'd told John Leedmont, though, the man had actually listened to reason.

She laughed at him. "You totally owe this deal to me, studmuffin."

"Shut up," he murmured, kissing her again.

She ripped two buttons off the cuff of his sleeve as she pulled his shirt off. "Oops. Can I at least tell you that you contributed to SPERM?"

That caught his attention. He stopped midway through untying her bikini top. "What?"

"Society for the Protection of the Environment and Range of Manatees," she said, moving his hand to cover her left breast. "You gave 'em five thousand dollars."

"For a minute I thought we were supporting a fertility clinic or something."

Samantha laughed again, the sound reverberating through his hand and straight into his heart. "Isn't it great? Who would have thought that the Palm Beach matrons had a sense of humor?"

"Not me." He returned to his untying, slipping her scanty top off and lowering his mouth to her bare breasts. "So your lunch went well, then, I presume?" he muttered.

"Just shag me, baby. We'll talk later."

That didn't bode well, but neither did he want to be distracted right now. Four hours of hard discipline, keeping a rein on his temper and his impatience, working slowly and patiently to wear down a very stubborn and suspicious CEO and board of directors—he was ready to let loose.

He slipped a hand into her bikini bottoms and cupped her. She was wet. If he waited another minute without being inside her, he was going to explode. Thankfully, her bottoms were tied together with what felt like dental floss, and getting them off only took a second. With her help, Richard unbuckled his belt, unzipped his trousers, and shoved them down to his thighs.

With a grunt he shoved forward, inside her. Samantha gave a gasping moan, digging her fingers into his back and wrapping her ankles around his hips. He pumped hard and fast, feeling her contracting around him with delicious heat. "Come for me," he ordered, taking her mouth in a hard, deep kiss.

She did come, with a half-strangled scream, and Richard closed his eyes, pushing himself forward. He ejaculated at the tail end of her orgasm, sending them both into a heaving, writhing pile of tangled limbs and sweat.

"Jesus," she gasped after a minute, still clinging to him.

"Sorry for the quickie," he managed, carefully settling his weight on her. She could take it.

"The hell you say. That must have been some negotiation."

"It was. Toward the end, there, all I could think of was getting back here and shagging you."

Samantha chuckled, lifting her head to kiss his jaw. "Then I'm glad I was here, for Reinaldo's sake."

"It wouldn't have been the same." Putting out an arm to catch himself, he rolled off the couch and onto the floor. He took her with him, still straddling his hips, still encasing him.

"Want to go swimming with me?" Samantha asked, sitting up with her hands braced on his chest. "We could cover up the cameras and go in the buff."

"The Donners are coming over for a barbecue at six," he returned, watching her face.

Her expression tightened a little, then relaxed again. "All of them?"

"Yes. Even Chris. He's on winter break from Yale. I invited them for a swim, as well." Slowly, he ran his palms along her shoulders, drawing them down over her breasts.

"Okay." She leaned into his palms, sighing with a deep satisfaction that made him seriously consider cancelling dinner.

"Are you going to tell me about your luncheon now?"

Green eyes held his. "Did you go looking at real estate with Laurie Kunz?"

To borrow one of Samantha's favorite words, *crap*. "I'm looking for a place for Patricia. You know that."

"I know that. What, precisely, made you choose Laurie Kunz as your ideal realtor?"

Lying there flat on his back with his pants around his knees and his cock still inside her, he wasn't going to lie. "I thought she might know something about the robbery."

"But the police are handling that case, Richard. They are doing a splendid job, and do not need help from amateurs." She put a hand to her mouth. "Hm. It seems like I've heard that before. Who was it that said that to me?"

"I just thought I might lend a hand."

"You're a hypocrite."

Richard sat up, frowning. "Why, because I decided to talk to her?"

"Because when I look into things on my own it's dangerous and a probable disaster and none of my business, but you get to go house-hunting with a possible murderer and it's fine that you don't tell me?"

"I'm telling you now."

"Because I caught you."

Okay, so she was correct. That didn't mean he had to admit it to her. "Would it make a difference if I said she seemed a little suspicious?"

"It makes things more interesting," she said after a moment.

"And why is that?"

"Because I passed Laurie a note at lunch offering to help her with any problems caused by her brother."

He looked her in the eye. "You did what?"

When Samantha pulled away from him and stood, he was certain he wasn't going to like her answer. She walked naked and graceful into the bathroom and came out pulling on a bathrobe. "I didn't say anything specific. I wanted to see how she would react. First I gave a faux Gugenthal ruby to Patricia to wear, and had her say that Daniel had given it to her. When Laurie saw it, her eyes practically popped out."

Worry and a fair bit of anger clenched into his gut. Standing, he yanked his trousers back up and fastened them. This wasn't a naked-type conversation, any longer. "She's not going to react well if she's the killer."

"It was Daniel. I'm almost positive. She'll just want a way out, maybe to keep herself from getting the blame."

She could be positive if she wanted, but he intended to reserve judgment until he'd looked through Laurie's financial records. And now he definitely wasn't going to tell her about the Kunz paperwork unless or until he got results. He had a wager to win. "So how or when will you know she's decided to bring you in?"

"My note gave her twenty-four hours. I told her that after that I would take my suspicions to the insurance company. I'm sure they'd offer a reward for saving them the kind of money involved in all this."

Richard joined her to look over the pool deck. "Does she know that you and Walter are friends?"

"She probably knows we work in the same office."

"If she did the deed, she's not going to want you around to talk about it."

"I know what I'm walking into."

For a long moment Richard stayed silent as he slowly pulled her warm, terry-cloth-wrapped body back against his. "I appreciate that you told me all this, wager or not."

"I didn't want you walking into a potential fire without knowing. Especially if you're still going to work with Laurie on your real estate stuff."

"I have to, don't I? We can't risk making her suspicious." Not until he'd satisfied himself about whether she was involved.

Samantha twisted in his arms to face him, her upturned face serious. "You're not going to say we should call Castillo and let him know what's going on?"

He smiled. "I know how reluctant you are to make statements without proof. Or to put yourself in the position of being the star witness."

"Yes, that does make me twitchy, doesn't it?"

"Not as twitchy as it used to, if you can joke about it." Bending his head down, he kissed her. "Brace yourself, because I'm going to say it again."

"Rick—"

"I love you, Samantha Jellicoe."

Predictably, she made a show of untangling herself from his grasp. He let her loose. It *was* a show, he realized, probably for the first time. She was getting used to hearing him say it, and it didn't bother her as much as it had before. Which meant either that she no longer considered being close to someone—to him—a trap, a confinement that would somehow harm her, or that she didn't mind being trapped.

The intercom buzzed. Grateful the interruption hadn't come a few minutes earlier, Richard went to the phone and hit the button. "Yes?"

"Sir? Detective Frank Castillo is at the front gate. He says he has an appointment with Miss Sam."

"Send him in, Reinaldo," Samantha said over his shoulder. "We'll meet him in the library."

Richard straightened. " 'An appointment'?"

Sam gave him her quicksilver grin. "I might have called him and asked him to come by. Winning by any means and all that. And Walter. The ambush sex made me forget."

"Very likely." He walked over and grabbed the front of her robe, pulling it wide open. "You should probably put some clothes on before I make you forget again."

"You, too." She ran a hand down his bare chest. "You look like one of those romance cover models like that—bare feet, belt undone, no shirt."

"Just so it's not Fabio I look like."

"No. One of those black-haired British noblemen." She kissed his chin, then scampered toward the closet. "Oh, wait! You are one of those."

"Smart ass."

"I was kind of surprised you waited until this afternoon to call me," Frank Castillo said, taking a seat at the large library research table and accepting an iced tea from Reinaldo.

"So you know that Walter Barstone and I are friends?"

He gave a short laugh that managed not to sound all that amused. "Give me a break. Tom Donner's been calling everybody who owns a phone to try and get information. Donner means Addison, and it didn't take my shiny detective badge to figure out that that meant Jellicoe."

"Stoney's an old friend helping me set up my security business," she lied, wishing she and Rick had had a little more prep time to get the back story straight. Neither, though, would she have wanted to pass up the ambush sex.

Frank took a swallow of iced tea. "Look, Sam, I'm not an idiot. I don't expect you to make any confessions, but I'm running a murder investigation. Don't mess with witnesses or evidence, and don't lie to my face. Walter Barstone's been under surveillance before, and while he's just about as slick as you, we could still make a fair case against him even without this new stuff."

Her heart dropped into her stomach. "Are you?" she managed, just barely keeping her voice steady. "Going to make a case against him regardless of how the Kunz investigation turns out?"

"I don't know yet. I'm homicide, remember?" He looked down for a moment, stirring his tea with the straw. "I'll see what I can find out."

"Thanks, Frank."

"Is that why you called? We could have done this over the phone."

"I want to know who tipped you off that Stoney had some of the Kunz property."

"It was an anonymous tip. We get them all the time, but they usually don't pay off like that." Blotting his moustache with a napkin, he sent Samantha a curious look. "It surprised the hell out of me when I realized who we were arresting. I mean, you made such a big deal about being concerned over Kunz's death, and then poof, it's your guy fencing the stolen prop—"

"Stoney didn't do anything," Samantha broke in. "He was set up."

"I don't suppose you can prove that?"

"Not yet. Not in court, anyway."

"Sam, I ain't a judge."

She took a deep breath. "Okay. And I'm trusting you, so don't shaft me—or nobody's gonna be happy with the way this turns out."

"I'll ignore that and just say tell me what you know."

Sitting beside her, Rick stirred for the first time. It was funny; he was the one with the reservations about trusting the cop this time around. "I still think Donner should be here," he murmured.

"He'll be here in twenty minutes," she returned, squeezing his knee beneath the table. "And don't worry; I can run faster than Frank."

"Let's hope we don't have to find out whether that's true," the detective noted, slipping his ever-present notepad out of his jacket pocket. "Let me have it."

"You found Stoney holding a Giacometti statue, right?"

"A who statue?"

"Giacometti. Alberto Giacometti. Trust me, he's big."

"Okay."

She could have told him that Stoney never hid business shit in his front closet, not when he had a hidden room in the attic, but that probably wouldn't help anything. "The statue wasn't taken in the original robbery, and I know that because it was there at least until Charles Kunz's wake. Daniel took me into his dad's old office and asked me if I knew what it was and how much it might be worth."

"And you told him what?"

"I told him a full-sized Giacometti had gone for as much as three million."

The detective sat back in his chair. "I'm not sure you should be telling me this, Sam. You're admitting that you saw this statue and then the next day your guy gets arrested with it in his possession. That doesn't look good."

"But Stoney also had a Gugenthal ruby with him, didn't he?"

Frank eyed her. "How did you know that?"

"I'll tell you in a minute. Look at it from the perspective

of a professional thief." She gave a brief grin. "Pretend I'm acquainted with one. I know exactly where the rubies are, how to easily liberate them, and I decide they're probably the simplest and most lucrative items in the house to dispose of. Easy to hide, easy to disperse in small quantities. I walk right past an unprotected Giacometti that's not even listed in the insurance papers yet. And then a couple of days later I go back and steal it *after* the family realizes how much it's worth."

"But why would someone plant it on Barstone?"

"Because it makes you look at him—and maybe me—for the murder and robbery."

He nodded. "And the ruby connects him—you—to the night of the crime. The Giacometti only connects him to the house."

"Right."

Frank jotted down a few notes. "Can you prove *anything* you're saying?"

Samantha drew a slow breath. Castillo hadn't let her down yet. There was always a first time, but hopefully this wouldn't be it. She needed him to know what was going on, and she needed them to be able to trust one another, even at the cost of the bet. "Not yet, but I think Daniel did it, and I think Laurie suspects him." The whys and wherefores could wait until later—if ever.

"And?" the detective prompted after a moment.

Sheesh. Everybody was getting to know her way too well. "And so I kind of offered to help Laurie dispose of any stolen items and keep her brother out of prison."

The tip of Castillo's pencil broke. "You *what*?"

"Hey, you're always telling me you need proof."

"Yeah, but . . ." Frank swore softly in Spanish. "If they

trap you into doing something illegal and then drop a dime on you like they did on your friend, you're screwed, Sam."

"They won't trap me into anything. I'm the trap*per*. They're the trap*pees*."

Rick was also gazing at her. "Don't forget that this isn't just a robbery. It's a murder, too."

"That's why I'm doing this—for Charles. All I want is answers—and proof."

"No." Rick stood, walking to the floor-length windows and back. "I know how you push people into revealing things, Samantha. Pushing like that to find a murderer will get you killed."

"Excuse me for interrupting," Frank broke in, "but whatever everybody's hunches might be, I haven't found a stitch of evidence that either of the Kunz kids had anything to do with killing their dad. No motive, nothing. Maybe they just took advantage of circumstances and robbed the safe."

"Maybe," Samantha admitted reluctantly, "but I don't think so."

"Cash went missing at the same time, you said," Rick put in as he continued pacing. "I have to say, extra cash is fairly easy to fold into a real estate business. And Laurie Kunz has one of those."

Rick might know everything about the sharks in the business world, but she knew about theft and greed and the way people's minds worked. They made a pretty good team, actually. "And Daniel's got a cocaine habit. A bad one."

Castillo pulled another pencil out of his pocket. "That could explain his need to take the rubies—especially knowing the insurance company would lock down the estate—but it still doesn't prove a murder. His father bought him a yacht, after all. And he's got a stable of polo ponies or something."

"He's got a pair of them," Rick said. "We're actually playing on the same team Monday afternoon, for the Fireman's Fund charity."

"I think we need to look at the insurance papers," Samantha mused, "because Daniel said the boat wasn't his—yet. And I'd bet a Picasso that the ponies don't belong to him, either. Charles wasn't a fool. He had to know about Daniel's drug habit. Maybe Dad was pinching the money hose to force Daniel into rehab or something. Can we check to see if he's been to any clinics lately? Or whether he was scheduled to enter a clinic and didn't?"

"That's gonna be sticky, but I can pull a few strings."

"So can I," Rick added after a moment. "And don't forget Laurie in all this."

"Let's say I'm buying into all this speculation," Castillo said. "And let's say it makes more sense than anything my guys and I have been able to put together. What's our next step?"

"That's easy," Samantha replied, storing Frank's response in her mind for use against Rick later. She _was_ ahead of the cops. "We wait for a phone call. How do you feel about barbecued steak?"

Eighteen

Saturday, 7:15 p.m.

$\mathcal{R}$ichard sat in one of the wrought-iron bistro chairs on the pool deck and watched as Samantha did a cannon-ball into the deep end in tandem with Mike and Olivia Donner. From what Samantha had said, she hadn't had much of a childhood, but she made up for it when the Donner kids were around. He noted that Chris Donner, the oldest of the brood, had abruptly decided he wasn't too mature and digni-fied to take a dip in the pool, either—and he knew that it had happened the moment the Yale law student had seen Saman-tha in her red bikini.

They made an odd group tonight: The thief, the police de-tective, the lawyer, and the British nobleman. Rick took a sip of beer. Extremely odd, and yet over the past three months it had all become rather . . . normal.

"Hey," Samantha said, trotting up to drip water on his shoulder, "are you going to sit there and brood all night?"

"I'm barbecuing."

Her cool lips kissed his ear. "It's just a little more murder and mayhem," she whispered. "They're becoming my specialty."

He twisted his head to look up at her. "You'll have to forgive me if I'm not terribly happy about the way you put yourself in harm's way."

"Take it easy. She hasn't even called yet. She might not."

"And if she doesn't?" For a brief moment he hoped that Laurie and Daniel Kunz had decided to flee the country rather than go up against Samantha Jellicoe. If they knew her as well as he did, they might consider it.

"I've been thinking about that." She lowered her voice still further. "A little B and E for a good cause could be just the thing."

His hands went cold. "Sam, you prom—"

She put a finger to his lips. "This isn't just about Charles, now. It's about saving Stoney. And I never promised. I said I would try."

Bloody, fucking hell. "Don't—"

"I'll tell you first." She straightened again. "At least get some trunks for Frank. You two are still teammates, right?"

Richard sent a glance at the detective, sipping an iced tea at one of the bistro tables and chuckling at the kids in the pool. He'd put himself in charge of Samantha's cell phone, and it sat at his elbow, charged up and ready to ring if anyone called.

"Right. He'd probably sink straight to the bottom, but I'll ask if he's interested."

She kissed him again, this time on the mouth. "Thanks, sweetie. She'll call. Then you'll only have my safety to worry about. And turn the hot dogs."

Shit. He got to his feet and went to check the barbecue. Mike and Livia had demanded hot dogs rather than steaks, and after a mere moment of Samantha-instigated chaos, dinner had turned into dogs and burgers, leaving Hans busy in the kitchen making something called macaroni salad.

Richard flipped the burgers and turned the hot dogs, then made his way over to Frank. "I keep plenty of extra suits, if you want to take a dip."

"Thanks, but technically I'm still on duty."

With a nod, Richard returned to his seat with Katie and Tom and took another draw of his beer. Samantha had returned to the pool, and was playing blind man's bluff with the three Donner kids.

"So whose idea was it to invite the cop?" Tom murmured, working on his own beer.

"Samantha's. We're waiting for a phone call."

"So I gathered. Anybody in particular?"

"Yes."

Tom scowled. "You know, if we're butting in during your little murder and robbery rodeo of fun, we can go."

Kate put a hand on her husband's arm. "Don't be so cranky. I'm sure Rick would let us know if anything dangerous were going on."

He heard the warning in her voice, the mother protecting her brood. "Nothing more dangerous than a phone call, Katie."

She smiled. "Thanks for your generous SPERM donation, by the way. It was the hit of the luncheon."

Tom blinked. "What the hell are you talking about?"

"The manatee society, hoss," she returned, laughing. "Rick and Sam donated five thousand dollars."

The attorney was shaking his head. "You people really need a better acronym."

"It gives the blue-haired old ladies a thrill," Kate said. "And gets the cause attention. So it all works out."

"Except for the husbands like me who have to say their wife's looking for SPERM contributions."

"That's part of the fun." She squeezed his wrist. "Now go and lifeguard so Rick and I can chat for a minute."

"Yeah, okay." Tom snagged his beer and went to sit on the end of the diving board.

"What are we chatting about?" Richard asked, settling deeper into his chair.

"Are you actually looking for a house for Patricia?"

"Did Samantha tell you that?"

"Actually, your realtor did. We chatted before the luncheon."

"You know Laurie Kunz?"

She leaned closer. "Don't change the subject, Richard."

He forced a grin, though he didn't consider his question unimportant. Kate's opinion of Laurie could have been useful. She had great instincts. She was also still glaring at him, and he shook himself. "What was the subject?"

"Patricia."

"She asked me for help. But I really don't think it's your concern."

"You know, I thought Samantha was out of line when she went driving with Patricia. Then she shows up at SPERM with Pa—"

"Will you please call it something else?"

"Fine. Laurie says you're helping dear Patricia find a place to live in Palm Beach. Then Sam shows up at the manatee society with Patricia and says you know they're working together."

"And your point is?"

"My point is, are the two of you insane?" When Frank glanced at them, she gave a self-conscious glance at the rest of the pool deck occupants, then lowered her voice. "I know you didn't appreciate Sam associating with Patricia, because I know you. So you turn around and try to find her a place what, a mile from where you and Sam are living?"

"She asked for my help," he repeated, clenching his jaw. He didn't need advice on his damned relationships.

"If you can't resist your chivalrous impulses, fine, find her a place to live. Buy her a nice house. But for God's sake, don't set that viper loose in your own backyard. She's not here to do you any good. She's here to help herself. And she'll slip in between you and Sam so smoothly you won't even realize it until Sam decides she's had enough and vanishes."

"Nobody's vanishing, Kate."

"Trust me, Rick. I know how the female mind works. Patricia's been here what, two weeks? And already she's jumped into Sam's work, and into your time."

Reluctantly Richard had to admit that Kate had a point. A good point. He looked over at Samantha again, treading water about three feet from Mike and easily eluding the fourteen-year-old as he searched for the other swimmers.

"I never thought of Patricia as being that slick," he said slowly.

"Come on. She's a professional at getting what she wants, and she's desperate. You're the only failure she's had, and I don't think she's given up on you, yet."

Richard straightened. "She's not getting *me* back. That's ridiculous. I'd never trust her again, even if it wasn't for Samantha."

"She doesn't have to get you back to ruin you and Sam. But play it however you want. I'm just saying you should be a little more cautious. I mean, when you caught her and Peter, I hope you realize that couldn't have been the first time they fooled around on you."

He'd considered that during the divorce, and it was probably the closest he'd ever come to doing Patricia physical harm. Being reminded of it didn't serve to improve his mood any. "You've given your advice, Kate. I trust you'll leave the rest to me."

Reinaldo and another employee, Valez, emerged onto the pool deck just then with a bowl of macaroni salad and a tray of condiments. Richard blew out his breath. "All right, burgers are burning," he called, standing.

They clustered around three closely spaced tables, handing bottles of ketchup and jars of mustard around. He'd always enjoyed entertaining the Donners, but with Samantha present, and even considering Frank Castillo's unexpected visit, he couldn't put a word to the sense of deep satisfaction the evening gave him. It was probably the first time Solano Dorado had actually felt like . . . home.

"What are you smiling at?" Samantha asked, shoveling a mound of macaroni salad onto her plate. "I thought you were being pissed off this evening."

"I'll save it for later," he returned. "Any more thoughts on how you're going to refurbish the landscaping here?"

"I'm thinking garden gnomes. They could peer around all the ferns and stuff."

Thank goodness he was already working on his second beer. The veneer of alcohol enabled him to give a calm nod. "Perhaps the Seven Dwarfs and Snow White."

"Hey, that's good. I was thinking more like leprechauns, but I like the whole enchanted forest thing."

Beside her, eight-year-old Livia in a pink one-piece swim suit and a pair of blond ponytails, was laughing. "You guys are crazy."

"You should make like a Japanese garden," Mike contributed.

"Great, squirt," Chris said from the neighboring table. "That would totally go with the Spanish-style house."

"Oh, and like garden gnomes go with anything."

"She was joking." The oldest Donner offspring looked at Samantha. "Weren't you, Sam?"

She shrugged, still grinning. "Who knows? I'm pretty sure gnomes go with everything."

"Mike could loan you his *Star Wars* action figures," Olivia offered.

"I can not. You loan her your doll collection."

"I have a stone tortoise my uncle made for me," Castillo put in unexpectedly. "I'd be willing to donate that. It's bright blue."

"A blue tortoise?" Olivia exclaimed, giggling.

Frank nodded. "I think my uncle's crazy."

"Then he'd fit right in here." With a laugh, Kate passed the bottle of ketchup.

Samantha's cell phone didn't ring. They sat out by the pool through dinner and through an ice cream sundae dessert, and through a soak in the Jacuzzi for Samantha and the kids, and nothing interrupted them.

Finally the Donners gathered up their clothes and shoes. "This was fun, Uncle Rick," Livia said, planting a kiss on his cheek.

"Yeah, thanks, Rick," Mike added as his mother nudged him forward.

Chris offered his hand. "Good luck this semester," Rick said, shaking it.

"Thanks. I'll need it." After a hesitation, the twenty-year-old took Samantha's hand as well. "It was great meeting you, Sam."

She grinned. "You too, Chris. You're way cooler than your dad."

He laughed, blushing. "Thanks."

"Yeah, thanks a lot," Tom put in. "I'll see you in the office first thing Monday, right?"

"Right," Rick agreed. That would be for the meeting about Walter, and how to ensure he got out of jail on bail. "Samantha and I will be there by eight."

The attorney nodded. "Bring your checkbook."

"I will."

"I'd better get out of here, too," Castillo said, shaking hands.

"Thanks for staying," Samantha told him, wrapping her fingers around Richard's arm, probably so she wouldn't have to shake the detective's hand. She'd come a long way, but not quite that far.

"You call me as soon as you hear anything," Frank returned. "I'm not kidding."

"I get it." She nodded.

Not that she'd said she would call, but Richard let that pass. He was just happy to have the rest of the night alone with her.

Samantha checked her cell phone again and pocketed it in the thin jacket she'd donned. "Technically she's got until early afternoon tomorrow to call me back, if she does it at all."

"I looked at the TV listings for tonight," he said, escorting her up the poolside stairs to their bedroom balcony. "*King Kong vs. Godzilla* is on in about fifteen minutes."

"You wouldn't kid a girl about something like that, would you?"

"Never."

Yes, that was his Sam, the best cat burglar in the world, now mostly retired, and fanatic Godzilla fan. And justice-bringer for a murdered millionaire whom she'd only known for a few minutes, despite the cost to herself and her small circle of friends. Even considering what had happened, Charles was lucky to have her on his side.

Richard frowned. She'd said Charles had been uneasy that night. Had he known someone was going to kill him? Had that been why he'd approached Samantha? That made her some sort of avenging angel, he supposed. It suited her, and in truth he couldn't exactly imagine her doing nothing but planting garden gnomes. What would she do, then, if her next client only needed an alarm system?

"I'm going to check my e-mail," he said as they walked inside the master bedroom suite. Leaning down to pick up the TV remote, he tossed it to her. "Be right back."

"I need to shower the pool off me, anyway."

In his office, Richard turned on the computer and then slid open the top drawer of his desk. All evening he'd been weighing whether to leave the party in favor of the Kunz papers. If he didn't take a look at them before Laurie called, he could be allowing Samantha to step into more danger than she realized. Of course, he could simply have told her he had the files in his possession, but if they turned out not to have any significant information, he'd be losing a step on her— and he couldn't afford to do that. Nor would he risk letting Castillo know he had the files; he was supposed to be aiding the legal side of the wager, and he was certain getting those papers without some sort of warrant couldn't be good for the police department's case.

Tom had managed to get just about everything he'd asked for: Paradise Realty financial statements, Charles Kunz's will, and some of the Kunz family trust paperwork. Slowly he began paging through it, looking for anything that might point to a motive for robbery and murder. The real estate records would probably have been indecipherable to anyone without a background in business and finance, but to him it said marginal success, with a net large enough to keep the company in business, and small enough to keep it from being anything to gloat about. Hm. According to gossip, Charles's little girl was a real estate wizard. It didn't look that way to him. But was that enough to point to robbery and murder?

"Kong's in Tokyo," Samantha's quiet voice came, and he jumped.

"Christ. I thought you said you'd always knock," he snapped, whipping his gaze up to see her leaning in the doorway. He had no idea how long she'd been there.

"It was open."

Her auburn hair was damp and loose around her shoulders, her body swathed in a thin cotton robe and, he was certain, nothing else. He drew a slow breath. "Come take a look at this," he said reluctantly. Much as he wanted her to lose the wager, from her expression she'd already realized something was up. It was either talk or have her jimmy his bloody desk open later.

She moved around to look at the papers over his shoulder. "Financial statement?" she asked after a moment.

"Paradise Realty."

"Oh, you bad boy. Did Donner get these for you?" Leaning her hands on either of his shoulders, she kissed his ear. "And I thought he was such a Boy Scout."

"He wasn't happy about it." Richard frowned. "It's not as successful as she lets on, but that just makes her a poor businesswoman—not a murderer."

"I thought you suspected her."

He shifted. "I might be leaning in your direction, now. You were right about Daniel's funds being restricted," he went on, turning to the trust paperwork. "I don't have everything here, but there's definitely something he's supposed to be doing in order to receive his monthly stipend."

"Like maybe attend a drug rehab program?"

"Probably. But the trust doesn't collapse because Charles is dead. Killing him doesn't free up Daniel's funds."

"Not right away. What about a will?"

"It's complicated, but essentially upon Charles's death the trust becomes all-encompassing. The monthly payouts are higher, but the conditions and restrictions are the same."

"Hm. Daniel probably figured the cash and jewelry would be enough until he could charm the court into agreeing to amend the trust."

"Could be," Richard agreed. "Laurie mentioned getting out of real estate to take over her father's chairmanship."

"So it could be a position she was after, rather than money."

Richard looked up over his shoulder at her. "I thought *you* suspected Daniel."

"I'm an equal opportunity suspector." Slowly she slid her hands down his chest to hug him. "You kind of went above and beyond to get these, didn't you?"

"I didn't want you walking into anything blind." It sounded good, anyway.

He felt her smile against his cheek. "You're such a fucking liar. What, were you going to find the key piece of evidence and slip it to Frank so you could win the bet?"

He began to think there might be such a thing as a partner being *too* bright. "Maybe," he conceded.

"You are so going to lose."

Samantha was sound asleep when her phone rang. She sat up in bed, noting the time on the clock's glowing digital face even as she reached for the phone. "*Hola?*"

"I have some conditions." It was Laurie.

Rick slid a hand along her bare back as he sat up beside her. "Are you fucking crazy?" Samantha hissed in a low voice. "It's three o'clock in the morning."

She eyed Rick. In a second his gaze sharpened, and he nodded. "Who is it, Samantha?" he asked, throwing in a yawn for good measure.

"It's a wrong number," she returned. "I'll call you back in five," she whispered, and hung up.

"Laurie, I presume?" he said, flicking on the bed stand light.

"Yes. That was a test, I'm sure, to find out if I would talk in front of you."

"Because your note also told her I was a stuffed shirt who didn't know anything about your nefarious activities and would probably report her and her brother to the authorities?"

"Wow. You sound really British at three in the morning." He also looked really good, with the beginnings of beard stubble and crazy disheveled bed hair. "And no. It's more about whether I'm willing to take a walk on the dark side. You're the good side."

"Luke Skywalker?"

Despite the joking, she knew he was worried. As for her, at the first second the phone rang she'd been wide-awake and ready to go. This was the kind of thing she lived for. "More like young Obi-Wan. I'm Anakin Skywalker, I guess." She frowned. "No, Han Solo. He's cooler, and he turned out to be a hero."

"I can't believe we're talking about this right now," he muttered. "Do you think she bought the delay as assurance that you can be trusted?"

"We'll see." She checked the clock. "Two more minutes. And remember, you're not in earshot, no matter what I might say."

"I know how to play the game, my dear."

Of course he did. "Sorry. I just don't want to mess it up."

"You won't. Just keep in mind that I don't want *you* messed up."

She gazed at him for a long moment, alert, highly intelligent blue eyes obscured by strands of wild black hair in an actor-handsome face, bare-chested and athlete-muscular, surrounded by deep blue sheets and pillows of fine satin. "So in an ideal world, what would you be doing right now?"

"Exactly what I'm doing, except that you wouldn't have a phone in your hand."

Sam grinned. "And what would I have in my hand?" she asked slyly, lowering her gaze to the sheet across his hips.

"My hand," he returned promptly. "It's usually about sex, but not always. It *is,* however, always about being with you."

Before she could reply to that—not that she had any idea what to say—he leaned over and kissed her. His mouth was soft and gentle, a warm caress, a reassurance of support and . . . love.

He'd said before that he loved her, and she'd been able to see in his eyes and his expression that he was serious, but this was different. She felt this, and that made it inescapably real. And the oddest thing of all was that it didn't frighten her.

"Make your call," he prompted after a second slow kiss.

She cleared her throat. "Right." *Get it together, Sam.* With a deep breath she shook out her shoulders and then dialed the number her phone had stored.

"Hello?"

"Okay, what conditions?"

"If I thought Daniel might be in some difficulty, having the police around looking for the thief and the killer wouldn't be very helpful."

Sam understood instantly. Clenching her free fingers into a hard fist, she nodded into the phone. "Okay. Barstone stays in jail—if you make it worth my while. Finding a new fence is a pain in the ass. Is that it?"

Laurie was silent for so long that Samantha began to wonder whether she would take the bait or not. "I need a guarantee that I can trust you," she finally returned. "My brother's future is at stake. And mine, too, if you and I go into business together."

"For me, this is about money. Your brother pulled a job out from under me, so if I turn you in, I don't get anything."

"Turning Daniel in would be a risky proposition, anyway," Laurie said, cynical amusement in her voice. "I wouldn't recommend limiting the funds of a spoiled rich kid who's got a five-hundred-dollar-a-day coke habit."

"Then we should probably include him in this," Samantha noted, putting a smile into her voice as adrenaline pounded through her system. Daniel *had* shot Charles. "I get twenty percent for fencing the rubies, the paintings, and whatever else you two can lift from the house without making the insurance company suspicious. And that's not negotiable."

"All right. But I've already been tailed once. If you screw with me, you're not going to live long enough to regret it."

So *she'd* rented the black BMW. "Ooh, you scared me. Are we doing business, or not?"

"Do you expect me to drop off a bucket of jewelry at Solano Dorado? Or maybe I could send it to you FedEx. I'm sure the police won't notice a thing."

Laurie had a definite cynical streak. "Are you going to that stupid polo match Monday?" Sam asked, glancing at Rick and mouthing *What time does it start?*

He held up two fingers.

"Of course. Daniel's on one of the teams, and everyone who's anyone attends."

"Good. Bring a picnic basket with some fruit and shit in

it. Core the apples. I like apples. I'll meet you under the refreshment canopy at two-thirty."

"I'll be there. And don't screw me over, Jellicoe."

"Hey, I was wondering how I was going to keep myself entertained while Rick's off playing sticks and ponies."

She hung up. Her hands were shaking from the adrenaline rush.

Rick took the phone from her and set it on his nightstand. "The apple thing was very clever. That's thinking on your feet."

"Thanks. I just hope it works."

He slid his arms around her waist, tugging her back against his side. "So do I. Especially if I have to be out on the field playing 'sticks and ponies' while you're accepting stolen property connected with a murder."

"Only for pretend," she said, hoping that was the truth. She was going to have to let Castillo in on it, or she *would* be breaking the law.

And he was right about the "connected with" bit. The stolen goods didn't equal murder. Finding the gun would, but that meant a whole other set of problems. It was a damned good thing she liked trouble.

"Rick, you don't need to go with me," Samantha said, leaning her elbows on the kitchen island while Hans loaded sodas into a picnic basket. "I'm a big girl."

"I know that," Rick returned, finishing a quick perusal of the Sunday paper. "Two of us together make a better cover."

She studied his expression. Calm, a little amused, and beneath all that a stubborn determination to somehow make things right. Well, if he wanted to go along with her, so be it. She could probably use the backup. "Fine," she conceded. "But I'm the boss."

He lifted his hands in mock surrender. "I'm merely going on a picnic."

"Right. Me, too."

Hans closed the wicker lid and handed the basket off to Rick. It seemed nuts, even pretending to go for a picnic lunch while Stoney sat in jail, and while Laurie and Daniel were taking the time to plan who knew what for the polo match tomorrow. But she didn't have to be a cop to know they needed the damn gun to make the case, and Daniel wasn't likely to hand it over any way but bullet first.

Rick picked the old banana-yellow SLK because it was a convertible. Putting the picnic basket prominently in the space behind her seat, they tooled along toward South Lake Trail. They passed a dozen locals bicycling, and one of them nearly crashed into the high sea grass as he tried to wave at them.

Samantha checked her watch. "Okay, enough of your fans have seen you to give us an alibi. Let's head to Coronado House."

"How certain are you that Laurie and Daniel aren't home?"

"I talked to Aubrey. They always attend Sunday church service."

He glanced at her as he turned the car onto Barton Avenue. "This hasn't exactly been an ordinary week for them."

"I know. But I bet they figure they need all the forgiveness they can get from the man upstairs."

"I can't help thinking this is a very bad idea." His lips twitched at her snort. "You really want this badly, don't you?"

"Yes."

"Because it's a rush, or because you want to find the gun and prove a murder?"

"Can't it be both?"

With a deep breath he flipped on the left-hand turn signal. "You worry me, Samantha."

She couldn't help grinning. "I know. Seriously. I know. After this I'll only break into *your* houses." *And maybe the occasional one to return things Patricia stole, and shit like that.*

"Wait," Samantha's soft voice came from inside the high stone walls bordering the Coronado House grounds. "Wait . . . okay, now."

Richard hit the wall halfway up, dug in the toes of his shoes, and grabbed the short iron spikes topping the thing. With another push he went over the top, landing with a fair amount of dignity on his bum inside.

Samantha grabbed his arm and yanked him into a cluster of ferns. "Your first try," she said, amusement crinkling her voice. "I'm impressed."

"Ouch," he whispered, refusing to rub his haunch.

She gave him a swift kiss on the cheek. "I'm serious," she said, crouching low beside him. "That wasn't an easy climb."

"Did you fall on *your* arse?"

"No, but I've jumped way more walls than you have. You didn't break anything, and you didn't get caught. It counts."

"Fine." It didn't help his ego much, but as he glanced back at the ten-foot wall topped with three-foot spikes, Richard decided he had nothing to be ashamed of. Christ.

"Okay. See the light box there?" she asked, gesturing with one gloved hand. "I'll go first, and then I'll signal you when to follow. When you get there, get behind it and look back at the wall. Wait until the camera starts to swing away from you, then run straight for the chimney. And I mean run."

Richard took in the fifty-foot expanse of grass and low

flowers between the lighting box and the house. As a home-
owner, he would have thought it far too wide for anyone to
cross undetected. Looking at it from Samantha's point of
view, he could see that it was the shortest open space in the
garden, the way no window above had a straight-on view, the
camera to the north with an overgrown juniper between it
and the clearing. "Ready when you are," he murmured.

Flashing him a smile, Samantha returned her attention to
the cameras. "You totally dig this, don't you?" she breathed.

She took off before he could answer. Moving low to the
ground, she worked her way around the flower beds to the
lighting box. It didn't provide much cover, but since the camera only saw in two dimensions, whoever was monitoring the
screens would have to be paying extremely close attention to
see her crouched there. Of course, he was a foot taller than
she was, but he wasn't going to sit this one out.

Much as he'd hate to admit it, he did "dig" this. It was
arousing. And addictive. No wonder she was having such a
hard time giving it up.

With a barely perceptible push, Sam stood upright and ran
for the house. She hadn't been kidding about the importance
of speed. Richard didn't realize he'd been holding his breath
until he let it out, relieved, when she reached the small hol-
low beside the chimney.

Aware that she would probably already be in the house if
he hadn't insisted on tagging along, Richard waited for her
signal and then scrambled forward to the lighting box. That
had been fairly easy, though he sternly resisted the urge to
grin at her. Damn it, he was supposed to be dissuading her
from doing this sort of thing, not encouraging it. Drawing in
his legs, he eased around the side to watch the camera. As
soon as it swung past him, he broke into the open, running

toward the house and thankful that he still used the downstairs gym at Solano Dorado.

He slid in between the bushes and pressed himself against the wall beside her. "How was that?" he asked.

"Olympic." She had a small scratch on one cheek, probably from the shrubbery, but she made no effort to disguise the fact that she was having a great time. "Okay. According to the blueprints, we're leaning against the family room. Four windows down is the bathroom. That's where we're heading."

It made sense. Small, enclosed, and since it was in the main part of the house, employees probably didn't use it. He wouldn't ask how she meant to open the window; the longer she spent having to stop and explain things, the greater the chance they'd get caught.

They pushed along the wall to the fourth window, and he boosted her up to the casing. A few seconds later he heard a small pop, and the shards of glass fell at his feet. She pushed up the frame and scrambled through the opening.

A second later she leaned out again. "Wait until I put a towel over the casement," she whispered. "I don't want any Rick Addison blood lying around."

"I'm fairly thick-skinned," he whispered back, then hopped up and in without waiting for her. "Somebody's going to notice that the window's broken," he commented as she closed it behind them.

"I'll stick a branch through it on the way out."

For the first time Richard began to realize what a stroke of luck it had been that he'd caught her in the Rawley House library three weeks ago—or at Solano Dorado three months ago. She moved like a shadow, flitting past in the blink of an eye.

"So where's the gun going to be?"

She went to the bathroom door and cracked it open. "Somewhere he could take peeks at it to remind himself that he had the balls to off his dad, close enough where the cops could almost find it but not quite. He's an adrenaline junkie, too."

Too. Like her.

She'd been right about the security once they got inside the house; the motion detectors were turned off for the convenience of the staff, and he didn't see any sign that security patrolled the hallways. Only the distant sound of salsa music coming from the direction of the kitchen gave away the fact that there was anyone else there at all.

Outside Charles's office he slowed, but she continued in the direction of the back stairs. On the second floor she started peering through bedroom doorways. Richard caught on and headed up the far side of the hall. On a shelf just inside the third door he spied a yachting trophy. "Samantha."

She joined him at the door, then slipped inside and closed it behind them. "You *are* a natural at this," she said. "Check the closet, and I'll take the desk and the chest."

He was glad he'd remembered to bring gloves. Daniel probably had his own office in the house, but Richard agreed with Samantha that checking the bedroom first made the most sense. Adrenaline junkie or not, Daniel would want to be comfortable enough with the surroundings to figure he could hide the gun from the police. Gazing around the closet, Richard flipped on the light and started digging behind clothes. When she muttered his name a few minutes later, he joined her at the desk. "Daniel has a lot of polo shirts," he commented.

Samantha gave a quick smile. "Does this look short to you?" she asked, pulling open the bottom desk drawer.

"How do you—" Abruptly he realized what she meant.

The desk itself was about twenty-four inches deep, but the drawer looked a good six inches short of that. "Can you lift it out?"

She knelt and slid the mahogany drawer free, tilting it up in the last inch or so to free it from the runner. That done, she bent down to peer into the opening. "Bingo."

Samantha reached into the desk and pulled out a small metal box. Standing, she set it on the smooth mahogany surface.

Stepping in, Richard flipped the catch open and lifted the lid. A .45 lay in a loosely wrapped cloth, packets of what had to be cocaine stuffed in around it. "He keeps both bad habits together, anyway."

Samantha, though, was looking into the box, her expression still and solemn. "Jesus," she finally whispered. "He did it. He killed his own dad." She visibly shook herself. "And we're going to make sure he doesn't shoot one of us with this thing."

"But we can't move it without compromising the police investigation."

She picked up the lighter, pushed into one corner of the box. "Naughty Daniel, doing coke in his dad's house," she said, flipping it to him and closing the box again.

He caught it, watching as she uncoiled a copper-looking wire from her wrist and straightened the last few inches of it. At her gesture, he sparked the lighter, and she held the wire over the flame until it began to glow. Then she threaded it into the latch and twisted until the wire snapped. They repeated the procedure several times, until bits of hardening soldered wire jammed both hinges and the latch so solidly it would probably take a metal saw to break into the thing.

"Very nice, MacGyver. Will that do it?" he asked.

"Thanks. It's pretty seat-of-your-pants, but I think so.

Give it another minute to cool off, and we'll put it back and get the hell out of here."

"The police will know it's been tampered with."

"Yes, but it'll still hold a gun that has Daniel's prints on it, and it'll match the ballistics of the one that killed Charles. And they won't be able to prove we were anywhere near it."

"You're a wonder," he said, kissing her cheek.

"Yep, I can gum up the works like nobody's business," she said, putting the box back and stepping out of the way while he replaced the drawer. "Let's get out of here. We should do the picnic thing for real, just to cover our bases." Samantha kissed him back, on the mouth. "And I'm suddenly feeling kind of horny."

"Suddenly? I'm not sure I'll fit back through the window."

"Mm. Don't tease me, man. I hope you know a good private beach."

Nineteen

Monday, 8:13 a.m.

"So let me get this straight," Tom said, slamming a law book closed and not making any effort to conceal his annoyance. "You *don't* want Walter Barstone released from jail?"

After the argument he and Tom had had about that very thing, Richard decided to leave the talking up to Samantha. He sat back in one of the law office's comfortable client chairs and folded his arms.

"Correct," she said, obviously wanting to fight, and ready to settle for Tom.

He could understand that; Stoney was her family, and now in order to reassure Laurie that the police had another suspect to look at besides her brother, the plan involved not rescuing him. They'd discussed alternatives most of yesterday afternoon, and whatever his personal feelings about Walter, for Samantha's sake he'd made a genuine effort to come up with a way around this. Finally she'd been the one to come out and admit that Stoney needed to stay in jail.

"Shit." The attorney rounded on Richard. "You're going along with this?"

"It's Samantha's decision," he returned, keeping his voice cool. One of them had to remain calm.

"After all the calls I made and all the favors I called in, now you aren't going to do anything?"

"That's what I said," Samantha shot back.

A knock came at the closed office door, and Bill Rhodes stuck his head in. "Sorry I'm late. I was getting together some more information. Let's go over everything; we have to be in court in less than an hour."

"We're not going to court," Tom snapped, starting to stand up and then dropping into his chair again.

Rhodes came in the rest of the way and closed the door behind him. "What?"

"Go ahead, Jellicoe, tell him."

"It's not her fault, Tom," Richard finally put in. "I'm the one who asked you to follow up on this."

"That's right, you did. You came to my house and ordered me to get this guy out of jail."

Samantha turned in her chair and looked at him. Richard met her gaze, but didn't say anything. Whatever he'd done, he'd done for her, but it didn't matter at the moment—and they both knew it.

"You do realize I can probably get him back on the street with a minimal bond," Rhodes went on, leaning one haunch on the edge of Tom's credenza. "His last arrest was twenty years ago, and he's been a Florida resident for the past three years."

"I know all that," Samantha returned, impatience and annoyance touching her voice.

"Then what—"

"Just don't do anything, okay?" she blurted. "He has a court-appointed attorney, right?"

"Yes, but I wouldn't trust one overworked defense attorney to be able to—"

"That's fine. Let his own lawyer worry about it."

Both attorneys turned to Richard. "I don't understand, Rick," Rhodes said.

"It's complicated. We might still need your help, but not today."

"But today is his bond hearing."

"And if somebody else is arrested for what they say he did," Samantha broke in, "he'll go free regardless."

"But not today."

"No, not today," Samantha repeated, her voice rising. "That's the point. Dammit, you guys are supposed to be smart. Just don't show up in court! That's it! The end."

With a growl she stomped past the lot of them and slammed out the door. Richard stood, as well. "Sorry, gentlemen, but that's the way it needs to be. I'll explain it in a day or two."

"You'd damned well better, Rick." Donner slammed his fist into the desk again. "I used to be able to figure out what you were thinking. I didn't always agree with it, but at least it made some sort of sense."

"This does, too. Trust me."

When he caught up to Samantha, she was already seated in the SLR in the parking garage. He climbed into the driver's seat, and didn't ask how she'd managed to open the hi-tech car without setting off the alarm. Not after what he'd participated in yesterday. They sat there for a moment while he gave her the time to explode if she felt the need. Instead she curled her feet under her bottom and looked out the window.

Finally he started the car. "Where to?"

"The courthouse," she said, not moving otherwise.

That surprised him. "Are you certain?"

"When nobody shows up to get him out of jail, I at least want him to see my face."

A tear ran down that same face, and she impatiently wiped it away. The deep anger that had been building in Richard since he'd realized someone was trying to hurt Samantha crawled closer to the surface. They might have taken the gun out of play, but there were other ways to wound her—and Laurie or Daniel had found a good one.

"He'll understand, you know. When he sees you, he'll realize you have a plan. It'll be all right."

"After I practically promised to bust in there and break him out." She blew out her breath. "Let's go."

He didn't even know where the courthouse was, and had to access the SLR's GPS system to track it down in Delray Beach. Parking was full, but he managed to find a curbside space a block and a half down from the main building.

"You don't have to go in," she said as the doors flipped up and she climbed out of the car.

"Yes, I do." He offered his hand.

She gripped it hard, and they walked up the street to the main doors. This had to be as difficult for her as going into a police station for the first time—she'd mentioned that during her father's trial she hadn't dared go near court, in case someone testifying against him happened to recognize her. She wasn't in that kind of danger today, but the high security and the armed police everywhere didn't make this a picnic, either.

Tom had given him the courtroom number, and he asked at the information desk where they might find it. "Third floor," Samantha muttered as they headed for the stairs. "Too far to jump."

"There will be no jumping in my presence."

A light flashed in his eyes, and he started. Bloody great. Of course reporters would be assigned to hang around the courthouse. And of course they would be interested to see what Rick Addison might be doing there.

"Shit," Samantha breathed. "Like I need this on top of everything else."

"Just ignore them."

"Why are you here, Mr. Addison?" a reporter said, rushing them. Immediately the rest of the herd followed.

"No comment," he returned, keeping her close as he continued down the hallway. "Excuse me."

"But—"

Rick slowed, catching the reporter with an annoyed glare. "No comment."

The press backed off. He watched as they noted which courtroom he and Samantha were heading for and then ran downstairs to confirm who was on the docket this morning. One thing was for sure—Tom wasn't going to like any of this.

As soon as they were through the courtroom doors her shoulders sagged. "Are you all right?" he asked.

"I want to know which Kunz set him up," she growled, sliding onto the bench at the back of the room. "Whoever did it, they are going to be very, very sorry. And I am going to see the look in their eyes when they get caught."

The sight of the large bald black man in the orange jumpsuit was probably the worst thing Samantha had ever seen. Or so she thought, until she saw the expression in his eyes when he caught sight of her. "Oh, boy," she breathed, sinking lower on the bench.

"He'll get it," Rick insisted, though even he was beginning to sound a bit dubious. And he was supposed to be the cheerleader.

When the bailiff called the case number, the court-assigned defense attorney made his way through the low, swinging gate. Stoney looked at him, then turned around to look at Sam again. He lowered both eyebrows, clearly asking her what the hell was going on.

Sorry, she mouthed. Anything more substantial would have to wait until after the polo match and whatever came from that.

Rick held her hand, their fingers twined together. She was used to standing on her own two feet, making her own decisions, facing the resulting consequences. For probably the first time, though, it occurred to her that she wouldn't have been able to do this on her own.

The prosecutor read the list of charges, and she winced. Robbery, possession of stolen property, breaking and entering, with a possible charge of murder to follow. "Jesus," she whispered.

"You knew it would be like this," Rick returned equally quietly. "Take it easy."

His defense attorney then said that Walter pleaded not guilty, and noted exactly what Bill Rhodes had, that Stoney had had a clean record for the past twenty years, that he was an established resident of Palm Beach.

With barely a pause for the prosecutor to refute those two points, the judge denied bail and ordered Stoney remanded into custody. Stoney sent her a last annoyed look over his shoulder and vanished into the bowels of the courthouse.

The look actually reassured her a little. He knew she hadn't abandoned him, at least. As for the rest, if she couldn't follow through with the Kunzes, what happened to him next would be her fault.

"That sucked."

"Yes, but you've done your part, and now it's Laurie's turn."

"Yes, it is. And she'd better follow through." She stood, abruptly wanting to get out of the solid, somber building. "Breakfast. And then we'd better talk to Castillo."

They retrieved the car, and she let Rick choose the breakfast spot. To her surprise he pulled up in front of John G's on South Ocean Boulevard. "You're kidding me," she said.

"What? I can't know about good breakfast spots?"

"You've eaten here before?"

He nodded, escorting her to the front door. "Several times."

"But *I've* eaten here. Their cinnamon-nut French toast is fab."

"Yes, it is."

The waitress seated them by the window and left them to look over the menu. Rick seemed amused at her surprise—he obviously didn't get it. "What if we ate here at the same time?" she finally asked.

"We didn't. Have you had the stuffed croissant?"

"Yes, and how do you know we were never here together?"

He smiled. "Because I would have noticed you."

She couldn't help grinning back at him. "You are so smooth."

"Don't you forget it." He looked up as the waitress brought coffee. "Thank you, and a Diet Coke for the lady, if you please."

"Ooh, and gallant, too."

She didn't know how he managed it, but abruptly the day didn't seem nearly as gloomy. Hell, she was smiling. For a moment Samantha wondered again what in the world Patricia could have been thinking to screw things up so badly with him.

"What?" he asked, and she realized she'd been staring at him.

Samantha shook herself. "So tell me about a typical polo

match. And the layout of the grounds, too. I want to know what I'll be walking into this afternoon."

"Well, it's a weekday event for charity, so we won't be in the stadium. It'll be a field with umbrellas and tables on one side, and a canopy or two for refreshments and more seating."

"Reporters?"

"Tons of them. In addition to me, Trump shows up on occasion, and a handful of other celebrities, most of them just here for the Season."

Another thought abruptly occurred to her. "You promised me some ex-girlfriends at the Everglades Club, and Patty showed up. So how many of those actresses and models you've left strewn in your wake will be around?"

His jaw twitched. "Some, probably. They can't resist seeing me in my polo uniform. But how many former girlfriends must one have before they can said to be strewn?"

"The exact number that you have," she retorted. She'd seen photos of him with them, on the Internet, in every national rag, and even the more reputable magazines. And she knew there'd only been maybe half a dozen of them, though with the intensive coverage, the numbers seemed much higher than that.

"Don't worry, love. I won't be paying attention to anyone but you, busily trapping thieves and killers and strewing them in *your* wake."

"Yeah, and don't you forget *that*."

"So you made all these plans without telling me." Frank paced back and forth in the small police interrogation room and glared at them.

Personally, Richard thought the detective needed to be a little more lenient. This was quite possibly Samantha's least favorite place to be in the world, and yet she'd gone into the room voluntarily, and she was currently doing a fair impression of one of those *Law and Order* detectives, standing with her hands braced on the back of one of the metal chairs.

"You knew the general plan. Now we're telling you the details," she said gruffly.

"You could have told them to me before you passed them on to the Kunz kids. Or yesterday, maybe."

"We were doing that day of rest thing," Samantha retorted.

"Or she could have skipped telling you about them at all," Richard noted, ignoring that her idea of rest was breaking into a mansion. "The point being, we're here. What's the next step?"

"A wire," the other two said in unison.

That was a little frightening. "I'm not that familiar with American criminal law, but don't you have to have a court order or a warrant or something for that?"

Frank reached into his jacket pocket and pulled out a folded piece of paper. "Nope. All you need is an okay from your captain. And like you said, I knew the general plan. I figured something like this would be involved."

"Now we're smokin'," Samantha put in, taking the paper and reading through it. "Except for one problem."

"And what might that be?" Castillo asked, leaning against the one-way mirror.

"Your request doesn't say anything about how helpful I've been to your investigation, and how the police department will hold me harmless from any statements I might make in the course of nailing somebody's ass to the wall." She released the paper, and it floated down to the table.

"I thought about asking for it, but even though you've helped me out before, you're not real popular around here. Especially not when your partner is already in jail on this same case."

Richard looked at Samantha, abruptly worried. If pushed, would she choose Walter's freedom over her own? She blamed herself for him being arrested, and as of an hour ago for not getting him out on bail. He wouldn't allow her to go to prison for this—for anything.

She pursed her lips, looking down at the paper for a long moment. "Then I want something I can turn on and off."

Castillo shook his head. "That would mean wearing a tape recorder. I wouldn't get a live feed, so I wouldn't know when to come in and make the arrest—and I wouldn't know when you have the evidence I need to make the case. Plus any defense attorney would be able to say we tampered with the evidence, and he'd be right."

"Then I can't wear a wire."

"This isn't about getting your buddy out of trouble, Sam. It's about catching thieves and murderers and shit. It's just a happy coincidence that doing that will help your friend."

"I get that," she shot back at him. "Trust me. We'll come up with a signal, and you'll know. I can't help Stoney unless you get your evidence. I can follow the game plan, but I'm not wearing a wire unless I get some assurances."

Frank glared at her, while she looked right back at him. Even knowing what was at stake, Richard found the conflict interesting. Samantha definitely had a way of attracting strong personalities.

"All I can do is say I'll give it my best shot," the detective finally said.

"That's not good enough," Richard finally put in.

"She can wear a tape recorder, but it has to stay on. If we get enough evidence without using the tape, I'll personally lose it."

Richard slid a glance at Samantha. She stood with her

head lowered, the very image of deep, serious thought. Finally she looked up and nodded at him.

"The modified game plan," Rick said slowly, "is that once this is over, *I* get the tape. My attorney will review it, and then we will hand it over to you."

"I don't like it." The detective folded his arms across his chest.

"You think I do?" Samantha retorted. "Like I want Tom Donner to decide whether I'm going to be in trouble or not."

"Shit. I get the tape unmodified. Not matter what it says."

"You get the tape," Samantha repeated, only the clench of her fingers around the back of the chair letting Richard know how little she liked this plan.

Frank blew out his breath. "Okay. If you screw up, you're going to have to hire me or something, because I'm going to be shit out of a job."

"Deal," Samantha said, offering her hand.

The detective shook it. "Don't let me down, Sam."

"I'll add you to the list of people I can't let down today," she returned, sending a glance at Richard.

She couldn't let him down if she tried, but that wasn't what she wanted—or needed—to hear at the moment. It was bravado time, and they both knew it. "Just be glad you don't have to ride a horse," he said.

"Or hit that ball with that stick thing. I know, I'm getting off easy." Samantha turned her chair around and sat. "Okay, let's plan this out."

Twenty

"You should probably quit playing around with that," Rick suggested.

Samantha hooked the tape recorder back onto her belt. She knew all about video surveillance, but she needed to catch up on audio tracking. When Castillo had handed her a pager, she'd actually had to ask him how it worked. "It's neat," she commented, looking down at it again.

He tossed his polo helmet into his sport bag. "Yes, it's very neat. Don't turn it on by accident."

"I'm familiarizing myself with it. I almost wish it looked more like a recorder, though." Taking it off again, she popped it open to see the minitape inside. "There's got to be a way for me to flick it on and off without looking like I'm having a seizure or something, and without the cops being able to tell."

"Let's see it."

She handed it over. Rick had been a little quiet since they'd left the police station, and she knew he was worried. Hell, *she* was worried, but at least they wouldn't have to sit around and speculate much longer. It would have to be settled one way or another this afternoon.

"I have an idea," he said, looking up from the pager again.

"What?"

"Leave it here."

"Rick—"

"Don't wear it. I'll hire every attorney in the States to defend Walter, and every private detective in the world to find something on the Kunzes. Don't risk yourself like this, Samantha."

For a minute she didn't say anything. The thought, the worry, that had been eating at her since she'd gone to live with him in Devon wrenched through her gut again. "If I end up arrested in all this, what will you do?" she asked, even though she was fairly certain that she didn't want to know the answer. Everyone looked out for themselves first. It was the first law of thievery, and of just about everything else.

He shoved a pair of socks into the bag. "I don't know, Sam. I'll say that your present doesn't worry me as much as your past."

"I broke into a house yesterday," she returned. "That's pretty present." And that wasn't even all she'd done in the past week, though it was safe to assume that was all he knew about.

His shoulders lifted with the deep breath he took. "Don't ask me what I would do if your past caught up to you, because I—you—" He closed his eyes for a second. "You have my heart. So just don't balls it up, okay?"

Wow. She walked up and hugged him tightly around the waist. After a second his arms slid around her, holding her tight and safe. Safe. She'd never felt as safe as she had since she'd met Rick Addison. Slowly she rose up on her tiptoes and kissed him. "Okay," she whispered against his mouth.

"And I still don't like one spot of this."

"Well, I'm not sure you'll be all that safe riding that horse around."

"I can see I'll be giving you some riding lessons after this. Don't change the subject."

Samantha just held onto him for a minute, pretending it was lust and that she wasn't actually drawing strength from his support and his presence and his faith. "Can I name my horse Trigger?"

"You can name it Godzilla, for all I mind."

Reinaldo knocked on the bedroom door. "Mr. Addison, it's after one o'clock. Ben has the limousine ready."

"We'll be right there," Rick called.

"Duty calls," Samantha said, reluctantly slipping out of his embrace and snagging the pager in the same motion. "I can't wait to see you in your polo pants."

"I could still withdraw."

She snickered. "You never withdraw."

Rick slammed his fist into the bedroom wall with enough force to break through the plaster. "Dammit, I'm serious!"

Startled, she grabbed his hand. "Hey, stop that. I like those fingers." She turned his wrist, examining the deep abrasions across his knuckles. "That was stupid."

"More stupid than purposely setting yourself up to be arrested? Do you have to play *everything* so close to the edge?"

She smiled at him even as she dragged him toward the bathroom. "I'm not setting myself up to be arrested. I'll be careful."

"That's not good enough. I want to be right there, not out on the field where I can't do anything."

Her knight in shining armor. "We're just going to be talking," she said quietly, occupying herself with rinsing plaster dust off his hand and scrambling for a Band-Aid, and pretending that she wasn't half ready to cry. He *did* love her. He truly did. "The stuff I need you for will be afterward, when the cops want the tape."

"Saman—"

Finished sticking the Band-Aid around his knuckle, she yanked on his hair to pull his face down. She kissed him ferociously, feeling both the passion and the worry in his response.

"Let's go. I don't want to be late," she said after a breathless moment. "Don't forget your outfit."

She could practically see him pulling himself together, returning to Richard Addison the rich, suave, athletic businessman who always knew precisely what he was doing. And she wondered how many people *he* ever allowed to see the other side of him. Two, maybe? Or just her?

"It's a uniform, not an outfit," he said, following her back into the main room. He grabbed the duffel bag with one hand, and her fingers with the other.

"Time to go catch the bad guys," she said, heading for the door and hoping the powers that be considered her to be in the good guy camp, at least for today.

When they arrived at the field, Rick went straight to the locker room to change, leaving Samantha to wander around the near edge of the field. It was set up pretty much as he'd said, with two large canopies covering the refreshment and donation tables, and a field of umbrella tables and chairs filling the space between them. What she hadn't expected was that two fields were apparently going to be used, with the seats in the middle of the two. Great. The cops could only come in from two sides.

The dress of the day was sophisticated urban—which had made fitting in the pager difficult. It didn't quite go with her white and safari-green Prada dress, but hell, she supposedly owned a business. From what she knew of Laurie Kunz, the realtor would probably have a pager on her, as well.

Her compromise was to attach it to the strap of her purse, but even that looked stupidly ... obvious to someone as used to blending and keeping to the shadows as she was. With a sigh she hooked it over the inside edge of her purse, keeping the top unsnapped. If Castillo's contraption couldn't pick up anything from inside, that would be his own damned fault for giving her inferior equipment.

Rick had been right about the press and the celebrities, too, but she stifled her frown as paparazzi began aiming cameras in her direction. It was all part of the Addison package, and little as she liked it, at least she was getting used to it. Actress-model Julia Poole sat at one of the tables, her rocker boyfriend and a bottle of Corona beside her. Sam spent a moment looking at the tall, black-haired beauty. Julia and Rick had dated on and off for nearly a year, though from the tabloid photos it hadn't been anything close to exclusive.

Five tables away from the Poole party, Patricia sat with a few members of what Rick called "Patty's Pack," which consisted of probably a dozen total women who had joined together for the common cause of commiserating with Patricia and badmouthing Rick and her. They were welcome to their fun; personally, she thought the common thread was a lack of a single personality to divide among them.

Castillo was easy to pick out; in his tan cop suit and cheap shoes, he stood out as exactly what he was. Laurie would expect his presence, though, since even with Stoney in jail, no one had been officially charged with Charles's murder yet. Samantha presumed that Frank had backup, but if they were around, at least they were dressed appropriately enough to blend.

In the old days it would have freaked her out, knowing cops were around. Today she just hoped they would be far enough away that they couldn't overhear, and close enough that they could move in before any valuable evidence vanished. At least they wouldn't have to worry about one particular gun. Score one for the semi-good guys.

Rick appeared from the stables, a bay polo pony in tow. For a long moment she just watched him approach. His leather boots came up past his knees to protect him from mallet blows, and the white trousers beneath the loose green polo shirt made him look just . . . yummy. Even the green helmet with his wavy black hair beneath was attractive. And this guy was going home with her.

"What do you think?" he asked, holding the mallet easily over his right shoulder.

"I so want you to wear this to bed tonight," she murmured, leaning up along his lean body to kiss him.

He chuckled, taking the moment while he patted his horse's neck to look past her shoulder into the crowd. "Any sign yet?"

"No Laurie. How about Daniel?"

"No. He's on my team, so once we're out on the field I'll do my best to keep him occupied."

"What's your horse's name?" she asked, tentatively patting the near shoulder or wither or whatever it was called.

"Middlebrook-on-Thames," he replied.

"What?"

"Tim, for short. He has a nasty long pedigree."

"Hence the stupid name."

Rick raised an eyebrow. "*I* have a nasty long pedigree."

"I know that, Richard William Addison, Viscount Halford, Marquis of Rawley."

He kissed her again. "You got it straight, Samantha Elizabeth Jellicoe of Palm Beach."

At that moment Daniel and Laurie emerged from the stables, Daniel with a gray pony behind him, and Laurie with a picnic basket over one arm. "Bingo," she said softly.

To his credit, Rick didn't turn to look. "Be careful," he murmured, kissing her on the forehead. "I'd best go warm Tim up."

"You be careful, too," she said, stepping back to watch him swing gracefully into the saddle.

"I'll be watching."

With that Rick and Middlebrook-on-Thames trotted onto the field, to the general applause of the spectators. Sam started. She'd forgotten people were watching them. A flock of photographers approached, and she just barely stifled her urge to run.

"What are you wearing, Miss Jellicoe?" one of the women asked.

A dress was her first response, but she knew what they wanted, and the sooner they got it, the sooner they would leave her alone. "Prada," she answered, standing still for a minute so they could take her picture. Damn, life was strange.

"You and Mr. Addison were at the courthouse this morning. Have you set a date yet?" another of them asked.

Samantha blinked. Courthouse and a date. *A date.* Jesus Christ. "No," she blurted, knowing her face must be turning white. "I'm still trying to figure out how he cheats at Scrabble."

From the general laughter, she must have said the right thing, and with a short nod she made her escape. That was one conversation she was not going to repeat to Rick. Ever. Just the thought—

The referee blew his whistle, and the two teams assembled in the middle of the field. The same thing was going on behind her, but this was the game that had her attention. For a moment she wished she didn't have to do anything but watch Rick play.

That, though, was for somebody with a different life than hers. With a sigh she flipped on the recorder, then went to find a table with a decent view and wait for Laurie to bring by her apples—just like the wicked queen from *Snow White*. The only difference was that Samantha knew better than to take a bite.

"So is it odd or fitting that Rick and Daniel are on the same team?" Laurie asked, taking the chair opposite Samantha and setting the picnic basket on the table in front of her.

"I don't think it's either," Sam replied, keeping her gaze on the players as they raced back toward the red team's goal. "Rick's not part of this. That's the deal, remember?"

"I remember. I saw your court appearance on the midmorning news. It's a shame you couldn't arrange for bail for Mr. Barstone."

"Don't push it, or I'll increase my cut to thirty percent."

"Not likely."

Samantha turned her gaze to Laurie. "Just make sure you and Daniel keep up your end of the deal. Did you bring me some apples?"

Laurie lifted the lid of the picnic basket and pulled out a shiny red apple. "Are you certain you can take care of this?"

"Oh, yes."

"Next time pick something less messy," she commented, handing the apple to Sam.

It was heavy. Too heavy to be just an apple. Easily hiding her relief behind years of practice, Samantha set the fruit on the table at her elbow. Okay, she had robbery evidence. Now she needed murder evidence. Time to play her hand. "How are you going to make sure that Daniel doesn't kill you the same way he did your dad? The company will go to you now, after all. Won't it?"

With a smile, Laurie set the picnic basket down on her lap. "We're very close. Besides, if another Kunz turned up dead, not even Daniel could charm his way out of an arrest."

"Sure, that makes sense to you and me, but I don't have a

drug habit. You're kind of stuck, aren't you? I mean, you either arrange to pay for his coke or start dodging bullets."

Sam caught sight of Patricia waving a handkerchief at Daniel, and his responding mallet wave back. That figured. Patty would play all sides until one of them came back to bite her in the butt.

"I'd rather talk about profit margins," Laurie returned.

"That's pretty calm talk for somebody with a basketful of ruby reds in her lap."

"If I'm disposing of stolen goods, then you're receiving them."

Wow, she was confident. Didn't Laurie care at all that her brother had killed their father? Or was her nonchalance about Daniel because *she* had pulled the trigger? That made a damned lot of sense, but Sam needed to be sure. Time to turn up the heat.

"You know, Walter knows exactly how much a Giacometti is worth," she said slowly.

"Which would be why he stole it."

"Except he would have stolen it the same night that the rubies and paintings went missing. He wouldn't go back for it a week later."

"Now that I think about it, there's no Giacometti statue listed in the insurance paperwork. That must have belonged to someone else."

"That's lame," Sam replied, warming to the conversation. She loved puzzles, especially right before they were solved. "How many people were at the wake? I'd guess at least fifty of them went into your dad's old office and saw the statue sitting there. Want to try again?"

"I—"

"Oh, wait, now it's my turn." Samantha sat back in her chair, hoping she looked the picture of cool confidence—

which wasn't easy considering how many assumptions and leaps of faith she was about to make. Still, she knew thieves, and she knew their mentality. She doubted this one was all that different. "*You* killed Charles because he wouldn't bail out Paradise Realty. How many months in a row were you late paying your office rent? No wonder you jumped so fast when Rick called. Good thing you didn't have any other appointments to cancel—oh, no, that's a bad thing, isn't it? Your dad knew you were getting desperate for money. That's why he called me in, to make sure you couldn't do anything to him before he got all the wills and trusts amended. He didn't get it though, did he? How bad it would look for the daughter of one of the country's most successful businessmen to fail at her own business, especially with the price of property around here?"

"You can't prove any of that," Laurie said, the color in her cheeks deepening.

She was getting angry, which was what Sam was aiming for. "Sure I can. I have the rubies."

Laurie shifted, her hand drifting into the basket. "Give me that apple back," she murmured.

"Nope. I like apples."

Both hands went into the basket, followed by the distinctive sound of a pistol being cocked. "Give me back the apple."

Fuck. Rick had been right. It *had* been Laurie all along. "If you use that, nobody's gonna believe you didn't murder your dad. Daniel's your last scapegoat, Laurie. Don't blow it. If you turn yourself in now, you can claim you panicked and you were trying to get rid of the rubies to help your brother. He's the only family you have."

"Nice story."

"*I* think so. You might have gotten away with it all, if Daniel hadn't decided he couldn't wait for the insurance settlement and needed cash for his little nasal problem," she continued. "That must have pissed you off, doing this great robbery and still having to take the one Gugenthal item not reported stolen and have Aubrey Pendleton sell it to that antique shop. All those goods, and no one to help you turn them into cash."

Laurie smoothly stood, shifting the basket over one elbow and keeping her opposite hand buried in its depths. "Ooh, hurray, you're so smart. Pick up your apple and let's go for a walk."

"Fine with me." Fewer people to help her out, but she didn't expect much of that. At least bystanders were less likely to get shot if they moved the arena somewhere else. Sam got to her feet, snagging the apple and her purse as she did. "Let's go."

"Samantha?" They both turned as Patty approached, white purse over her arm and distaste all over her face.

"I'm a little busy now, Patty."

"I need a word with you." Patricia sent a glance at Laurie. "Right now."

"Then come with us," Laurie interrupted.

"Oh, that's not—"

The muzzle of the pistol emerged from the basket, just long enough for Patty to see it. "We're going for a walk," Laurie continued, smiling.

Patricia turned white, but she headed in the direction Laurie indicated, toward the stables. Of course. There would be plenty of places to hide—or slip away after committing a murder.

Across the tent, Frank ambled to his feet, but Sam shook her head. If there was one thing they couldn't afford right now it was a gun battle. She could see Rick at the far side of the field, his attention on the game at hand. Good. She didn't want him hurt.

The three of them made their way down the line of tables

and out from under the canopy. Laurie stayed a little behind, while Patty crowded close to Sam. The Ex was probably planning on throwing her in the way of any bullets.

"I knew having anything to do with you was a mistake," Patty whispered fiercely, her cheeks gray.

"You're the one who got chummy with the Kunz kids. Don't complain to me."

They rounded the first of the stables, out of sight of the polo players and their audience. "I'm glad you're here, Patricia," Laurie commented. "Now I can make it look as though you two killed one another."

Great. It was even pretty clever. Samantha could picture the scenario: Patricia dated Daniel to get an in with the family, then brought in the thief for a robbery-murder, and then they got greedy over the proceeds and maybe even over Rick and shot one another. "You really think we could kill each other with the same gun?" she asked. Anything to delay, to throw a wrench into Laurie's plans.

"Anything could happen in a struggle."

Sam inched away from Patricia, giving herself room to move. "No way. I'd kick her ass in a fight." Without warning she whipped around, letting gravity slide her purse from her elbow to her hand. Carrying through with the motion, she slammed Laurie in the side of the head.

Laurie stumbled, the basket falling to the muddy ground. She kept her grip, though, on the gun. "Duck!" Sam yelled, shoving Patricia sideways.

Propelled mostly by instinct, Samantha slammed herself against Laurie, grabbing the gun hand in hers and shoving upward. The pistol fired, the bullet burning along her arm as it shot skyward. Overbalanced, the two of them hit the soft ground. Laurie yanked backward, trying to free the gun, but Sam refused to let go.

They rolled. For a sickening second Laurie shoved Sam's face full into the mud. *Christ*. Fighting panic, she shoved with her free hand, turning Laurie onto her back again. Shaking mud from her eyes, she kicked, freeing one of her pumps. It thunked onto the ground beside her, and she grabbed it, holding Laurie down with her shoulder and her knees grinding into Laurie's hips.

"Hey!" she yelled, angling the heel of her pump toward Laurie's face. "You want this in the eye? Let go of the gun!"

"Bitch!"

Sam slammed Laurie in the shoulder with the heel, knowing that it hurt. "Let go of the gun or the next time I take out an eye!"

Another weight landed across their tangled arms, and through the mud she glimpsed Castillo and a herd of suddenly armed and capable-looking audience members. The cavalry. Thank God.

"Okay, Sam, we've got the gun," Castillo grunted, lifting her bodily around the waist.

"Get the apples!" she panted, staggering away and trying to find her balance with one shoe missing. All she needed was for a herd of stray polo ponies to eat the evidence.

Laurie shot to her feet, only to be grabbed by a pair of cops. "I didn't do anything," she snapped. "She attacked me!"

"She killed her dad," Sam managed, swiping a thick layer of mud off her face and arms. "It's on the—"

Charging straight at her full speed, his mallet raised over his head, was Daniel Kunz.

Twenty-one

Monday, 2:57 p.m.

Richard was one stroke away from making a goal when he heard the gunshot. Wrenching around, he looked at Samantha's table. It was empty. His heart jolted. Tapping Tim's ribs, he angled for the edge of the field.

"Look out, Rick!" one of his opponents, Bob Neggers, yelled.

He jerked his head around just in time to take a mallet across the shoulder rather than the back of his head. It knocked him off balance, and he grabbed the low pommel to keep from falling to the ground. By the time he straightened, swearing, Daniel was at the far edge of the field and headed for the stables.

Richard sent Tim charging after them. Running spectators and paparazzi scattered as Daniel galloped through them, Rick on his heels.

"Sam!"

Even as Richard yelled to warn her, Samantha dove sideways and rolled beneath the swinging mallet. Rick had a fleeting, surreal moment to note that she made it look grace-

ful even in a mud-covered dress. Daniel yanked his horse
around and went after her again. Police yelled, aiming pis-
tols at Kunz, but with the press everywhere filming, they
weren't likely to shoot.

Which meant it was up to him. "I don't think so," Richard
growled as Daniel and his mount rounded after Samantha.
He sent Tim crowding into the other horse and rider. The
mallet swung at his head again, but this time he saw it coming and ducked.

Richard urged Tim forward again, cutting Daniel off from
pursuing Samantha. Clearly, though, pushing and blocking
wasn't going to suffice.

He swung his own mallet, catching Daniel in the thigh.
The wood handle cracked and split. Annoyed, he flung it to
the ground and leapt. He hit Daniel in the ribs, and they both
went crashing to the ground. As Daniel climbed to his feet,
Richard charged and hit him full in the chest, throwing them
both down again.

Richard yanked the mallet out of Daniel's hand, then
found himself grabbed around the arms and shoulders and
pulled backward. He fought against the grip, furious.

"Rick!"

Castillo's face came into focus in front of him. With another curse Richard subsided, shrugging what felt like half
the Palm Beach police force off him. "All right! All right."

"We'll take it from here," Frank continued, still eyeing
him warily.

Richard didn't have any more time for him. Instead he
whipped around, and nearly crashed into Samantha as she
approached. Thank God.

"Are you all right?" he asked, gripping her arms and
pulling her closer.

"I'm fine. That was some nice riding, Tex." She reached

up and brushed a finger across his cheek. "You're cut, though."

"I nearly caught a rock in the eye," he said, still unable to take his gaze off her, to make sure she hadn't been clubbed or trampled. "You're cut, too."

She glanced at her arm. "Just a graze."

Jesus. "You got what you needed?"

"We got the rubies," Castillo said, joining them again. "And an attempted murder by Laurie Kunz, plus an assault by Daniel Kunz. That'll do for starters. Where's the tape?"

One of his officers brought up Sam's purse, which looked as though one of the horses had trampled it. No matter what kind of evidence the recorder might have held, Tim was getting an extra ration of oats tonight.

"That's just great," Castillo grumbled, pouring the remains of his wire into a bag. "Did you plan this?"

"Just lucky," Samantha returned, clearly relieved. "And hey, if that's not the gun used to kill Charles, there's another one behind the bottom drawer of Daniel's desk at Coronado House. There's some cocaine there, too."

"And you know this because?"

"Oh. It was on the tape. Sorry."

"I bet." The detective handed off the bag. "Do you know how expensive those things are?"

"Bill me," Samantha returned. "After you get my friend out of jail."

"It'll take a day or two, but I think we'll manage that." He glanced around. "I'd better get the Kunzes out of here before the press ruins my case."

Paparazzi surrounded them. "I'm not much in the mood for this, either," Richard said, taking Samantha's hand. "What say we go give Tim some of those apples?"

"No!" Castillo bellowed.

"He was kidding, Frank. Lighten up," Samantha said, and turned back to Rick. "And yes, let's get the hell out of here."

His brusque "No comment," together with the glares he was handing out, seemed to cow the press for the second time that day, and as soon as Richard handed Tim off to a groom, he and Sam hurried toward the parking lot and the waiting limousine. They were followed, of course, but he was more concerned with not being overheard than with not being seen.

"You're certain you're all right?" he repeated.

"I'm fine. Really. I mean, sheesh, the first time we did something like this I ended up with a fractured skull, and the second time a pickup truck tried to run me over. Some mud and a stampeding horse is nothing."

"And the bullet graze?"

"Well, it stung, but—"

Her head was yanked backward out of his sight, followed by the rest of her.

"How dare you?" Patricia shrieked, still hauling Samantha by the hair.

Sam twisted, grabbing her hair to pull it free from Patricia's grip. She'd lost hair three months ago fighting with Patty's soon to be ex-husband, and it had hurt like hell. She wasn't doing it again. "Back off," she ordered.

From her red face, Patricia wasn't having any. "You pushed me into the mud! And you just left me there and took credit for everything!"

"And where were you when Laurie tried to shoot us? Oh, that's right, you were safe behind the stable. And you're welcome."

"You—"

Sam slapped Patricia's pointing finger down. "Touch me again and nobody in Palm Beach is going to want you around for anything but cleaning their toilets." She took a breath. "You'll still get credit for figuring out that Daniel had something to do with the theft and murder. A promise is a promise."

"I—I'd better. And I want that videotape."

"No fucking way, Patty. I'm not an idiot." Sam moved around her, rejoining Rick. "Let's get out of here."

"You're really going to give her credit?"

She shrugged. "A little. The less testifying I have to do, the better."

"Right," he returned, then uncharacteristically cleared his throat. "I seem to have lost my realtor."

Sam sent a glance over her shoulder at Laurie, protesting everything as Castillo set her into the back of a police car. This conversation wasn't about Laurie Kunz, though; she could tell that just from Rick's hesitation. "And?" she prompted.

"And so I thought I might look for another one. In New York, say."

"New York's nice." She swiped mud off her arm and slung it to the ground. "We don't spend much time there, do we?"

"No, we don't."

"Even better, studmuffin."

Rick smiled, sending his gaze down the muddy length of her and lingering for a moment at her chest. "You look hot, by the way."

Great. She obviously had a wet T-shirt thing going. "If you're going to stay in that uniform, I'll stay in this outfit."

"Do I get to hose you down?"

Sam pressed against his side, making sure he was getting good and muddy. "We'll take turns. So you finally got to play the knight in shining armor thing for real," she noted. "Horse and all."

Rick laughed. "Ain't I cool?"

Epilogue

Thursday, 8:40 a.m.

Samantha drove into the parking structure and left the Bentley. Early as it was, she still felt miserably behind; she hadn't even been to her own damned office in five days.

She rode up the elevator and walked down the hall, pulling out her keys as she went. Inside the office suite everything was quiet and neat, all the furniture where it belonged and now a tasteful forest green, all of the empty files put into cabinets and ready for client information.

As she reached the reception desk, though, she frowned. Both she and Stoney suddenly had double mail slots, one marked *mail* and the other marked *messages*. In her message slot were a half-dozen phone messages in a neat hand, detailing name, time called, return phone number, and message. And they all wanted to make an appointment regarding her services.

Holding the messages, she went through the side door into the office area, making the circle of the back. No one was there. Stoney had taken the day off, and considering that he'd only gotten out of jail yesterday afternoon, she wasn't going to argue with him. He'd smacked her across the fanny, but since he'd hugged her, too, she knew their shady little world was still intact.

Diet Cokes still lined the little break room refrigerator door, so she took one and popped the tab. As she turned, she caught sight of the Gauguin print hanging in the opposite hallway.

"Hello," Rick's voice came from reception. "Might I get some service up here?"

With a grin she made her way to the desk. "I thought you had a meeting with Donner."

"I'm taking a coffee break," he returned, leaning over the phone to kiss her. He swivelled one arm from behind his back, producing a crisp currency bill. "One hundred dollars."

"I was wondering whether you'd pay up on the bet." She took it, snapping the Benjamin Franklin. "This is going to buy me some new underwear."

"Saucy." He brought his other arm around in front of him. A pretty potted asparagus fern sat in his hand.

"What's this?" she asked, taking it from him.

He shrugged. "I neglected to get you an office-warming present. And I know you like plants, so there you go." Rick rocked back on his heels, looking absurdly pleased with himself. "I picked it out myself."

Feeling unexpected tears pushing at the back of her eyes, Samantha set the plant on the closest file cabinet. "Come here, studmuffin," she said, leaning across the desk to grab him by the lapels.

She kissed him, drinking in his warmth and his presence and his touch as he cupped the sides of her face and kissed her in return. He'd known just what present she would appreciate the most, and he'd gone out and gotten it for her.

Rick slid his hands down around her waist and lifted, drawing her forward over the desk to his side of the reception area. She leaned into him, meeting his deepening embrace eagerly.

"So you're okay with my tiny little operation?" she asked, her voice not quite steady. "Two weeks ago you were pushing for that worldwide conglomerate thing."

He gazed at her for a long moment. "No guarantees that I'll stop pushing, but I'm okay with anything you want to do, Samantha—as long as I get to be a part of your life and you stay clear of things that will get you put in jail."

She reached up and traced his lean jaw with her fingertips. "I love you, Rick Addison," she murmured. The roof didn't cave in, lightning didn't strike, and her father didn't magically appear from the beyond to chastise her. In fact, it didn't hurt at all to say it. It actually felt . . . warm, and comforting.

He smiled. "I love you, Samantha Jellicoe."

That felt even better.

The office door opened again. "Well, look who's here," Aubrey Pendleton said, strolling into reception.

Samantha drew a breath. "Are you the office fairy?"

The handsome blond man grinned. "Excuse me?"

"The one who hung up the painting and took all the messages?"

"Oh, yes, well, then I am the office fairy. Guilty as charged."

Rick cleared his throat. "And you are?"

"Sorry," Sam interjected. "Rick Addison, Aubrey Pendleton. Aubrey, Rick."

The two men shook hands. "Is that your Barracuda outside?" Aubrey asked.

Rick nodded. "It's a new acquisition. My 'sixty-five Mustang was recently totaled."

"It's flash. I've got a 'sixty-two El Dorado. Took me a year, but I rebuilt the engine myself."

Leaning closer as Aubrey straightened the mess they'd made of the reception desk, Rick's lips brushed Sam's ear. "He is *not* gay," he whispered, then straightened again. "You helped Samantha out," he said. "Thank you."

"My pleasure. I admire her spunk."

"Spunk. That's me, all right." Sam pulled the messages out of her jacket pocket. *Rick was wrong about Aubrey. Probably.* "Hey, are these legit?"

Aubrey nodded. "You bet," he drawled. "They're practically beating down your door."

Rick took her free hand, picking up his briefcase with his other. "Sam, could I see you in your office for a minute?"

Without waiting for an answer, he started dragging her toward the hall door. She didn't fight him, but looked back at the walker. "Do you want a real job?" she asked.

"Miss Samantha, you hired me three days ago," Aubrey answered. "I just didn't have a chance to tell you."

"Cool."

Once they were in her office, Rick locked the door. "You're hiring him?"

"You heard him—I already did."

"Sam—"

"Come here and kiss me again," she ordered, walking over to close the office blinds. No sense giving Donner a thrill this early in the morning.

He joined her by the window, kissing her lips softly. She liked that he didn't make a big deal about what she'd said. After all, it wasn't like she'd agreed to marry him or something.

Just as she was about to melt, he backed off a little. "By the way," he whispered, "I thought you might like to take a look at this."

She grinned. "I've seen it before."

"Not that." He reached into his jacket and pulled out a folded newspaper. "This."

With a frown she took it, unfolding yesterday's *Palm Beach Post*. Across the top of the section it said "Society Page." Beneath that, the headline PUMMELING ON THE POLO GROUNDS shouted at her, with a large black and white photo of herself and Laurie going at it in the mud. Patricia was in view behind them—or her backside was, anyway, as she crawled out of danger. "Great," she muttered.

"Read the part I highlighted," he instructed, indicating the paragraph with the tip of one finger. "Out loud."

Samantha cleared her throat. " 'When asked whether she and Addison had set a date after their morning's trip to the courthouse, Jellicoe's response was a resounding, "No. I'm . . ." She trailed off.

"Finish it."

Fuck. " ' "I'm still trying to figure out how he cheats at Scrabble," she said, dodging any further questions.' "

" 'Cheats'?" he repeated, taking the paper back.

"Well, yes. Cheats."

"Aha." Moving away, he picked up his briefcase. "Sit down."

Furrowing her brow, she complied, sinking into the chair behind her desk. "What are you doing?"

He lifted a Scrabble board and a sack of letters out of the briefcase and set them on the desktop. "It's not cheating when I'm simply better at the game than you. All of we English are. And I'm going to prove it, Yank."

She grinned, picking up her Diet Coke and taking a swallow. "Oh, this is war, Brit. Bring it on."

MEN ARE LIKE A BOX OF CHOCOLATES . . .

You never know what you're going to get, but they're all tasty!

There are over six billion people on this planet and half of them are men (yeah!). But how is a gal to choose among so many? Are you drawn to the quiet and sensitive bespectacled gentleman next door? Or are you just dying to tame that bad boy with the tattoo? Are you a fan of Russell Crowe or Tobey Maguire? Perhaps you like them all . . .

In these four Avon Romance Superleaders, we've compiled a little sampling of the yummiest men around to tempt even the pickiest heroine. Turn the pages and meet four irresistible heroes—a sexy cop, a debonair billionaire, a rakish reformed pirate and a scandalous dark lord . . .

*If you like the smooth
sophistication of a mousse-filled
chocolate, then you'll love*

DON'T LOOK DOWN
by Suzanne Enoch
Coming January 2006

Ex-thief Samantha Jellicoe and British billionaire Richard
Addison are back for another sexy, twisted escapade of
romance, stolen jewels and male escorts in sizzling Palm
Beach. Sam is trying to set up a legitimate security business,
but when her first client ends up dead, Sam can't rest until
she figures out whodunit—a task complicated by Rick's
heated scrutiny.

"I caught you red-handed in Florida three months ago, and
now here in Devon. It's probably a good thing you did retire
from the cat burglary business."

Oh, that was enough of that, the superior British ass.
Samantha leaned up to kiss Rick, feeling the surprise of his
mouth and then his arms slipping across her shoulders as his
body relaxed. She slid the rope off her arm and twisted it
around his hands, ducking from beneath his grip.

"Sam—"

She whipped the free end of the rope around him, pulling
it tight and knotting his hands across the front of his ribs.
"Who's slipping now?" she asked.

"Take this off," he snapped, the gloating humor leaving his voice and his expression.

"Nope. You've disparaged my abilities." She pushed against his chest, and he sat down heavily in one of his Georgian reading chairs. "Apologize."

"Untie me."

Ooh, he was mad. Even if she'd been inclined to do so, letting him loose now seemed a supremely bad idea. Besides, she'd been working on a healthy adrenaline high that he'd managed to wreck. Before he could push to his feet, she tied him to the chair with the rest of the rope. "Maybe this'll convince you not to confront people breaking into your house unless you have something more substantial than charm to defend yourself with."

"You're the only one who breaks into my house, and I'm beginning to find it less amusing."

"Of course you are," she mused, stepping back to admire her handiwork. "I'm in charge."

Dark blue eyes met hers. "And apparently into bondage. Naughty, naughty."

"Apologize, Rick, and I'll let you go."

His jaw twitched, his gaze lowering to her mouth. "Let's say I'm calling your bluff. Do your worst."

"Ah." This was getting interesting. "My worst is pretty bad," she commented, her adrenaline beginning to recover. Tying up Rick Addison. Why hadn't she thought of this before? "Are you sure you're up for it?"

"Definitely," he returned, pushing toward her against the rope.

Slowly, Samantha leaned in and licked the curve of his left ear. "Good."

He turned his head, catching her mouth in a hard kiss. "So

is this what I should expect every time you meet with a client?"

Samantha pulled her pruners from her back pocket, amused at the sudden wariness in his eyes. "Apparently," she returned, snipping the neck of his sweatshirt and then opening up the front of the material to expose his chest and washboard abs. The first time she'd set eyes on him she'd thought he looked more like a professional soccer player than a businessman, and she still couldn't quite control the way his body affected her.

"Then I definitely encourage you to expand this business of yours."

"I don't want to talk about business right now."

If you enjoy the seemingly
innocent surface of a cherry cordial
hiding a sinfully sweet center,
then you'll love

SEX, LIES, AND ONLINE DATING
by Rachel Gibson
Coming February 2006

Hardluvnman. Bigdaddy 182. Welcome to the world of online dating. Lucy has gone on a series of blind dates—and has pretty much given up—when she meets Quinn. At first he seems promising, but then he tells her his tales of woe, and she figures she's dating another loser. Except this time, Lucy doesn't realize she's dating a cop—one who is after a female killer—and, though she doesn't know it, Lucy may be a suspect. Is Quinn out to protect her or to get her?

Lucy pushed back the sleeve of her jacket and looked at her watch. Ten after seven. Ten minutes late. She'd give hard-luvnman another five, and then she was leaving.

She'd learned her lessons about dysfunctional men. She wanted a nice, normal guy who didn't drink too much, wasn't into extremes of any kind, and didn't have mommy/daddy issues. A man who wasn't a compulsive liar or serial cheater. Who wasn't emotionally retarded or physically repugnant. She didn't think it was too much to ask that he have sufficient verbal skills, either. A mature man who knew that grunting an answer did not pass for conversation.

Lucy took a drink of her coffee as the door to Starbucks swung open. She glanced up from the bottom of her cup to the man filling up the doorway as if he'd been blown in from a "mad, bad and dangerous to know" convention. The bill of his red ball cap was pulled low on his forehead and cast a shadow over his eyes and nose. His tanned cheeks were flushed from the cold, and the ends of his black hair curled up like fish hooks around the edge of the hat. Rain soaked the wide shoulders of his black leather bomber's jacket. The jacket's zipper lay open, and Lucy's gaze slid down a bright strip of white T-shirt to the worn waistband of faded Levi's. As he stood there, his gaze moving from table to table, he shoved his fingers into the front pockets of the worn denim, his thumbs pointing to his button fly.

Mr. hardluvnman had finally arrived.

Like his photo on the Internet site, Lucy could not see him clearly, but she knew the second his gaze focused on her. She could feel it pinning her to her chair. She slowly lowered her cup as he pulled his hands from his pockets and moved toward her. He walked from his hips, all long and lean, with a purpose to each step. He navigated his way through chairs and coffee drinkers but kept his gaze on her until he stood across the small table.

The shadow of his cap rested just above the deep bow of his top lip. He raised a hand and slowly pushed up the brim of his cap with one finger. By degrees, the shadow slid up the bridge of his nose and past thick black brows. He looked down through eyes the color of a smoldering Colombian blend.

Lucy was a writer. She worked with words. She filled each of her books with a hundred thousand of them. But only two words came to mind. *Holy crap!* Not eloquent, but fitting.

"Are you Lucy?"

"Yeah."

"Sorry I'm late," he said. His voice was deep, testosterone rough. "My dog got into the garbage just as I was leaving, and I had to clean up after her."

Which Lucy supposed could be true but, she reminded herself, probably wasn't. Not that it mattered. After tonight, she would never see this hunk of hardluvnman again. Which was kind of too bad, since he was the best-looking thing she'd seen outside of a men's magazine.

"I'm Quinn." He held his hand toward her, and the sides of his jacket fell open across his chest to reveal hard pecs and abs of steel all wrapped up in his tight T-shirt. The kind of pecs and abs that begged the question: Why did a guy like him have to go online to find a date? It didn't take her long to come up with the answer. Inside that hard body, there was something wrong with him. Had to be.

Lucy took his hand in hers. His warm palm pressed into hers. Calloused. Strong. The kind that actually might belong to a plumber. She took her hand back and wrapped it around her cup. "Aren't you going to get a coffee?"

"I'm good." As he sat, his dark scrutiny touched her face, her hair, and cheeks, then slid to her mouth. His voice dropped a little lower when he asked, "Are you good?"

*If you're a fan of the nutty,
rough-around-the-edges taste of a
chocolate nut cluster,
then you'll love*

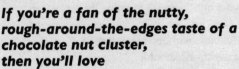

HER MASTER AND COMMANDER
by Karen Hawkins
Coming March 2006

The Duke of Rochester's oldest illegitimate son, wounded war hero and one-time pirate Tristan Llevanth, has no idea that he's about to become "legitimized." Under the guidance of the duke's butler Reeves, his bothersome yet delectable neighbor Prudence Thistlewaite molds a reluctant Tristan into a real lord. Lessons turn into kisses, which quickly turn into hot, searing passion . . .

Prudence met his gaze without flinching. "I am here to see to it that you stop running from your responsibilities. I want the issue of the sheep resolved. I came here to see to it that you do something about it."

"I rather thought you came here because you enjoyed my company. My wit."

Her gaze narrowed. "I have asked you time and again to keep your sheep out of my garden."

"And I've said it before and again; shut the blasted gate—*firmly.*"

She stamped her foot, her boot landing in a puddle and

splashing mud upon the edges of the moss green skirts barely visible beneath the voluminous blue cloak. "Captain, the gate *was* shut. *Firmly.*"

"Are you saying my sheep are jumping the fence into your garden?"

"Yes. The white one with the black face."

Tristan looked over his shoulder. "Stevens!"

The first mate appeared as if by magic. "Aye, Cap'n?"

"Do I have a white sheep with a black face?"

Stevens scratched his chin, his brow furrowed. "Hmm. Seems I seen one of that cut not too long ago."

"Is it possible that this particular sheep can jump a fence the height of the one surrounding Mrs. Thistlewaite's garden?"

"By Peter's watery grave, no!" the first mate said, chuckling at the thought.

Mrs. Thistlewaite's full lips pursed into a scowl. "Captain, I do not appreciate your levity. I do not know how your sheep manages to creep past my fence, but he does. And then he grazes through my spice bed like a great scythe, eating all of my herbs and trampling the flower beds."

"Hmm." Tristan noted the rising color in the widow's face. He stifled a grin. Perhaps he enjoyed teasing her so much because she looked so very prim and perfect, her hair so severely bound, her cloak buttoned to her throat, her mouth a determined line that almost dared to be invaded. Plundered. *Tasted.*

He found himself staring at her mouth. The bottom lip was fuller than the top and gently rounded underneath. He wondered if it was as sensitive as it looked, how she would react if he kissed her and then gently—

Startled at the direction his thoughts were taking, he pulled himself back into the present. "Mrs. Thistlewaite, as you can see, sheep do not jump good fences, nor do they crawl beneath closed gates, nor do they fly through the air to land in the midst of a garden. I, myself, have a garden, and the sheep never bother it, so I feel there are no grounds for your complaints. You will have to deal with the sheep issue on your own."

"Captain," Mrs. Thistlewaite said, her voice frigidly perfect, "I can see that I wasted my time coming here."

"You not only wasted it, but you have made yourself unwelcome. If you keep pestering me with this sheep nonsense, I shall train my dogs to herd those bloody animals onto your land every blasted morning."

"Oh! I cannot believe you'd— How dare you?" She drew herself up, her eyes flashing fire, her mouth set. "You, sir, are no gentleman."

No gentleman. The words flamed across his mind. His father had been a gentleman. "Fortunately for us all, I've never wanted to be a gentleman. Not now. Not ever."

If you crave the complexity and full flavor of a dark chocolate truffle, then you'll love

SWORD OF DARKNESS
by Kinley MacGregor
Coming April 2006

The first in a dazzling new series, Lords of Avalon, introduces Seren, a lovely young apprentice destiny has chosen as the future mother of one of the most powerful Merlins . . . Kerrigan is a Lord of Darkness sent by the evil Morgen le Fey to capture and hold Seren until the Lords of Avalon give Morgen what she needs to rule the world of man and demon. But, recognizing her purity, Seren is what Kerrigan has yearned for throughout time—yet can he save her in the face of evil?

"Thank you, my lord," Seren said to the knight holding her. "You have truly saved my life this day. I can never repay you for your kindness."

The chase didn't seem to concern him at all as he guided his horse with expert hand through the town. "And how is it I have saved your life?"

"Those men who were after me. They were mad."

"How so?"

"They claimed that I was to be the mother of the wizard Merlin. Mayhap they were only drunk, but . . ." She shivered as she considered what had almost befallen her. "Thank the Lord and all his saints that you came when you did. I shudder to think what they would have done to me had I gone with them."

He gave her a knowing look. "Aye, there was a higher power that brought me to you this day. Of that I have no doubt."

Seren had just started to relax when she heard the sound of hooves behind them.

The knight turned to look.

"It's them!" she breathed, her panic returning as she saw the two knights again in pursuit. "Why won't they let me go?"

"Have no fear. I won't let them take you."

His words thrilled her. Who would have believed that such a handsome knight would defend a simple peasant maid? "You are truly a kind and noble knight, sir."

But as he looked down at her, Seren could have sworn that his eyes flashed red before he spurred his horse to an even greater speed. The other two knights continued to give chase. They raced through town until they flew over the bridge that took them out into the countryside.

Seren cringed. "I'm not to leave the town," she told the knight. "My master will have me beaten for leaving without his permission."

"There is nothing I can do. Should we return, they will take you. Is that what you want?"

"Nay."

"Then hold tight until we lose them."

Seren did as he said. She wrapped her arms about his waist and inhaled the scent of leather, man, and beast. His horse flew over the open meadow, racing toward the dense woods that lay before them.

All of a sudden, something exploded by their side.

"Accero, accero domini doyan," the knight said in his deep, resonate voice.

Seren gasped in terror as the gargoyle decorations on the horse's bridle lifted themselves off and took flight. They screeched like banshees before they headed toward the men pursuing them.

"What is this?" she asked.

"You're lost in a dream." His voice was inside her head. "Sleep, little one. Sleep." Seren blinked her eyes as exhaustion overtook her. She tried desperately to remain awake but couldn't.

Before she knew what was happening, darkness consumed her.

In an eerie black mist, the visible world faded. The veil that separated the two realms mingled until Kerrigan found himself once more on the black soil of Camelot.

USA *Today* bestselling author of
The Trouble With Valentine's Day

RACHEL GIBSON

Sex, Lies, and Online Dating

Welcome to the world of online dating. Lucy has gone on a series of blind dates, and has pretty much given up, when she meets Quinn. At first he seems handsome, but then he tells her his tales of woe, and she knows she's dated another loser. Except this time, Lucy's actually dated a cop—one who is after a female killer—and, though she doesn't know it, Lucy somehow fits the profile. Is Quinn out to protect her or to get her?

Buy and enjoy SEX, LIES, AND ONLINE DATING
(available January 31, 2006), then send the coupon below along with your proof of purchase for SEX, LIES, AND ONLINE DATING to Avon Books, and we'll send you a check for $2.00.

Mail receipt and coupon for *Sex, Lies, and Online Dating* (0-06-077291-3) to: AVON BOOKS/HarperCollinsPublishers Inc., P.O. Box 767, Dresden, TN 38225

NAME
_____

ADDRESS
_____

CITY
_____

STATE/ZIP
_____

*Offer valid only for residents of the United States and Canada. Offer expires 4/30/06

SLO 0106